TOME OF ALCHEMY

AUTHORS:
Courtney Campbell
Matt Finch

DEVELOPERS:
Zach Glazar
Matt Finch
Michael Russell
John Ling

EDITOR:
Jeff Harkness

LAYOUT:
Suzy Moseby

INTERIOR ART:
Sid Quade
C. J. Marsh
Adrian Landeros
Terry Pavlet
Brett Barkley
Josh Stewart
Lloyd, Metcalf
Hector Rodriguez

COVER ART:
Artem Shukaev

ART DIRECTOR:
Casey Christofferson

NECROMACER Games

ISBN: 978-1-6656-0091-0
5e Hardcover
PRINTED IN CHINA

TABLE OF CONTENTS

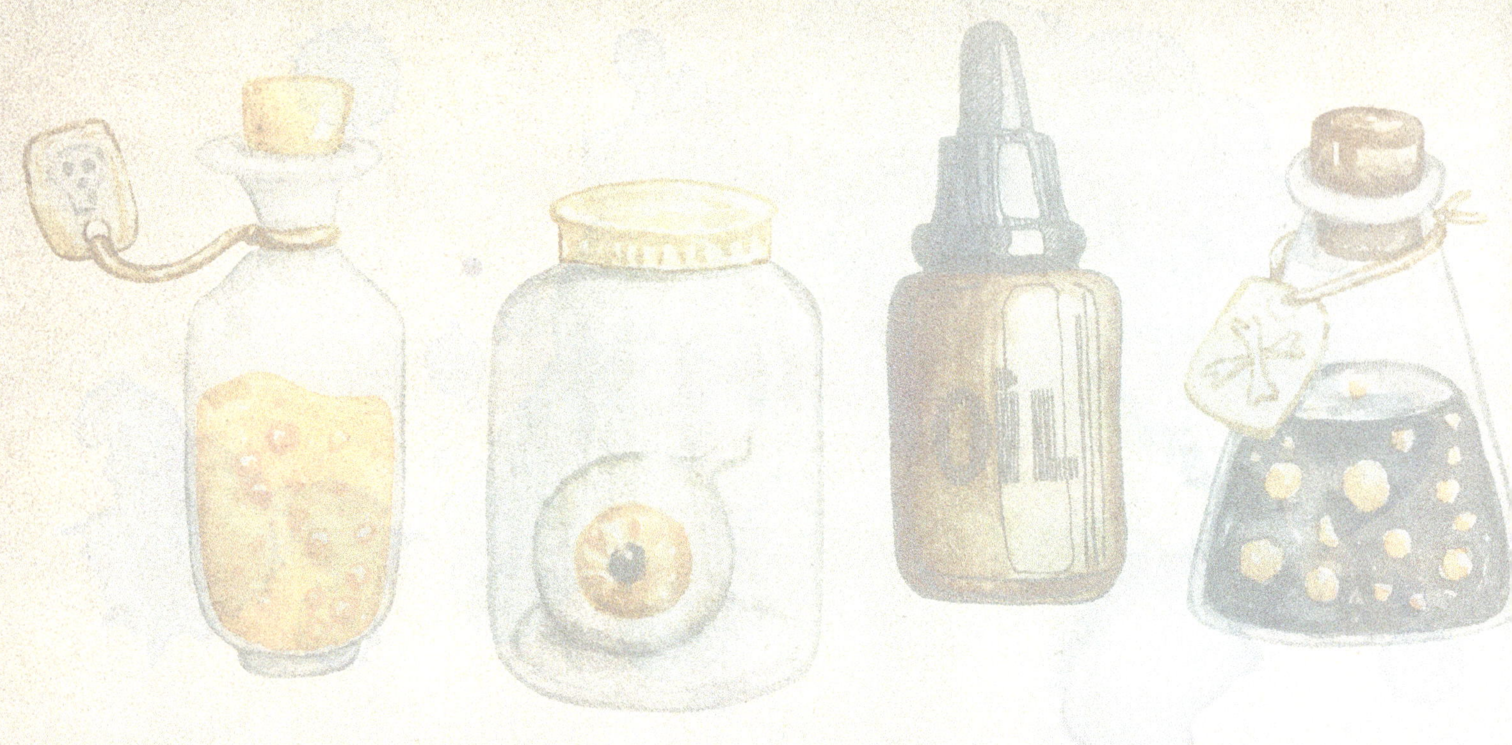

INTRODUCTION

The purpose of alchemy was similar to the purpose for the practice of all mystical arts: unity with the divine. It was not just a matter of concocting strange potions and reagents in dank laboratories.

The fact that it was some of the earliest proto-scientific study of chemistry and medicine was just a convenient byproduct.

Alchemists desired to change lead into gold or, more broadly, base metals into noble metals, because it was a physical manifestation of the spiritual purification of the soul. Their hope was to use the same or a similar process on themselves.

Alchemy, then, is the study and process of change. Whether searching for the universal solvent to break things down, transmuting substances into other substances, or even seeking the means to extend life, it is the philosophical and practical search for knowledge.

Of course, once acquired, this knowledge was put to as many different uses as those who practiced it. For every spiritual seeker, there was one whose skills were put to practical use. For every alchemist who developed new medicines, others sold snake oil that did nothing or was even harmful.

WHY ALCHEMY?

Alchemy has always been something tangential to fantasy roleplaying. Something cool but incomplete. It was something the wizard player asked about and the Game Master waved aside, because, where do you start? The items have to be balanced, meaning you would have to create a system of creation from whole cloth!

Where does the alchemist go when looking to craft something interesting? An item here and there scattered throughout half a dozen supplements? A PDF on the internet with 11, 25, or 40 items in it?

Let there be no question: This is an advanced tome, filled with more than a thousand items for your enterprising alchemist.

More importantly, this isn't a tool only for characters: This is a book of ideas for gaming. I wrote this because I wanted a tool and a reference for my own table. I hope you find alchemy an essential part of your gaming library, too.

HOW TO USE THIS BOOK

Looking at this book may be a bit overwhelming. I suggest two general guidelines:

First, assume that the book is filled with lost lore and not available to the players in total, and introduce sections, alchemical formulas, or items from the book a little at a time. A lot of items and options are in this book, and it is assumed that they are not all freely available and common knowledge. That's the best way to avoid a player using some strange corner case of items and class abilities to unbalance the game. Remember, you have the final word.

Second, it is strongly encouraged that you not just allow characters to purchase or craft any item from this book unless you are interested in a campaign with a wildly varying power level. Fantasy characters can already push the boundaries of the upper limits of effectiveness with feats, class features, and existing magical items. Allowing them to acquire items cheaply that further leverage their abilities will put too much stress on this system. It is OK to use an item to bypass an encounter; after all, they spent the gold and used the resource. But creating a situation with an endless supply of an item can be a disaster. A number of the tools in this book are designed to allow you to control the frequency of such items and how they may be used and created.

General rules cover situations and ideas the players might come up with and provide reasonable explanations for outcomes to help you with situations that might otherwise result in you saying "You just can't" or "I don't know." Materials and essences cover an expansion to the crafting system. These provide ways to enhance spells and alchemical items and limit your characters crafting their way endlessly to being overpowered for their level.

The next section is the items. Hundreds of new (and a few classic) items are found here. Each contains rules for use and crafting.

Finally, we get into some of the more interesting and esoteric powers of wizards and alchemists. Here, you will find ideas that can drive anything from character concepts to campaigns!

Courtney Campbell

CHAPTER ONE: ALCHEMY BASICS

BACKGROUND AND SKILLS

The study of alchemy is an individual pursuit. Most alchemists historically worked in a special code passed on from their mentors that was highly individualized. Alchemical formulas were gathered from experimentation. Their practice is much like that of the spellcasters: individualized, didactic, empirical, and arbitrary.

Alchemists are limited only by the nature and rules of alchemical processes and their equipment. A thorough examination of both follows.

> ### WHAT IS AN ALCHEMIST?
>
> *For the purposes of this book, "alchemist" refers to any character that has proficiency in using Artisan's Tools (Alchemist's Supplies). For clarity, we refer to this proficiency simply as "Alchemist's Supplies."*

BACKGROUND

Alchemists are usually guild artisans (if they are more focused on the commercial side of the trade) or sages that have specialized in alchemy (if they are more focused on the pure research). A guild artisan should take a tools proficiency in Alchemist's Supplies. If the character's background is as a sage, the alchemist specialty should be considered to grant a tools proficiency in alchemist's supplies.

AVAILABILITY OF ITEMS

One of the advantages of alchemical items is that they provide useful, one-shot items that are available for purchase in cities and towns. However, this does not mean that you can purchase 50 bottles of *alchemist's fire* just because you have the gold. Unlike traditional magical items, alchemical items aren't permanent, which means a vendor would keep only a few in stock at any point. So how do you determine their availability?

To determine item availability for purchase, reference the item type and rarity on the following table. For each purchase attempt, roll 1d100. If they are less than the relevant number, the item is available for purchase. The number available for purchase is dependent on the size of the settlement and is listed next to the percentage.

If you instead go the other route and wish to stock a shop to simulate the distribution of goods, then use the following values to determine the number of different kinds and quantity of items. Roll on the relevant table in this book to determine the items (i.e. 75% of the items are available; roll to randomly determine which 25% are not). Legendary items are available as you see fit.

Given the power of many of the alchemical items in this book, even the non-magical ones, it is recommended that you follow this table *only as a rough guideline* for the sorts of items that might be available.

TABLE 1—1: ALCHEMICAL ITEM AVAILABILITY

Item Rarity	Thorp	Hamlet	Village	Small Town	Large Town	Small City	Large City	Metropolis
Common	25% / 1	50% / 1	75% / 1d3	80% / 1d4	90% / 1d6	95% / 2d6	99% / 2d10	100% / 5d10
Uncommon	10% / 1	25% / 1	50% / 1	75% / 1d3	80% / 1d4	90% / 1d6	95% / 2d6	99% / 2d10
Rare	*/*	1% / 1	5% / 1	10% / 1	15% / 1	40% / 1	65% / 1d3	80% / 1d4
Very Rare	*/*	*/*	1% / 1	5% / 1	10% / 1	15% / 1	30% / 1	75% / 1d3

* Indicates item appears only at your discretion.

It is also important to remember that if you are allowing characters to craft items once they have learned the formula, then once they purchase an item in town, this effectively allows them to craft copies of it once they destroy it to learn the formula. This makes cities very desirable goals for players, as well as a method you can use to selectively introduce items.

CRAFTING AND RESEARCHING

THE ALCHEMICAL LABORATORY

The tools of the alchemist are many and varied. The lab is not just for show. Creating alchemical items is a difficult and involved process requiring many different steps such as calcination, fermentation, exaltation, and more. Each of these processes takes time and requires certain specialized equipment to perform.

The type of equipment in a fully featured lab can be quite diverse. In addition to the standard chemistry accoutrements you might expect — vials, burners, cylinders, flasks, forceps, funnels, pipettes, stirring rods, droppers, glass and steel plates, evaporating dishes, spatulas, clamps, test tube racks and files — you might find musical instruments, mechanical oddities, forges and associated equipment, reed meditation mats, braziers, shrines, plaques and signs with alchemical references, brushes, brooms, and various cleaning apparatuses, chairs, seats, food, and even temporary quarters.

In order to craft items, an alchemist is assumed to have a simple, basic repertoire of tools if he or she is in a civilized area. However, you may rule that basic alchemical equipment is unavailable in certain situations and places. If this is the case, the alchemist can still attempt to create the item but has disadvantage on any checks made to do so. An alchemist with a proper laboratory has advantage on checks made to craft items. Typical portable alchemists' supplies and a portable lab merely allow the check to be made.

An alchemy lab costs 200 gp and contains 40 pounds of equipment. It requires a building with at least 400 square feet. Portable alchemy labs are available but are rare and difficult to find. However, they do not require an entire building to construct or use. They cost 75 gp and weigh 20 pounds in addition to the alchemist's supplies required to stock it. These do not require a proficiency above and beyond alchemist's supplies; their use is included in that tool proficiency.

The specific items included in an alchemist's lab should generally be abstract, as part of the alchemist's supplies in a set of tools, with the more elaborate constructions just considered a sufficient laboratory supplied by paying the cost. Anything more detailed is likely to bog the game down in minutiae. However, a bit of flavor and terminology will be helpful both to the player and to the Game Master, so a general list of items is described below.

Athanor: An athanor is an oven capable of reaching high temperatures. The athanor was often the signal component of an alchemist's lab, and it would be possible to have magical athanors that grant a bonus to crafting alchemical items.

Braziers: These are metal trays placed over a fire to heat large quantities of substances, usually solids. For liquids, one would ordinarily use a cauldron.

Burners: Small flames required for heating liquids are usually fired with bits of coal, and are relatively reliable.

Calipers: These are used for precise measurement of length. As a measuring tool, they are subject to inaccuracy unless they are made with tremendous care by an artisan whose own measuring tools are accurate in the first place.

Cauldron: A pot used for mixing liquids, since braziers are more prone to spillage and leaks.

Crucible: Crucibles are used to hold and mix molten metal, so they need to be able to handle very high heat.

Distilling Apparatus: A still is basically identical to the equipment used in producing alcoholic drinks.

Flasks and Beakers: Most of these are normal items of blown glass, but others had specific uses in distillation that required unusual shapes. These more specialized flasks could be quite expensive and require skilled glass blowers to produce them. Measuring flasks are also subject to markings too imprecise for the high level of accuracy required in alchemy.

Lenses: Lenses aren't needed for most alchemical work, but when an item requires etching or other related work a good lab would include at least a magnification lens. Magical lenses might also allow an alchemist to gain knowledge about precise ratios of materials or other information that can be achieved in modern-day labs. Such items might, like magical athanors, grant bonuses to crafting rolls made in a lab.

Orrery and Astrolabe: Orreries are mechanical models of a solar system, while astrolabes are celestial measuring devices used before the development of the sextant. An astrolabe is a disk with measurements along the outside of the disk, and a pointer in the center. In a fantasy world, an astrolabe could comprise multiple disks related to aspects of the stars not comprehended within the ordinary world.

Scales and Balances: In addition to the obvious importance of measuring substances by weight, magical scales might exist which are capable of balancing and measuring non-material substances such as ethereal and astral presences.

Star Charts: Astrological charts depicting constellations at various times of the year are an important part of alchemy. Obtaining charts that are more accurate than others (or dealing with those that turned out to be less so) can be a good adventure hook.

Test Tubes: Racks of small, glass tubes are a mainstay of the well-prepared laboratory, especially when conducting research. If they aren't well-cleaned between uses they are a good explanation for an alchemical mishap (see **Appendices**).

RESEARCH

One of the assumptions of the Fifth Edition game is that characters immediately have access to all spells, alchemical formulas, crafting formulas, and other information. Research is never necessary.

This is very empowering for players, but it creates a situation: as more material for the game becomes available where something with a very specific and limited use can be paired with something else to create a synergistic effect in which the interaction becomes much more powerful than either base item.

In addition, it prevents the existence of powers, magic, and items that the players don't know about. How can they have the joy of discovery if all they need to do is learn a spell is purchase a scroll?

Limiting the amount of material available to players has its own pitfalls. It's complicated and can frustrate the players since they won't know what their characters can and cannot use when reading the books. Before you make any decisions about limiting access to spells and gear, take a moment to consider the eventual effects. Requiring spell and alchemical research reduces the power level of "book" spellcasting classes and people using the alchemy skill, whereas characters not dependent on research become more powerful by comparison. Less money will be available for the whole party.

That said, spell and alchemical item research is a good idea. Spell research is already implicit in the rules, being that spellcasters can cast spells only of an appropriate level. This background research is also the driving force behind spellcasters gaining new spells at some levels.

If you'd like to have some simple restrictions on knowledge that the characters have and don't want to disrupt your game too badly, here are some suggestions:

All items in the core rules should be available for all classes. For other items, use the following guidelines: For crafted items such as those made with alchemist's supplies or smith's tools, a character does not know any formula with a crafting DC higher than their current proficiency modifier + 15. You must possess or find a copy of a magical item before you can discover how to craft a magical item.

This gives you more control over which items can be available in the game and prevents the players from using bonuses from crafting something too powerful too soon.

OVERVIEW

What is actually involved in researching a new alchemical item, magical item, or spell? The process usually involves a mixed approach to discovering the secret or unknown method of production. Usually the spell or item is heard about first in conversation. The initial portion of research is spent gathering information and doing research in libraries. Many times, these libraries are owned by specific individuals who have their own requirements for research and lending. A process of experimentation and testing then takes place until eventually the alchemist succeeds at making a discovery.

Another method of researching a new alchemical item, magical item, or spell is to take a copy of the item in the wild and destroy it to find out how it works. This is how a scroll functions. But for magical items and alchemical items, allowing a character to destroy the item to determine the formula is an excellent way to learn how to craft it.

However, assuming a character does not have a copy of the magical item, alchemical item, or spell he or she is attempting to study, the following procedure can simulate the research of an item.

PREPARING FOR RESEARCH

The player knows which item he or she wants to research. This represents their character hearing a rumor or story about the spell or item at some point in his past. The character decides to track down how to create such an item. The character begins attempting to gather information about the item or spell. This can include the history, when it was crafted or used, the creator, where it was created — any of these facts are useful when attempting to duplicate their work.

In order to track down this information, the character must succeed at an Intelligence (Investigation) or Charisma (Persuade) check to gather information. The base DC of this skill check for spells is 10 + twice the spell's level. The base DC of this skill check for alchemical and magical items depends on the item's rarity (see **Table 1–2**). A success on this check means that the creator now knows the item exists and understands enough about it to begin researching how to make it. Unlike a normal attempt to gather information, this check takes 1d4 days per attempt. If the character fails by 5 or more on this check, there is no information in this area to be had and the character must try again in another city or settlement. This check may be modified by the size of the settlement. A small hamlet is much less likely to have someone who knows about a rare item.

TABLE 1–2: INFORMATION GATHERING DC

Alchemical or Magic Item Rarity	DC to Track Down Information
Common	10
Uncommon	12
Rare	15
Very Rare	20
Legendary	25

RESEARCHING

The next step is the research itself. This requires a character to succeed at an Intelligence (Arcana) check to discover the creation process (see **Tables 1–3** or **1–4** depending on whether the research is for a spell or an item). In order to make this check, the character needs access to an arcane library. An arcane library is a collection of nonmagical books on a variety of arcane topics. A large town might have an arcane library with a value of 10,000 gp while a village might have an arcane library with a value of 2,500 gp. Of course, some towns or villages may have a library above or below its size because of its cultural history. Many times these libraries are open only to citizens. In some cases, they are in the hands of private owners or merchants. Very rarely will a library — especially an arcane library — be open to the public.

Characters may build their own arcane library to avoid and defer costs of using public or private libraries in the settlements they visit. If they do not, they must use the available facilities in settlements to perform their research. Each item researched needs a certain size arcane library in order for any information on the item to be found. The players may use their arcane library total and combine it with the arcane library in a settlement to do their research.

The DC required to complete the research for spells is DC 10 + twice the spell's level. For alchemical items and magical items, the DC for the Intelligence (Arcana) check depends on the item's rarity (see **Table 1–5**).

The size of the library required to do the research is the DC of the Intelligence (Arcana) check required for successful completion of the research squared multiplied by 100 gp. A large town likely has a large enough library to research a 1st-level spell (12^2 x 100 = 14,400 gp), whereas a small city might be required to research 3rd level spells (16^2 x 100 = 25,600 gp). If the character lacks an appropriately sized arcane library, then the check is penalized by 1 for every 1,000 gold short the library is.

TABLE 1–3: SPELL RESEARCH AND SETTLEMENT REQUIRED

Spell level	Research DC	Arcane Library Required	Minimum Settlement Size*
1st	12	14,000 gp	Small city
2nd	14	17,000 gp	Small city
3rd	16	25,000 gp	Small city
4th	18	32,000 gp	Medium city
5th	20	40,000 gp	Large city
6th	22	48,000 gp	Large city
7th	24	57,000 gp	Metropolis
8th	26	67,000 gp	Metropolis
9th	28	78,000 gp	Metropolis

* May be adjusted based on culture and local technology

TABLE 1–4: MAGICAL ITEM RESEARCH AND SETTLEMENT REQUIRED

Alchemical or Magic Item Rarity	Research DC	Arcane Library Required	Minimum Settlement Size*
Common	10	6,000 gp	Large town
Uncommon	12	14,000 gp	Small city
Rare	15	22,000 gp	Small city
Very Rare	20	40,000 gp	Large city
Legendary	25	62,000 gp	Metropolis

*May be adjusted based on culture and local technology

If the check fails, the character may retry freely. Each time this check is made, the character spends a number of days equal to 30 minus the result of the check. On a successful check, the character has discovered the spell or item and may create it! For spells, this means going through the process of scribing a scroll. For alchemical and magical items, this means crafting the item normally.

Sera, a 1st-level wizard, decides she would like to research *magic missile*. She must first track down how to create such a spell. She makes a Charisma (Persuade) check with a difficulty of 12. Her first check is a 4. This failure costs her 30 – 4 = 26 days, and because she failed by more than five means that nobody in this hamlet has heard of *magic missile*. After 26 days, she travels to a larger town and tries again. This time she gets a 14. This result is enough to find some clue about the spell. She knows it exists and understands enough about the spell to begin making it.

She begins researching *magic missile*. The small town she is in has an arcane library equivalent to 5,000 gp. The spell *magic missile* is 1st level, requiring a library equal to 12^2 x 100 = 14,400 gp, which means it isn't big enough to perform the spell research. Instead of going to a larger city, she completes a quest to rescue a sage. The sage has a personal library worth 4,000 gp. The town now has an arcane library equal in value to 9,000 gp, giving her a –5 penalty to her research. She could have continued the research with a –9 (14,000 – 5,000) penalty for the small size of the arcane library, but the sage needed rescuing anyway.

Having the materials she needs at hand, she begins her research. Her Intelligence (Arcana) skill is a +5. She needs to succeed at a DC 12 Intelligence (Arcana) check. Her first die roll is a 13, resulting in a successful Intelligence (Arcana) check of 13 + 5 – 5 = 13. She spends 30 – 13 = 17 days and researches *magic missile*. She pays for the cost of the scroll and now has a scroll of *magic missile*.

To research an *amulet of health* (rare), she must succeed on a DC 15 Charisma (Persuade) check, have access to an arcane library of 22,500 gp, and succeed at a DC 15 Intelligence (Arcana) check.

CRAFTING AN ITEM

Each item has a rarity associated with it (see **Table 1–5**). To craft an item, the alchemist must complete the necessary research (see below), have the appropriate materials (often quite expensive), and make a successful Intelligence (Alchemist's Supplies) check. The DC of the check depends on the rarity of the item being created. The crafting cost and a list of special ingredients are listed for each alchemical item where they are described in the following chapters.

TABLE 1–5: ITEM RARITY

Item Rarity	DC to Craft
Common	10
Uncommon	12
Rare	15
Very Rare	20
Legendary	25

Sometimes your players may want to create a spell or craft an item that isn't in any book. If this is the case, then the procedure should be similar to the above. Because the item doesn't exist, skip the gathering information section, and the character instead proceeds with the research. Design the final item with the player giving you the information you need. It is suggested that you make sure this item is balanced for its cost and rarity. Once you have that, perform research as normal, requiring an arcane library 10,000 gp more valuable than normal. Also, increase the research DC by +5. On a successful result, the player successfully researches a new never-before-seen item and may begin crafting it.

Chapter Two discusses the ingredients required to create alchemical items.

FIRE

Fire is pretty straightforward in the rules, but as described it's not really very fire-like. Here's a way to make fire a bit more interesting.

Any time fire is on something inflammable — clothing, human skin, horses — the size of the fire may increase. Fire growth follows the progression found in **Table 1–6**. In general, check for progression every minute unless it makes sense to use a different time frame.

TABLE 1–6: FIRE PROGRESSION

Type	Damage	Result	Spread
Flame	1d3	Extremity on fire. This is ignored when the fire burns out	Moves to next category on a 3, burns out entirely on a 1
Burning	1d6	Torso on fire	Moves to next category on a 6, burns down to a flame on a 1
On Fire	2d6	Person on fire	Moves to next category if either die rolls a 6, down a category if the roll is a 2
Conflagration	3d6	Area on fire (everything nearby takes 1d3 damage)	Becomes an Inferno if any die rolls a 6, burns down a category if the roll is a 3
Inferno	3d8	Area on fire (everything nearby takes 1d3 damage)	Fire spreads on a roll of 6+, down a category if the roll is a 3

SOME CAVEATS

If everything inflammable in the area is destroyed, the fire goes out.

If something highly inflammable is burning, you may add a bonus for things to catch fire.

So, if a character throws *alchemist's fire* at a target and rolls a 6 for her damage roll, the next round she rolls 2d6 to determine how much damage she does. For a player who rolls a 1, the next round the fire does 1d3 damage to the target.

As long as there is still something for the fire to burn, growth results always supersede burnout results. If someone is on fire and the dice come up with a 6 and 1, then the fire becomes a conflagration the next round, and he takes 3d6 damage. Also note in the table that as fire grows, it also becomes more likely to spread.

This makes fire an effective and deadly weapon.

GAS CLOUDS

All gas is not the same. Here are some guidelines for handling issues involving gaseous substances and their dispersion rates.

TYPES OF CLOUDS

There are four different kinds of vapors of interest: smoke, poison gas, alchemical gas, and magical clouds.

SMOKE

Smoke is produced by fire and is lethal. It is important to note that smoke is not produced by spells such as *burning hands* or *fireball*. These spells channel inner dimensional energy from the Plane of Fire; the resulting explosion produces heat and flame, but no object experiences combustion so there is no smoke.

Smoke and exposure to it is unpleasant, and anyone who can escape flees long before they are injured by exposure to the smoke. If you are trapped in a smoky area, lung damage from irritants begins almost immediately, and asphyxiation begins immediately after. This quickly leads to difficulty breathing, headache, and confusion, followed by fainting, seizures, coma, and death.

A character exposed to smoke must make a DC 5 Constitution saving throw every round. For every consecutive round spent within the smoke, the DC increases by +2. On a failed check, the character falls prone and is stunned. The character must succeed at a DC 14 Wisdom saving throw or become *confused* as the spell. The character continues to make the Wisdom save every round he or she is in the smoke until the character becomes confused. The character also continues making Constitution saves every round. On a second failed Constitution save, the character falls unconscious. On the third failed Constitution save, the character begins suffocating and starts dying after a number of rounds equal to his or her Constitution modifier.

Smoke is opaque and provides total concealment.

POISON GAS

Deadly and fast-acting, and often transparent or invisible, poison gases affect and kill their targets extremely rapidly. These can be any gaseous substance — even oxygen can be deadly!

Poison gas is highly reactive and will not remain inside a sealed chamber indefinitely. This extreme reactivity is also why it is so deadly. Lesser concentrations of smoke or poison gas disperse proportionally faster.

Various nonmagical, non-alchemical substances are considered and treated as poisonous gases. They are listed below.

Asphyxiant: An asphyxiant gas has little to no negative effect chemically on the body. They are often inert. They asphyxiate by displacing oxygen. The creature is breathing, but there is no oxygen in the air, so it starts to suffocate. The first symptoms include drowsiness and difficulty hearing. The character's heart rate increases in an attempt to transfer more oxygen. Then a headache, dizziness, shortness of breath, and confusion. Finally, the creature's sight dims, and it begins to tremor and sweat. Unconsciousness follows soon after.

Use the standard rules for holding one's breath and suffocation.

Blister: This gas is nefarious because exposure to it has no immediate effects. Only hours later do symptoms appear. It is also important to note that this gas does not occur naturally. It is detectable by the scent of garlic, mustard, or horseradish. Initial symptoms include mucus membrane irritation, large fluid blisters, tearing and eye damage, and difficulty breathing.

Once exposed to blister gas, there is no immediate effect, but hideous blisters and sores cover the body several hours later. These blisters are painful and debilitating, and each creature must make a DC 16 Constitution saving throw each round it is exposed. Unless magical healing is performed, 2d6 hours later the creature's Strength, Dexterity, and Constitution are reduced by two for each failed saving throw and by one for each successful one. The ability score reduction heals one point for each after a creature completes a long rest. *Lesser restoration* completely heals any one ability score, while *greater restoration* heals all ability score damage.

Blood: When inhaled, this chemical is absorbed into the blood. The gas often prevents the body from processing oxygen, which causes victims to suffer from suffocation. After inhalation, the victim experiences dizziness, weakness, and nausea. Headaches begin shortly before seizures and coma. Exceptionally strong exposure can cause death within seconds.

A creature that starts its turn in the cloud must make a DC 16 Constitution saving throw or take 27 (5d10) poison damage and become poisoned. Victims must save each round with a cumulative +1 increase to the DC for each consecutive round spent within the gas. A round spent outside the gas reduces DC to the starting level. The poisoned condition lasts until the creature completes a short or long rest.

Choking: This gas works primarily by inflaming the mucus membranes and the lungs. The mouth and lungs burn, and the victim experiences shortness of breath, dizziness, headache, and unsurprisingly, coughing. These symptoms are caused by gases that turn to acid in the lungs. Damage is immediate and deadly.

A creature that starts its turn in the cloud must make a DC 16 Constitution saving throw or suffer 55 (10d10) poison damage. Victims must save each round with a cumulative +1 increase to the DC for each consecutive round spent within the gas. A round spent outside the gas reduces DC to the starting level.

Nerve: This normally water-soluble liquid acts as a central nervous system toxin. It can be turned into a gaseous spray very easily and hangs around in the air much like a normal gas. The first symptoms are a runny nose and extremely dilated pupils. Then, there is a rapid onset of sweating, nausea, and vomiting. Finally, before death, involuntary urination and defecation occur, followed by seizures, coma, and death.

A creature that starts its turn in the cloud must make a DC 16 Constitution saving throw or suffer 55 (10d10) poison damage. A target who survives must make a DC 16 Wisdom saving throw or suffer a degenerative nervous condition and lose 4 Intelligence, Wisdom, and Charisma. The ability score reduction heals one point for each after a creature completes a long rest. *Lesser restoration* completely heals any one ability score, while *greater restoration* heals all ability score damage.

Tear: This gas irritates the mucus membranes, causing uncontrollable crying, sneezing, coughing, difficulty breathing, eye pain, and blindness. It is often not lethal unless exposure to a massive quantity occurs.

A creature that starts its turn in the cloud must make DC 16 Constitution saving throw or become blinded and poisoned. Victims must save each round with a cumulative +1 increase to the DC for each consecutive round spent within the gas. A round spent outside the gas reduces the DC to the starting level. After a rest period of six minutes of flushing the eyes with water, these conditions dissipate.

Vomiting: These gases are rarely toxic but cause uncontrollable vomiting. These gases are usually thick and can often bypass protective measures. The subsequent vomiting usually forces the target to remove its personal protection, which allows a second gas to be more effective.

A creature that starts its turn in the gas must succeed on a DC 16 Constitution saving throw or become incapacitated. Check every round the victim is exposed to the gas. An incapacitated creature that leaves the area of the gas can attempt the saving throw again at the end of each of its turns, ending the effect on a success.

TABLE 1–7: GAS TYPES

Lethal

Gas	Type	Onset	Weight Relative to Air	Color / Odor	Notes
Arsine	Blood	Days	Heavier	Colorless/Odorless	Bloody urine
Carbon Monoxide	Blood	10 minutes	Lighter	Colorless / Odorless	Cherry-red skin
Chlorine Gas	Choking	10 minutes	Heavier	Yellow-Green / Bleach	Flammable; byproduct of bleach and ammonia (chloramine gas)
Hydrogen Cyanide	Blood	10 minutes	Heavier	Colorless / Bitter almonds	
Hydrogen Fluoride	Choking	10 Minutes	Lighter	Colorless / "Offensive"	Flammable
Hydrogen Sulfide	Blood	10 minutes	Heavier	Colorless / Rotten eggs	Nullifies sense of smell; flammable
Nitrogen Mustard	Blister	12 hours	Heavier	Yellow-Brown / Garlic, Horseradish, Mustard	Liquid; Soluble in Water
Oxides of Nitrogen	Choking	120 minutes	Lighter	Red-brown / Fishy	
Phosgene	Choking	5 rounds	Heavier	Colorless / Fresh Mown Hay	
Sarin, Soman, Tabun	Nerve	1 round	Heavier	Colorless / Odorless	
Sulfur Dioxide	Choking	10 minutes	Heavier	Colorless / Brimstone	Nonflammable
Sulfur Mustards	Blister	12–360 minutes	Lighter	Yellow-Brown / Garlic, Horseradish, Mustard	

Non-Lethal

Gas	Type	Onset	Weight Relative to Air	Color / Odor	Notes
Adamsite	Vomit	1 round	Lighter	Canary-Yellow / Odorless	
Ammonia	Tear	1 round	Lighter	Colorless / Ammonia	
Carbon Dioxide	Asphyxiant	10 minutes	Lighter	Colorless / Odorless	
Chloropicrin	Vomit	1 round	Heavier	Colorless / Pungent Stinging	
Bromine	Tear	20 minutes	Heavier	Dark-rust Red / Bleach	
Propane	Asphyxiant	10 minutes	Lighter	Colorless / Odorless	Flammable
Methane	Asphyxiant	10 minutes	Lighter	Colorless / Odorless	Flammable

ALCHEMICAL GAS

Alchemical gases are created from grenades, powders, and dusts. They expose anyone entering the cloud to the effects of the grenades, powders, and dusts. The specifics of the effects are identical to the listed grenade from which they are crafted, excepting the area of effect and duration. The effect lasts until the gas is dispersed. Grenade types are listed in **Table 3-3**.

MAGICAL GAS

Magical gases are created by spells and come in many different forms. The gas cloud lasts for the spell's duration and resists dispersion unless noted otherwise in the spell description. This means that wind and breezes can move them, but they maintain cohesion. They fill the volume as directed by the spell. They don't grow to a larger size or spread out; they don't become thinner or more diffuse; and if pushed or blown into a different shape, they resist. Exposure to a smaller space than their volume reshapes the cloud, but it desires to fill its volume in the easiest possible way, meaning it seeks to expand into the area of lowest pressure.

GAS DISPERSION

Over time, fresh air entering a room disperses nonmagical smoke and gas. However, as the fresh air mixes with the gas before forcing it out, it is this mixture that leaves the room.

For safe entry, a smoky room has to be 90% fresh air, and an area with poison gas must be 99% fresh air. Characters entering a room once it starts to clear may receive bonuses on saving throws: +2 for 50% clear, and +4 for 80% clear or greater.

Five different categories of ventilation exist (see **Table 1–6**). Each reaches these thresholds at different rates.

TABLE 1–8: GAS CLOUD DURATION

Ventilation	Smoke	Poison Gas	Alchemical Gas	Example
No Ventilation	Perpetual*	1 month	20 minutes	Sealed Crypt
Poor Ventilation	100 minutes	280 minutes	10 minutes	Dungeon
Standard Ventilation	50 minutes	140 minutes	5 minutes	Standard Room
Good Ventilation	10 minutes	30 minutes	3 minutes	Alchemist's Lab
Superb Ventilation	1 round	10 minutes	1 round	Outside on a Windy Day

* This smoke eventually settles and covers the surfaces in the sealed area with ash.

CHAPTER TWO: MATERIALS AND ESSENCES

In order to craft an alchemical item (including potions, salves, and so forth), the alchemist needs to have the required materials and significant ingredients, which will have been identified during the research phase of crafting (see Chapter One). There are two fundamental types of significant ingredients: mineral essences and vital essences.

Every alchemical formula contains a mix of mineral essences (rare earths, metals, and gemstones) and vital essences (which are ordinarily prepared elements from living creatures). Quantities are given in drams of distilled essence, or carats of powdered gemstone.

BASIC MATERIALS

You can't make something out of nothing. Every item you create has a cost in gold pieces to cover the raw materials necessary during item creation. This cost includes basic supplies such as talc, fuel for burners, purified platinum tongs, gem dust, purified liquids, and other one-use rarefied items. These are the normal costs necessary and are not listed in the item description.

MINERAL ESSENCES

RARE EARTH

Anyone with alchemical training can collect rare earths (wizards able to practice item creation, alchemists, etc.). Rare earths consist of elemental substances such as antimony, cinnabar, pitchblende, and various salts and metal oxides. They also contain trace amounts of all the elements and can be found in small quantities in all types of soil and sand. Collecting rare earths takes a day of labor. For every eight person-hours spent, with a successful DC 10 Intelligence (Investigation) check a character can generate one dram of rare earth, with an additional one dram for every 5 by which the check exceeds the DC. Rare earths appear as a bit of rich earth suffused with small crystals that reflect different colors of light. They have a rich fresh ethereal smell and require no special storage containers or requirements. They do not expire. On the open market, they can be purchased for 10 gp, but there is no cost (beyond time) to collecting them. The cost of rare earths is included in the crafting price.

GEMSTONES

Twelve essential alchemical gemstones have specific spiritual resonances that people have known about for ages. The gemstones are agate, amethyst, diamond, emerald, jade, malachite, moonstone, onyx, pearl, ruby, sapphire, and turquoise. These alchemical gemstones can be ground into a fine powder for use in many alchemical formulas. The process of creation requires a certain amount of gemstone dust per item. Each powdered carat costs 10 gp. An alchemist can generate this by powdering these gemstones or purchase gemstones or gemstone powder from town. An alchemist who finds a ruby worth 253 gp can dust that gemstone, turning it into 25 carats of ruby gemstone powder suitable for crafting. The extra dust from the value of the gem is lost to the dusting process. Note that a gemstone cannot be partially ground down without completely destroying its value.

When reading the alchemical formulas for items, a gem showing in the formula is assumed to be 50 carats worth (500 gp). An entry reading "Diamond (x100)" would mean 5,000 carats of powdered diamond with a value of 50,000 gp.

In certain rare cases or in the case of crafting alchemical gemstone talismans, uncut or unpowdered gemstone is required.

RARE METALS

Sometimes the alchemist needs certain rare metals such as silver, gold, or platinum to craft items. These metals are very powerful magical activators. Rarely, pure samples of these metals can be purchased, sometimes from dwarves or other creatures of the earth, but most commonly the source for these metals are coins. Coins, however, are very impure. To produce one pure dram of this metal from common coins requires 10 coins. For example, to extract five drams of platinum, one needs 50 platinum coins. The coins are melted down, and the impurities are removed. A crafter with no in-game source for pure metals must make do with transmuting coinage into pure metals. The cost of these coins is included in the crafting price.

Note that in the above cases, a crafter who collects the necessary materials can use it to reduce the crafting price. Also note that if the crafter doesn't have access to a hamlet or larger community, then it's possible that the crafter can't purchase the rare materials and must possess them to craft the item.

TABLE 2–1: MINERAL ESSENCES

Material	Price
Gemstones	As gemstone
One dram of gold	10 gp
One dram of iron	1 gp
One dram of silver	1 gp
One dram of platinum	100 gp
Rare earths	10 gp

VITAL ESSENCES

Vital essences are necessary mystical components from living (or unliving) creatures, required to make powerful alchemical items function. The various types are discussed below.

The entire creature is not needed to collect and distill the essence, just the applicable part such as the ears, heart, or teeth. For the alchemist, all of the creature's essence can be distilled from this single part. No essence remains in the rest of the creature, as the collected portion now holds the essential energy. Distilling the rest of the hell hound produces nothing!

Vital essences have additional uses beyond their use in crafting. Having more of the appropriate essences can lower the cost of crafting even beyond what is listed. In addition, essences can be used to empower spells as they are cast. This is discussed in **Chapter Six: Alchemy in Structures.**

If you are using alchemy at a very abstract level and want your alchemist to be able to purchase relevant ingredients, you may use the table below to ascertain prices for necessary vital essences.

TABLE 2–2: VITAL ESSENCES

Vital Essence	Price	
Aberration	10 gp	
Beast	1gp	5 sp
Celestial	10 gp	
Construct	10 gp	
Dragon	10gp	5 gp
Elemental	5 gp	
Fey	5 gp	
Fiend	10 gp	
Humanoid	1 gp	
Monstrosity	5 gp	
Monstrous Humanoid	5 gp	
Ooze	5 gp	
Plant	1 gp	
Undead	5 gp	

If vital essences are not generally available for sale, the characters will have to hunt monsters in order to obtain them.

Harvesting a monster's components must be done within one hour of death and takes 10 minutes per hit die and a successful DC 15 Intelligence (Arcana) check per hit die. Components may then be brought back to the lab for distillation.

VITAL ESSENCE TYPES

Many living (or undead) creatures contains essences that are used in alchemical formulas. There are 38 of these vital essences. All vital essences fall into one of eight categories: the four elemental essences (fire, water, earth, and air), the three alchemical essences (sulfur, salt, and mercury) and the category of azoth, which is primarily related to magical influences.

Table 2-3 shows which essences fall into which of the eight categories.

Every alchemical formula comprises a combination of vital essences (in addition to mineral essences). Many of these formulas specify one of the *categories* of vital essences as an ingredient rather than a specific vital essence. In this case, any vital essence from that category can be used to satisfy that part of the formula. If a particular vital essence, as opposed to just a category, is included in the formula then that specific essence is required.

TABLE 2–3: VITAL ESSENCE TYPES BY CATEGORY

Category	Vital Essences
Elemental Essences	
Air	Electricity
	Flight
	Illusion
	Speed
	Stealth
Earth	Acid
	Armor
	Disease
	Plant
	Strength
Fire	Agility
	Decay
	Light
	Pain
	Purity
Water	Cold
	Emotion
	Fear
	Memory
	Toxin
Alchemical Essences	
Mercury	Control
	Dream
	Mind
	Telesthetic
	Transmutation
	Transportation
Salt	Body
	Death
	Prophesy
	Protection
	Prowess
	Stasis
Sulphur	Healing
	Life
	Love
	Luck
	Perception
	Planar
Unique	
Azoth	Azoth

DISTILLING VITAL ESSENCES

If vital essences are not generally available for sale, the characters will have to hunt monsters in order to obtain them.

HARVESTING ESSENCES

Harvesting a monster's components must be done within one hour of death. The number of components that can be harvested depends on the size of the creature, per the table below. Each component requires one character working for 10 minutes to harvest. At the end of each ten-minute period, have the character harvesting make a DC 15 Intelligence (Arcana) check. On a success, they have successfully harvested one component. On a failure, that component is ruined. A character proficient in Nature or Survival may help the character making the Arcana check. Harvested components may then be brought back to the lab for distillation. They do not have any important alchemical properties other than raw potential until they are distilled.

DISTILLATION

When you distill down a harvested monster's components, you choose one of its available vital essences. One vital essence is available for each harvested component. Distilling an essence takes one hour and requires a successful DC 15 Intelligence (Alchemist's Supplies) check.

TABLE 2–4: NUMBER OF HARVESTABLE COMPONENTS

Size	Available Components
Tiny	1
Small	2
Medium	4
Large	8
Huge	1
Gargantuan	20

When you distill down a harvested monster's components, you choose one of its available vital essences per hit die. Distilling an essence takes one hour for each component and a DC 10 Intelligence (Alchemist's Supplies) check.

When distilling an essence from harvested components, a generic essence (such as Fire) yields 2 drams of the essence per hit die, and a specific essence (such as Agility) yields only 1 dram per hit die.

As an example, let's assume that the characters have killed a huge red dragon. A red dragon, as you will see later, can produce the following vital essences: Azoth, Fire/ Armor, Fear, Flight, Perception, Prowess. Azoth and Fire are categories, and the other essences are specific. Armor, for example, is an essence in the Earth category. The characters might be able to harvest as many as 12 different components from the dragon, assuming total success on the harvesting die rolls, since it is a huge creature. Once the components are in the alchemist's lab, they can be stored for use until they are needed. At that time, the alchemist can distill them down for whatever particular project they are needed for, and can choose what essences — out of the available choices — to distill the components into.

One possibility, using the first of the 12 components, would be to distill a generic Fire essence. The dragon's hit die will yield 2 drams of generic Fire essence since Fire is a generic category. The same is true of azoth since it is also a general category (even though azoth has no sub-essences). On the other hand, the alchemist might decide to distill the one hit die worth of components into an essence of Armor. Since Armor is a specific essence, doing so will only yield 1 dram of Armor essence instead of the 2 Fire essence. However, the dram of Armor essence has more potential uses than a dram of generic Fire essence, since it can also substitute in formulas as a generic Earth essence (Armor is a sub-category of Earth). Most alchemical formulas require the use of a generic essence such as "Earth (any)," and the Armor essence can be used to fill that requirement since Armor is a subcategory of Earth.

ALTERNATE ESSENCES

The examples of essences given are just that, examples. As lord of your milieu, some monsters will be included and others may not. Allow characters to extract any reasonable essence from creatures while keeping the verisimilitude of your campaign world in mind. If goblins are as common as dirt and their hearts work as healing essences, then the characters will be awash in healing potions.

You might restrict or keep this list secret, forcing the players to discover in play what essences are recoverable from which creature. This can put alchemists in a position where they waste essences experimenting.

It is recommended that you remain somewhat flexible with essence availability. After all, the character chose to learn alchemy to be able to create items. Without essences available, they cannot. A suggested list of reasonable essences for common creatures follows. These are suggestions only.

NOT USING ESSENCES

Removing this system makes it easier for characters to just craft the items they need in town. Keeping the essence system in the game drives the characters to collect the essences they need, giving them an in-game reason to track down and kill certain creatures.

GIBBERING MOUTHER

ANKLYOSAURUS

EFREETI

SOURCES OF VITAL ESSENCES

The following table lists monsters that can be used to distill each of the vital essences.

TABLE 2–5: SOURCES OF VITAL ESSENCES

Essence	Monster
Acid	Ankheg, Black Dragon, Black Pudding, Copper Dragon, Earth Elemental, Gibbering Mouther, Gray Ooze, Green Dragon, Ochre Jelly, Purple Worm, Roper
Agility	Fire Elemental, Aarakocra, Balor, Giant Eagle, Giant Wolf Spider, Goblin, Kobold, Pteranodon, Saber-toothed Tiger
Air	Air Elemental, Cloaker, Cloud Giant, Cockatrice, Darkmantle, Djinni, Gold Dragon, Griffon, Harpy, Hippogriff, Invisible Stalker, Pegasus, Pteranodon, Roc, Sprite, Storm Giant, Wyvern
Armor	Ankheg, Ankylosaurus, Behir, Bulette, Chuul, Dragons (all), Dragon Turtle, Earth Elemental, Giant Crab, Giant Crocodile, Gorgon, Iron Golem, Triceratops
Azoth	Balor, Deva, Dragons (all), Drow, Ghast, Ghost, Ghoul, Guardian Naga, Homunculus, Lich, Mummy, Owlbear, Planetar, Pseudodragon, Shadow, Skeleton, Solar, Spectre, Spirit Naga, Tarrasque, Unicorn, Vampire, Wight, Will-o'-Wisp, Wraith, Zombie
Body	Chuul, Clay Golem, Ettin, Flesh Golem, Gnoll, Hill Giant, Giant Elk, Giant Lizard, Hobgoblin, Mammoth, Manticore, Minotaur, Ogre, Plesiosaurus, Tarrasque
Cold	Frost Giant, Ice Devil, Ice Mephit, Remorhaz, Silver Dragon, Water Elemental, White Dragon, Winter Wolf,
Control	Aboleth, Harpy, Lamia, Lycanthropes (all), Wraith
Death	Death Dog, Ghost, Sea Hag, Tarrasque, Shadow, Skeleton, Spectre, White Dragon, Wight, Will-o'-Wisp, Wraith, Zombie,
Decay	Balor, Bone Devil, Fire Elemental, Ghast, Ghoul, Giant Hyena, Giant Vulture, Gnoll, Mummy, Roper, Rust Monster, Skeleton, Violet Fungus, Wight, Zombie
Disease	Earth Elemental, Giant Rat, Horned Devil, Mummy, Otyugh
Dream	Djinni, Efreeti, Night Hag, Nightmare, Spectre, Treant
Earth	Allosaurus, Ankheg, Ankylosaurus, Basilisk, Black Pudding, Bulette, Clay Golem, Dryad, Dust Mephit, Earth Elemental, Gargoyle, Giant Badger, Giant Goat, Gibbering Mouther, Gorgon, Grick, Iron Golem, Otyugh, Purple Worm, Roper, Rust Monster, Satyr, Shambling Mound, Shrieker, Stone Giant, Stone Golem, Triceratops, Xorn, Treant, Violet Fungus
Electricity	Air Elemental, Behir, Blue Dragon, Bronze Dragon, Kraken, Oni, Shambling Mound, Storm Giant, Will-o'-Wisp
Emotion	Androsphinx, Djinni, Efreeti, Lycanthropes (all), Night Hag, Satyr, Sprite, Succubus/Incubus, Water Elemental
Fear	Allosaurus, Dragons (all), Hippogriff, Lich, Nalfeshnee, Pit Fiend, Saber-toothed Tiger Vampire, Water Elemental
Fire	Azer, Balor, Barbed Devil, Bearded Devil, Bone Devil, Brass Dragon, Chain Devil, Chimera, Dretch, Efreeti, Erinyes, Fire Elemental, Fire Giant, Glabrezu, Gold Dragon, Hell Hound, Hezrou, Horned Devil, Ice Devil, Imp, Lemure, Marilith, Nalfeshnee, Nightmare, Pit Fiend, Quasit, Red Dragon, Remorhaz, Salamander, Steam Mephit, Succubus/Incubus, Vrock
Flight	Aarakocra, Air Elemental, Cloaker, Dragons (all), Flying Snake, Griffon, Hippogriff, Manticore, Roc, Sprite, Stirge, Wyvern
Healing	Couatl, Deva, Guardian Naga, Hydra, Lemure, Solar, Tarrasque, Troll, Unicorn
Illusion	Aboleth, Air Elemental, Chain Devil, Green Hag, Grey Ooze, Lamia, Sea Hag
Life	Couatl, Deva, Ghost, Giant Boar, Guardian Naga, Kraken, Lich, Solar, Spectre, Spirit Naga, Tarrasque, Troll

Essence	Monster
Light	Azer, Balor, Darkmantle, Duergar, Fire Elemental, Giant Fire Beetle, Planetar, Shadow
Love	Couatl, Dryad, Satyr, Solar, Tarrasque
Luck	Centaur, Couatl, Satyr, Sprite, Merfolk, Tarrasque
Memory	Erinyes, Invisible Stalker, Mummy, Spectre, Water Elemental
Mercury	Aboleth, Androsphinx, Blink Dog, Chimera, Doppelganger, Drider, Gynosphinx, Lamia, Medusa, Mimic, Minotaur, Night Hag, Oni, Owlbear, Rakshasa
Mind	Drow, Giant Owl, Gynosphinx, Harpy, Kraken, Lich, Rakshasa, Treant
Pain	Balor, Barbed Devil, Dragon Turtle, Drow, Duergar, Fire Elemental, Giant Wasp, Goblin, Green Hag, Hell Hound, Merrow, Stirge
Perception	Androsphinx, Bugbear, Centaur, Couatl, Giant Bat, Giant Frog, Giant Octopus, Giant Toad, Giant Weasel, Gibbering Mouther, Gynosphinx, Red Dragon, Shrieker, Solar, Tarrasque
Planar	Azer, Barbed Devil, Bearded Devil, Bone Devil, Chain Devil, Couatl, Deva, Djinni, Dretch, Dust Mephit, Efreeti, Erinyes, Glabrezu, Hell Hound, Hezrou, Horned Devil, Ice Devil, Ice Mephit, Lemure, Magma Mephit, Marilith, Merrow, Nalfeshnee, Planetar, Pit Fiend, Quasit, Salamander, Steam Mephit, Succubus/Incubus, Tarrasque, Vrock, Xorn
Plant	Dryad, Earth Elemental, Shambling Mound, Shrieker, Treant, Violet Fungus
Prophecy	Centaur, Gynosphinx, Marilith, Storm Giant, Tarrasque
Protection	Black Pudding, Clay Golem, Gelatinous Cube, Gibbering Mouther, Solar, Tarrasque, Triceratops
Prowess	Bulette, Cloud Giant, Dragons (all), Fire Giant, Frost Giant, Giant Shark, Glabrezu, Griffon, Hill Giant, Iron Golem, Killer Whale, Kraken, Lion, Roc, Stone Giant, Stone Golem, Storm Giant, Tarrasque
Purity	Balor, Deva, Dryad, Fire Elemental, Pegasus, Planetar, Unicorn
Salt	Clay Golem, Ettin, Flesh Golem, Hill Giant, Manticore, Ogre, Otyugh, Stirge, Tarrasque
Speed	Air Elemental, Allosaurus, Behir, Pteranodon, Sprite
Stasis	Basilisk, Brass Dragon, Cockatrice, Gargoyle, Gelatinous Cube, Ghast, Ghoul, Giant Spider Gorgon, Medusa, Silver Dragon, Stirge, Tarrasque
Stealth	Air Elemental, Bugbear, Cloaker, Darkmantle, Doppelganger, Gargoyle, Gray Ooze, Grick, Invisible Stalker, Mimic
Strength	Ankylosaurus, Behir, Cloud Giant, Earth Elemental, Ettin, Fire Giant, Flesh Golem, Frost Giant, Giant Ape, Giant Constrictor Snake, Hydra, Mammoth, Minotaur, Ogre, Orc, Owlbear, Salamander, Shambling Mound, Stone Giant, Stone Golem, Xorn
Sulfur	Couatl, Griffon, Guardian Naga, Magma Mephit, Spirit Naga, Storm Giant, Tarrasque, Troll
Telesthetic	Drider, Otyugh, Pseudodragon
Toxin	Bearded Devil, Dretch, Drider, Ettercap, Giant Centipede, Giant Poisonous Snake, Giant Scorpion, Giant Spider, Hezrou, Imp, Medusa, Pseudodragon, Purple Worm, Spirit Naga, Vrock, Water Elemental, Wyvern
Transmutation	Bronze Dragon, Cockatrice, Copper Dragon, Doppelganger, Gold Dragon, Imp, Lycanthropes (all), Mimic, Ochre Jelly, Oni, Quasit, Rakshasa, Vampire
Transportation	Blink Dog, Nightmare, Phase Spider, Roc, Vampire, Wraith
Water	Chuul, Dragon Turtle, Frost Giant, Gelatinous Cube, Gray Ooze, Green Hag, Giant Sea Horse, Hydra, Ice Mephit, Kraken, Lizardfolk, Merfolk, Merrow, Ochre Jelly, Plesiosaurus, Sahuagin, Sea Hag, Steam Mephit, Water Elemental

In many situations it will be useful to cross-reference which vital essences are yielded by a particular monster, for which you will want to use **Table 2-6**.

GIANT SCORPION

BULETTE

GIANT SEAHORSE

Monster	Vital Essences Yielded
Aarakocra	Agility, Flight
Aboleth	Mercury/ Control, Illusion
Air Elemental	Air/ Electricity, Flight, Illusion, Speed, Stealth
Allosaurus	Earth/ Fear, Speed
Androsphinx	Mercury/ Emotion, Perception
Ankheg	Earth/ Acid, Armor
Ankylosaurus	Earth/ Armor, Strength
Azer	Fire/ Light, Planar
Balor	Azoth, Fire/ Agility, Decay, Light, Pain, Purity
Barbed Devil	Fire/ Pain, Planar
Basilisk	Earth/ Stasis
Bearded Devil	Fire/ Planar, Toxin
Behir	Armor, Electric, Speed, Strength
Black Dragon	Azoth/ Acid, Armor, Fear, Flight, Prowess
Black Pudding	Earth/ Acid, Protection
Blink Dog	Mercury/ Transportation
Blue Dragon	Azoth/ Armor, Electricity, Fear, Flight, Prowess
Bone Devil	Fire/ Decay, Planar
Brass Dragon	Azoth/ Armor, Fear, Fire, Flight, Prowess, Stasis
Bronze Dragon	Azoth/ Armor, Electricity, Fear, Flight, Prowess, Transmutation
Bugbear	Perception, Stealth
Bulette	Earth/ Armor, Prowess
Centaur	Luck, Percipience, Prophesy
Chain Devil	Fire/ Illusion, Planar
Chimera	Fire, Mercury
Chuul	Water, Armor, Body
Clay Golem	Earth, Salt/ Body, Protection
Cloaker	Air, Flight, Stealth
Cloud Giant	Air/ Prowess, Strength
Cockatrice	Air/ Stasis, Transmutation
Copper Dragon	Azoth/ Acid, Armor, Fear, Flight, Prowess, Transmutation
Couatl	Sulfur/ Healing, Life, Love, Luck, Perception, Planar
Darkmantle	Air/ Light, Stealth
Death Dog	Death
Deva	Azoth/ Healing, Light, Planar, Purity
Djinni	Air/ Dream, Emotion, Planar
Doppelganger	Mercury/ Stealth, Transmutation
Dragon Turtle	Water/ Armor, Pain
Dretch	Fire/ Planar, Toxin
Drider	Mercury/ Telesthetic, Toxin
Dryad	Earth/ Love, Plant, Purity
Duergar	Light, Pain
Dust Mephit	Earth/ Planar
Earth Elemental	Earth/ Acid, Armor, Disease, Plant, Strength
Efreeti	Fire/ Dream, Emotion, Planar
Elf, Drow	Azoth/ Mind, Pain
Erinyes	Fire/ Planar, Memory
Ettercap	Toxin
Ettin	Salt/ Body, Strength
Fire Elemental	Fire/ Agility, Decay, Light, Pain, Purity

ALLOSAURUS

DRIDER

Monster	Vital Essences Yielded
Fire Giant	Fire/ Prowess, Strength
Flesh Golem	Salt/ Body, Strength
Flying Snake	Flight
Frost Giant	Water/ Cold, Prowess, Strength
Gargoyle	Earth/ Stasis, Stealth
Gelatinous Cube	Water/ Protection, Stasis
Ghast	Azoth/ Decay, Stasis
Ghost	Azoth, Death, Life
Ghoul	Azoth/ Decay, Stasis
Giant Ape	Strength
Giant Badger	Earth
Giant Bat	Perception
Giant Boar	Life
Giant Centipede	Toxin
Giant Constrictor Snake	Strength
Giant Crab	Armor
Giant Crocodile	Armor
Giant Eagle	Agility
Giant Elk	Body
Giant Fire Beetle	Light
Giant Frog	Perception
Giant Goat	Earth
Giant Hyena	Decay
Giant Lizard	Body
Giant Octopus	Perception
Giant Owl	Mind
Giant Poisonous Snake	Toxin
Giant Rat	Disease
Giant Scorpion	Toxin
Giant Sea Horse	Water
Giant Shark	Prowess
Giant Spider	Toxin, Stasis
Giant Toad	Perception
Giant Vulture	Decay
Giant Wasp	Pain
Giant Weasel	Perception
Giant Wolf Spider	Agility
Gibbering Mouther	Earth/ Acid, Perception, Protection
Glabrezu	Fire/ Planar, Prowess
Gnoll	Body/ Decay
Goblin	Agility, Pain
Gold Dragon	Azoth, Air, Fire/ Armor, Fear, Flight, Prowess, Transmutation
Gorgon	Earth/ Armor, Stasis
Gray Ooze	Water/ Acid, Illusion, Stealth
Green Dragon	Azoth/ Acid, Armor, Fear, Flight, Prowess
Green Hag	Water/ Illusion, Pain
Grick	Earth/ Strength
Griffon	Air, Sulfur/ Flight, Prowess
Guardian Naga	Azoth, Sulfur/ Healing, Life

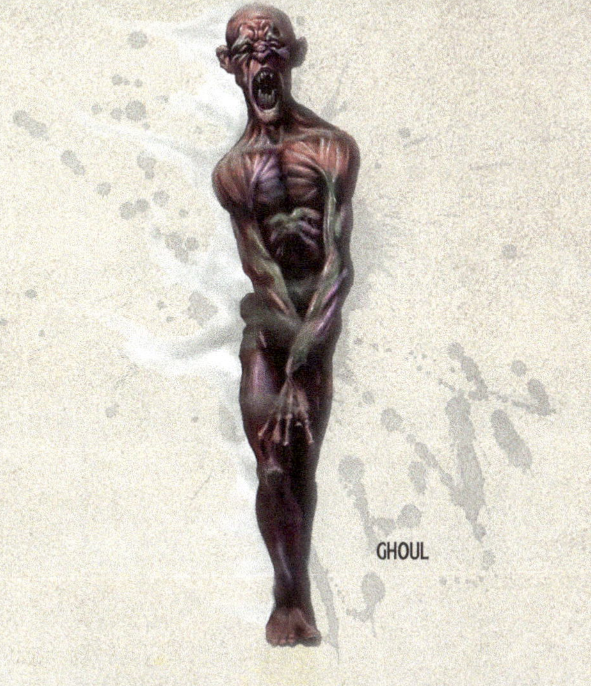

GHOUL

GIANT CRAB

GIANT FROG

GUARDIAN NAGA

MUMMY

Monster	Vital Essences Yielded
Gynosphinx	Mercury/ Mind, Percipience, Prophesy
Harpy	Air/ Control, Mind
Hell Hound	Fire/ Pain, Planar
Hezrou	Fire/ Planar, Toxin
Hill Giant	Salt/ Body, Prowess
Hippogriff	Air/ Fear, Flight
Hobgoblin	Body
Homunculus	Azoth
Horned Devil	Fire/ Disease, Planar
Hydra	Water/ Healing, Strength
Ice Devil	Fire/ Cold, Planar
Ice Mephit	Water/ Cold, Planar
Imp	Fire/ Toxin, Transmutation
Invisible Stalker	Air/ Memory, Stealth
Iron Golem	Earth/ Armor, Prowess
Killer Whale	Prowess
Kobold	Agility
Kraken	Water/ Electricity, Life, Mind, Prowess
Lamia	Mercury/ Control, Illusion
Lemure	Fire/ Healing, Planar
Lich	Azoth/ Fear, Life, Mind
Lion	Prowess
Lizardfolk	Water
Lycanthropes (all)	Emotion, Transmutation
Magma Mephit	Sulfur/ Planar
Mammoth	Body, Strength
Manticore	Salt/ Body, Flight
Marilith	Fire/ Planar, Prophesy
Medusa	Mercury/ Stasis, Toxin
Merfolk	Water
Merrow	Water/ Pain, Planar
Mimic	Mercury/ Stealth, Transmutation
Minotaur	Mercury/ Body, Strength
Mummy	Azoth/ Decay, Disease, Memory
Nalfeshnee	Fire/ Fear, Planar
Night Hag	Mercury/ Dream, Emotion
Night Mare	Fire/ Dream, Transportation
Ochre Jelly	Water/ Acid, Transmutation
Ogre	Salt/ Body, Strength
Oni (Ogre Mage)	Mercury/ Electricity, Transmutation
Orc	Strength
Otyugh	Earth, Salt/ Disease, Telesthenic
Owlbear	Azoth, Mercury/ Strength
Pegasus	Air/ Purity, Transportation
Phase Spider	Transportation
Pit Fiend	Fire/ Fear, Planar
Planetar	Azoth/ Light, Planar, Purity
Plesiosaurus	Water/ Body
Pseudodragon	Azoth/ Telesthenic, Toxin
Pteranodon	Air/ Agility, Speed
Purple Worm	Earth/ Acid, Toxin

Monster	Vital Essences Yielded
Quasit	Fire/ Planar, Transmutation
Rakshasa	Mercury/ Mind, Transmutation
Red Dragon	Azoth, Fire/ Armor, Fear, Flight, Perception, Prowess
Remorhaz	Fire/ Cold
Roc	Air/ Flight, Prowess, Transportation
Roper	Earth/ Acid, Decay
Rust Monster	Earth/ Decay
Saber-Tooth Tiger	Agility, Fear
Sahuagin	Water
Salamander	Fire/ Planar, Strength
Satyr	Earth/ Emotion, Love, Luck
Sea Hag	Water/ Death, Illusion
Shadow	Azoth/ Death, Light
Shambling Mound	Earth/ Electricity, Plant, Strength
Shrieker	Earth/ Perception, Plant
Silver Dragon	Azoth/ Armor, Cold, Fear, Flight, Prowess, Stasis
Skeleton	Azoth/ Death, Decay
Solar	Azoth/ Healing, Life, Love, Perception, Planar, Protection
Specter	Azoth/ Death, Dream, Life, Memory
Spirit Naga	Azoth, Sulfur/ Life, Toxin
Sprite	Air/ Emotion, Flight, Luck, Speed
Steam Mephit	Fire. Water/ Planar
Stirge	Salt/ Flight, Pain, Stasis
Stone Giant	Earth/ Prowess, Strength
Stone Golem	Earth/ Prowess, Strength
Storm Giant	Air, Sulfur/ Electricity, Prophesy, Prowess
Succubus/Incubus	Fire/ Emotion, Planar
Tarrasque	Azoth, Sulfur/ Body, Death, Prophesy, Protection, Prowess, Stasis
Treant	Earth/ Dream, Mind, Plant
Triceratops	Earth/ Armor, Protection
Troll	Sulfur/ Healing, Life
Tyrannosaurus Rex	Earth/ Fear, Prowess
Unicorn	Azoth/ Healing, Purity
Vampire	Azoth/ Fear, Transmutation, Transportation
Violet Fungus	Earth/ Decay, Plant
Vrock	Fire/ Planar, Toxin
Water Elemental	Water/ Cold, Emotion, Fear, Memory, Toxin
Werebear	Emotion, Transmutation
Wereboar	Emotion, Transmutation
Wererat	Emotion, Transmutation
Weretiger	Emotion, Transmutation
Werewolf	Emotion, Transmutation
White Dragon	Azoth/ Armor, Cold, Death, Fear, Flight, Prowess
Wight	Azoth/ Death, Decay
Will-o'-Wisp	Azoth/ Death, Electricity
Winter Wolf	Cold
Worg	Azoth
Wraith	Azoth/ Control, Death, Transportation
Wyvern	Air/ Flight, Toxin
Xorn	Earth/ Planar, Strength
Zombie	Azoth/ Death, Decay

SHADOW

ZOMBIE

CHAPTER THREE: ALCHEMICAL EQUIPMENT

Alchemical equipment refers to items and pieces of gear that can be produced only by someone proficient with alchemist's supplies or other specialized skills. Many of them do not detect as magical at all — these are items that do not have an alchemical formula, which is listed as "not applicable." The other items in this category are produced by non-magical, purely alchemical means, but they still detect as magical due to the presence of the vital essences contained in them. Truly magical items are listed in Chapter Four.

The various types of alchemical equipment are alchemical devices, grenades, incense, liquids and tonics, ointments and pastes, powders, solvents, and tinctures.

Each table below lists an item's name, its rarity, the crafting cost, and its weight. Descriptions provide more details about each item and include any non-standard requirements to craft the item. The rarity simply communicates how frequently such items are available for purchase and determines the DC to research and craft the item. The cost is precalculated in gold pieces. Non-standard requirements are included in the price and include rare gem dusts and essences.

The cost includes the price of all reagents, special requirements, and ingredients. Normal ingredients are presumed to be available and constitute what is being spent as part of the base cost to craft the item. Special ingredients such as other alchemical concoctions, gemstones, rare earths, and essences cost money and might be restricted or difficult to find. Collecting these and using them can lower the crafting cost of many of these items. For each one already in hand, reduce the crafting cost by the appropriate value.

The components for alchemical items are listed in order by mineral essences, vital essences that comprise an entire category of possible components, and then specific alchemical esssences that do not have substitutes. The azoth category is listed as having "any" possible sub-components even though it does not have actual subcomponents. This is done in case you decide to add subcategories to azoth, which has some characteristics that could be subdivided (including animation, undeath, sound and magic in general).

READING THE FORMULAS

An entry such as Air (any) (x2) indicates that any Air essence may be used, but two are required. Therefore, the alchemist might use two general Air essences, a general Air essence coupled with, for example, Speed, two of the same specific essence (such as two Speed essences), or two different specific Air essences (such as Speed and Stealth).

An entry such as Air (any 2 different) requires two different sources of the essence. Thus, a general Air essence might be coupled with a specific Air essence such as Speed, or two different specific essences might be used such as Speed and Stealth.

YOUR OWN FORMULAS

When you choose to make your own alchemical formulas or determine esssences that might be derived from monsters not on the list, there are a few general guidelines for using the general categories. Air is generally associated with motion, Earth is less thematic but tends toward bodily features, Fire is intuitively associated with qualities attributed to fire, Mercury has to do with mental qualities and change, Salt is similar to Earth but has more of an emphasis on skill rather than innate properties of matter, and Sulfur generally has to do with external forces. There are absolutely a number of specific vital essences that contradict these general guidelines for understanding the overall categories, which gives you considerable flexibility to make associations that "feel" right.

Many of the specific vital essences may appear counterintuitive as they are used in the items. This is because a category such as Light also includes its own opposite: there is no essence of "Blindness" or "Darkness," because these may be counteracted alchemically by manipulating the essence of Light. In other words, essences are often used to contradictory effect.

TYPES OF ALCHEMICAL EQUIPMENT

ALCHEMICAL DEVICES

Alchemists often combine their substances with particular devices such as inks, arrows, and ropes. They are often more powerful and useful than standard equipment. Many alchemists make their living selling such goods to local merchants.

GRENADES

These are thrown weapons that often cause damage to nearby targets. Because they are alchemical items, a character's Strength bonus never affects the damage. For items that damage adjacent areas, a character may choose to target a surface at a particular grid intersection; hit AC 5 and all targets within five feet take the splash effect. If targeting a surface, no target takes direct damage.

Characters are automatically considered proficient in throwing these and use their Dexterity to modify their chance to hit. A character cannot throw an object its size or larger. Items weighing more than one pound are thrown with disadvantage.

Selecting and drawing a grenade, pellet, or stone to throw is identical to drawing a weapon and can be part of a move action.

Grenades are specially scored to break on impact; any use of the grenade activates it. A grenade cannot be recovered after battle. A character carrying grenades that rolls a 1 on a saving throw versus force, fire, or other area damage may see the grenades trigger.

If a thrown item misses the target, roll 1d8 for the direction of the miss. A roll of 1 is directly north of the target (overthrown), with the other numbers going clockwise around the compass points. Thus, a roll of 5 would be short of the target. Roll 1d3 x 5 for miss distance in feet.

Grenades and thrown weapons have a range of 20/60 feet. Stones have a range 30/90 feet. Pellets have a range of 10/30 feet.

You may fire a grenade from a sling, but it does not fly well. You have a –8 penalty on to-hit rolls when doing this.

INCENSE

These are organic materials that release a scent or smoke when heat is applied to them. Incense is made from aromatic flora material. Incense takes an action to light and burns for one hour, no matter what variety is used. The effect begins at the beginning of your next turn.

Incense affects an area. Incense in an open area fills a 15-foot radius. However, if the area is enclosed or the air is particularly still, it can affect a maximum radius of 25 feet.

Incense can be snuffed out as an action by ordinary means. After being doused, crushed, or covered, the effects of incense end in 1d4 + 1 rounds.

LIQUIDS AND TONICS

Liquids and tonics are usually found in simple glass vials, bottles, or jars with one dose. These are usually labeled. Unfortunately, these labels usually have nothing but exaggerated claims of their effectiveness. Since these are manufactured for a profit, they are usually branded with the name of a local alchemist. Until consumed, it is difficult to determine the effects of these substances, so imbibe them at your own risk. Liquids of the same type, make, and manufacture will be somewhat similar, though formulation varies greatly from alchemist to alchemist.

Unless otherwise noted in the descriptions of individual tonics, the effects last for 1d4 + 4 minutes. The whole dose must be consumed for any effect to occur.

OINTMENTS AND PASTES

Ointments and pastes are substances that produce an alchemical effect when they are smeared over a surface. They take an action to apply. Ointments are applied to the skin and pastes to objects.

Note that in order to apply an ointment to the skin, clothing and armor must be removed.

Unless otherwise noted, ointments and pastes have a duration of one hour. Like magical oils, unless otherwise noted, these may be rinsed off with a mild alcohol solution such as wine if there is a desire to end their effects early.

POWDERS

Unless otherwise noted, powders appear as a dry, thick bulk solid composed of unconstrained flowing particles that move freely when shifted. Color and consistency may vary.

Powders are delivered to the target by a variety of methods. They may be sprinkled, added to food or drink, delivered by blowgun, or thrown.

Powders delivered via blowgun have a maximum range of 10 feet and affect the first target in front of you. You may instead target two adjacent creatures within five feet of you, but if there is a saving throw, each creature has advantage on it. If you don't have proficiency with a blowgun (martial ranged weapon), on a natural roll of 1 the powder affects you as if you were the target. Powders may also be thrown like grenades with a range of 10/30 feet. A direct hit is necessary to affect a single target. Any miss and the powder is harmless.

To be thrown as a grenade-like weapon, the powder must be prepared this way specifically ahead of time and contained in a light, breakable shell. Otherwise, there are loose piles of powder that are suitable for sprinkling or for use in a blowgun. A powder thrown as a grenade-like weapon does not need to penetrate armor in order to hit a target, unless specifically noted.

Unless otherwise noted, the target makes its saving throw when the powder hits it, and the effect occurs at the start of the target's next turn. Unless noted, the effects of powder last for 1d4 + 1 rounds.

SOLVENTS

Solvents are substances that, when applied to materials, rapidly weaken them or break them down. While acids and bases may act as solvents, damage caused by solvents is acid damage. Solvents are not represented by name, but by a class. Each type has a varying damage, type, and efficacy.

TINCTURES

A tincture is an extract formed using a substance soaked in alcohol. These are not always consumed. They are often added to other liquids and substances both magical and alchemical for their effects. The duration for a tincture is permanent, unless otherwise noted.

It usually takes one standard action to imbibe or apply a tincture, but it takes a few seconds before the tincture takes effect. Tinctures take effect at the start of the alchemist's next turn after activation.

ALCHEMICAL DEVICES

Anyone with proficiency in Alchemist's Supplies can produce the following devices. They are considered nonmagical items and tools. They are treated as standard equipment. Since these items are usually produced under contract with an alchemist and are not generally available, prices vary considerably. As a general rule, an alchemist would produce such an item at roughly five times the crafting cost, or three times the casting cost if the purchaser is providing the necessary elements of the alchemical formula used in production of the item.

TABLE 3–1: ALCHEMICAL DEVICES

Name	Rarity	Purchase Cost	Crafting Cost	Weight
Alchemist's Bandage	Common	Varies	40 gp	0.5 lb.
Alchemist's Fire Skewer	Uncommon	Varies	40 gp	1 lb.
Arcane Focus	Very Rare	Varies	2,500 gp	3 lbs.
Armor Padding	Uncommon	Varies	50 gp	1 lb.
Armorbreacher	Rare	Varies	15 gp	1 lb.
Arrow, Alchemical	Uncommon	Varies	5 gp	0.15 lb.
Arrow, Armor Piercing (20)	Uncommon	Varies	6 gp	3 lbs.
Arrow, Bleeding	Rare	Varies	160 gp	0.15 lb.
Arrow, Durable (20)	Common	Varies	20 gp	3 lbs.
Arrow, Dye (20)	Uncommon	Varies	20 gp	3 lbs.
Arrow, Flare (20)	Uncommon	Varies	20 gp	3 lbs.
Arrow, Lodestone (20)	Uncommon	Varies	200 gp	3 lbs.
Arrow, Marking	Uncommon	Varies	20 gp	0.15 lb.
Arrow, Pheromone	Uncommon	Varies	15 gp	0.15 lb.
Arrow, Shrieking (20)	Uncommon	Varies	10 gp	3 lbs.
Arrow, Slowburn	Rare	Varies	100 gp	0.15 lb.
Arrow, Splintercloud	Uncommon	Varies	25 gp	0.15 lb.
Arrow, Stinker	Uncommon	Varies	2 gp	.15 lb.
Arrow, Tangleshot	Uncommon	Varies	20 gp	0.15 lb.
Arrow, Thunder	Uncommon	Varies	5 gp	0.15 lb.
Arrow, Venipuncture	Uncommon	Varies	1 gp	0.15 lb.
Blade, Alchemical	Rare	Varies	500 gp	0.1 lb.
Bladeball	Uncommon	Varies	15 gp	1 lb.
Blinding Bag	Uncommon	Varies	15 gp	2 lbs.
Bolt Cutters, Heavy Duty	Uncommon	Varies	15 gp	5 lbs.
Bolt Cutters, Small	Uncommon	Varies	6 gp	1 lb.
Bomb Launcher	Uncommon	Varies	10 gp	0.5 lb.
Boots, Alchemical	Uncommon	Varies	450 gp	4 lbs.
Boots, Sonic	Uncommon	Varies	450 gp	4 lbs.
Boots, Springing	Uncommon	Varies	450 gp	4 lbs.
Bullet, Alchemical	Uncommon	Varies	35 gp	0.5 lb.
Bullet, Concussive	Uncommon	Varies	150 gp	0.05 lb.
Buoyant Balloon	Uncommon	Varies	10 gp	1 lb.
Calculus	Rare	Varies	50 gp	4 lbs.
Chalk, Dark Flame	Uncommon	Varies	5 gp	0.05 lb.
Chalk, Enduring	Rare	Varies	5 gp	0.05 lb.
Chalk, Glow	Uncommon	Varies	5 gp	0.05 lb.
Chalk, Ice	Uncommon	Varies	5 gp	0.05 lb.
Cloak, Deception	Rare	Varies	350 gp	1 lb.
Cloak, Fragrant	Rare	Varies	350 gp	1 lb.
Cloak, Slowfall	Rare	Varies	450 gp	1 lb.
Cold Fire	Common	Varies	10 gp	2 lbs.
Empyrean Stone	Common	Varies	100 gp	3 lbs.
Fabric, Noncombustible (Sq. Ft.)	Uncommon	Varies	10 gp	7 lbs.
Fabric, Shadow (Sq. Ft.)	Uncommon	Varies	15 gp	4 lbs.
False Tooth	Uncommon	Varies	30 gp	—
Falsifier's Parchment (Sheet)	Uncommon	Varies	10 gp	0.05 lb.
Flame Blade	Uncommon	Varies	50 gp	0.1 lb.
Flamethrower, Large	Very Rare	Varies	1,500 gp	500 lbs.
Flamethrower, Personal	Very Rare	Varies	1,000 gp	200 lbs.
Gloves, Alchemical	Rare	Varies	650 gp	1 lb.
Glow Globe	Common	Varies	3 gp	1 lb.
Glow Orb	Rare	Varies	200 gp	1 lb.
Heat Stone	Common	Varies	300 gp	0.1 lb.
Helm of Lenses	Rare	Varies	500 gp	3 lbs.
Homing Rods	Uncommon	Varies	250 gp	2 lbs.
Hose, Personal Waterblast	Rare	Varies	1,000 gp	200 lbs.
Hose, Waterblast	Rare	Varies	1,500 gp	500 lbs.
Ink, Cloud Chaser	Uncommon	Varies	250 gp	0.1 lb.
Ink, Disappearing	Uncommon	Varies	50 gp	0.2 lb.
Ink, Firelight	Uncommon	Varies	15 gp	0.2 lb.
Ink, Glowing	Uncommon	Varies	50 gp	0.1 lb.
Ink, Incendiary	Rare	Varies	50 gp	0.1 lb.
Ink, Magelight	Rare	Varies	30 gp	0.2 lb.
Ink, Moonlight	Rare	Varies	25 gp	0.2 lb.
Ink, Underscript	Rare	Varies	75 gp	0.2 lb.
Ink, Waterproof	Common	Varies	25 gp	0.1 lb.
Lantern, Solar	Uncommon	Varies	250 gp	2 lbs.
Lockrender	Uncommon	Varies	250 gp	2 lbs.
Marbles, Detonating	Rare	Varies	30 gp	2 lbs.
Mask, Gas	Uncommon	Varies	100 gp	8 lbs.
Mask, Superior Gas	Rare	Varies	125 gp	3 lbs.
Oil, Long-Burning	Uncommon	Varies	50 gp	1 lb.
Oil, Quick-Freeze	Rare	Varies	50 gp	1 lb.
Oil, Shadow	Common	Varies	5 gp	1 lb.
Oil, Stink	Uncommon	Varies	15 gp	1 lb.
Oil, Thieves'	Very Rare	Varies	55 gp	1 lb.
Paper, Acidproof	Uncommon	Varies	12 gp	0.2 lb.
Paper, Fireproof	Uncommon	Varies	10 gp	0.2 lb.
Paper, Waterproof	Uncommon	Varies	8 gp	0.2 lb.
Pox Burster	Rare	Varies	50 gp	1 lb.
Ring, Poison Needle	Uncommon	Varies	150 gp	0.1 lb.
Ring, Rogue's	Uncommon	Varies	300 gp	0.1 lb.
Ring, Secret Compartment	Uncommon	Varies	10 gp	0.1 lb.

Robe, Alchemical	Uncommon	Varies	65 gp	4 lbs.
Rope, Cave Fisher Reel	Rare	Varies	250 gp	0.1 lb.
Rope, Liquid	Uncommon	Varies	75 gp	5 lbs.
Rope, Stoneweave	Rare	Varies	12 gp	7 lbs.
Rope, Terrafugia	Uncommon	Varies	100 gp	5 lbs.
Rope Ladder, Flittermouse	Uncommon	Varies	175 gp	15 lbs.
Shard, Various	Common	Varies	45 gp	0.5 lb.
Shield, Alchemical	Uncommon	Varies	500 gp	15 lbs.
Shield, Hypnosis	Very Rare	Varies	+800 gp	15 lbs.
Smokestick (5)	Common	Varies	100 gp	2.5 lb.
Smokestick, Noxious	Uncommon	Varies	80 gp	0.5 lb.
Sparkthrower, Large	Rare	Varies	1,500 gp	500 lbs.
Sparkthrower, Personal	Rare	Varies	1,000 gp	200 lbs.
Spike, Locking	Uncommon	Varies	800 gp	15 lbs.
Spike, Self-Driving (10)	Rare	Varies	150 gp	5 lbs.
Spike, Silent (10)	Uncommon	Varies	80 gp	5 lb.
Spray Bellows, Alchemical	Uncommon	Varies	80 gp	6 lbs.
Sunrod (40)	Common	Varies	80 gp	40 lb.
Swiftlight	Common	Varies	15 gp	2 lbs.
Tanglewire (10 feet)	Uncommon	Varies	25 gp	5 lbs.
Thermotic Container	Common	Varies	80 gp	0.5 lb.
Tindertwig (10)	Common	Varies	10 gp	0.5 lb.
Towel, Alchemical	Uncommon	Varies	15 gp	3 lbs.
Trapblaster	Rare	Varies	150 gp	3 lbs.
Trapspringer	Uncommon	Varies	100 gp	Various
Vacuum Rod	Rare	Varies	500 gp	3 lbs.
Wall, Portable	Rare	Varies	400 gp	40 lbs.
Water Purification Sponge	Common	Varies	25 gp	1 lb.
Weather Rune	Uncommon	Varies	20 gp	0.5 lb.

Alchemist's Bandage: This bandage is slathered in a blood-clotting paste. You can use an action to apply it to a dying creature. The creature is stabilized and regains 1d4 hit points.
Alchemical formula: Earth (any), Salt (any), Sulfur (any), Healing

Alchemist's Fire Skewer: These two-foot iron spikes can be wielded like daggers. When you hit, they automatically activate and begin burning. The target takes 1d4 piercing damage when struck and 1d6 fire damage for each of the following two rounds. A creature can use an action to remove the skewers from the target to end the fire damage.
The skewers are used up on a successful strike. They can be thrown like daggers, but if they strike a target, they do not begin to burn.
Alchemical formula: Fire (any), Fire (any), Rare Earth

Arcane Focus: This ring is a magical focus made for a spellcaster. You may make one for yourself. Any spell cast using the focus is cast as if one higher level of spell slot was used for a specific arcane school of magic, such as the illusion school or the necromancy school.
Alchemical formula: Azoth (any 5), Gold, Rare Earth

Armor Padding: This is not an item but a technique you can learn to modify heavy armor. Successfully padded heavy armor does not provide disadvantage on Stealth checks when worn.
Alchemical formula: Not applicable

Armorbreacher: This device tears apart and weakens heavy armor. Make a melee weapon attack against a target in heavy armor. On a hit, the armor takes a permanent −2 penalty to the AC it offers. Armor reduced to an AC of 10 is destroyed. The *armorbreacher* is used up on a successful attack.
Alchemical formula: Iron (10), Rare Earth

Arrow, Alchemical: This arrow has a hollow tip. Upon striking a target, the tip shatters and the target is affected by the alchemical grenade used (see **Table 3-3**). A given arrow can be used only with a single type of alchemical grenade. The entire grenade is used up in the construction of the arrow. The cost of the grenade is not included in the crafting cost of the arrow; this must be purchased separately.
The arrow does 1d4 piercing damage, and the ranges are reduced by 25%. The alchemical mixture does half damage, or if no damage is applied, the target has advantage on their saving throw.
Alchemical formula: Not applicable

Arrow, Armor Piercing (20): You receive a +2 bonus to hit with this arrow versus any target with an armor or natural armor bonus of +4 or greater.
Alchemical formula: Iron (10), Rare Earth, Armor

Arrow, Bleeding: This sharpened hollow tube looks like the narrow proboscis of some giant insect, but it actually comes from a carnivorous plant. If you hit a living creature with this arrow, it does normal damage and the target loses 1 hit point at the beginning of each of its turns until a creature uses an action to bandage the target or the target is healed for at least one hit point.
Alchemical formula: Air (any), Pain, Healing, Silver

Arrow, Durable (20): These arrows are tightly wrapped in strands of alchemical glue. Durable arrows don't break with normal use, whether or not they hit their target; unless a durable arrow goes missing, you can retrieve and reuse it again and again. Durable arrows can be broken in other ways (such as deliberate snapping, hitting a fire elemental, and so on). A magical durable arrow becomes nonmagical after a hit, and it can be reused or imbued with magic again.
Alchemical formula: Air (any), Earth (any), Body, Turquoise

Arrow, Dye (20): This arrow ends in a crystalline bubble filled with a viscous alchemical dyeing agent. When you hit a creature with a dye arrow, it takes no damage but is splashed with enough black, blue, green, or red marker dye to coat about one square foot. The stain caused by marker dye cannot be washed off except with magic for the first 72 hours but fades completely after two weeks.
Alchemical formula: Azoth (any), Earth (any)

Arrow, Flare (20): This is an arrow that leaves a bright streak of light behind it in the air. A creature making a ranged attack against a target lit by a flare arrow get a +1 bonus to hit. The effect lasts for one minute or until a creature uses an action to remove and cover the arrow.
Alchemical formula: Fire (any), Fire (any)

Arrow, Lodestone (20): This heavy iron arrowhead is sealed with an alchemical resin. You can use a bonus action to pull a small string to break the seal and trigger a reaction in the arrowhead that greatly increases its magnetic properties. You gain a +4 bonus to hit when firing a lodestone arrow at a target wearing metal armor or at a target made of metal, but the magnetized arrow deals only half damage on a successful hit. The increased magnetism fades one round after you activate a lodestone arrow, after which it becomes a normal arrow.
Alchemical formula: Rare Earth, Iron, Earth (any)

Arrow, Marking: These are not arrows for a bow, but triangular pointing arrows. When you use an action to place one on a surface, it sinks down flush with the surface. When made, they may be configured to glow in the visible or infrared spectrum. They may be removed with a keyword. *Dispel magic* destroys them, or they can be pried out with a successful DC 15 Strength check.
Alchemical formula: Azoth (any), Mercury (any)

Arrow, Pheromone: The arrowhead of this arrow is coated with potent substances that react to blood and sweat, releasing a strong aroma that most predators recognize as the scent of tasty injured prey and that other creatures perceive as merely unpleasant. The target is more likely to be preferentially targeted by carnivorous beasts and other creatures with low intelligence that eat meat. This effect lasts for one hour or until the target spends one minute washing it off. If you hit with this arrow, it does normal damage.
Alchemical formula: Mercury (any), Love

Arrow, Shrieking (20): When fired, this arrow causes a terrible keening noise as if people were shrieking in pain as it flies through the air. All opponents must make a DC 12 Wisdom saving throw. On a failure, the creature is frightened until the start of your next turn. This arrow also attracts nearby wandering monsters. If you hit with it, it does normal damage.
Alchemical formula: Rare Earth, Air (any), Fear

Arrow, Slowburn: A small receptacle of alchemical material behind the head of this arrow heats up when exposed to air and eventually combusts; barbs on the arrowhead pierce the pouch when it hits a target. If you hit a target with a *slowburn arrow*, it deals damage as normal, but at the beginning of your next turn, the arrow bursts into flames and deals 3 (1d6) fire damage to all creatures within a five-foot radius. A creature can use an action to remove the arrow and throw it up to 15 feet in any direction.
Alchemical formula: Rare Earth, Fire (any), Fire (any), Mercury (any)

Arrow, Splintercloud: The shaft of this arrow is formed from numerous small bone fragments painstakingly glued together. On a successful hit, a *splintercloud arrow* deals normal damage. As it flies, it tears itself apart and creates a burst of razor-sharp bone shards centered on the target. Each creature within five feet, must succeed on a DC 15 Dexterity saving throw or take 1d3 piercing damage.
Alchemical formula: Air (any), Decay or Death

Arrow, Stinker: When you hit a target with this arrow, it does normal damage and the target is splashed with a strong scent of rotting eggs. Anyone attempting to track the target within 24 hours has advantage on their Survival checks to do so.
Alchemical formula: Sulfur (any), Decay

Arrow, Tangleshot: This arrow is tipped with a tiny vial of an alchemical adhesive. If you hit with the arrow, it does no damage, but the target is splashed with goo. If the creature is Medium or smaller, it is restrained (escape DC 12).
Alchemical formula: Earth (any), Mercury (any), Stasis

Arrow, Thunder: This arrow emits a deafening bang if it strikes its target. Anyone within 10 feet must succeed on a DC 14 Constitution saving throw or take 1d4 force damage and be deafened for one minute. The arrow does not otherwise do any damage. The range increment of the missile is cut in half.
Alchemical formula: Air (any), Salt (any), Strength

Arrow, Venipuncture: This arrow drains and collects a single ounce of the target's blood if it strikes a creature.
Alchemical formula: Not applicable

Blade, Alchemical: This modification to a melee weapon allows the weapon to store an alchemical grenade. When you strike a target with the modified weapon, you may choose to affect only the target with the effects of the grenade. The cost of the alchemical grenade is not included in the crafting cost — it must be added to the weapon after it is made. You can use a bonus action to load a new grenade into the weapon.
Alchemical formula: Not applicable

Bladeball: This small iron ball is about two inches in diameter. It is a thrown weapon with a range of 20/60 feet. On a successful hit, it does 3 (1d6) bludgeoning and piercing damage as spikes and blades explode out of the ball.
Alchemical formula: Iron, Air (any), Fire (any), Sulfur (any)

Blinding Bag: If this bag is thrown over someone's head, it clamps itself shut! Make a ranged or melee weapon attack. The bag has a maximum range of 10 feet. If you hit, the bag snaps shut over the target's head, blinding it. A creature can remove the bag with a successful DC 14 Strength check to end the blindness. This destroys the bag.
Alchemical formula: Iron, Mercury (any)

Bolt Cutters: This tool damages nonmagical metal bars. It comes in two sizes: small and heavy duty. The small bolt cutters do 15 damage to bars up to one-half inch thick with an AC up to 18; the heavy duty ones do 30 damage on bars up to one inch thick with an AC up to 22.
Alchemical formula: not applicable

Bomb Launcher: This is a one-use item "shell" that extends the range of a thrown alchemical device or grenades. These odd-looking, egg-shaped contraptions have cleverly placed fins that improve a grenade's accuracy. Goblin alchemists use these special containers to make their bombs more accurate when thrown long distances. Using a *bomb launcher* when throwing a grenade increases the bomb's range to 30/90 feet. Bomb launchers are destroyed when used.
Alchemical formula: not applicable

Boots, Alchemical: These boots are exceptionally well-made and stable. They provide you with protection against your own tricks. First, while wearing these boots you have advantage on any saving throw to avoid being knocked prone or to fall down. Also, you treat difficult terrain that is caused by alchemical items as normal terrain.
Alchemical formula: Iron, Rare Earth, Earth (any), Agility, Strength

Boots, Sonic: While wearing these boots, you can adjust the sound that they make. You can lower the noise produced to almost nothing, granting advantage on Stealth checks, or they can be increased in volume till every footfall sounds as if a storm giant was walking around. It takes an action to adjust the volume.
Alchemical formula: Rare Earth, Air (any), Mercury (any), Stealth

Boots, Springing: When triggered, these boots cause powerful springs to shoot the wearer high into the air. While wearing them, you gain a +5 bonus to Strength (Athletics) checks made to jump. When you land, however, you must succeed on a DC 14 Dexterity (Acrobatics) check to reset the boots. If you fail, you are held three inches off the ground by the springs and your movement is halved until you remove the boots or spend one minute resetting them. On a success, the boots are reset and may be used again.
Alchemical formula: Iron, Air (any), Flight

Bullet, Alchemical: This hollow glass sphere is designed to be fired from a sling. You must select which grenade to use at the time the item is created. The entire grenade is used up in the construction of the bullet. The cost of the grenade is not included in the cost of the item.
The bullet does normal damage on a hit and the alchemical mixture does half damage, or if no damage is applied, the target receives advantage on their saving throw.
Alchemical formula: not applicable

Bullet, Concussive: If this bullet strikes, it detonates and knocks the target prone. On a successful hit, the target is subject to the damage from the bullet and must succeed on a DC 14 Strength saving throw or be knocked prone. The bullet's range is cut in half.
Alchemical formula: Rare Earth, Air (any), Salt (any), Strength

Buoyant Balloon: This fist-sized alchemically treated animal bladder is tightly sealed around a small wooden grip. By using an action to give the handle a sharp twist, you break a tiny glass ampoule just inside the bladder, filling the bag with buoyant gas and causing it to swell into a three-foot-diameter sphere. Once filled, the balloon floats upward at a speed of 60 feet per round. The balloon can lift up to 20 pounds of weight as it rises, though carrying more than 10 pounds reduces its speed to 30 feet per round. Multiple balloons attached to a single object add their carrying capacities together when determining how much weight they can lift. If a balloon is not held or bound in place in some manner, it continues to rise until it reaches a height of 600 feet, or until 10 minutes pass, after which it pops or deflates and is destroyed.
Alchemical formula: Air (any), Air (any)

Calculus: This oversized mechanical sling is designed to fire grenades and liquid flasks. It can fire *alchemist's fire*, powders, solvents, and other alchemical items. This has whatever effect the item has but with a range of 40/120 feet. This is an exotic gnomish weapon, and gnomes are considered to have natural proficiency with it.
Alchemical formula: not applicable

Chalk, Dark Flame: This chalk appears to write invisibly, but is clearly visible with darkvision.
Alchemical formula: Rare Earth, Mercury (any), Sulfur (any)

Chalk, Enduring: This chalk makes indelible marks. Exposure to solvents, cleaners, motion, or other types of removal methods will not work. The marks can be erased with *dispel magic* followed by a normal cleaner.
Alchemical formula: Rare Earth, Azoth (any)

Chalk, Glow: This chalk and writing made with it glows in the dark.
Alchemical formula: Rare Earth, Light

Chalk, Ice: This chalk is able to write on ice.
Alchemical formula: Rare Earth, Water (any)

Cloak, Deception: This cloak can be taken off and with one round of preparation appear to move on its own. The cloak stays standing where set and appears to be a cloaked creature from a distance. The cloak can also be set to move in a somewhat realistic way no more than five feet in any direction and then back. To determine that the cloak is not a person requires a successful DC 13 Wisdom (Perception check). This DC can be increased if the person setting up the cloak takes two full rounds to do so. The user can then make a Stealth check and add half the result to the perception DC to notice that the cloak is not a person.
The cloak immediately collapses if struck by any weapon blow or attack.
Alchemical formula: Iron, Azoth, Illusion, Mind

Cloak, Fragrant: This is a cloak with a long-term scent neutralizer. It eliminates natural orders and leaves an odorless freshness behind. Animals dependent on scent to locate prey, such as when blinded, treat you as invisible while you wear this cloak.
Alchemical formula: Air (any), Fire (any), Salt (any), Stealth

Cloak, Slowfall: This cloak blooms out behind you when you fall, expanding like a pair of wings. This allows you to slow your speed and drift. If an unexpected fall happens, it negates the first 10 feet of falling damage. If you intentionally jump, it allows you to fall 40 feet safely and allows you to move five feet horizontally for every 10 feet you fall.
Alchemical formula: Iron, Rare Earth, Air (any), Flight

Cold Fire: These are small cubes or sticks. When you use an action to douse one in water, it begins to glow. It sheds bright light out to a 20-foot radius and dim light another 20 feet for two hours. This light produces no heat.
Alchemical formula: Rare Earth, Fire (any), Light

Empyrean Stone: This stone is attuned with a heavenly body when it is created. The stone glows when this body is in the sky, no matter how far underground the stone is taken. It is often attuned to the sun or the moon to determine the passage of time.
Alchemical formula: Diamond, Moonstone, Rare Earth, Light

Fabric, Noncombustible: This produces a rough cloth that is textured like stiff burlap. This cloth is resistant to fire and does not burn. It melts if exposed to extremely high temperatures, but it does not catch on fire. A full suit made of this cloth provides resistance to nonmagical fire damage and prevents the wearer from igniting while it is worn.
Alchemical formula: Fire (any), Salt (any), Water (any), Body

Fabric, Shadow: This matte fabric absorbs light and assists the user in hiding and stealthy movement. A cloak or single piece of clothing like a cloak provides a +1 bonus to Stealth checks made in dim or darker light, while a whole suit provides advantage on these checks.
Alchemical formula: Air (any), Azoth (any), Light, Stealth

False Tooth: This is a hollow tooth. It is implanted in the mouth and may contain anything that can fit in the space of a tooth.
Most often it is used to contain a single dose of an alchemical dust, liquid, powder, or poison. You may use a bonus action to crack open the tooth and with an action may blow the contents such that you and one creature within five feet are affected. The price does not include the contents of the tooth.
Alchemical formula: Pearl

Falsifier's Parchment: When this paper is exposed to mild heat, it turns nearly transparent. This is of particular use to forgers. At the end of an hour, it becomes opaque again and is indistinguishable from normal paper. Using this paper gives you advantage on using a Forgery Kit to create false documents.
Alchemical formula: Air (any), Fire (any)

Flame Blade: This small metal tube has a tab. When you use a bonus action to pull the tab, the reaction inside the tube causes a gout of flame to shoot from the end for one minute. You can make a melee weapon attack with it, doing 3 (1d6) fire damage on a successful hit.
Alchemical formula: Rare Earth, Fire (any), Mercury (any), Flight

Flamethrower, Large: This 10-foot-by-10-foot immobile device can throw flame. It has a nozzle attached to a 10-foot-long hose. You stand adjacent to the projector and fire a 60-foot line or 30-foot cone of fire. Each creature in the area must make a DC 16 Dexterity saving throw, taking 14 (4d6) fire damage and igniting on a failure or half as much and not igniting on a success.
You can use an action to change from a line to a cone. During this time, the weapon cannot be fired. When full, this item can be used six times. You can refill two uses with an action. A refill weighs eight pounds and costs 160 gp. This 500-pound projector can be mounted on wheels for an additional 500 gp. This allows it to be pushed or pulled forward or backward. It may turn in place.
Obviously, such a large volume of flammable liquid is very combustible. When taking any fire or lightning damage, roll d20. If the value is less than the amount of damage taken, the device explodes and is destroyed. Each creature within 30 feet must make a DC 16 Dexterity saving throw, taking 7 (2d6) fire damage per round of ammunition currently within it on a failure or half as much damage on a success. The flamethrower has an armor class of 14.
For an additional 500 gp and 200 pounds of weight, you can build a device that has eight rounds of ammunition. For an additional 1,000 gp and 500 pounds of weight, you can build one that holds 10 rounds of ammunition.
Alchemical formula: Rare Earth (x20), Earth (any) (x20), Fire (any) (x20), Sulfur (any), Mercury (any)

Flamethrower, Personal: This smaller flame-throwing device is mounted on a five-foot-by-five-foot cart. It has a nozzle attached to a 10-foot-long hose. You stand adjacent to the projector and fire a 40-foot line or 20-foot cone of fire. Each creature in the area must make a DC 16 Dexterity saving throw, taking 7 (2d6) fire damage and igniting on a failure or half as much and not igniting on a success.
You can use an action to change from a line to a cone. During this time, the weapon cannot be fired. When full, this item can be used four times. You can use an action to refill two uses. A refill weighs eight pounds and costs 160 gp. Obviously, such a large volume of flammable liquid is very combustible. When taking any fire or lightning damage, roll d20. If the value is less than the amount of damage taken, the device explodes and is destroyed. Each creature within 30 feet must make a DC 16 Dexterity saving throw, taking 7 (2d6) fire damage per round of ammunition currently within it on a failure or half as much damage on a success. The flamethrower has an armor class of 14.
Alchemical formula: Rare Earth (x10), Earth (any) (x10), Fire (any) (x10), Sulfur (any), Mercury (any)

Changing the intensity of the light requires a bonus action. After the flash is used, the orb is dark for one hour, after which it resumes its normal functions.
Alchemical formula: Gold, Rare Earth, Air (any), Fire (any), Light

Heat Stone: When placed firmly on the ground and given a slight sprinkle of water, this small stone heats up. The area that heats up is the section painted with water. It will boil water or heat food but does not catch flammables on fire or burn living creatures.
Alchemical formula: Rare Earth, Ruby, Fire (any)

Helm of Lenses: A variety of lenses are attached to this helm. You may use them to gain a +2 bonus on any of the following skill checks: Intimidation, Investigation, Perception, Survival (tracking only), Thieves' Tools, or relevant tools depending on vision. You receive an equal penalty to attack rolls and other skills, and always act last in the round.
This helm also has a variety of slots where other normal and magical cusps and lenses can be inserted and used hands free.
It takes an action to change a lens.
Alchemical formula: Diamond, Rare Earth, Mercury (any), Perception, Prowess

Homing Rods: These two rods vibrate in harmony and always attempt to point toward each other. They can be set to either vibrate or ring as they get closer to each other. They stop vibrating if they are on separate planes.
Alchemical formula: Diamond, Iron, Rare Earth, Water (any 2 different water essences)

Hose, Personal Waterblast: This smaller water sprayer sits on a five-foot-square cart. It has a nozzle attached to a hose that is 10 feet long. You stand adjacent to the projector and fire a 40-foot line or 20-foot cone of water. A creature in the area must make a DC 16 Dexterity saving throw. A creature in the way of the line that fails its saving throw takes 1d8 bludgeoning damage and is knocked prone. The area within the cone is difficult terrain and a creature in the cone who fails its saving throw takes 1 bludgeoning damage and is pushed back five feet.
You can use an action to change from a line to a cone. During this time, the weapon cannot be fired. When full, this item can be used four times. You can use an action to refill a use. A refill weighs 40 pounds and is free. The personal waterblast hose has an armor class of 12 and is fully destroyed if it takes 25 hit points of damage.
If the item takes any damage, it is disabled, being that it requires pressure (generated by steam) in order to fire. The materials used are too fragile to consider using any other substance in the portable waterblast hose other than water.
Alchemical formula: Rare Earth, Fire (any 2 different fire essences), Sulfur (any) (x5), Water (any) (x10), Strength

Hose, Waterblast: This large immobile device can spray a powerful gout of water. It takes up a 10-foot square. The device has a nozzle attached to a hose that is 10 feet long. You stand adjacent to the projector and fire a 60-foot line or 30-foot cone of water. Anyone in the area must make a DC 16 Dexterity saving throw. Targets in the way of the line that fail take 2d6 bludgeoning damage and are knocked prone. The area in the cone is difficult terrain and a creature in the cone that fails its saving throw takes 1 bludgeoning damage and are pushed back five feet.
You can use an action to change from a line to a cone. During this time, the weapon cannot be used. When full, this item can be used six times. You can use an action to refill a use. A refill weighs 40 pounds and is free.
This 500-pound projector can be mounted on wheels for an additional 500 gp. This allows it to be pushed or pulled forward or backward. It may turn in place.
If the item takes any damage, it is disabled, being that it requires pressure (generated by steam) in order to fire. The interior may be acid coated for an additional 3,000 gp, but then each use takes 40 pounds of solvent — for the weakest solvent, that's a crafting cost of 400 gp. Solvent cannot be pressurized to the same degree as water, so the damage from the spray is halved (1d6 for the line), though targets are covered in the solvent. The solvent damage is tripled, but still lasts for the same duration as the normal solvent does. Also, the hose must be replaced after two uses and doing so takes a full minute. The waterblast hose has an armor class of 12 and is fully destroyed if it takes 25 hit points of damage.
For an additional 500 gp and 200 pounds of weight, you can build a device that has eight rounds of ammunition. For an additional 1,000 gp and 500 pounds of weight, you can build one that holds 10 rounds of ammunition.
Alchemical formula: Rare Earth, Fire (any 3 different fire essences), Sulfur (any) (x10), Water (any) (x20), Strength

Gloves, Alchemical: You can use a bonus action to cause these gloves burst into elemental energy. Once activated these gloves are covered in elemental energy for three rounds. If you hit with a melee attack during this time, you do an addition 1d6 damage of the appropriate type, along with relevant secondary effects noted below. Each round you take 1 damage of the appropriate type. These gloves may be activated again after a minute has passed. Materials and effects are listed below.

TABLE 3–2: ALCHEMICAL GLOVE ENERGIES

Element/ Damage Type	Essence	Effect
Acid	Acid	Target takes an additional 1 acid damage at the beginning of each of its turns until a creature uses an action to clean the acid from the target.
Fire	Fire (any 2 different fire essences)	Target must succeed on a 14 Dexterity saving throw or ignite.
Cold	Cold	Target must succeed on DC 14 Constitution saving throw or its movement is reduced by half until the end of its next turn.
Lightning	Electricity	Each creature within 5 feet of the target takes 1 lightning damage.

Alchemical formula: Rare Earth (20), applicable essence (see **Table 3-2**)

Glow Globe: A glow globe casts bright light in a 15-foot radius and dim light for an additional 15 feet
Alchemical formula: Fire (any)

Glow Orb: This is similar to the glow globe, but substantively more useful. This sphere is adjustable between a dim glow all the way to a blinding flash. A creature within 30 feet of the blinding flash that can see must succeed on a DC 16 Dexterity saving throw or be blinded. A blinded creature can make a DC 16 Constitution saving throw at the end of each of its turns, ending the effect on a success. At maximum steady state, it sheds bright light in a 60-foot radius and dim light for an additional 60 feet. It floats anywhere you wish within 10 feet of you. It has an armor class of 12 and 10 hit points.

Ink, Cloud Chaser: When added to water, this ink runs through the water like a darting fish toward the place where the water is closest to the sky.
Alchemical formula: Pearl, Rare Earth, Water (any), Perception

Ink, Disappearing: This ink leaves a normal looking mark after it dries. One minute later, the ink disappears. The ink can be made to reappear with the application of Salt essence.
Alchemical formula: Rare Earth, Mercury (any), Water (any)

Ink, Firelight: This ink leaves no mark after it dries. The marks reappear only when exposed to flame.
Alchemical formula: Air (any), Mercury (any), Salt (any), Water (any)

Ink, Glowing: This ink glows a light green or orange when put to paper. It allows whatever is written to be read in the dark.
Alchemical formula: Rare Earth, Light

Ink, Incendiary: This ink appears completely normal at first glance. However, once dusted with simple talc powder, the ink flares up and burns the sheet of paper and any attached papers to ash.
Alchemical formula: Rare Earth, Fire (any), Sulfur (any)

Ink, Magelight: This ink leaves no mark after it dries. The marks reappear only when exposed to magical light such as *continual flame* or *light*.
Alchemical formula: Rare Earth, Azoth (any), Fire (any)

Ink, Moonlight: This ink leaves no mark after it dries. The marks reappear only when exposed to moonlight.
Alchemical formula: Moonstone, Azoth (any)

Ink, Underscript: This ink leaves no mark when anyone writes with it. However, it is highly visible to anyone who has darkvision.
Alchemical formula: Rare Earth, Mercury (any), Water (any), Stealth

Ink, Waterproof: This ink is waterproof and will not run when exposed to water.
Alchemical formula: Earth (any), Mercury (any), Salt (any), Water (any)

Lantern, Solar: This lantern requires no fuel source except the sun. Exposure to eight hours of sunlight allows it to cast light for 12 hours. The core must be replaced monthly at the cost of 10 gp.
Alchemical formula: Gold, Rare Earth, Fire (any), Light

Lockrender: This explosive shaped charge is used to bypass doors. When set against a lock and lit, it burns for 1d4 + 1 rounds before igniting. At the end of this time, it creates a blast that blows up the lock.
The lockrender makes a Strength check to break open the door with a +10 bonus.
Those standing within 10 feet of the blast must make a DC 12 Constitution saving throw or be knocked prone and take 7 (2d6) force damage.
Alchemical formula: Iron, Rare Earth, Fire (any), Strength

Marbles, Detonating: These marbles may be used in different ways. You may throw one as an action, doing 1d4 fire damage on a hit, and 1 force damage to everyone within five feet. Or they may be used like normal marbles. A creature entering a square with marbles scattered on it must succeed on a DC 10 Dexterity saving throw or fall prone. The marbles then all detonate, doing 3 (1d6) fire damage. In either case, they continue to burn and smolder for one full minute, causing that five-foot area to be difficult terrain and illuminating the area within 10 feet brightly and double that distance dimly.
Alchemical formula: Earth (any), Fire (any), Sulfur (any), Transmutation

Mask, Gas: This mask provides protection from inhaled toxins. All saving throws versus gas attacks, noxious fumes, or stenches are made with advantage. This mask functions while worn for 24 hours before needing to be replaced.
Alchemical formula: Air (any 2 different Air essences), Earth (any), Water (any), Protection

Mask, Superior Gas: This mask is lighter than a standard gas mask. It provides advantage on all saving throws versus gas attacks, noxious fumes, or stenches. It also allows the wearer to breath underwater for two minutes. This mask functions while worn for 24 hours before needing to be replaced. Each minute used to breathe water reduces this length by eight hours.
Alchemical formula: Air (any 3 different Air essences), Earth (any), Water (any 2 different Water essences), Protection

Oil, Long-Burning: When added to a torch or lamp, this oil fuels the burning reaction and causes it to burn for a greatly extended duration. One dose causes a campfire to burn for 24 hours, six torches to burn for 12 hours each, or it can keep an oil lamp burning for 72 hours.
It is not at all volatile and does not explode (and is even harder to light). It does not affect magical flames and has no effect on fires larger than a campfire.
Alchemical formula: Rare Earth, Fire (any), Salt (any), Water (any), Light

Oil, Quick-Freeze: This bottle of viscous blue oil sublimates slightly when exposed to air. When poured over water, the oil pools on the surface and takes six seconds to spread out from the point of origin in a 20-foot radius. At the end of this time, the oil flash-freezes the surface of the water, creating an ice sheet over the affected area. Any five-foot square of this ice can support up to 200 pounds of weight. Weight in excess of this amount causes the entire sheet to crack and quickly break up. This ice sheet becomes unstable and breaks up on its own after one hour, or after 20 minutes in a hot climate. Any creature whose bare skin comes in contact with this oil takes 3 (1d6) cold damage.
Alchemical formula: Rare Earth, Salt (any), Water (any), Cold

Oil, Shadow: When burned in a lantern, this oil works like normal oil in all ways such as burning time, but instead of producing a bright yellow light, it produces a dim blue-green light.
Alchemical formula: Earth (any), Fire (any), Water (any), Stealth

Oil, Stink: This glass container of foul-smelling oil shatters easily upon impact. You can throw a vial of stink oil to a square within 30 feet. Any creature that can smell within five feet of the target location must succeed on a DC 14 Constitution saving throw or be nauseated for 1d4 + 1 rounds. While nauseated, the creature is poisoned.
Alchemical formula: Rare Earth, Salt (any), Water (any), Decay

Oil, Thieves': When burned in a lantern, this oil works like normal oil in all ways such as burning time, but the light produced is visible only to the wielder.
Alchemical formula: Rare Earth, Azoth (any), Salt (any), Water (any), Stealth

Paper, Acidproof: This paper is not damaged by acid for one minute. The price is for a single sheet.
Alchemical formula: Earth (any), Salt (any), Acid

Paper, Fireproof: This paper is does ignite from nonmagical fire for one minute. Any saving throw made to resist having it burn from magical fire is made with advantage. The price is for a single sheet.
Alchemical formula: Earth (any), Fire (any), Salt (any), Protection

Paper, Waterproof: This paper is waterproof, and the ink on it will not run if exposed momentarily to rain, water splashes, ice, or snow. The pages will not be ruined by such exposure. When submerged in water, it repels the water for up to one minute. The price is for a single sheet.
Alchemical formula: Earth (any), Water (any), Salt (any), Protection

Applications of multiple proofing treatments are possible. Simply take the most expensive treatment and double the quantity for two applications, triple it for three, etc.

These same treatments may also be applied to leather scroll cases.

Pox Burster: A *pox burster* is an alchemically preserved animal bladder or gourd that has been filled with toxic, rotting materials. You can throw a pox burster with a range of 10/30 feet. A direct hit forces a target to succeed on a DC 13 Constitution saving throw or contract sewer plague. Every space adjacent to the target square of the *pox burster* is covered in disease-causing filth. For the next minute, any creature that takes damage while in one of these spaces must make a DC 9 Constitution saving throw or contract sewer plague.
Alchemical formula: Salt (any), Decay, Disease, Toxin

Ring, Poison Needle: Any nonmagical ring and any poison may be used. The poison is not what is being created here and the ring, once crafted, is empty: it is the price and the difficulty involved in adding the needle mechanism that is reflected in the table. Loading poison into the ring takes an action. You may use a bonus action to twist the stone to exude a needle with one dose of poison. The needle may spring from the inside, outside, or both. You can make a melee weapon attack to inject the poison into a target. The needle itself does no damage.
Alchemical formula: not applicable

Ring, Rogue's: This slightly oversized ring conceals a few lockpicks and other tools coiled inside its band. These discreet tools — made of a metal alloy that springs straight once the tool is removed from the band — are sufficient to attempt checks that require thieves' tools, and long enough to pick locks on manacles fastened around the wearer's hands. You have advantage on any Sleight of Hand or Stealth checks made to conceal the ring's nature from anyone searching you.
Alchemical formula: Rare Earth, Platinum, Earth (any), Stealth

Ring, Secret Compartment: Any nonmagical ring may be used or created. The price and difficulty to add the compartment are listed in **Table 3-1**. This ring can store one dose of any potion, elixir, philter, liquid, tonic, tincture, dust, powder, or any other substance deemed feasible and keep it fresh and protected from harm for seven days. The compartment is waterproof.
Alchemical formula: not applicable

Robe, Alchemical: This robe is especially designed to hold up to 10 alchemical items weighing one pound or less in protected pockets. You have advantage on any saving throws made to avoid their destruction while the items are in the pockets.
The robe also has several harnesses to hold larger objects. You can carry items as if your Strength was one higher.
Alchemical formula: Protection, Strength

Rope, Cave Fisher Reel: This is a needle-thin, strong, transparent rope that supports 1,000 pounds. When paired with gloves and boots coated in a mixture of alchemical glue and solvent, cave fisher reel rope provides a +10 bonus to Strength (Athletics) checks made to climb.
Alchemical formula: Rare Earth, Earth (any), Transmutation

Rope, Liquid: This liquid is in a squeezable pouch, most often a waterskin. When you use an action to uncap and squeeze it empty, it produces a length of green paste that firms up into a rope-like substance at the end of your next turn. The liquid can produce up to 500 feet of rope.
The rope lasts for 24 minutes when exposed to air then begins to flake and fall apart into dust.
Alchemical formula: Rare Earth, Mercury (any), Water, (any), Transmutation

Rope, Stoneweave: Dwarves make this rope from discarded metals. The rope has 12 hit points and can be burst with a DC 25 Strength check. It can support up to 1,000 pounds.
Alchemical formula: Iron, Earth (any), Strength

Rope, Terrafugia: This rope appears normal while coiled. However, once an end is free, it falls upward. The rope always falls away from the ground. If unraveled outdoors, the rope falls away into the sky, though the slightest weight or pressure holds it down. This is primarily useful for underground exploration and travel.
Alchemical formula: Rare Earth, Air (any), Flight

Rope Ladder, Flittermouse: This is a rope sculpture knotted in the form of a bat. When you use an action to toss it into the air, it flies unerringly to any target that is not a creature within 60 feet and attempts to attach itself. It can attach to stone or rock and hook to ledges or other surfaces easily. Once attached, a 60-foot rope ladder unfurls and falls down. It takes one minute to re-knot the *flittermouse rope ladder* for use.
Alchemical formula: Rare Earth, Air (any), Azoth (any), Prowess

Shard, Various: These useful items can be used for various purposes when immersed in water. Upon immersion, you may choose to boil the water, chill the water, or flavor it as stock. A *various shard* is useful for about 30 days before the potency starts to fade.
Alchemical formula: Diamond, Earth (any), Fire (any), Water (any)

Shield, Alchemical: This modification to a shield allows it to store an alchemical grenade (see **Table 3-3**). When a melee attack misses the wielder by 1 or 2, the attacker and anyone within five feet of the outside of the shield is affected as if struck by the grenade (i.e., not the wielder, but the target and the squares to either side of the target). The alchemical grenade must be purchased separately and is not included in the cost.
Alchemical formula: not applicable

Shield, Hypnosis: This modification to a shield allows the shield to hypnotize opponents. As an action, you can activate the shield, turning the black and white spiral on the front. All within 20 feet who can see the shield must succeed on a DC 16 Wisdom saving throw or be captivated by the shield. While captivated, a creature cannot take a reaction or an action. If the creature moves, it must move toward the shield. If a captivated target takes damage, it snaps out of its reverie. A captivated target can repeat the saving throw at the end of each of its turns, ending the effect on itself on a success.
Alchemical formula: Rare Earth, Control, Mind

Smokestick: This alchemically treated wooden stick instantly creates thick, opaque smoke when you use an action to ignite it. The smoke fills a 10-foot cube, and everything within the cube is heavily obscured. The stick is consumed. The smoke dissipates naturally after one minute or immediately with wind of moderate or greater speed (at least 10 mph). See **Chapter One: Alchemy Basics** for alternate dispersion rates of smoke.
Alchemical formula: Rare Earth, Fire (any), Salt (any)

Smokestick, Noxious: This alchemically treated wooden stick instantly creates thick, opaque smoke when you use an action to ignite it. The smoke fills a 10-foot cube, and everything within the cube is heavily obscured. Any creature that starts its turn in the area or enters the area for the first time on its turn must make a DC 14 Constitution saving throw. On a failure, the creature is poisoned. A poisoned creature remains poisoned until it leaves the area. The stick is consumed. The smoke dissipates naturally after one minute or immediately with wind of moderate or greater speed (at least 10 mph). See **Chapter One: Alchemy Basics** for alternate dispersion rates of smoke.
Alchemical formula: Rare Earth, Fire (any), Salt (any), Toxin

Sparkthrower, Large: This 10-foot-by-10-foot immobile device can throw bolts of electricity. It has a nozzle attached to a 10-foot-long rubber-coated copper wire. You stand adjacent to the projector and fire electricity in a line that is 60 feet long by five feet wide. Any creature in the line must make a DC 16 Dexterity saving throw, taking 14 (4d6) lightning damage on a failure or half as much damage on a success.
This weapon has no limit on the number of uses; however, it must be charged. It is charged manually by working the cycler and the pump. With a crew of three, the weapon can be charged and fired every other round. With a crew of two, the weapon can be fired and charged every third round. A single operator can charge and fire the weapon every fourth round. A charge is held for one minute.
This 500-pound projector can be mounted on wheels for an additional 500 gp. This allows it to be pushed or pulled forward or backward. It may turn in place.
If the *sparkthrower* is damaged, the user and anyone adjacent must make a DC 16 Dexterity saving throw or take 1d6 lightning damage. The device no longer functions when broken. It has an armor class of 12 and 25 hit points.
Alchemical formula: Rare Earth, Air (any) (x20), Earth (any) (x20), Sulfur (any) (x20), Electricity (any) (x2)

Sparkthrower, Personal: This smaller *sparkthrower* device sits on a five-foot-by-five-foot cart and allows you to throw bolts of electricity. It has a nozzle attached to a 10-foot-long rubber-coated copper wire. You stand adjacent to the projector and fire electricity in a line that is 60 feet long by five feet wide. Any creature in the line must make a DC 16 Dexterity saving throw, taking 7 (2d6) lightning damage on a failure or half as much damage on a success.
This weapon has no limit on the number of uses; however, it must be charged. It is charged manually by working the cycler and the pump. With a crew of two, the weapon can be charged and fired every other round. A single operator can charge and fire the weapon every third round. A charge is held for one minute.
If the *sparkthrower* is damaged, the user and anyone adjacent must make a DC 16 Dexterity saving throw or take 1d6 lightning damage. The device no longer functions when broken. It has an armor class of 12 and 25 hit points.
Alchemical formula: Rare Earth, Air (any) (x10), Earth (any) (x10), Sulfur (any) (x10), Electricity (any)

Spike, Locking: These spikes are enchanted so that when they spike a door closed, the door is affected by the spell *arcane lock*. Each spike can be used only once, and its enchantment vanishes after it is used to magically hold a door closed. The effect ends if the spike is removed but otherwise persists without end.
Alchemical formula: Iron, Azoth (any), Stasis

Spike, Self-driving: These spikes require no hammer to drive themselves in. Once placed in the appropriate position, you can use a bonus action to trigger the spike. One round later, a bright flame shoots out the back, and the spike drives itself into the ground, drilling as it goes. This is somewhat quiet, producing little sound, but it does create a very bright light. These spikes can be used as a dagger to attack. They do 1d3 piercing damage on a hit, and the next round the spike begins to drill into an opponent, doing 1d4 piercing damage and 1d6 fire damage. The target also must succeed on a DC 12 Wisdom saving throw or be dazzled by the bright light until the end of its next turn. While dazzled, the target has disadvantage on attack rolls. It must be activated after being stuck into an opponent. A target may remove a self-driving spike as part of their move action.
Alchemical formula: Gold, Iron, Fire (any 2 different Fire Essences), Strength

Spike, Silent: An alchemist can create specially treated spikes. When used, climbed on, hammered into a surface, or interacted with in any way, they produce no sound. They also completely absorb any sound made from them being driven into a surface.
Alchemical formula: Iron, Stealth

Spray Bellows, Alchemical: This device consists of one watertight central ammunition bladder and several air bladders linked by specialized nozzles. When you use an action to compresses the air bladders, the *alchemical spray bellows* sprays its ammunition in a 10-foot cone. Most adventurers use the bellows to spray powder over invisible foes or holy water over incorporeal undead, but it can also spray oil, itching powder, sneezing powder, or other mundane dusts and liquids.
Loading the ammunition bladder takes an action and requires either a four-pint jug of liquid (weighing up to four pounds) or a four-pound sack of powder; insufficient ammunition causes it to misfire harmlessly. Refilling the air bladders can be done as part of a move action. Readying and firing an alchemical spray bellows requires two hands.
Loading an *alchemical spray bellows* with unstable compounds such as acid or *alchemist's fire* destroys the device.
Alchemical formula: not applicable

Sunrod (40): This one-foot-long, gold-tipped iron rod glows brightly when you use an action to strike it. It sheds normal light in a 30-foot radius and dim light for an additional 30 feet. It glows for six hours, after which the gold tip burns out and is worthless.
Alchemical formula: Gold, Rare Earth, Light

Swiftlight: This is a fast-lighting torch that sheds light for 20 minutes. It can be lit as a free action when drawn, one time only.
Alchemical formula: Fire (any), Speed

Tanglewire: You can use an action to string *tanglewire* across an opening up to 10 feet wide. A creature that traverses the area must succeed on a DC 16 Dexterity (Acrobatics) check or take 2 (1d4) slashing damage. A creature that takes damage is restrained (escape DC 13).
Alchemical formula: Iron, Rare Earth

Thermotic Container: This metal container maintains the temperature of liquids added to the bottle for up to eight hours.
Alchemical formula: Rare Earth, Earth (any), Fire (any), Water (any), Stasis

Tindertwig: The alchemical substance on the end of this small, wooden stick ignites when struck against a rough surface (which you can do as a free action). Creating a flame with a *tindertwig* is much faster than creating a flame with tinder and a flint and steel or by using a magnifying glass. A tindertwig burns for 1d2 rounds and sheds light as a candle. *Tindertwigs* are waterproof but must be dried before you can strike them.
Alchemical formula: Rare Earth, Fire (any)

Towel, Alchemical: This amazing towel is comfortable and serves as a normal towel, except it has amazing absorbent properties. It can hold up to 60 times its weight in water and liquids. This means it can absorb approximately three cubic feet of water, or more than 22 gallons. It's easily washable, won't scratch any surface, and you'll say, "Wow!" every time you use it.
Alchemical formula: Air (any), Water (any), Transmutation

Trapblaster: These are two jagged, two-foot-long poles attached to powerful springs. When thrown, they begin bouncing and ricocheting against any surface in a five-foot square. Anyone in the square must succeed on a DC 16 Dexterity saving throw or take 2d6 bludgeoning damage. The *trapblaster* cuts tripwires, damages trap mechanisms, and hits surfaces with 150 pounds of force. The *trapblaster* walks to a randomly selected square at the end of every round. Roll 1d10 on the grenade scatter table; a 9–10 means it stays in the same square. If it moves into a wall, move it five feet in the opposite direction. It is very mobile and has an armor class of 15 and 15 hit points. The *trapblaster* operates for one minute before breaking.
Alchemical formula: Iron, Flight

Trapspringer: These rubberized globes can be thrown at a surface within 30 feet. They come in a variety of weights. Each pound of the *trapspringer* triggers traps as a 25-pound object plus the strength of the thrower squared. If a person with a Strength of 16 throws a one-pound *trapspringer*, it impacts the trap as if 281 pounds (25 + 256 = 281) had triggered it. That same person throwing a five-pound *trapspringer* would impact an area with a 381-pound force (125 + 256 = 381). If thrown at a target, they do 1 bludgeoning damage on a hit, plus 1 additional for every 50 pounds of force. A person with a Strength of 16 throwing a one-pound *trapspringer* would do 6 bludgeoning damage. *Trapspringers* weighing more than five pounds require two hands to throw. As a thrown weapon, a *trapspringer* has a range of 10/30 feet.
Alchemical formula: Rare Earth, Strength

Vacuum Rod: This rod has the ability to produce a powerful vacuum. When you use an action to trigger this item, you gain a +5 bonus to your armor class against all missile attacks. The area in a 30-foot cone in front of you becomes difficult terrain, and all Dexterity checks and saving throws are made with disadvantage. Objects that are not worn or carried that weigh less than one pound are sucked into the rod and vaporized. After every round of use, there is a noncumulative 1% chance that the rod ceases functioning and is broken and worthless.
Alchemical formula: Rare Earth, Azoth (any) (x2), Salt (any), Sulfur (any), Transportation

Wall, Portable: This is a large brick that weighs 40 pounds and takes up two cubic feet of space (12 inches x 18 inches x 16 inches). When set on the ground and activated as an action, it turns into a barrier that is two feet thick, 10 feet wide, and four feet high. Standing behind this barrier provides partial cover, while ducking behind it provides full cover. The barrier is solid and treated as stone. It takes one minute to collapse the wall back down to its portable form.
Alchemical formula: Rare Earth, Earth (any 2 different Earth essences), Strength, Transmutation

Water Purification Sponge: This fist-sized blue sponge absorbs up to one pint of water. Squeezing the water out of the sponge filters and purifies it, making it safe for drinking, washing, and similar activities. Filling and emptying the sponge takes an action. The filtration is enough to remove mundane impurities and common diseases, but does nothing to protect against poisons, magic, and other exotic threats. Each sponge can cleanse 25 pints of water before deteriorating and becoming useless.
Alchemical formula: Rare Earth, Water (any), Purity

Weather Rune: By reading the color changes in this stone, the alchemist is able to predict the weather over the next 24 hours with 90% accuracy. Note that no roll must be made to determine the current weather.
Alchemical formula: Air (any), Earth (any), Salt (any), Water (any)

GRENADES, PELLETS, AND STONES

Any item marked as a grenade can be converted into a mine that detonates if approached within five feet. A mine is placed as an action on a grid intersection. Anyone within five feet is affected by direct damage. Anyone between five feet and 10 feet is affected by splash damage. It adds 300 gp to the crafting cost. You can avoid setting it off with a successful DC 18 Dexterity (Stealth) check, and it can be disabled with a successful DC 18 Dexterity check with thieves' tools. On a failure of more than 5, the mine is triggered.

Any item marked as a grenade can be converted into a gas, which persists and applies the grenade effect to all those within range of the grenade. This process is difficult and dangerous. On a failure by 5 or more during creation, the alchemist is affected by a double strength version of the grenade instead of rolling on the Alchemical Mishap table. Converting grenades into gases costs an additional 1,000 gp. This creates a gas cloud with a radius of 30 feet that is 10 feet high. The cloud persists for 30 rounds or until it is dispersed; this varies based on the local ventilation level (see **Gas Clouds** in **Chapter One: Alchemy Basics**). Anyone within the cloud receives the effect of the grenade each round while within the cloud. Grenades that are already gasses cannot be modified in this way. Creating gaseous grenades increases the creation check DC by 5.

TABLE 3–3: GRENADES, PELLETS, AND STONES

Name	Rarity	Purchase Cost	Crafting Cost	Weight	Type
Aboleth Gel	Very Rare	Varies	400 gp	1 lb.	Grenade
Alchemist's Alarm	Rare	Varies	200 gp	1 lb.	Grenade
Alchemist's Barricade	Rare	Varies	180 gp	1 lb.	Grenade
Alchemist's Befuddlement	Rare	Varies	200 gp	1 lb.	Grenade
Alchemist's Censorship	Uncommon	Varies	200 gp	1 lb.	Grenade
Alchemist's Fire	Common	Varies	25 gp	1 lb.	Grenade
Alchemist's Firewater	Uncommon	Varies	25 gp	1 lb.	Grenade
Alchemist's Fist	Rare	Varies	50 gp	1 lb.	Grenade
Alchemist's Inferno	Rare	Varies	600 gp	1 lb.	Grenade
Alchemist's Knife	Uncommon	Varies	40 gp	1 lb.	Grenade
Alchemist's Mortar	Rare	Varies	80 gp	1 lb.	Grenade
Alchemist's Stupor	Rare	Varies	100 gp	1 lb.	Grenade
Alchemist's Sunburst	Uncommon	Varies	250 gp	1 lb.	Grenade
Alchemist's Surprise	Uncommon	Varies	150 gp	1 lb.	Grenade
Alchemist's Terror	Uncommon	Varies	150 gp	1 lb.	Grenade
Armor Stripper	Rare	Varies	200 gp	0.05 lb.	Grenade
Black-Light	Uncommon	Varies	300 gp	1 lb.	Grenade
Blanch Bomb (Silver)	Rare	Varies	100 gp	0.5 lb.	Grenade
Blessed Sphere	Rare	Varies	200 gp	1 lb.	Grenade
Blister Broth	Rare	Varies	50 gp	1 lb.	Grenade
Bottled Lightning	Common	Varies	40 gp	1 lb.	Special
Chronobreak	Very Rare	Varies	600 gp	1 lb.	Grenade
Demi-Bomb	Rare	Varies	500 gp	1 lb.	Grenade
Dye Bomb	Uncommon	Varies	25 gp	1 lb.	Pellet
Earth Sphere	Uncommon	Varies	150 gp	1 lb.	Grenade
Fireburst Pellet	Uncommon	Varies	10 gp	1 lb.	Pellet
Fire Interruption Gas	Rare	Varies	25 gp	1 lb.	Grenade
Firestone (5)	Common	Varies	100 gp	5 lb.	Stone
Flame Globe	Rare	Varies	500 gp	1 lb.	Grenade
Flaming Morass	Rare	Varies	500 gp	1 lb.	Grenade
Flash Pellet	Rare	Varies	50 gp	1 lb.	Pellet
Frost Sap	Uncommon	Varies	40 gp	1 lb.	Grenade
Frozen Fire	Rare	Varies	75 gp	1 lb.	Grenade
Frozen Prison	Rare	Varies	500 gp	1 lb.	Grenade
Glow Glue	Uncommon	Varies	35 gp	1 lb.	Grenade
Gravity Globe	Very Rare	Varies	500 gp	1 lb.	Grenade
Knockout Globe	Rare	Varies	200 gp	1 lb.	Grenade
Lethargy Globe	Rare	Varies	1,000 gp	1 lb.	Grenade

Name	Rarity	Purchase Cost	Crafting Cost	Weight	Type
Levitation Grenade	Very Rare	Varies	200 gp	1 lb.	Grenade
Liquid Ice	Uncommon	Varies	40 gp	1 lb.	Grenade
Mephitic Smoke	Rare	Varies	150 gp	1 lb.	Grenade
Misery Vial	Very Rare	Varies	450 gp	1 lb.	Grenade
Mitelight	Uncommon	Varies	80 gp	1 lb.	Grenade
Nightblinder	Rare	Varies	100 gp	1 lb.	Grenade
Noisemaker	Uncommon	Varies	20 gp	1 lb.	Pellet
Puppet Blood	Very Rare	Varies	150 gp	1 lb.	Grenade
Putrid Sphere	Uncommon	Varies	600 gp	1 lb.	Grenade
Pyrotechnic Dazzler	Uncommon	Varies	50 gp	1 lb.	Pellet
Sabotage Pulse	Very Rare	Varies	600 gp	1 lb.	Grenade
Shadow Shell	Uncommon	Varies	200 gp	1 lb.	Grenade
Shrieking Betty	Uncommon	Varies	30 gp	1 lb.	Grenade
Sleepsmoke	Uncommon	Varies	50 gp	1 lb.	Grenade
Slickshell	Uncommon	Varies	10 gp	1 lb.	Grenade
Slime Bane	Uncommon	Varies	15 gp	1 lb.	Grenade
Smoke Pellet	Uncommon	Varies	25 gp	1 lb.	Pellet
Snarlweave	Uncommon	Varies	200 gp	1 lb.	Stone
Spore Stone	Uncommon	Varies	50 gp	1 lb.	Stone
Sticky Mist	Rare	Varies	400 gp	1 lb.	Grenade
Stink Bomb	Uncommon	Varies	50 gp	1 lb.	Grenade
Stun Gas	Uncommon	Varies	600 gp	1 lb.	Grenade
Tanglefoot Bag	Uncommon	Varies	50 gp	1 lb.	Grenade
Tanglefoot Bag, Acidic	Rare	Varies	200 gp	4 lbs.	Grenade
Teleportation Grenade	Very Rare	Varies	500 gp	1 lb.	Grenade
Thunder Globe	Very Rare	Varies	100 gp	1 lb.	Stone
Thunderstone (5)	Uncommon	Varies	150 gp	5 lb.	Stone
Void Bomb	Very Rare	Varies	1,000 gp	1 lb.	Grenade
Voltaic Orb	Very Rare	Varies	600 gp	1 lb.	Grenade
Wind Sphere	Uncommon	Varies	200 gp	1 lb.	Grenade

Aboleth Gel: This grenade is made from the corpse of an aboleth and the eldritch gel it produces to allow its slaves to breathe water. Five grenades can be produced from the corpse of one aboleth.
It affects just the target hit with no splash effect. The target must succeed on a DC 16 Constitution saving throw or lose the ability to breathe air for six minutes while gaining the ability to breathe water for these same six minutes. On a successful save, they do not lose the ability to breathe air.
Alchemical formula: An Aboleth, Agate, Rare Earth, Transmutation

Alchemist's Alarm: When this globe is shattered, all creatures sleeping within 60 feet are silently and immediately awakened from sleep. They are temporarily cleansed of any fatigue or exhaustion for one minute. This grenade has no effect on creatures that are awake.
Alchemical formula: Rare Earth, Azoth (any), Mercury (any), Sulfur (any), Mind

Alchemist's Barricade: When thrown, this green gel hardens into jagged spikes to create a partial barricade about four feet high. It takes up one five-foot square. A creature that moves through the spikes takes 3d6 piercing damage and destroys the barricade. The barricade has an armor class of 12 and 30 hit points. The spikes do not provide complete protection, but the barricade does provide partial cover.
Alchemical formula: Rare Earth (5), Sulfur (any), Plant, Transmutation

Alchemist's Befuddlement: This is a black, bubbling sphere of aqueous oily liquid that fumes and smokes upon striking a target. On the next round, the target must succeed on a DC 16 Wisdom saving throw or be confused as the spell for 1d4 + 4 rounds.
Alchemical formula: Mercury (any), Sulfur (any), Mind

Alchemist's Censorship: A target struck by this grenade loses its voice for 1d4 + 1 rounds. They can still communicate but no louder than a whisper. If they attempt to cast a spell, there is a 20% chance of spell failure. They are unable to shout or yell commands in battle. During a chaotic situation, it may be difficult to hear them from more than 10 feet away.
Alchemical formula: Salt (any 2 different Salt essences), Sulfur (any), Stasis

Alchemist's Fire: This sticky, adhesive fluid ignites when exposed to air. On a hit, the target takes 1d4 fire damage at the start of each of its turns. A creature can end this damage by using its action to make a DC 10 Dexterity check to extinguish the flames.
Alchemical formula: Rare Earth, Fire (any 2 different Fire Essences), Sulfur (any)

Alchemist's Firewater: This works as *alchemist's fire* but is non-reactive with air. This substance ignites when exposed to water. Grenades made from this substance are filled with water that ignites the firewater when thrown. On a hit, the target takes 1d6 fire damage at the start of each of its turns. A creature can end this damage by using its action to make a DC 14 Dexterity check to extinguish the flames. Every creature within five feet of the point where the flask hits takes 1 fire damage at the start of their next turn. Attempting to extinguish the fire using water increases the damage dealt the next round by +2.
Alchemical formula: Fire (any), Sulfur (any), Water (any), Transmutation

Alchemist's Fist: A target struck by this grenade takes 1d4 force damage and must succeed on a DC 14 Constitution saving throw or be knocked prone. Those within five feet take no damage but must succeed on a DC 10 Constitution saving throw or fall prone.
Alchemical formula: Air (any), Earth (any), Sulfur (any), Strength

Alchemist's Inferno: A flask of hot, long-burning flame. On a hit, the target takes 3d6 fire damage at the start of each of its turns. A creature can end this damage by using its action to make a DC 16 Dexterity check to extinguish the flames. Every creature within five feet of the point where the flask hits takes 1d6 fire damage at the start of their next turn. Leaping into a lake or magically extinguishing the flames automatically smothers the fire.
Alchemical formula: Fire (any), Sulfur (any), Pain, Strength

Alchemist's Knife: When this grenade strikes a target, shrapnel flies everywhere. The target takes 1d4 piercing and slashing damage and loses 1 hit point at the start of each its turns until it receives healing or a creature succeeds on a DC 10 Wisdom (Medicine) check to stop the bleeding. Each creature within five feet of where the flask hits takes 1 slashing damage.
Alchemical formula: Iron, Salt (any), Sulfur (any), Decay

Alchemist's Mortar: This round bomb has an adjustable fuse. It can be set to detonate instantly or at the start of your next turn or the turn after that. It does 2d6 fire damage to any target within five feet of the detonation, with 1d6 piercing damage in a 10 foot radius around the detonation.
Alchemical formula: Iron, Fire (any), Sulfur (any), Body, Strength

Alchemist's Stupor: This is a concussive explosive that works only if it hits the target. On a successful hit, the target must make a DC 12 Constitution saving throw. On a failure, the target is stunned until the end of its next turn, while on a success it is only incapacitated.
Alchemical formula: Mercury (any), Salt (any), Sulfur (any), Stasis

Alchemist's Sunburst: This grenade contains the concentrated power of sunlight. When this grenade is thrown, it bursts in a brilliant shining explosion, showering a 15-foot radius with bright sunlight until the start of your next turn.
Alchemical formula: Gold, Air (any), Fire (any), Sulfur (any), Light

Alchemist's Surprise: This is a special admixture of *alchemist's fire* and acid. A creature hit with this substance takes 1d4 fire damage and 1d4 acid damage immediately. Every creature within five feet takes 1 fire splash damage and 1 acid damage. At the start of the target's next turn, it takes 1d4 fire damage.
Alchemical formula: Rare Earth, Earth (any), Fire (any), Sulfur (any), Acid

Alchemist's Terror: This grenade is filled with a terrifying hallucinogenic oil. On a direct hit, the target must succeed at a DC 16 Wisdom saving throw or gain the frightened condition. Creatures within five feet must succeed at a DC 12 Wisdom saving throw or be frightened. A frightened creature can repeat the saving throw at the end of each if its turns, ending the effect on a success.
Alchemical formula: Mercury (any), Sulfur (any), Water (any), Fear

Armor Stripper: When *armor stripper* strikes a target wearing armor or having natural armor such as scales or a tough hide, the armor takes a –2 penalty to the AC it offers. This effect lasts for 1d4 + 1 rounds. Huge or bigger creatures require two doses for the same effect.
Alchemical formula: Earth (any), Mercury (any), Acid, Plant

Black-Light: When thrown, this grenade creates a 20-foot radius of darkness where it shatters. The alchemist who prepared this grenade can see in this darkness as if it were daylight. The darkness lasts until the end of your next turn.
Light dispels this effect.
Alchemical formula: Rare Earth, Mercury (any), Sulfur (any), Light

Blanch Bomb (Silver): The nearly invisible gas contained in this fragile glass sphere temporarily but drastically deteriorates the defenses — manufactured and natural — of those affected.
A *silver blanch bomb* is thrown as a splash weapon. Upon contact with a hard surface, the bomb fills a 10-foot radius with a hazy cloud of gas. This cloud lasts for 1d4 + 1 rounds and can be dispersed as *fog cloud*. A creature is the area that is resistant to nonmagical attacks that are not silver loses this resistance while it is in the cloud. A creature that is immune to nonmagical attacks that are not silver becomes resistant to them.
Alchemical formula: Rare Earth, Silver, Azoth (any), Salt (any), Sulfur (any)

Blessed Sphere: This divine mixture is very delicate and often carried in small glass spheres covered in golden wire. It is harmful to all those who carry evil in their hearts. Upon striking an undead or fiend, it does 2d6 radiant damage to the target and 1d6 radiant damage to every undead or fiend within five feet.
Alchemical formula: Fire (any), Sulfur (any), Light, Life

Blister Broth: A target struck by this grenade breaks out in blisters. They must make a DC 14 Constitution saving throw, taking 2d4 acid damage and developing blisters on a failure or half as much damage and not developing blisters on a success. This grenade does 1 acid damage to those within five feet.
The blisters become painful and burst two minutes after a target is affected, reducing the target's movement by 10 feet for one hour and giving the target disadvantage on attack rolls and ability checks for the same duration. The condition is ended by any amount of magical healing.
Alchemical formula: Rare Earth, Earth (any), Salt (any), Water (any), Acid

Bottled Lightning: Electricity crackles along a metal filament inside this small glass bottle. You can open the bottle as an action to unleash a small bolt of lightning toward an enemy within 20 feet of you. This is a ranged weapon attack that deals 1d8 lightning damage on a hit. Any creature in a line between you and the target (including the target) must make a DC 15 Constitution saving throw or take 1 thunder damage from the terrific clap of thunder the bolt generates.
Alchemical formula: Silver, Air (any), Sulfur (any), Electricity

Chronobreak: This grenade causes the target struck to be frozen in the time stream. The target must make a DC 16 Constitution saving throw. On a failed save, the target is frozen in time. They are aware of their surroundings but unable to move or affect them. The target is also unable to be affected by them, although their frozen form can be picked up and moved. On a successful save, they are sluggish, giving the target disadvantage on Strength and Dexterity ability checks and saving throws. In either case, the target may repeat the saving throw at the end of each of its turns, ending the effects on a success.
Alchemical formula: Agate, Emerald, Jade, Onyx, Azoth (any), Stasis

Demi-Bomb: This grenade creates a black explosion in a five-foot radius. A creature in the area takes 1d8 thunder damage and is stunned if it has less than 5 Hit Dice and is deafened if it has less than 10 hit dice. Undead take 3d8 thunder damage. The *demi-bomb* continues to act for 1d4 + 1 rounds, and anyone entering the area is restrained (escape DC 15).
Alchemical formula: Onyx, Rare Earth, Azoth (any), Death

Dye Bomb: These pellets explode when jostled or upon striking a target. Each contains an indelible dye that cannot be made invisible. Anything such as clothing, skin, or porous material covered in this dye is stained. Any nonporous surface is covered in the dye and can be cleaned off using an alcohol base.
The dye cannot be washed out through normal means and is usually of a conspicuous color selected by the alchemist. The color fades from skin in 1d4 + 6 days. This is useful for drawing attention to thieves, shapeshifters, and invisible opponents.
Alchemical formula: Azoth (any), Sulfur (any), Transmutation

Earth Sphere: This grenade explodes in a 5-foot radius. It bursts, doing 1d4 + 1 bludgeoning damage to all targets adjacent to the intersection, and scattering dirt and stone over the ground. This creates difficult terrain in that area.
Alchemical formula: Rare Earth, Earth (any), Sulfur (any), Strength

Fire Interruption Gas: This grenade instantly extinguishes all fires in a 10-foot-by-10-foot square. Any nonmagical fire in the square is extinguished. It does this by displacing all the available oxygen. The entire square is completely filled with opaque smoke that acts as an asphyxiant. This persists until dispersed based on prevailing conditions, usually in one minute (see **Gas Dispersion** in **Chapter One: Alchemy Basics**). If the grenade is used and there is no fire, there is no reaction and the grenade is wasted.
Alchemical formula: Mercury (any) (x2), Salt (any) (x2)

Fireburst Pellet: This pellet explodes in searing bursts and gouts of flame if it is thrown into a nonmagical flame. All creatures standing within 10 feet of the flame must make a DC 14 Dexterity saving throw, taking 7 (2d6) fire damage on a failure or half as much damage on a success.
Alchemical formula: Fire (any) (x2), Sulfur (any)

Firestone: When struck sharply, this stone bursts into flame, doing 1d6 fire damage to all targets in a single five-foot square and igniting any inflammable objects. Fires lit by a *firestone* then burn normally.
Alchemical formula: Rare Earth, Ruby, Fire (any)

Flame Globe: When this grenade strikes a target, it does 2d6 fire damage and 2 fire damage to adjacent targets within 5 feet. It burns for three rounds, doing 1d6 fire damage at the end of the target's turn.
The target may attempt to use an action to extinguish the flames to prevent the additional rounds of damage. A successful DC 15 Dexterity saving throw accomplishes this. Immersion in water extinguishes the fire.
The flames within a 5-foot radius burn anyone who stands in area, doing 1d6 fire damage. A creature may attempt to avoid the damage by passing through the area and succeeding on a DC 16 Dexterity saving throw.
Alchemical formula: Emerald, Ruby, Fire (any)

Flaming Morass: When this grenade strikes a surface or a target, it fills a 20-foot radius area with flaming goo until the end of the turn after your next turn. A creature that enters a burning square on its turn or starts its turn in a burning square takes 1d4 fire damage. The area is considered difficult terrain.
Alchemical formula: Emerald, Jade, Onyx, Ruby, Fire (any)

Flash Pellets: When thrown, this pellet causes a click to draw attention. A bright, stunning light then appears. Anyone unprepared within 60 feet who fails a DC 13 Constitution saving throw is blinded. A blinded creature may repeat the saving throw at the end of each of its turns, ending the effect on a success. If the explosion occurs in a dim or darker area, the saving throws are made with disadvantage.
Alchemical formula: Rare Earth, Fire (any), Salt (any), Light

Frost Sap: This flask contains two different substances that mix and adhere when they strike their target. Upon striking the target, it does 1d6 cold damage. The next round, the target takes another 1d6 cold damage. It does no splash damage.
The substance is sticky and hard to remove but may be scraped off as an action with a successful DC 15 Dexterity saving throw.
Alchemical formula: Salt (any), Sulfur (any), Water (any), Cold

Frozen Fire: This grenade sprays out a mist when it strikes a target. The mist instantly catches fire, burning the target for 1d6 fire damage and doing 1 fire damage to those adjacent. The next round, the remaining liquid gets very cold, damaging the target for another 1d6 cold damage and doing 1 cold damage to those initially splashed.
The liquid mist can't be scraped off, but an action using a mild alcohol or solvent solution to clean it off eliminates the additional damage.
Alchemical formula: Malachite, Ruby, Fire (any), Cold

Frozen Prison: When this grenade strikes a Medium or smaller target, the target is quickly trapped in a layer of ice. The target is restrained (escape DC 16). Because they are encased in ice, any attacks against them instead damage the ice, which frees them. The ice has AC 14 and 9 hit points. Each point of damage lowers the escape DC by one.
While imprisoned, the target takes 1 cold damage at the beginning of each of their turns. In very cold or wet areas, the prison might trap people for double or even quadruple normal duration. Each additional hit with a frozen prison grenade adds +1 to the escape DC and 9 hit points.
Alchemical formula: Amethyst, Onyx, Water (any), Cold (2)

Glow Glue: This sticky substance is thrown against a single target. On a hit, the target glows with a pale outline. The alchemist can determine the color. Attacks against the target have advantage, and the target cannot benefit from becoming invisible. The glow lasts for one minute.
Alchemical formula: Earth (any), Water (any), Light

Gravity Globe: This grenade subjects the target to increased weight. On a hit, the target must make a DC 16 Constitution saving throw. Creatures within five feet make a DC 12 Constitution saving throw. On a failed save, the target suffers from crushing gravity. The target's speed drops by 20 feet, and the target has disadvantage on ability checks, attack rolls, and saving throws that use Strength, Dexterity, or Constitution. A creature that fails its saving throw may repeat it at the end of each of its turns, ending the effect on a success.
Alchemical formula: Emerald, Jade, Sapphire, Turquoise, Stasis

Knockout Globe: When this powerful globe shatters, it fills a single five-foot square with a powerful transparent gas. Anyone exposed to this gas must succeed on a DC 12 Constitution saving throw or fall unconscious for 1d4 + 1 rounds. It disperses naturally in three minutes (see **Gas Dispersion** in **Chapter One: Alchemy Basics**). An unconscious creature can be revived with a successful DC 10 Medicine check.
Alchemical formula: Emerald, Moonstone, Sapphire, Air (any), Toxin

Lethargy Globe: When thrown, this grenade bursts in a five-foot radius cloud of cloying mist. The target must succeed on a DC 16 Constitution saving throw or be affected by a *slow* effect, as the spell. Creatures within five feet must succeed on a DC 14 Constitution saving throw or be *slowed* as the spell also. Slowed targets have the effect until the end of their next turn.
Alchemical formula: Agate, Jade, Air (any), Stasis

Levitation Grenade: This grenade creates a 10-foot square of antigravity that lasts for 1d4 + 1 rounds. Targets fall to the ceiling, taking falling damage as normal, but then may fight and act on the ceiling until the effect ends. Targets entering the area of effect have the same occur to them, and the effect ends if they leave the area of effect.
Alchemical formula: Emerald, Rare Earth, Sapphire, Flight

Liquid Ice: Also known as "alchemist's ice," this sealed jar contains crystalline blue fluid that starts to hiss and evaporate once opened. During the 1d6 rounds after it is opened but before it evaporates completely, you can use it to freeze up to a five-foot cube of liquid or to coat a Medium or smaller object in a thin layer of ice. You can also throw *liquid ice* as a weapon. A direct hit deals 1d6 cold damage; creatures within five feet of where it hits take 1 point of cold damage from the splash.
Alchemical formula: Sulfur (any), Water (any), Cold

Mephitic Smoke: This grenade shatters when it strikes a target, spewing flaming smoke out in a 20-foot radius. Everyone within the area takes 1d4 fire damage, and the area is filled with a thick, black, choking smoke. The smoke is opaque. A creature that enters the area for the first time on its turn or starts its turn in the area must succeed at a DC 16 Constitution saving throw or be poisoned. A poisoned creature can repeat the saving throw at the end of each of its turns, ending the effect on itself on a success. The smoke disperses naturally in three minutes (see **Gas Dispersion** in **Chapter One: Alchemy Basics**).
Alchemical formula: Air (any), Fire (any), Salt (any), Toxin

Misery Vial: This cursed grenade is a small sphere covered in enchanted runes. The grenade shatters upon striking the target, splattering the target with a grimy light oil.
The next round, the target must make a DC 16 Wisdom saving throw. Failure means the curse takes hold. For the next 1d4 + 4 rounds, the target takes twice the damage it inflicts on others. Rents and sympathetic wounds of similar types appear on the target's flesh. There is no splash damage.
The target must be a living creature, and the effect can be dispelled by *dispel magic*, *remove curse*, or a stronger spell.
Alchemical formula: Diamond, Emerald, Azoth (any), Decay

Mitelight: This grenade creates a buzzing column of glowing gnats and mites. Anyone in the square with the mites must succeed at a DC 16 Wisdom saving throw or be stunned until the end of their next turn. The area within the cloud is lightly obscured and sheds dim light for 10 feet. The cloud lasts for 1d4 + 1 rounds.
Alchemical formula: Rare Earth, Air (any), Fire (any), Light

Nightblinder: This grenade has no effect on normal sighted creatures. A creature with darkvision that is struck by this grenade must succeed on a DC 16 Constitution saving throw or lose its darkvision for one minute.
Alchemical formula: Rare Earth, Fire (any), Mercury (any), Sulfur (any)

Noisemaker: When struck against a hard surface, these make a terrible racket that lasts for six rounds — not enough to deafen targets but enough to draw the attention of anyone within 60 feet. Anyone attempting a Stealth check for stealthy movement receives advantage, and targets that fail a DC 16 Constitution saving throw automatically fail their Perception check to notice the target.
Note that the noise reaction continues for several moments and likely draws the attention of wandering or nearby monsters.
Alchemical formula: Iron, Air (any), Earth (any), Sulfur (any), Stealth

Puppet Blood: When this grenade strikes a target, the target is coated in an adhesive oil. Immediately, tendrils of gooey paste writhe toward the ceiling. If there is a surface above the victim within 50 feet, the victim must succeed at a DC 15 Dexterity saving throw or be restrained (escape DC 15) and pulled up toward the ceiling. Even if they succeed at their check and remain on the ground, they have disadvantage on attack rolls, ability checks, and saving throws that rely on Dexterity. A restrained creature must succeed at a DC 10 Concentration check to successfully cast a spell.
The goop dissolves in 1d4 + 1 rounds, dropping the victim, prepared or not.
Alchemical formula: Azoth (any), Earth (any), Salt (any), Stasis

Putrid Sphere: When thrown, this grenade bursts into a flesh-eating liquid that does 2d8 + 3 necrotic damage to the target and 1d4 + 1 necrotic damage to those within five feet.
Alchemical formula: Onyx, Ruby, Azoth (any), Decay

Pyrotechnic Dazzler: When thrown, this small pellet produces a dazzling flash of pulsing light. Everyone within sight of where the dazzler strikes must succeed at a DC 16 Constitution saving throw or be dazzled for 1d4 + 1 rounds. A dazzled creature has a –1 penalty to attack rolls and Perception checks.
Alchemical formula: Rare Earth, 2 of any Fire *or* 1 Light, Sulfur (any)

Sabotage Pulse: This grenade disables constructs. Any non-construct target hit takes 1d4 lightning damage. Constructs when hit take 1d8 + 2 force damage and take 3d8 + 6 lightning damage. The construct must succeed at a DC 14 Constitution saving throw or by incapacitated. An incapacitated construct can repeat the saving throw at the end of each of its turns, ending the effect on itself on a success.
Alchemical formula: Diamond, Platinum, Rare Earth, Azoth (any), Electricity

Shadow Shell: This grenade is filled with an inky, dark liquid. When it strikes a target, it does 2d6 + 2 necrotic damage. The target must succeed at a DC 14 Constitution saving throw or be blinded until the end of its next turn.
Alchemical formula: Fire (any), Mercury (any), Disease, Decay

Shrieking Betty: When this grenade is thrown, it causes a deafening shrieking sound that lasts for three rounds. While the grenade is going, all targets within a 10-foot radius of the grenade are deafened.
Alchemical formula: Air (any), Salt (any), Sulfur (any)

Sleepsmoke: This grenade releases a vapor that does not actually put anyone to sleep due to how quickly it disperses. Instead, it produces a vapor on a direct hit and a failed DC 15 Constitution saving throw that causes a single target to be stunned until the end of its next turn and then poisoned thereafter. A poisoned creature can repeat the saving throw at the end of each of its turns, ending the effect on a success.
Alchemical formula: Salt (any), Sulfur (any), Water (any), Stasis

Slickshell: This is the grenade version of alchemical grease (see **Ointments and Pastes** in **Chapter Three: Alchemical Items**). It is a quick-drying oil that is extremely slick. When thrown at a surface, it covers a single five-foot-by-five-foot square. Anyone standing in, entering, or leaving that square must succeed on a DC 14 Dexterity saving throw or fall prone. The oil dries and becomes useless in 1d4 rounds.
Alchemical formula: Sulfur (any), Water (any), Agility, Stasis

Slime Bane: This mixture is designed to dissolve the bonds of any ooze, pudding, or slime-like creature. On a successful hit, it does 2d8 + 2 necrotic damage to an ooze. On the following round, the ooze must succeed on a DC 16 Constitution saving throw or take another 1d8 necrotic damage. Against all other creatures, it does 1d4 acid.
Alchemical formula: Earth (any), Salt (any), Sulfur (any), Decay

Smoke Pellet: This pellet creates thick clouds of opaque smoke that cover a 10-foot-cube area for two rounds. This fog blocks vision and provides total concealment to anything more than five feet away; otherwise, it provides partial concealment. The alchemist sets the color of the smoke.
Alchemical formula: Rare Earth, Air (any), Earth (any), Salt (any), Stealth

Snarlweave: This small item creates a shockwave that causes all plants within a 10-foot-square area to begin writhing. Anyone in the area is affected as if subject to an *entangle* spell (DC 14) for 1d4 + 1 rounds.
Alchemical formula: Earth (any), Salt (any), Sulfur (any), Plant

Spore Stone: This is not an actual stone but a calcified shell around spores. When thrown on the ground, it releases a cloud of spores that cover a five-foot radius from detonation. A creature that enters this cloud for the first time on its turn or who starts its turn in the cloud must succeed on a DC 16 Constitution saving throw or be poisoned. A poisoned creature may repeat the saving throw at the end of its turn, ending the effect on a success.
Alchemical formula: Earth (any), Water (any), Plant, Toxin

Sticky Mist: This grenade covers a 10-foot-square area in mist for two rounds. Anyone caught within this mist or passing through it during the two rounds is affected. After two rounds, the mist begins to harden, sticking fast for one hour. Those covered in the mist have disadvantage on attacks, ability checks, and saving throws that rely on Dexterity. Their movement is halved. An affected creature can use an action to attempt a DC 17 Strength check to break free of the bonds. If an affected creature attempts to cast a spell, they must succeed at a DC 10 Concentration check or the spell fails.
Alchemical formula: Emerald, Turquoise, Air (any), Strength

Stink Bomb: This bomb fills a 10-foot-square area with a thick disgusting stench. This stench is completely transparent and provides no obfuscation of any kind. Anyone within this area must succeed on a DC 16 Constitution saving throw or gain the poisoned condition. This lasts for the number of rounds the target is in the cloud and for the round after they leave. The cloud disperses in 2d4 rounds if not sooner by prevailing conditions.
Alchemical formula: Sulfur (any), Decay, Toxin

Stun Gas: This clear red liquid instantly evaporates when exposed to air and forms a gas cloud. When thrown, it creates a 10-foot-radius sphere of gas that dissipates in one round. During that round, the gas cloud is opaque and provides total concealment.
Anyone caught inside the gas must make a DC 14 Constitution saving throw or be stunned for 1d4 + 1 rounds.
Alchemical formula: Air (any), Salt (any), Sulfur (any), Stasis

Tanglefoot Bag: A *tanglefoot bag* is a small sack filled with tar, resin, and other sticky substances. When you throw a *tanglefoot bag* at a creature, the bag comes apart and goo bursts out, entangling the target and then becoming tough and resilient upon exposure to air. Creatures struck by the *tanglefoot bags* must make a DC 15 Dexterity saving throw; on a failure they are restrained, while on a success their movement speed is halved. The bags can be removed from an affected creature with a successful DC 15 Strength check, but failing the check causes the affected creature to take 7 (2d6) slashing damage. Huge or larger creatures are unaffected by a *tanglefoot bag*. A flying creature is not stuck to the floor, but it must make a DC 15 Dexterity saving throw or be unable to fly (assuming it uses wings to fly) and falls to the ground. A *tanglefoot bag* does not function underwater.
The goo becomes brittle and fragile after 2d4 rounds, cracking apart and losing its effectiveness. An application of universal solvent applied to a stuck creature dissolves the alchemical goo immediately.
Alchemical formula: Rare Earth, Mercury (any), Stasis

Tanglefoot Bag, Acidic: This is a small bag filled with acidic adhesive. It works much like a *tanglefoot bag* but a creature restrained by it takes 1d6 acid damage at the start of each of its turns.
Alchemical formula: Rare Earth, Mercury (any), Acid, Stasis

Teleportation Grenade: When this grenade strikes an area, all creatures within a five-foot radius are randomly teleported five to 40 feet. Determine direction by rolling a 1d8. Determine distance in feet by rolling a 1d8 and multiplying by 5. Targets that end up in solid areas or areas occupied by other creatures take 4d6 force damage and are shunted to the nearest open space. In any case, the experience is jarring, and targets must succeed at a DC 16 Constitution saving throw or be nauseated. A nauseated creature has disadvantage on attack rolls, ability checks, and Constitution saving throws. Rumors exist of more powerful versions of this grenade that kill creatures by teleporting them into solid objects.
Alchemical formula: Diamond, Emerald, Pearl, Transportation

Thunder Globe: When this stone strikes a hard surface, it creates a thunderous clap. Each creature within a 20-foot-radius spread takes 1d8 thunder damage and must succeed at a DC 15 Constitution saving throw or be deafened for one hour. A deafened creature, in addition to the obvious effects, has disadvantage on initiative rolls and has a 20% chance to miscast and lose any spell with a verbal component that it tries to cast.
Alchemical formula: Rare Earth, Sapphire, Air (any), Salt (any), Strength, Prowess

Thunderstone: When a *thunderstone* strikes a hard surface (or is struck hard), it creates a deafening bang. Each creature within a 10-foot-radius spread must make a DC 15 Constitution saving throw or be deafened for one hour. A deafened creature, in addition to the obvious effects, has disadvantage on initiative rolls and has a 20% chance to miscast and lose any spell with a verbal component that it tries to cast.
Since you don't need to hit a specific target, you can simply aim at a particular five-foot square.
Alchemical formula: Rare Earth, Sapphire, Salt (any), Strength

Void Bomb: This more advanced version of a *demi-bomb* (see **Grenades, Pellets, and Stones** in **Chapter Three: Alchemical Items**) creates a literal black hole. When thrown, they spin up in the air and beep till the start of the thrower's next turn. Anyone standing in the square the grenade lands in when it goes off is obliterated. A black hole then occupies that square for 1d3 + 1 rounds. A Large or smaller creature passing adjacent to this square must succeed at a DC 17 Strength saving throw or get sucked into the square and killed. A Medium or smaller creature passing within 20 feet must succeed at a DC 13 Strength saving throw or get pulled one square toward the black hole. If a creature has something immobile to hold onto, the creature can use an action to attempt a Strength check of the same DC as the saving throw to avoid the effect.
Alchemical formula: Diamond, Emerald, Onyx, Rare Earth, Azoth (any), Planar

Voltaic Orb: This grenade bursts and covers a single five-foot square in a hemisphere of crackling electricity that lasts for 1d4 + 1 rounds. Any target adjacent to the sphere takes 1d4 lightning damage at the start of its turn. A target in the sphere takes 2d4 lightning damage at the start of its turn. A creature that enters or leaves the five-foot square with the hemisphere takes 6d4 + 6 lightning damage.
Alchemical formula: Emerald, Ruby, Sapphire, Electricity

Wind Sphere: This grenade explodes and covers a 20-foot square. It creates tumultuous winds that swirl around the area. This clears out any standing gasses and causes all ranged attacks that pass through this area to have disadvantage. A creature in the area has disadvantage on ability checks, attack rolls, and saving throws that rely on Dexterity. A creature that moves into an affected square must succeed on a DC 13 Strength saving throw or be knocked prone. The winds last for 1d4 rounds.
Alchemical formula: Emerald, Jade, Sapphire, Air (any), Strength

INCENSE

Incense is found in bundles of 2d3 sticks or cones. When crafting these items, the alchemical formulas below produce a batch of six sticks unless otherwise noted.

TABLE 3–4: INCENSE

Name	Rarity	Purchase Cost	Crafting Cost	Weight
Aromatherapy	Common	Varies	150 gp	0.05 lb.
Beastbane	Uncommon	Varies	60 gp	0.05 lb.
Healing	Very Rare	Varies	300 gp	0.05 lb.
Insanity	Rare	Varies	250 gp	0.05 lb.
Phasebound	Very Rare	Varies	300 gp	0.05 lb.
Phasic Disruption	Rare	Varies	150 gp	0.05 lb.
Poison	Rare	Varies	500 gp	0.05 lb.
Prognostication	Uncommon	Varies	250 gp	0.05 lb.
Sleep	Rare	Varies	200 gp	0.05 lb.
Spellbreaker	Rare	Varies	100 gp	0.05 lb.
Stinkstuff	Uncommon	Varies	60 gp	0.05 lb.
Thoughtfocus	Common	Varies	60 gp	0.05 lb.
Trollbane	Uncommon	Varies	50 gp	0.05 lb.
Unfettered Joy	Uncommon	Varies	50 gp	0.05 lb.
Verminbane	Common	Varies	50 gp	0.05 lb.
War	Uncommon	Varies	50 gp	0.05 lb.
Wolfsbane	Uncommon	Varies	100 gp	0.05 lb.

Aromatherapy Incense: A variety of these incenses exist, and each provides a minor bonus of a certain type to an ability score or skill. Anyone who mediates for one minute within the range of this incense receives a +1 bonus to the specific statistic or a +2 bonus to a specific skill.

This specific statistic or skill must be selected when the item is created; e.g. the alchemist could create an aromatherapy of strength and gain a +1 alchemical bonus to Strength after meditating.

The effects of this incense last one hour.

Alchemical formula: Rare Earth, Mercury (any), Salt (any), Plant

Beastbane Incense: This incense produces a cloud and scent that animals find distasteful. Any beast must succeed at a DC 16 Constitution saving throw in order to enter the cloud. Once within the cloud, all animals receive a −1 penalty to attack rolls and saving throws. If you are in the cloud and cause damage to a beast, it can enter the area without making a saving throw.

Alchemical formula: Rare Earth, Air (any), Fire (any), Mercury (any), Emotion

Healing Incense: This incense produces a golden cloud that smells of lavender. All those within the area of effect of this incense are soothed and calmed. Any healing they receive is doubled.

Alchemical formula: Jade, Rare Earth, Healing *or* Plant

Insanity Incense: This incense produces a vapor that clouds the minds of those who enter its radius. Those that fail a DC 16 Wisdom saving throw are subject to *confusion* as the spell.

Alchemical formula: Rare Earth, Mercury (any), Mind

Phasebound Incense: While this incense burns, it produces light smoke of a pleasant scent and has no other obvious effect. However, anyone who is not located on the Prime Material Plane where the incense burns notes a golden cloud pouring out from the incense. This cloud is viscous and solid. Anyone covered by this smoke is forced from other planes into the Prime Material Plane.

This incense prevents blinking, etherealness, astral travel, shadow walking, phasing, and other forms of dimensional travel. Outside of the radius, in other dimensions the cloud appears as a solid wall filling the area it covers. Anyone engaged in physically occupying more than one plane at once is shunted into the Prime Material Plane. If the creature is normally multi- or extraplanar, it is unable to enter the area. If the effect causing the planar shift is magical, it is dispelled. Extradimensional items are rendered inert for one minute after leaving the cloud.

Alchemical formula: Jade, Rare Earth, Azoth (any), Planar, Stasis

Phasic Disruption Incense: This incense burns a purple cloud that smells of metallic silver. Any creatures out of phase with the Prime Material Plane, such as an ethereal or incorporeal creature, suddenly finds themselves corporeal while within the area of this incense. They are subject to any and all attacks from creatures on the Prime Material Plane. However, there is no compulsion on them staying within range of the incense; they may enter and leave freely. The incense does not affect anything other than ethereal or incorporeal creatures and has no effect other than making them susceptible to physical attacks.

Alchemical formula: Onyx, Rare Earth, Silver, Azoth (any), Planar, Stasis

Poison Incense: Anyone who starts their turn within the cloud or who enters the cloud for the first time must succeed on a DC 16 Constitution saving throw or take 2d6 poison damage.

Alchemical formula: Rare Earth, Air (any), Water (any), Toxin

Prognostication Incense: Those who burn this incense receive a +2 (or +10%) bonus on any rolls to succeed at divination spells cast within the area of effect of the incense.

Alchemical formula: Rare Earth, Air (any), Fire (any), Sulfur (any), Prophesy *or* Perception

Sleep Incense: Anyone who smells this pleasant incense must make a DC 14 Constitution saving throw or fall fast asleep. This sleep is natural and may be ended normally. A creature that stays in range of the incense must make a saving throw at the beginning of each of its turns.

Alchemical formula: Moonstone, Rare Earth, Air (any), Stasis

Spellbreaker Incense: This creates a cloud that disturbs concentration. A creature must succeed on a DC 12 Concentration check at the beginning of each of its turns to maintain concentration on a spell.

Alchemical formula: Rare Earth, Air (any), Fire (any), Water (any)

Stinkstuff Incense: This incense smells like garbage and rotting meat. When this incense is lit, 2d10 rats or other appropriate vermin arrive within 1d10 + 1 rounds. They are not under the control of the summoner and are somewhat agitated by the scent of the incense.

Alchemical formula: Rare Earth, Air (any), Fire (any), Decay

Thoughtfocus Incense: This pleasant-smelling incense is an aid to the mind. Any Intelligence-based ability check made while exposed to this incense has advantage.

Alchemical formula: Rare Earth, Mercury (any), Mind

Trollbane Incense: This incense produces a greasy, thin, green cloud that smells pungent. While unpleasant to all, it is especially repulsive to trolls, who must succeed at a DC 14 Constitution saving throw to even approach. Once within the cloud, trolls receive a −1 penalty to attack rolls and saving throws. If you are in the cloud and cause damage to a troll, it can enter the area without making a saving throw.

Alchemical formula: Rare Earth, Earth (any), Fire (any), Mercury (any)

Unfettered Joy Incense: This incense produces a scent cloud that affects any being who is not under the effects of an oath, geas, or any other form of behavioral coercion. When they breathe the gas, they begin to laugh joyously, though the people in the cloud may choose to stifle this laughter a moment after it begins.

Alchemical formula: Rare Earth, Air (any), Fire (any), Emotion

Verminbane Incense: This incense produces a cloud and scent that vermin find distasteful. Any vermin must succeed at a DC 14 Constitution saving throw in order to enter the cloud. Once within the cloud, all vermin receive a −1 alchemical penalty to attack rolls and saving throws. If you are in the cloud and cause damage to the vermin, they can enter the area without making a saving throw.

Alchemical formula: Rare Earth, Air (any), Sulfur (any), Water (any), Emotion

War Incense: This incense produces a red-tinged cloud of smoke that spells like blood. All those within the area of effect of this incense are affected by bloodlust and are given a +1 bonus on to-hit damage rolls. This effect lasts for three minutes after leaving the incense. A person may be affected by this incense only once in a 24-hour period.

Alchemical formula: Earth, Earth, Mercury, Rare Earth

Wolfsbane Incense: This incense burns for eight hours. While it is burning, it gives those within the cloud the ability to resist lycanthropic change. It provides a 50% chance that the change will not occur. This works on willing and unwilling targets. Once suppressed, the ability to change is lost for 24 hours.

Alchemical formula: Rare Earth, Silver, Air (any), Mercury (any), Emotion

LIQUIDS AND TONICS

TABLE 3–5: LIQUIDS AND TONICS

Name	Rarity	Purchase Cost	Crafting Cost	Weight
Air Crystal	Uncommon	Varies	50 gp	0.1 lb.
Alchemist's Kindness (20)	Common	Varies	20 gp	0.1 lb.
Amnesia Tonic	Rare	Varies	25 gp	0.1 lb.
Analgesic	Common	Varies	5 gp	0.1 lb.
Antiemetic Snuff	Common	Varies	50 gp	0.1 lb.
Antiplague	Uncommon	Varies	50 gp	0.1 lb.
Antitoxin	Uncommon	Varies	50 gp	0.1 lb.
Bast's Kindness	Common	Varies	3 gp	0.1 lb.
Bone Bomb	Uncommon	Varies	50 gp	0.1 lb.
Dead Water	Rare	Varies	100 gp	0.1 lb.
Death Flame	Uncommon	Varies	50 gp	0.1 lb.
Dragon's Heart	Uncommon	Varies	50 gp	0.1 lb.
Elf's Heart	Uncommon	Varies	50 gp	0.1 lb.
Embalming Fluid	Common	Varies	50 gp	10 lbs.
Emetic	Uncommon	Varies	50 gp	0.1 lb.
Endurance Booster	Uncommon	Varies	50 gp	0.1 lb.
Energy Drink	Uncommon	Varies	400 gp	0.1 lb.
False Slumber	Rare	Varies	600 gp	0.1 lb.
Fool's Water	Rare	Varies	50 gp	0.1 lb.
Fruity Mouth Paste	Rare	Varies	100 gp	0.1 lb.
Lifeline	Rare	Varies	250 gp	0.1 lb.
Liquid Breath	Rare	Varies	100 gp	0.1 lb.
Low Light Tonic	Uncommon	Varies	100 gp	0.1 lb.
Oasis Refreshment	Uncommon	Varies	80 gp	0.1 lb.
Oil, Fire-Breathing	Uncommon	Varies	50 gp	0.1 lb.
Olfactory Acuity	Uncommon	Varies	25 gp	0.1 lb.
Olfactory Dulling	Common	Varies	5 gp	0.1 lb.
Piling	Rare	Varies	50 gp	0.1 lb.
Slumber Swig	Uncommon	Varies	200 gp	0.1 lb.
Smelling Salts	Uncommon	Varies	25 gp	0.1 lb.
Sweet Rest	Uncommon	Varies	75 gp	0.1 lb.
Thief's Heart	Uncommon	Varies	50 gp	0.1 lb.

Air Crystal: These unpleasant-tasting, alchemically grown crystals release breathable air when chewed. A pouch of air crystals provides one minute of breathable air. Placing air crystals in your mouth takes an action; chewing them each round is a free action. Any attempt to speak while chewing air crystals negates any remaining duration.
Alchemical formula: Amethyst, Air (any) (x3)

Alchemist's Kindness: Favored by young rakes and other well-to-do inebriates, this crystalline powder resembles salt. Mixed with water, it makes a fizzing cocktail that eliminates the effects of a hangover within 10 minutes of drinking it.
Alchemical formula: Rare Earth, Earth (any), Sulfur (any)

Amnesia Tonic: This tonic causes the user to have difficulty remembering the previous day after sleeping. Upon awaking, the drinker must struggle to remember any events from the previous period of wakefulness. A successful DC 14 Intelligence saving throw allows the imbiber to recover a single piece of information. The DC may be increased to recover more specific information.
Alchemical formula: Mercury (any), Water (any), Memory

Analgesic: This is an alchemist's painkiller. It provides advantage to a saving throw to continue functioning while in pain (such as from blister broth, see **Grenades, Pellets, and Stones**). It can also provide relief for migraines and post-surgical pain.
Alchemical formula: Fire (any), Water (any), Body

Antiemetic Snuff: This snuff can be used to shake off the effects of nausea. If you take it before being exposed to an effect that would nauseate you and allows a saving throw, you have advantage on the saving throw. A single dose provides this benefit for one hour.
Alchemical formula: Rare Earth, Earth (any), Salt (any), Body

Antiplague: If you drink a vial of this foul-tasting, milky tonic, you gain advantage on Constitution saving throws against disease for the next hour. If already infected, you may make an immediate saving throw with advantage to throw off the effects of one disease.
Alchemical formula: Earth (any), Fire, Sulfur, Disease, Healing

Antitoxin: If you drink a vial of antitoxin, you have advantage on Constitution saving throws against poison for one hour.
Alchemical formula: Earth (any), Sulfur (any), Water (any), Protection, Toxin

Bast's Kindness: This tonic dramatically reduces the chances of conception during sexual intercourse if taken daily for one month by either party. The effects last as long as it is taken daily thereafter. Each bottle contains 30 doses.
Alchemical formula: Water (any)

Bone Bomb: When this tonic is applied to an inanimate skeleton, it causes several effects. The bones take on a glossy sheen, and they become easier to damage.
If the skeleton is raised from the dead, it suffers a −2 penalty to its armor class. If the skeleton is destroyed, the bones shatter. Everyone adjacent to the skeleton must succeed on a DC 16 Dexterity saving throw or take 1d6 piercing damage.
Alchemical formula: Rare Earth, Azoth (any), Mercury (any), Decay

Dead Water: When this liquid is added to water, it instantly removes all the oxygen from the liquid in a 10-foot cube. Still waters remains oxygen deprived for 24 hours. More active waters clear themselves out in a few rounds, usually six. Water-breathing creatures in the area immediately begin to suffocate.
Alchemical formula: Iron, Rare Earth, Water (any), Salt (any)

Death Flame: This fluid is applied to undead creatures. Undead coated in this fluid explode into flame if they are struck in combat. This greenish-blue flame does no damage to them, but any melee attack they make does an additional 1d6 fire damage for one minute.
Alchemical formula: Onyx, Azoth (any), Fire (any), Sulfur (any)

Dragon's Heart: This tonic provides advantage on Constitution saving throws for one hour.
Alchemical formula: Rare Earth, Earth (any), Salt (any), Body

Elf's Heart: This liquid provides advantage on Wisdom saving throws for one hour.
Alchemical formula: Rare Earth, Salt (any), Water (any), Mind

Embalming Fluid: This fluid is used to preserve corpses, whether for later dissection, taxidermy, necromancy, or magic such as *raise dead*. Embalming fluid is technically a poison, and using it makes a corpse unpalatable to most animals and vermin, though corpse-eating undead don't mind the taste. Treating a corpse with embalming fluid takes one hour and a successful DC 15 Wisdom (Medicine) check. The embalmed corpse decays at half the normal rate (each day dead counts as half a day for the purpose of *raise dead*).
Alchemical formula: Rare Earth, Earth (any), Salt (any), Water (any), Stasis

Emetic: This liquid induces vomiting. If unopened when swallowed whole by a creature, opening this vial causes the creature to vomit you out unless it passes a DC 16 Constitution saving throw. The creature is sick and gains the nauseated condition for 1d4 + 1 rounds. While nauseated, it has disadvantage on attack rolls. There are 10 doses in a vial. If some doses of this have been used and then it is used on a creature that swallows you, the DC to resist vomiting is decreased by 1 for each dose already used.
If imbibed after ingesting a poison, this allows a second saving throw with advantage.
Alchemical formula: Rare Earth, Water (any)

Endurance Booster: This tonic grants you advantage on Strength (Athletics) checks made to swim, climb, or hang in place, and on Constitution saving throws to avoid suffocation or exhaustion. After this hour, you gain a level of exhaustion. If you had a level of exhaustion when you took this tonic, your exhaustion level is reduced by one for the duration, but then you regain that level and one more at the end of the duration. Of the people who drink this tonic, 25% react strongly to it, and it lasts 1d4 hours for them. This is only rolled the first time an imbiber takes an endurance booster.
Alchemical formula: Rare Earth, Sulfur (any) (x2), Strength

Energy Drink: This liquid banishes any sort of fatigue or exhaustion in the user. However, if the user engages in further activity that causes fatigue, it accumulates as normal. The consumption of another beverage can also banish this fatigue. After 24 hours, the imbiber becomes completely overwhelmed and getting the benefits of a long rest takes four hours longer per drink beyond the first that was consumed.
Alchemical formula: Air (any), Fire (any), Mercury (any), Sulfur (any), Strength, Body

False Slumber: When consumed, this tonic causes the imbiber to fall into a deep sleep for 2d6 + 4 x 10 minutes. The character cannot be awakened short of *dispel magic* or a stronger spell. Another side effect of this tonic is that the user appears to be dead; a successful DC 15 Wisdom (Medicine) check reveals that the person lives.
Alchemical formula: Rare Earth, Mercury (any), Salt (any), Stasis

Fool's Water: This substance appears to be a totally normal vial of water. When poured out of the vial, however, it flows uphill until it reaches the highest surface nearby. Surface tension keeps it attached to the surface it is poured on. It pools on this surface, and if possible, begins to drip upward toward the sky.
This liquid can be poured on a wall inside a closed chamber, in which case it climbs and finds the highest point on the ceiling. It is water, so if it encounters a crevice, it flows through that crevice just as normal water would. If opened outside, it flows upward into the sky.
Alchemical formula: Rare Earth Air (any), Mercury (any), Flight

Fruity Mouth Paste: This liquid coats the inside of the imbiber's mouth and allows them to hold toxic substances in their mouth for up to an hour without any negative effects. Note that if the user swallows the toxic substance, it affects them normally. But even the most toxic chemicals may be held in the mouth for the duration. This is useful for spitting a spray of poison at opponents.
Alchemical formula: Rare Earth, Earth (any), Salt (any), Toxin

Lifeline: When consumed, this liquid tonic affects you for 24 hours. The first time you fall to 0 hit points during that time, you are unconscious but not dying. If you take additional damage while unconscious, the lifeline cannot help you.
Alchemical formula: Emerald, Jade, Life

Liquid Breath: This liquid fills your lungs with a highly oxygenated liquid that allows you to breathe in oxygenated liquids such as water. You are immune to the nonlethal environmental pressure and effects due to depths, e.g. the bends. This lasts for two hours. Note that 1d6 rounds after imbibing this substance, you can no longer breathe air.
Alchemical formula: Sapphire, Air (any), Water (any), Body

Low Light Tonic: This tonic grants the imbiber darkvision.
Alchemical formula: Rare Earth, Mercury (any), Sulfur (any), Perception

Oasis Refreshment: This wonderful liquid prevents all negative effects from heat, sunstroke, and dehydration for 12 hours. If you already have penalties from the effects of the sun, these are negated as the liquid rehydrates you and protects you from the environment for six hours.
Alchemical formula: Salt (any), Sulfur (any), Water (any), Body

Oil, Fire-Breathing: This hard-to-light oil burns well at a low temperature. It is often used by jesters and other fire-breathing entertainers. Those trained with the oil and wielding a flame source can use an action to breathe out a one-foot cone that is five feet wide at the end and deals 1d3 fire damage to a creature on a hit. A fumble means you accidentally burnt yourself for 1d6 fire damage. A vial contains 10 doses.
Alchemical formula: Fire (any) (x2), Salt (any), Water (any)

Olfactory Acuity Tonic: This tonic gives you a preternatural sense of smell. You have advantage on any Wisdom (Perception) checks that rely on smell.
Alchemical formula: Air (any), Earth (any), Salt (any), Perception

Olfactory Dulling Tonic: This tonic nullifies your sense of smell for one hour, making you immune to stench attacks and giving you advantage on saving throws versus an effect that causes nausea, vomiting, or illness.
Alchemical formula: Silver, Earth (any), Salt (any)

Piling Tonic: When this tonic is poured onto the floor, all light loose material within a 20-foot radius is gathered into a pile. This includes dust, fluff, and loose small objects of one pound or less. There is no limit to how much the potion can attract, but the objects must be non-living and unconstrained. Coins in a box, bag, drawer, or behind a door are not affected. It takes 10 minutes for everything to roll to the center near the liquid. It is advised to stand back. As soon as the gathering is over, the items may be redistributed freely.
Alchemical formula: Iron, Silver, Rare Earth, Azoth (any)

Slumber Swig: When this liquid is consumed or inhaled, you fall asleep for eight hours. You may resist if you succeed on a DC 16 Constitution saving throw. Each hour you may make another saving throw with a cumulative +2 bonus to wake up. Note that this must be held over the mouth for one round or imbibed to have an effect.
Alchemical formula: Rare Earth, Mercury (any), Water (any), Stasis

Smelling Salts: These sharply scented gray crystals cause people inhaling them to regain consciousness. *Smelling salts* grant you a new saving throw to resist any spell or effect that has already rendered you unconscious. If exposed to *smelling salts* while dying, you immediately become conscious, but must still make Death saving throws each round; if you perform any other strenuous action, you take 1 point of damage after completing the act and fall unconscious again. A container of *smelling salts* has dozens of uses if stoppered after each use but depletes in a matter of hours if left open.
Alchemical formula: Rare Earth, Salt (any), Sulfur (any)

Sweet Rest: When imbibed, this effervescent solution causes a heavy warmth to spread from your stomach outward to your limbs, resulting in feelings of security and well-being. If you sleep for at least one hour after consuming the solution, the next time within the next 24 hours that you attempt a saving throw, you have advantage.
Alchemical formula: Rare Earth, Salt (any), Sulfur (any), Healing

Thief's Heart: This liquid provides advantage on Dexterity saving throws for one hour.
Alchemical formula: Rare Earth, Air (any), Fire (any), Salt (any), Agility

OINTMENTS AND PASTES

TABLE 3–6: OINTMENTS AND PASTES

Name	Rarity	Purchase Cost	Crafting Cost	Weight
Alchemical Glue	Common	Varies	20 gp	0.5 lb.
Alchemical Grease	Common	Varies	25 gp	0.5 lb.
Armor Malleability	Uncommon	Varies	550 gp	0.1 lb.
Blessing	Rare	Varies	300 gp	0.1 lb.
Brittle Cream	Uncommon	Varies	150 gp	0.1 lb.
Buoyancy	Rare	Varies	400 gp	0.1 lb.
Clarity	Rare	Varies	400 gp	0.1 lb.
Counterscent	Common	Varies	25 gp	0.1 lb.
Durability	Uncommon	Varies	100 gp	0.1 lb.
Flame Paste	Uncommon	Varies	150 gp	0.1 lb.
Icewalking	Rare	Varies	375 gp	0.1 lb.
Insect Repellent	Common	Varies	50 gp	0.1 lb.
Insulating Paste	Uncommon	Varies	100 gp	0.1 lb.
Lockstick	Common	Varies	50 gp	0.1 lb.
Magical Aura	Rare	Varies	50 gp	0.1 lb.
Nightingale	Common	Varies	25 gp	0.1 lb.
Orcus' Protection	Uncommon	Varies	100 gp	0.1 lb.
Protection	Rare	Varies	650 gp	0.1 lb.
Quieting	Rare	Varies	250 gp	0.1 lb.
Scarsalve	Common	Varies	10 gp	1 lb.
Shrieking Paste	Common	Varies	50 gp	0.1 lb.
Sun Cream	Common	Varies	10 gp	0.5 lb.
Toxinshield	Uncommon	Varies	125 gp	0.1 lb.
Trollkiller	Rare	Varies	300 gp	0.1 lb.
Weapon Blanch, Silver (10)	Uncommon	Varies	50 gp	5 lbs.
Woodbronzer	Uncommon	Varies	60 gp	0.1 lb.

Alchemical Glue: This glue is stored as two flasks of syrupy liquid that form a strong bond when mixed together and allowed to cure. The glue is sufficient to coat one square foot of surface or (because of waste, spills, and inaccurate mixing) up to 20 smaller applications of approximately two square inches each. The glue is tacky after one minute and fully cured after one hour. Pulling apart a large glued surface (of at least one square foot) requires a DC 18 Strength check for tacky glue or DC 22 for cured glue. Pulling apart a small glued surface (anything less than one square foot) is a DC 13 Strength check for tacky glue or DC 15 for cured glue.
Alchemical formula: Rare Earth, Earth (any), Salt (any), Water (any)

Alchemical Grease: Each pot of this slick black goo can cover one Medium creature or two Small ones. If you coat yourself in *alchemical grease*, you gain advantage on Acrobatics or Athletics checks to avoid or escape a grapple. This lasts for four hours or until you wash it off.
Alchemical formula: Salt (any), Water (any), Agility *or* Plant

Armor Malleability Paste: This useful paste has a sharp, acrid odor. Its purpose is to remove some of the inherent stiffness in armor. The magics that allow it to do so work by weakening the armor itself.
Once applied, any disadvantage to Stealth checks caused by wearing heavy armor is removed. While it is active, the armor has a –2 penalty to the AC bonus it provides.
Alchemical formula: Rare Earth, Water (any), Body, Stealth

Blessing Ointment: Using this ointment grants the user a +2 bonus to AC and gives the user a +2 bonus to saving throws for one hour.
Alchemical formula: Rare Earth, Salt (any), Sulfur (any), Protection

Brittle Cream: Strength checks made to break an object coated with this cream have advantage. One vial has enough to coat one Medium or two Small objects. It takes one minute for the cream to take effect, and the effect lasts for one hour.
Alchemical formula: Earth (5), Mercury (5), Rare Earth, Rare Earth

Buoyancy Ointment: Coating a person or object with this oil provides a natural buoyancy and causes the target to float in water for 2d4 + 6 hours. One jar of ointment can cover 30 square feet or one Medium creature. The users gains +10 on any Athletics checks made to stay afloat.
Alchemical formula: Rare Earth, Air (any)(x2), Water (any)

Clarity Ointment: This cream-colored ointment has no efficacy on its own of any sort, but when it is used in conjunction with spells affecting vision such as *clairvoyance* or *arcane sight*, it doubles range and effect.
Alchemical formula: Rare Earth, Mercury (any), Sulfur (any), 2 Perception *or* 1 Prophesy

Counterscent Ointment: When applied, this ointment neutralizes and masks any odors produced by one Medium creature for two hours. During that time, the user exudes no scent or odor. Any Perception checks made to notice the creature that rely on smell have disadvantage.
Alchemical formula: Air (any), Fire (any), Salt (any), Stealth

Durability Paste: Strength checks made to break an object coated with this cream have disadvantage. One vial has enough to coat one Medium or two Small objects. It takes one minute for the cream to take effect, and the effect lasts for one hour.
Alchemical formula: Rare Earth, Earth (any), Salt (any), Decay

Flame Paste: This thick paste concentrates flame and burns extremely hot. It can be applied in any one-square-foot configuration, e.g. a line one inch high and 12 feet long or a one-foot square. It burns extremely hot, doing 3d6 + 3 fire damage per round. It must be applied thinly because it does not splatter or burn well upon initial air exposure. It must set for one round. *Flame paste* burns for three rounds.
While *flame paste* does burn hotter, it does not spread itself. When using the fire rules (see **Fire** in **Chapter One: Alchemy Basics**), simply apply increasing damage to the object, and if it burns hotter, allow the possibility of igniting flammable materials that are nearby.
Alchemical formula: Iron, Rare Earth, Silver, Fire (any)

Icewalking Paste: When applied to your hands and feet, this paste adheres to ice and allows you to cross and climb on icy surfaces as if under the influence of a *spider climb* spell.
Alchemical formula: Moonstone, Rare Earth, Air (any), Agility

Insect Repellent Ointment: This ointment can be applied to the skin to repel small biting insects. Tiny or smaller insects are held at bay for four hours. Larger insects or swarms must succeed at a DC 14 Wisdom saving throw to approach. If the character attacks the insects or intentionally agitates them, the insects automatically make their saving throws.
Alchemical formula: Rare Earth, Salt (any), Protection

Insulating Paste: When applied to the interior of armor, this paste gives the user advantage on all saving throws versus cold weather and cold damage for 24 hours.
Alchemical formula: Rare Earth, Earth (any), Fire (any), Cold

Lockstick Paste: When applied to a lock, this substance makes the lock more difficult to pick. Picks slide off, and gears and pins become more difficult to manipulate. Dexterity checks made to open the lock have disadvantage.
Alchemical formula: Rare Earth, Earth (any), Salt (any), Protection

Magical Aura Ointment: This ointment causes nonmagical items that are covered in it to detect as magical. When you create this ointment, you determine the type of aura this ointment creates.
Alchemical formula: Rare Earth, Azoth (any), Mercury (any), Transmutation

Nightingale Paste: When spread over a 10-foot-by-10-foot section of floor, this paste makes a loud squeaking noise and alerts nearby listeners. Creatures crossing this surface have disadvantage on Dexterity (Stealth) checks made to move silently. This paste lasts indefinitely but heavy foot traffic causes it to come off.
Alchemical formula: Air (any), Mercury (any), Stealth

Orcus' Protection Ointment: This ointment is formulated to provide protection from sunlight for light-sensitive humanoids and undead. It is a thick white ointment that provides 24 hours of protection. While under the protection of this ointment, creatures do not receive penalties on attack rolls or ability checks due to daylight, and vampires do not take damage from the sun. Note that direct exposure to bright sunlight might still have an effect, and radiant damage and *sunlight* spells affect the target as they do a normal aboveground creature.
Alchemical formula: Gold, Onyx, Rare Earth, Mercury (any), Protection

Protection Ointment: This light-blue ointment provides a +2 bonus to all saving throws for eight hours.
Alchemical formula: Rare Earth, Earth (any), Fire (any), Water (any), Protection

Quieting Paste: This paste is an oily black color and has a sharp metallic smell. Its purpose is to reduce the noise armors and clothing make. You have advantage on Dexterity (Stealth) checks made to move silently for one hour after spending one minute coating your armor and clothing in this paste.
Alchemical formula: Rare Earth, Sapphire, Mercury (any), Stealth

Scarsalve: When applied to scarred areas of the body, *scarsalve* causes those scars to fade from view for one day. If you gain benefits from having visible scars, you lose those benefits while under the effects of *scarsalve*, but you gain a +2 bonus on Deception checks made to disguise yourself.
Alchemical formula: Air (any), Mercury (any), Salt (any), 2 Body *or* 1 Healing

Shrieking Paste: At the beginning of your next turn after you expose this paste to air, it begins to shriek as loudly as a shrieker. It continues to do so for a full minute.
Alchemical formula: Rare Earth, Air (any), Azoth (any), Earth (any)

Sun Cream: Each application of this alchemical solution — which is typically compounded in combination with substances found in desert flowers, fruits, and roots — heals 1d4 damage that you have taken from heat exposure. If you succeed at a DC 15 Wisdom (Medicine) check while applying *sun cream*, you may add your Wisdom modifier to the damage healed. A creature cannot benefit from more than one application of sun cream in a 24-hour period.
Alchemical formula: Earth (any), Mercury (any), Salt (any)

Toxinshield Ointment: This ointment produces a waxy coating on your skin that gives you advantage on saving throws against contact poisons.
Alchemical formula: Rare Earth, Salt (any), Water (any), Toxin

Trollkiller Paste: When applied to a weapon, the paste causes damage that is difficult to heal on a successful strike. The edges of the wound are corrupted, and natural healing processes are inhibited. A creature that takes damage from a weapon coated with this paste since its last turn cannot regenerate. The paste lasts for one hour.
Alchemical formula: Onyx, Rare Earth, Earth (any), Fire (any), Decay

Weapon Blanch, Silver: This silver alchemical powder has a gritty consistency and appears at first glance to be simple metal shavings. When poured on a weapon and placed over a hot flame for a full round, the powder melts and forms a temporary coating on the weapon. Your next attack with this weapon is silver. Each dose of blanching can coat one weapon or up to 10 pieces of ammunition. Only one kind of weapon blanch can be applied to a weapon at one time, though a weapon made of one special material (such as adamantine) can have a different material blanch (such as silver) and count as both materials for the first successful hit.
Alchemical formula: Rare Earth, Silver, Mercury (any), Water (any)

Woodbronzer: When this paste is applied to any wooden object, it strengthens and protects wood. The wood's AC increases by +4 and any Strength check made to break it has disadvantage. This substance effects only rigid, porous, or organic materials (e.g., wood, coral). Note that a wooden shield coated with this material does not provide a greater bonus to AC than one that is not so coated.
Alchemical formula: Iron, Rare Earth, Earth (any), Plant

POWDERS

TABLE 3–7: POWDERS

Name	Rarity	Purchase Cost	Crafting Cost	Weight
Absorption	Uncommon	Varies	400 gp	0.2 lb.
Acid Neutralizing	Uncommon	Varies	20 gp	0.2 lb.
Avian Repellent	Rare	Varies	150 gp	0.2 lb.
Blandness	Very Rare	Varies	150 gp	0.2 lb.
Cleanliness	Common	Varies	50 gp	0.2 lb.
Clouded Vision	Uncommon	Varies	25 gp	0.2 lb.
Contrariness	Uncommon	Varies	50 gp	0.2 lb.
Convulsive Cachinnate	Common	Varies	100 gp	0.2 lb.
Deathsight	Uncommon	Varies	30 gp	0.2 lb.
Defoliant	Uncommon	Varies	30 gp	0.2 lb.
Dehydration	Rare	Varies	60 gp	0.2 lb.
Deicing	Uncommon	Varies	30 gp	0.2 lb.
Delirium	Rare	Varies	20 gp	0.2 lb.
Desalination	Uncommon	Varies	50 gp	0.2 lb.
Dire	Very Rare	Varies	150 gp	0.2 lb.
Dousing	Uncommon	Varies	10 gp	0.2 lb.
Enfeeblement	Rare	Varies	400 gp	0.2 lb.
Fatigue	Rare	Varies	400 gp	0.2 lb.
Fertilizing	Common	Varies	25 gp	0.2 lb.
Frailty	Uncommon	Varies	350 gp	0.2 lb.
Frothing	Uncommon	Varies	20 gp	0.2 lb.
Ground Fog	Uncommon	Varies	100 gp	0.2 lb.
Hallucination	Rare	Varies	30 gp	0.2 lb.
Incendiary (10)	Common	Varies	10 gp	2 lbs.
Insect Repellent	Rare	Varies	300 gp	0.2 lb.
Itching	Uncommon	Varies	25 gp	0.2 lb.
Magic Detection	Common	Varies	250 gp	0.2 lb.
Nausea	Common	Varies	30 gp	0.2 lb.
Nullifying	Uncommon	Varies	75 gp	0.2 lb.
Obscuring	Rare	Varies	500 gp	0.2 lb.
Paralysis	Uncommon	Varies	100 gp	0.2 lb.
Pesticide	Uncommon	Varies	10 gp	0.2 lb.
Piquant	Common	Varies	100 gp	0.2 lb.
Powdered Bloodhound Lure	Common	Varies	20 gp	0.2 lb.
Powdered Water	Rare	Varies	30 gp	0.2 lb.
Razor	Uncommon	Varies	50 gp	0.2 lb.
Smoke	Common	Varies	3 gp	0.2 lb.
Snap	Uncommon	Varies	5 gp	0.2 lb.
Sneezing	Uncommon	Varies	60 gp	2 lbs.
Spoilage	Uncommon	Varies	100 gp	0.2 lb.
Trail Dispersion	Uncommon	Varies	600 gp	0.2 lb.
Vertigo	Uncommon	Varies	40 gp	0.2 lb.

Absorption Powder: This powder is powerfully absorbent. When added to a liquid such as water or acid, it turns up to 100 cubic feet of it into a thick and inert paste-like mud.
Alchemical formula: Rare Earth, Air (any), Earth (any), Salt (any)

Acid Neutralizing Powder: This powder instantly neutralizes any acids or solvents it contacts. A character may spend an action applying it to themselves to eliminate ongoing acid or solvent damage.
Alchemical formula: Air (any), Earth (any), Salt (any), Acid

Avian Repellent Powder: This powder is particularly effective at repelling small birds. Each dose covers one acre and prevents any creature smaller than an eagle from landing there for one year.
Alchemical formula: Rare Earth, Air (any), Salt (any), Protection

Blandness Powder: When applied to anything edible, this powder removes any distinctive smell or taste. This destroys any olfactory or gustatory properties of the item. This can be used to disguise the taste or smell of poisons or to neutralize the odor of a body, drugs, or the shoes of teenagers. There is enough to cover the smell of one corpse or six plates of food.
Alchemical formula: Rare Earth, Earth (any), Salt (any), Illusion

Cleanliness Powder: A quick dusting of this powder leaves clothes and materials clean and dry. It removes mud, blood, stains — any substance marring the surface of the clothing and fabric. The dust is not abrasive and leaves no marks. One dose is enough to clean a single set of garments for a Medium creature.
Alchemical formula: Silver, Rare Earth, Salt (any), Sulfur (any)

Clouded Vision Powder: On a successful use, this powder causes blindness on a failed DC 10 Constitution saving throw. A blinded creature may repeat the saving throw at the end of its turn, ending the effect on a success.
Alchemical formula: Earth (any), Fire (any), Mercury (any), Illusion, Light

Contrariness Powder: When successfully used against a target, this powder produces a specific insanity that alters behavior. If a DC 16 Wisdom saving throw is failed, then the target behaves in some respect opposite the way they normally would. Their alignment may reverse or they may attack their allies instead of their opponents. The powder lasts up 1d6 + 4 rounds before the effect wears off, but the target may repeat the saving throw at the end of its turn, ending the effect on a success. There is a small chance upon repeated usage that the effect becomes permanent.
Alchemical formula: Rare Earth, Air (any), Earth (any), Mercury (any), Mind

Convulsive Cachinnate Powder: A target dosed with this powder is seized with an overwhelming compulsion to laugh. Everything becomes hilarious. The target may succeed at a DC 16 Wisdom saving throw to avoid the effects. If the saving throw is failed, the target begins laughing uncontrollably and falls prone on the ground. This lasts for only one round. After this round, they may stand up again, but they continue to laugh for the next 1d4 + 1 rounds. While laughing, they receive a –2 penalty on all attack rolls. This affects targets only with an Intelligence of 4 or higher.
Alchemical formula: Rare Earth, Air (any), Mercury (any), Emotion

Deathsight Powder: When this dust is inhaled or consumed, it causes the target to perceive all living creatures as walking corpses. A creature hit with the powder may attempt a DC 14 Dexterity saving throw to avoid inhaling it. Flesh appears to be rotting and sloughing off, gait is unsteady, and the process of decay has set in on every living creature the target sees. The target is under no compulsion to act hostile toward the visions and perceives all other visual and auditory stimuli as normal (i.e., he hears their speech and sees their reactions as normal).
The powder tastes like bananas and cumin and flavors food and drink accordingly.
Alchemical formula: Air (any), Mercury (any), Salt (any), Illusion

Defoliant Powder: This whitish powder is used to kill plants. It kills most small plants within 24 hours. One dose is enough to cover five square feet or one Large plant. Trees and various other large leafy plants die off over the following week.
This powder also has a damaging effect on any creature of the plant type. A plant creature hit with this powder takes 1d6 necrotic damage and must succeed on a DC 14 Constitution saving throw or take an additional 1d6 necrotic damage at the start of its next turn.
Alchemical formula: Earth (any), Salt (any), Plant, Decay

Dehydration Powder: This horrible powder dehydrates the target. Organic living creatures hit by this powder instantly become dehydrated as the powder absorbs water from their body through their pores and skin. The target must make a DC 16 Constitution saving throw or immediately take 2d6 necrotic damage and a level of exhaustion.

They must repeat this save in an hour if they do not acquire any water in the interim.

Creatures with an intelligence less than 4 subject to this powder feel as if they are dying of thirst and unless they succeed at a DC 12 Wisdom saving throw stop what they are doing and drink any available liquid — even poison.

Alchemical formula: Rare Earth, Fire (any), Salt (any), Death, Decay

Deicing Powder: This powder is heavy, but when dispersed over ice, it instantly melts one 10-foot-by-10-foot square to form a non-slick slurry. This powder can be used on solid ice to provide traction, but caution must be used if the surface of the ice is thin, as it increases the chance that you will fall through.

It also melts a solid cubic foot of ice in one minute and does 2d6 + 4 fire damage to creatures made of ice.

Alchemical formula: Fire (any), Mercury (any), Salt (any)

Delirium Powder: A target hit with this powder must make a DC 16 Wisdom saving throw. A creature that fails begins babbling, speaking continuously and randomly in any languages they know. Topics selected are random and may include the weather, dreams, fantasies, complaints, or even secret or useful information (10% chance per round). This effect lasts for 2d4 rounds.

A target knows what happened but is unable to stop themselves. They may become hostile immediately after the powder wears off.

Alchemical formula: Air (any), Mercury (any), Salt (any), Control

Desalination Powder: This wonderful powder turns one gallon of saltwater into green, brackish, foul freshwater that is safe to drink.

Alchemical formula: Rare Earth, Silver, Sulfur (any)

Dire Powder: A target hit by this powder must make a DC 17 Wisdom saving throw. On a failure, they develop an insatiable bloodlust and immediately attack the nearest target. If multiple targets from the victim are equidistant, select the target randomly. This powder lasts for 2d8 + 2 rounds. The victims continue to attack the nearest target until incapacitated or until the effect ends.

Alchemical formula: Rare Earth, Mercury (any), Salt (any), Water (any), Emotion

Dousing Powder: This dark gray powder is used to extinguish fires. When spread or dumped on a small flame, it immediately snuffs it out. It can be used to automatically prevent continuing fire damage. It automatically extinguishes a fire in a five-foot square. If you are using the optional fire rules (see **Fire** in **Chapter One: Alchemy Basics**), reduce the severity of a fire in a five-foot square by one level.

It also causes damage to creatures made of living fire. When used upon any creature made of fire, the powder does 2d8 + 2 cold damage.

Alchemical formula: Water (any), Salt (any) (x2)

Enfeeblement Powder: When this dust hits a target, they must make a DC 15 Constitution saving throw. On a failed save, they experience terrible weakness for one minute. This weakness is debilitating, giving them disadvantage on Strength-based ability checks, saving throws, and attack rolls. An enfeebled creature may repeat the saving throw at the end of its turn, ending the effect on a success.

Alchemical formula: Onyx, Platinum, Rare Earth, Water (any), Decay

Fatigue Powder: When this dust hits a target, they must make a DC 16 Constitution saving throw. On a failed save, the target gains a level of exhaustion.

Alchemical formula: Onyx, Platinum, Rare Earth, Fire (any), Stasis

Fertilizing Powder: This powder enriches soil and provides basic nutrition for plants. One dose is enough for an acre, and it must be applied weekly. Proper application of this powder increases the crop yield by 25%.

Alchemical formula: Earth (any), Plant (any), Sulfur (any)

Frailty Powder: When this dust hits a target, their immune system becomes heavily compromised. All Constitution saving throws the target makes have disadvantage. This effect lasts for one minute.

Alchemical formula: Iron, Onyx, Rare Earth, Water (any), Decay

Frothing Powder: This dry, salty powder causes any water it is dispersed into to violently froth and boil. This attracts any water predators or animals from up to a quarter of a mile away. Any animals caught in the 10-foot cube created by the powder must make a DC 14 Constitution saving throw or take 10 (3d6) fire damage on a failure or half as much damage on a success.

The first round the powder is applied, there is a slow disturbance in the water. For the next 1d4 + 1 rounds, the water boils and roils violently.

Alchemical formula: Earth (any), Fire (any) (x2), Water (any)

Ground Fog Powder: When this powder is thrown on the ground, it covers a 50-foot square in a low, rolling fog that flows along the ground and rolls downstairs and cascades into pits. The fog is in constant motion. Creatures attempting to spot invisible or hidden Medium or larger creatures in the area have advantage on Perception checks.

The ground is not visible beneath the fog. The fog has a height of three to four feet and covers anything on the floor completely. It is particularly effective at allowing creatures in gaseous form to hide, granting them a +10 bonus to Stealth checks.

Alchemical formula: Rare Earth, Air (any), Sulfur (any), Water (any), Stealth

Hallucination Powder: On a successful use of this powder, the subject must succeed at a DC 16 Wisdom saving throw or experience 1d4 + 1 rounds of terrifying hallucinations. This produces a result in the victim similar to fear. Spellcasting and combat are impossible, but the target may defend him or herself normally.

Bizarre psychology renders the power ineffective. It works only on humanoids and beasts; all others are immune. Using or making this powder carries a 1% chance that the user could go insane, as per *insanity*.

Alchemical formula: Air (any), Earth (any), Mercury (any), Illusion

Incendiary Powder: This quick-burning powder is used in the construction of fuses and bombs. If an ounce is exposed to open flame, it flares up and does 1d4 fire damage per ounce to anyone holding the powder. Large quantities of it can be quite dangerous near open flame, but by itself it makes a poor weapon. If thrown on a person who is currently on fire, it does 1d4 fire and force damage per ounce if they fail a DC 16 Dexterity saving throw. No more than two ounces of the loose dust can be thrown for this effect. Use the following table to determine the effects of large amounts of incendiary powder.

TABLE 3–8: INCENDIARY POWDER EFFECTS

Size	Ounces	Cost	Damage
Mini-Keg	32 ounces	32 gp	3d6
Keg	64 ounces	64 gp	4d6
Gallon	128 ounces	128 gp	6d6
Rundlet (18 gallons)	2,304 ounces	2,300 gp	8d6
Barrel (32 gallons)	4,096 ounces	4,100 gp	12d6

Alchemical formula: Fire (any), Salt (any), Sulfur (any)

Insect Repellent Powder: This powder is particularly effective at repelling small insects. Each dose covers one acre and prevents any insect smaller than one inch from entering for one year.
Alchemical formula: Rare Earth, Earth (any), Salt (any)

Itching Powder: This powder causes severe irritation and gives the target a −2 penalty to all attack rolls, saving throws, and ability checks until they take an action to wash off the powder.
Alchemical formula: Earth (any) (x2), Fire (any), Pain

Magic Detection Powder: An application of this powder causes any magical item, ward, creature, or aura to glow. The color of the glow indicates the type of magic as per *detect magic*.
Alchemical formula: Diamond, Gold, Rare Earth, Azoth (any)

Nausea Powder: A successful use of this powder causes retching and nausea. Targets must succeed at a DC 14 Constitution saving throw or become nauseated. A nauseated creature has disadvantage on attack rolls, ability checks, and Constitution saving throws. A nauseated creature may repeat the saving throw at the end of each of its turns, ending the effect on a success.
Alchemical formula: Earth (any), Fire (any), Water (any), Toxin

Nullifying Powder: This powder neutralizes alchemical reactions. It stops acid from continuing to do damage, puts out small fires, calms violent turbulent waters, and even calms upset stomachs. It affects one target except in the case of calming turbulent waves, where it affects a 300-foot radius.
Alchemical formula: Rare Earth, Air (any), Azoth (any), Earth (any), Fire (any), Mercury (any), Salt (any), Sulfur (any)

Obscuring Powder: This gray, ash-like powder has no remarkable qualities. If dashed upon the ground, it creates a 60-foot-diameter cloud that limits vision to less than one foot. The air is filled with an acrid odor that nullifies the ability to smell and makes it difficult to hear sounds within the cloud. Targets within the cloud have total concealment. The cloud lasts for 1d4 minutes and can be dispersed by a strong wind.
Alchemical formula: Rare Earth, Air (any), Sulfur (any), Stealth

Paralysis Powder: On a successful use, this powder requires the victim to succeed at a DC 12 Constitution saving throw or become paralyzed. A paralyzed creature may repeat the saving throw at the end of each of its turns, ending the effect on a success.
Alchemical formula: Rare Earth, Mercury (any), Salt (any), Stasis

Pesticide Powder: This powder causes diminutive vermin to die. When spread around an area, vermin walk through and pick up the powder on their extremities and transport it back to their lair. When they clean it off, it causes fatal damage to the surrounding vermin and they die. This is also harmful to small children and pets. Creatures that are Tiny or smaller that pass through an area are affected by the pesticide poison. An affected creature must make a DC 14 Constitution saving throw, taking 4d4 poison damage on a failure or half as much on a success.
Alchemical formula: Rare Earth, Salt (any), Death

Piquant Powder: When applied to anything edible, this powder increases any distinctive smell or taste. It allows the eater of the food to fully experience each unique flavor and odor in the food. It also intensifies the smell of toxins and poor preparation. There is enough powder to use on six meals. This grants advantage on any check to detect poisons, toxins, or alterations to the food.
Alchemical formula: Rare Earth, Mercury (any), Earth (any), Salt (any), Sulfur (any), Perception

Powdered Bloodhound Lure: This powder draws the attention of animals. Anyone covered in this powder is easily detectable by any natural animal. Beasts receive advantage on all Perception and Survival checks to locate the creature. In combat, beasts prefer to attack anyone covered in this powder.
Alchemical formula: Air (any), Earth (any), Emotion

Powdered Water: When a single drop of water is added to this white sparkling powder, it turns into a gallon of pure water. After the water is added, the mixture must be agitated and it produces a fair bit of heat. The powder is often added to a gallon-size container before reconstitution for ease of use.
Powdered water is useful to save weight on long treks and can be made in large enough quantities to ship to arid locals. It is difficult to transport by sea, as it must be kept dry.
A person in desperate need may swallow a dose and gain the equivalent of one quart of liquid. The extra is neutralized by the stomach acid.
Alchemical formula: Salt (any) (x2), Water (any) (x2)

Razor Powder: When this powder is spread over an area, razor-sharp crystals form. You can cover a single five-foot square with an action. A creature that moves through this area at full speed takes 1d8 slashing damage. A creature that treats it as difficult terrain does not take this damage. After one hour, the crystals dissolve. This powder is crafted with enough for 10 applications.
Alchemical formula: Diamond, Iron, Rare Earth, Salt (any)

Smoke Powder: When added to fire, this simple powder changes the color of the fire or produces smoke of any color the alchemist wishes. The smoke does not increase in volume or provide any sort of cover.
Alchemical formula: Plant

Snap Powder: One dose of this powder is enough to cover a five-foot-square area. Any creature that weighs more than 20 pounds sets off these tiny explosions and sparkly lights when moving through the area. Anyone attempting to move quietly or in the shadows is almost instantly discovered. Stealth checks have a −10 penalty.
Alchemical formula: Light

Sneezing Powder: This coarse, yellowish-red powder is a splash weapon that causes uncontrollable sneezing. A creature standing in the square of impact must succeed on a DC 12 Constitution saving throw to resist the powder, while those in adjacent squares must make DC 8 Constitution saving throws. Creatures affected by *sneezing powder* are incapacitated. An incapacitated creature may repeat the saving throw at the end of each of its turns, ending the effect on a success.
Alchemical formula: Rare Earth, Air (any), Salt (any), Sulfur (any), Toxin

Spoilage Powder: When sprinkled over food, this powder causes rapid spoilage. It is not instant, but within the hour, a cubic foot of food will be spoiled. Within a day, 100 cubic feet can be spoiled.
Alchemical formula: Salt (any), Decay

Trail Dispersion Powder: A good dusting of this powder removes a tracker's ability to follow a trail using normal sensory methods. Dogs become distracted and lose the scent, and tracks appear confusing and difficult to follow. This increases the tracking DC by 10. One container is enough to provide 10 uses.
Alchemical formula: Plant, Stealth

Vertigo Powder: On a successful use of this powder, the subject must succeed at a DC 16 Wisdom saving throw or experience severe dizziness. A dizzy creature has a 50% chance of falling prone at the beginning of its turn and has disadvantage on all attack rolls. A dizzy creature may repeat the saving throw at the end of each of its turns, ending the effect on a success. An unusual sense of balance can render this powder ineffective. It works only on humanoids and beasts.
Alchemical formula: Rare Earth, Air (any), Illusion

SOLVENTS

The alchemist must master each solvent grade in order, first solvent Type A, then B, and so on. An alchemist who masters the various solvent grades may make special organic and inorganic solvents that affect only the appropriate materials of that type. Upon crafting one of each, the alchemist may mix them to create the legendary alkahest or universal solvent, which is able to dissolve any substance practically instantly.

On a direct hit, the solvent causes damage for 1d6 rounds. Solvent times assume one full, eight-ounce dose of the solvent. Adjust times to dissolve items by the quantity of solvent; i.e., if 16 ounces of a solvent are used, items dissolve twice as fast. Greater amounts of solvent do not increase damage in combat; once affected by a solvent, throwing more only allows a new duration roll and does not increase the ongoing damage.

A target may take an action to wash with an astringent such as wine or vinegar or even large amounts of water to stop ongoing solvent damage.

Using solvents is not without risk. Solvents are carried safely only in glass or crystal vials due to their tendency to dissolve other materials. If the alchemist is subject to any shock such as a fall or takes any thunder damage and fails their save, the vials may break and cause damage to the alchemist.

Solvents are not usually available for sale on open markets due to their inherent nature.

TABLE 3–9: SOLVENTS

Name	Rarity	Crafting Cost	Time to Craft	Damage/ Round	Organic Matter*	Leather/ Rope*	Wood*	Bone*	Stone*	Gems*	Metal*
Alchemical Solvent	Common	20 gp	4 hrs.	0	—	—	—	—	—	—	—
Solvent Type A	Common	25 gp	4 hrs.	1d4	2 min.	6 min.	12 min.	24 min.	12 hrs.	—	—
Solvent Type B	Uncommon	50 gp	1 day	1d6	1 min.	4 min.	9 min.	12 min.	10 days	12 days	—
Solvent Type C	Uncommon	100 gp	2 days	2d4	5 rounds	2 min.	6 min.	9 min.	6 hrs.	10 days	12 days
Solvent Type D	Rare	200 gp	4 days	3d4	3 rounds	1 minute	2 min.	6 min.	9 min.	6 hrs.	10 days
Solvent Type E	Rare	500 gp	10 days	3d6	1 round	5 rounds	1 minute	2 min.	3 min.	9 min.	6 hrs.
Organic Solvent	Very Rare	1,000 gp	20 days	6d6	instant	1 round	1 round	2 rounds	—	—	—
Inorganic Solvent	Very Rare	1,000 gp	20 days	6d6**	—	—	—	—	Instant	1 round	1 round
Universal Solvent	Legendary	—	—	24d6	instant	instant	instant	instant	instant	instant	instant

* Time to dissolve one cubic foot of material.   ** Affects only inorganic creatures such as constructs

Alchemical Solvent: This bubbling purple gel eats through adhesives. Each vial can cover a single five-foot square. It destroys most normal adhesives (such as tar, tree sap, or glue) in a single round but takes 1d4 + 1 rounds to deal with more powerful adhesives (such as *alchemical glue*, *tanglefoot bags*, *spider webbing*, and so on). It has no effect on fully magical adhesives such as *sovereign glue*.
Alchemical formula: Fire (any), Mercury (any), Sulfur (any), Decay

Solvent Type A: This weak solvent does 1d4 acid damage on a direct hit for 1d6 rounds.
Alchemical formula: Earth (any), Fire (any), Mercury (any), Sulfur (any), Acid

Solvent Type B: This moderate solvent does 1d6 acid damage on a direct hit for 1d6 rounds. Anyone standing within a five-foot radius takes 1 point of acid damage.
Alchemical formula: Earth (any), Fire (any), Mercury (any), Acid (x2)

Solvent Type C: This strong solvent does 2d4 acid damage for 1d6 rounds on a direct hit. Anyone standing within a five-foot radius takes 1d4 acid damage.
Alchemical formula: Emerald, Earth (any), Fire (any), Mercury (any), Sulfur (any), Acid (x2), Decay

Solvent Type D: This powerful solvent does 3d4 acid damage for 1d6 rounds on a direct hit. Anyone standing within a five-foot radius takes 1d4 + 1 acid damage.
Alchemical formula: Emerald, Pearl, Earth (any), Fire (any), Mercury (any), Sulfur (any), Acid (x2), Decay (x2)

Solvent Type E: This dangerous and expensive solvent does a substantial 3d6 acid damage for 1d6 rounds on a direct hit. Anyone standing within a five-foot radius takes 1d6 + 1 acid damage.
Alchemical formula: Emerald, Pearl, Ruby, Earth (any), Fire (any), Mercury (any), Sulfur (any), Acid (x2), Decay (x2), Death

Organic Solvent: This powerful solvent does 6d6 acid damage to all living and organic creatures for 1d6 rounds on a direct hit. Anyone standing within a five-foot radius takes 2d6 + 2 acid damage. It dissolves any organic material at the rate of one cubic foot per round. This solvent must be contained in a glass, ceramic, or metal container. It has no effect on inorganic material.
Alchemical formula: Emerald, Pearl, Ruby, Turquoise, Acid, Plant

Inorganic Solvent: This substance dissolves any inorganic material at the rate of one cubic foot per round. It must be carried in an organic container such as a wooden vial, animal bladder, or wine skin. This solvent has no effect on organic material of any kind.
If used against any construct or inorganic object, it does 6d6 acid damage for 1d6 rounds on a direct hit. Any construct or inorganic object standing within a five-foot radius takes 2d6 + 2 acid damage.
Alchemical formula: Agate, Jade, Ruby, Turquoise, Azoth (any), Acid

Universal Solvent (Alkahest): This horrible substance is not made in a lab because it is too volatile to exist for very long. It destroys all matter that it comes into contact with — it is the alkahest. It is made by mixing together the organic and inorganic solvent.
For one round after they have mixed together, the substance is inert. After this period, it begins to dissolve anything it comes into contact with. It dissolves one cubic foot per second for 6d10 seconds.
A splash of this substances does 8d6 + 8 acid damage and a direct hit results in 24d6 acid damage for 1d6 rounds. A creature brought to 0 hit points by this solvent is completely disintegrated and can be brought back from the dead only with a *wish*.
There is no antidote.
Alchemical formula: Organic Solvent (1 dose), Inorganic Solvent (1 dose), Azoth (any)

TINCTURES

The creation process is a little different than the standard alchemical creation techniques, being that it takes time for the alcohol to work on the substance. In addition to the crafting time, it takes six weeks for the tincture to soak before it becomes effective. The alchemist may engage in any activity he wishes during this time.

The weight of tinctures is negligible and not included in **Table 3–10: Tinctures** below.

TABLE 3–10: TINCTURES

Name	Rarity	Purchase Cost	Crafting Cost
Tincture of Antemortem	Uncommon	Varies	25 gp
Tincture of the Clouded Mind	Rare	Varies	200 gp
Tincture of Extension	Very Rare	Varies	250 gp
Tincture of Far Reaching	Very Rare	Varies	250 gp
Tincture of Fire	Uncommon	Varies	150 gp
Tincture of Health (50)	Common	Varies	10 gp
Tincture of Lethality	Very Rare	Varies	200 gp
Tincture of Magnification	Very Rare	Varies	1,000 gp
Tincture of Poisonflesh	Very Rare	Varies	315 gp
Tincture of Purification (50)	Common	Varies	10 gp
Tincture of Putrefaction (50)	Common	Varies	10 gp
Tincture of Sanguineness	Rare	Varies	100 gp
Tincture of Slumber	Very Rare	Varies	450 gp
Tincture of Transference	Rare	Varies	2,500 gp
Tincture of Witch Bane	Uncommon	Varies	3 gp
Tincture of Wolfsbane (50)	Common	Varies	10 gp

Tincture of Antemortem: This tincture does nothing until the drinker expires and then it stays active for the drinker for one minute. Once that occurs, the tincture slows all mental and bodily processes, suspending the body a moment before death. Note that any further damage after this point results in death. Healing effects can be used during this time as normal, though the body does not visibly heal until the suspended animation ends. This state of suspended animation lasts for 24 hours. This state can be extended by 12 hours if the body is kept out of the light of the sun. If no healing is performed, the creature is at 0 hit points and dying.
Alchemical formula: Salt (any), Plant, Stasis

Tincture of Extension: When this tincture is added to a magic potion or other liquid, the duration of the effect is extended by 50%. The magic potion or liquid is not included in the casting cost.
Alchemical formula: Rare Earth, Azoth (any) (x2), Salt (any)

Tincture of Far Reaching: When this tincture is added to a magic potion or other liquid, the range of the effect (such as fire breathing oil) is extended by 50%.
Alchemical formula: Rare Earth (5), Azoth (any) (x2), Sulfur (any)

Tincture of Fire: This tincture is added to other liquids or foods as an incapacitating element, though some people voluntarily imbibe such substances.
If anyone eats or sips some liquid or food contaminated with this tincture, they must make a DC 14 Constitution saving throw or fall prone and writhe from the heat of the substance for 1d8 + 1 rounds. They take 1 fire damage each round. If this tincture is consumed straight and not diluted in another substance, the imbiber must succeed at a DC 5 Constitution saving throw or die from respiratory or heart failure. If they survive, they are incapacitated for 3d4 rounds, taking 1 fire damage per round.
Alchemical formula: Rare Earth, Fire (any) (x2), Salt (any)

Tincture of Health: This tincture enhances the respiratory functions and reduces inflammation of the bronchial passages. This tincture fights infections in the chest and lungs.
When taken, this tincture provides a noncumulative +2 bonus on the next saving throw versus a disease that a character makes while diseased.
Alchemical formula: Earth (any), Sulfur (any), Healing

Tincture of Lethality: When added to any poison, this tincture affects the body's natural defenses, making it harder to resist. Any poison with this added to it has +2 added to its saving throw DC.
Alchemical formula: Rare Earth, Salt (any), Water (any), Death

Tincture of Magnification: This tincture is intended to be mixed with a magical liquid. When combined, this tincture causes the magical liquid to have maximum effect. This means that the duration is the longest possible duration, and any numeric effects are not rolled but given their maximum values. For example, when mixed with a *potion of healing*, the potion heals 10 hit points.
Alchemical formula: Diamond, Platinum, Azoth (any) (x2)

Tincture of Poisonflesh: When mixed with up to three doses of poison, this powerful tincture turns your very flesh to the poison you mixed it with. When it is consumed, roll a DC 14 Constitution saving throw. Failure means you feel ill and are poisoned for the duration of the tincture. You are immune to the type of poison contained within the tincture for the duration. The cost varies based on the cost of the poison. The price is equal to the price of three doses of the poison, plus 315 gold for essences and Rare Earths.
If you are bitten or attacked and swallowed, the attacker is affected by the poison that flows in your flesh. They must make a saving throw versus the poison you ingested as if they had been attacked with it. If they fail, they experience the effects of the poison that you ingested.
Alchemical formula: Agate, Malachite, Rare Earth, Salt (any), Toxin

Tincture of Purification: This tincture purifies one gallon of water and removes all bacteria and impurities. It does not prevent water from being contaminated again, nor does it have any effect on magically polluted water. This tincture can be used to create the pure water necessary for the creation of potions.
Alchemical formula: Fire (any), Sulfur (any), Purity

Tincture of Putrefaction: This tincture instantly putrefies one gallon of water, making it unfit for consumption. Anyone who drinks water ruined with this tincture becomes violently ill and spends the next 2d4 rounds retching uncontrollably. The creature has disadvantage on attack rolls, ability checks, and Constitution saving throws.
Alchemical formula: Earth (any), Fire (any), Decay

Tincture of Sanguineness: When this tincture is added to any poison, it has the side effect of causing bleeding. A target that fails its saving throw versus the poison loses one hit point per round until healed or until a creature uses an action to make a successful DC 10 Medicine check to bandage its wounds. If the poison was ingested, the target instead loses 2d8 hit points at the start of the next round due to internal bleeding.
Alchemical formula: Iron, Malachite, Onyx, Rare Earth

Tincture of Slumber: When added to any poison or liquid, this tincture causes the target to slumber. The target must make a DC 16 Constitution saving throw or fall asleep. This has no affect when combined with a poison that already causes sleep. A target that fails the saving throw sleeps for eight hours and then must make a DC 16 Constitution saving throw. Failing that, they fall into a coma and can be awakened only by a *lesser restoration* or *remove curse* spell.
Alchemical formula: Moonstone, Pearl, Platinum, Rare Earth, Stasis

Tincture of the Clouded Mind: When mixed with up to four doses of poison, this tincture adds a side effect of confusion to the poison. A target that fails the saving throw versus the poison must make a second Constitution saving throw at the same difficulty to resist this tincture. If this save is failed, the imbiber has disadvantage on all saving throws and must succeed on a DC 12 concentration check to cast spells.
Alchemical formula: Rare Earth, Mercury (any), Water (any), Mind

Tincture of Transference: This tincture is intended to be added to a magical liquid. When consumed, the magical liquid does not affect the imbiber, but instead affects the target, determined by the organic essence added to the mixture as well as the thoughts of the imbiber. The target must be determined when the tincture is crafted. The target must be within 100 miles, and there is no saving throw against the tincture. If appropriate, the target may make a saving throw against the base magical liquid. There is always a small chance (1%) that this tincture fails to function and the magical liquid affects the imbiber.
Alchemical formula: Agate, Diamond, Pearl, Platinum, Azoth (any)
Additional Requirement: Hair, nail, or blood of target

Tincture of Witch Bane: This tincture, when given to someone under the effect of an enchantment effect, immediately allows a save with a +1 bonus. If the save is successful, the enchantment effect immediately ends.
Alchemical formula: Moonstone, Sulfur (any)

Tincture of Wolfsbane: This is a curative tincture. It has several effects depending on application. When added to water, this tincture acts as a diuretic and diaphoretic. In addition to causing urination and excessive sweating, it also provides a +2 bonus to any saves against lycanthropy if infected. This tincture can also be applied externally to heal wounds, bruises, arthritis, and irritations. It heals 1d4 hit points if used this way.
If the alchemist fails a DC 9 Intelligence (Alchemist's Supplies) check when applying this tincture, the tincture was prepared or applied incorrectly. If applied externally, the tincture deals 2d4 acid damage and no natural healing occurs that day due to blistering and inflammation. If taken internally it causes bleeding and possible death. Make a DC 12 Constitution saving throw three times, taking 1d4 acid damage for each failure. If all three saves fail, the creature's heart becomes damaged and it dies unless it passes a DC 12 Constitution saving throw.
Alchemical formula: Fire (any), Sulfur (any), Body, Plant

CHAPTER FOUR: MAGIC ITEMS

Alchemists have discovered many unique magic items and ways to use materials. They follow all standard rules for magic item creation. Like any spellcaster, the creator must possess the appropriate spells required to cast. The cost and difficulty to create magic items are based on their rarity.

CRAFTING COST OF MAGIC ITEMS

TABLE 4–1: MAGIC ITEMS RARITY

Item Rarity	Cost to Craft	DC	Minimum Spellcaster Level
Common	100 gp	10	3rd
Uncommon	500 gp	12	3rd
Rare	5,000 gp	15	6th
Very Rare	50,000 gp	20	11th
Legendary	500,000 gp	25	17th

CANDLES

Candles are most often made from animal fat. Candles usually have wicks, though primitive tallow candles can be made.

Candles can be snuffed out by ordinary means. The effects of candles are canceled immediately once snuffed out. Note that the effects candles produce (arcane warding, protection, etc.) do not prevent warded creatures or effects from putting the candles out.

ARCANE WARDING CANDLE

Wondrous item, very rare
This candle creates a shimmering globe with a 10-foot radius centered on the candle. It surrounds you and excludes all spell effects of 4th level or lower. The area or effect of any such spells does not include the area covered by the candle. Any spell may be cast from within the globe and can affect a target inside or outside the sphere. Anyone may enter or leave the area effect of the candle without penalty. This candle burns for one minute.
Alchemical Formula: Azoth (any), Fire (any), Protection

BLACK CANDLE

Wondrous item, rare (r
equires attunement by a creature capable of casting *bestow curse*)
This dark candle burns for one hour with a purple flame. When lit, you may cast *bestow curse* as a ritual every 10 minutes. The same person can be targeted with each of the six curses the candle can bestow. You must have the ability to cast the spell to use this candle.
Alchemical Formula: Fire (any), Salt (any), Sulfur (any), Death

BLADE CANDLE

Wondrous item, uncommon
When you use a bonus action to light this candle, the flame of this candle springs out to a length of three feet. It burns for one minute. You may use the candle as a rapier to make attacks except that it does fire damage. You are considered proficient in using this weapon.
Alchemical Formula: Fire (any), Mercury (any), Transportation

BLINKING CANDLE

Wondrous item, uncommon
When you hold this lit candle, roll a d20 at the end of each of your turns. On a roll of 11 or higher, you vanish from your current plane of existence and appear in the Ethereal Plane. At the start of your next turn, you return to an unoccupied space of your choice that you can see within 10 feet of the space from which you vanished. If no unoccupied space is available within that range, you appear in the nearest unoccupied space (chosen at random if more than one space is equally nearby). While on the Ethereal Plane, you can see and hear the plane from which you originated, which is cast in shades of gray, although you can't see anything there that is more than 60 feet away. You can affect and be affected only by other creatures on the Ethereal Plane. Creatures that aren't there can't perceive you or interact with you, unless they have the ability to do so.
Alchemical Formula: Fire (any), Mercury (any), Planar

BLUE CANDLE

Wondrous item, uncommon
This candle projects a blue aura in a five-foot radius while it burns. It burns for six hours. It protects against aberrations, celestials, elementals, fey, fiends, and undead. Creatures of those types have disadvantage on attack rolls against targets within the aura. Creatures within the aura also can't be charmed, frightened, or possessed by them. If a creature within the aura is already charmed, frightened, or possessed by such a creature, the creature has advantage on any new saving throw against the relevant effect.
Alchemical Formula: Fire (any), Salt (any), Planar

BRILLIANT CANDLE

Wondrous item, common
This candle burns for six hours and produces light equivalent to a torch but produces no heat. If this candle is countered and extinguished by magical darkness, it may simply be relit.
Alchemical Formula: Fire (any), Light
Small alterations to the formula may be made to produce a candle that emanates *darkness* as the spell in the same manner. The alchemical formula for this version of the item is Water (any), Light.

DETONATING CANDLE

Wondrous item, uncommon
This candle burns for 1d8 + 4 rounds then explodes in a sphere of flame on initiative 20. The flame extends 15 feet out from the center of the candle (covering a 30-foot diameter). Any creature in the area must make a DC 15 Dexterity saving throw, taking 8 (2d6) fire damage on a failure or half as much damage on a success. The candle is destroyed.
You may trim the wick on this candle to reduce the burning duration by one round or more. If, however, the random duration is rolled and results in being a duration of 0 or less, then the candle explodes instantly upon being lit.
Alchemical Formula: Fire (any), Earth (any), Memory

DIVINATION CANDLE

Wondrous item, very rare
When this candle is lit, it allows the wielder to cast a single spell from the school of Divination that the wielder can normally cast that they do not have prepared. The character may instead choose to cast a single Divination spell that they have prepared without using a spell slot.
The candle burns for an hour. Each time this ability is used, the candle burns down and loses 10 minutes of burning time.
Alchemical Formula: Fire (any), Mercury (any), Perception, Prophesy

FLAME ARROW CANDLE

Wondrous item, rare
This candle burns for 10 minutes. Once lit, this candle ignites any arrow fired within five feet of the candle. A lick of flame leaps up and lights the arrow once released. Each piece of ammunition fired within five feet of the candle does an additional 1d6 fire damage and can easily ignite a flammable object or structure but won't ignite creatures.
Alchemical Formula: Fire (any), Mercury (any), Flight

GOLD CANDLE

Wondrous item, rare
This candle burns for one minute. When lit, anyone within a 30-foot radius of this candle is healed for 1d4 + 1 hit points each round. This healing is positive energy and deals a similar amount of radiant damage to undead. Note that this affects any creatures within the range of the light.
Alchemical Formula: Gold, Fire (any), Healing, Life

HOLY CANDLE

Wondrous item, uncommon
This candle burns for six hours. Once lit, this candle repels undead within a 10-foot radius of the candle. An undead creature that attempts to enter the area must make a DC 14 Wisdom saving throw. On a failure, the creature is unable to enter the area.
Alchemical Formula: Silver, Fire (any), Life

RADIANT CANDLE

Wondrous item, rare
This candle burns for one hour. Once lit, this candle scalds undead within a 30-foot radius of the candle. An undead creature that starts its turn within this area or enters the area for the first time on its turn takes 1d6 radiant damage.
Alchemical Formula: Gold, Fire (any), Life

REFLECTION CANDLE

Wondrous item, very rare
This candle burns for six hours. When you light this candle, its smoke forms into an exact image of you. The image can move about, speak, and act as you wish within a 30-foot radius of candle. Your appearance is copied exactly, but the image is made of smoke and insubstantial, unable to attack, move objects, or affect the environment in any way. The form cannot cast spells. You can control the image from up to a half mile away. You can use a bonus action to provide a new instruction to the image or have it repeat a simple series of actions. As an action, you can transfer your senses to the image, allowing you to see and hear as if you were standing in the image's spot. While doing this, you are blind and deaf. You can recover your senses with an action.
Alchemical Formula: Fire (any), Mercury (any), Body, Illusion

SANCTUARY CANDLE

Wondrous item, rare
This candle burns for one hour. While you carry this lit candle, a creature attempting to attack you or target you with a harmful spell must make a DC 14 Wisdom saving throw. On a failed save, the creature must choose a new target or lose the attack. The candle does not protect you from area effects.
Alchemical Formula: Gold, Fire (any), Protection

SHIELDING CANDLE

Wondrous item, rare
This candle burns for an hour. While you hold this lit candle, a floating circle of force floats around you. Your armor class in increased by +5 and you take no damage from *magic missile*.
Alchemical Formula: Fire (any), Armor, Body

SLAYING CANDLE

Wondrous item, uncommon
The candle burns for one minute. When you use an action to light this candle, a spectral flame affixes to a target of your choice that you can see within 50 feet. Attacks against this creature are made with advantage. The target has disadvantage on saving throws. After the target is killed, the candle withers and turns to dust.
Alchemical Formula: Rare Earth, Fire (any), Body

VISION CANDLE

Wondrous item, uncommon
The candle burns for six hours. The light of this candle turns all invisible things within a 10-foot radius visible. This terminates any magical invisibility. This has no effect on naturally invisible or hidden creatures. *Invisibility* does not function within range of the candle.
Alchemical Formula: Rare Earth, Air (any), Fire (any), Perception

WIZARDRY CANDLE

Wondrous item, rare
This candle burns for six hours and any use, even for 15 minutes, burns down a full hour of the candle. When lit while preparing spells, a spellcaster within five feet of it may prepare three additional 1st-level spells, two additional 2nd-level spells, or one additional 3rd-level spell. It does not provide additional spell slots.
Alchemical Formula: Gold, Onyx, Azoth (any), Fire (any)

CUSPS, EYES, AND SPECTACLES

Cusps are gem-like hemispheres found in pairs that are placed over the eyes where they affix themselves. It takes an action to apply these to the face and you have a disadvantage on all vision-based Perception checks, attack rolls, and saving throws for the next minute. These may be worn for one hour before eye fatigue becomes too great. Six hours passing is enough time for the eyes to recover after removing the cusps. If you use them for more than one hour, after a second hour of use or when you remove them, whichever comes first, you are blinded for 1d4 days. The hour the cusps are used need not be consecutive; if used for less than 10 minutes, an hour is enough to allow the eyes to recover.

Spectacles are crystal discs in a frame placed over where the eyes rest. There is a 25% chance when they are found that they will have ear hooks. These can be constructed with ear hooks for an extra 10 gp. This allows the lenses to be used hands-free.

These can cause eye fatigue if used for greater than five minutes, giving you disadvantage on all vision-based Perception skill checks, attack rolls, and vision-based saving throws. The strain on the eyes requires an hour recovery time between uses to avoid the eye fatigue from beginning immediately upon putting the spectacles on.

Eyes may be worn without constraint and appear much like spectacles.

CUSP OF ANTIMAGIC

Wondrous item, legendary
This is not two cusps, but rather one large cusp that sits over the bridge of the nose and covers both eyes and a substantial portion of your forehead. As soon as they are applied, anything within the arc of the cusps is bathed in an antimagic field. You can select one 100-foot cone area to be looking at, and that area is covered in the field at the end of each of your turns. Within this area, spells can't be cast, summoned creatures disappear, and magic items don't function. Spells and other magical effects, except those cast by an artifact or deity, are suppressed. A slot expended to cast a suppressed spell is consumed. While an item is suppressed, it doesn't function, but the time it spends suppressed counts against its duration.
Anything within the cone is lightly obscured from your vision, and anything outside the cone is completely obscured from you unless you have additional eyes that can look in separate directions from the primary eyes.
Alchemical Formula: Diamond, Gold, Azoth (any) (x3), Planar, Prowess, Purity

CUSPS OF BLASTING

Wondrous item, rare
When worn, you can fire blasts of fire from your eyes. As an action, you can make a ranged attack against a target within 30 feet. On a hit, the target takes 4d6 fire damage.
Alchemical Formula: Fire (any), Light, Mind, Strength

CUSPS OF ENTHRALLMENT

Wondrous item, rare
These powerful cusps allow the user to mesmerize a single target. At will, you may use an action to create a *hypnotic pattern* per the spell that originates from the cusps. You must concentrate on the effect to maintain it. The spell save DC for the cusps is 14.
Alchemical Formula: Diamond, Mercury (any), Control, Illusion

CUSPS OF ILLUSION DETECTION

Wondrous item, rare
Anything you view while wearing the cusps is revealed as it really is. You can see through normal and magical darkness, illusions, spells that obscure creatures such as *blur* or *mirror image* and displacement effects. It does not penetrate solid objects.
Alchemical Formula: Ruby, Mercury (any), Illusion, Perception

CUSPS OF PRECOGNITION

Wondrous item, rare
While wearing these cusps, you see the next several moments happen in advance. If you spend a full round looking through these cusps, you receive a +2 bonus on initiative, attack rolls, saving throws, ability checks, and your armor class.
The goggles show several possible likely futures of several universes simultaneously, so it is impossible to predict if a door has a specific kind of trap. To use these in a non-combat situation, a minute of study must be completed to acquire the same bonus.
Alchemical Formula: Moonstone, Sulfur (any), Dream, Prophesy

EYES OF NIGHT VISION

Wondrous item, uncommon
When worn, these allow you to see in dim light and darkness as if it was bright light. The range on these cusps is unlimited. Vision when wearing these cusps is in shades of gray, making color impossible to distinguish.
Alchemical Formula: Air (any), Mercury (any), Perception

EYES OF SHADE

Wondrous item, rare
These lenses fit securely over your eyes, shading them from sunlight, light, and other light-based effects. Unlike normal cusps, these may be worn constantly. You have advantage on saving throws against any blinding, dazzling, or other sight-based effects, any penalties due to bright light, or any illusions relying on visual mesmerization or patterns. When removed, the wearer treats dim light as darkness and bright light as dim light for one minute.
Alchemical Formula: Jade, Platinum, Fire (any), Light

EYES OF SKYSIGHT

Wondrous item, rare
When these cusps are worn, they negate any vision impairments or obstructions within one-half mile, such as clouds, fog, hail, mists, or any obscuring vapor. It doubles the distance you can see in bright or dim light. Sandstorms, fogs, mists, and particulate matter are completely transparent to the wearer, providing no cover or concealment.
Alchemical Formula: Air (any), Illusion, Perception

EYES OF THE WITHERING GAZE

Wondrous item, uncommon
As an action, you may meet the gaze of any target that can see you. The target must succeed on a DC 14 Wisdom saving throw or become paralyzed. A target that succeeds must make a second DC 14 Wisdom saving throw or become frightened of you. A paralyzed or frightened creature may repeat the saving throw at the end of each of its turns, ending the effect on a success. If you move your gaze from the target, the effect automatically ends.
Alchemical Formula: Mercury (any), Fear, Stasis

SPECTACLES OF COMPREHENSION

Wondrous item, uncommon
The wearer of these spectacles is able to read any writing in any language. Secret messages that are not part of a written language, such as an arcane sigil, are not decoded.
Alchemical Formula: Azoth (any), Mercury (any), Perception

SPECTACLES OF LIFE SIGHT

Wondrous item, uncommon
These cusps give you an indication of the relative health of any creature you are able to see. It does not give numerical information, but you can tell if a target has more than three-quarters, more than one-half, or more than one-quarter of its initial hit points. You can also tell if a creature is regenerating, undead, unconscious, in possession of temporary hit points, healing, or losing hit points.
Alchemical Formula: Air (any), Fire (any), Perception

SPECTACLES OF SECRET DOOR DETECTION

Wondrous item, uncommon
These spectacles allow you to see extremely fine detail. You have advantage on Investigation or Perception checks that rely on sight to detect traps and secret doors.
These lenses quickly cause eye fatigue. The one minute they can be used allows you to inspect an area of a 10-foot cube, including floors, walls, and ceilings. If examining a single surface, you may cover 600 square feet, or six 10-foot-square walls. You must rest your eyes for six minutes before using the cusps again.
Alchemical Formula: Earth (any), Water (any), Perception

DUSTS

Dusts appear as collections of fine, granular, light, metallic particles. They do not clump. Color and consistency may vary, but they usually are metallic in nature. Dusts are delivered to the target by a variety of methods. They may be sprinkled, added to food or drink, delivered by blowgun, or thrown.

Dusts are heavy and are relatively dense. Dusts delivered via blowgun cover a 15-foot cone. If you don't have proficiency with the blowgun (martial ranged weapon), the dust affects you on a natural roll of 1. Dust may also be thrown like grenades with a range of 20/60 feet. Dust thrown as a grenade affects all targets within a five-foot radius. You must specifically prepare a dust ahead of time for it to be thrown as a grenade-like weapon. Each attack made in this way counts as a single use of the dust.

If you target a surface, you must hit AC 5 with the dust and it will affect all creatures within the five-foot radius. On a miss, the dust must land somewhere. Roll a 1d8 for direction and 1d4 x 5 feet for distance. When created, all dusts have their uses given in pinches (i.e., a dust with 10 + 1d10 pinches). If no number of uses is given, assume the whole dust must be used to cause the effect.

DUST OF AMNESIA

Wondrous item, rare
This dust causes the target to suffer complete memory loss for 2d6 minutes on a failed DC 15 Wisdom saving throw. They don't remember their name, where they are from, what they are doing, or any single fact about their lives. They are still able to breathe, eat, fight, cook, and cast spells. Except for skills involving lore, they continue to know how to perform any skill they possessed before; however, they lose access to all knowledge skills. Some people affected by this dust never recover. There is a small chance that the memory loss could become permanent until the application of an appropriate spell. Each bag of dust is found with 1d4 + 1 pinches available.
Alchemical Formula: Earth (any), Mercury (any), Salt (any), Memory

DUST OF ARCANE WEAKNESS

Wondrous item, common
A target struck by this dust must make a DC 15 Wisdom saving throw. On a failed save, the target's spiritual pattern is weakened. They have disadvantage on their next saving throw versus a spell or spell-like effect.
Alchemical Formula: Iron, Azoth (any), Earth (any)

DUST OF BLENDING

Wondrous item, uncommon
This dust is not found as loose grains or powder, instead it is found in golden crumbly dirt-like cakes approximately four inches in diameter and up to one inch thick. When thrown at a creature or object, the dust explodes in a shower of sparks and magic. The target begins to blend like a chameleon with the area. If the target is still, it has full concealment and a +10 bonus to Stealth checks. Creatures that are moving or fighting are easier to detect, receiving partial concealment and a +5 bonus to Stealth checks. There is also a 1% noncumulative chance per round that the dust is shaken off.
This effect lasts for 2d6 + 3 minutes. The dust may be removed and washed off at will. Each cake can affect one Medium creature or object.
Alchemical Formula: Earth (any), Mercury (any), Stealth

DUST OF BLIGHT

Wondrous item, rare
Targets hit by the dust who fail a DC 14 Constitution saving throw cannot regain hit points for 10 minutes. After the duration expires, healing again functions normally. Each bag of dust is found with 1d8 + 2 pinches available.
Alchemical Formula: Iron, Rare Earth, Earth (any), Death, Stasis

DUST OF BLIGHTED BONES

Wondrous item, very rare
This dust causes a terrible bone disease to take root within the target. The target must succeed on a DC 15 Constitution saving throw or, over the next 1d6 + 1 days, the target's bones slowly melt into jelly, causing an excruciating death. During this time, the person is vulnerable to all attacks. This begins 2d3 minutes after first exposure to the dust. At the end of the course of the disease, the target's bones turn to jelly. The target can no longer move. Their brain slowly dies as the skull is no longer solid enough to keep the brain together. The target can look forward to a very slow, excruciating, painful, and messy demise.
Remove curse, greater restoration, or *wish* ends the effect. *Lesser restoration* resets the progression of the disease but does not end the effect. *Dispel magic* ends the effect but does not reset the progression of the disease, leaving the bones in their weakened state.
Alchemical Formula: Earth (any), Death, Decay, Disease, Toxin

DUST OF BLINDNESS

Wondrous item, uncommon
Targets struck by this dust must succeed on a DC 18 Dexterity saving throw or be blinded for 2d6 minutes. Each bag of dust is found with 2d4 pinches of dust.
Alchemical Formula: Earth (any), Mercury (any), Stasis

DUST OF BLOOD LEECH

Wondrous item, very rare
This heinous dust draws out a creature's blood through its skin. It leaches the blood from the veins, flesh, and even the very bone marrow of the targets. When used, it forms a cloud 40 feet wide, 40 feet long, and 20 feet high. The cloud becomes inert the round after it is created. The dust adheres to the skin of anyone in the cloud when it forms as it begins to leach blood from their body, causing immediate weakness. Strength and Dexterity scores are cut in half. Thereafter each round until death, the victims must make a DC 16 Constitution saving throw. On the first failed save, the target falls prone. The second failed save causes paralysis. The third failed save results in death. The only cures for the dust are holy water, *dispel magic,* or *wish.* Survivors recover 1 point of their lost ability scores per day.
Alchemical Formula: Iron, Earth (any), Body, Decay, Stasis

DUST OF BREACHING

Wondrous item, rare
When you use an action to cast this dust against any magical or nonmagical physical barrier up to 10 feet thick, an opening appears. A five-foot radius cylindrical opening appears at the beginning of your next turn and disappears at the beginning of your following turn. Anything can pass through this space in the barrier. Creatures may enter or exit, arrows or spells may be cast through this space, and it can be seen through with no difficulty. The barrier is unharmed by any of this activity. Any barrier may be affected, whether a wall of fire, a wall of iron, a dungeon wall, an antimagic shell, or even a prismatic sphere.
Anyone within the portal at the end of the round must make a DC 18 Dexterity saving throw. A creature that fails dies, while on a successful save the creature takes 5d8 damage and is shunted to a randomly determined side of the barrier.
Alchemical Formula: Malachite, Azoth (any), Earth (any), Planar

DUST OF BURNING

Wondrous item, rare
When you use an action to spread this dust on an object, you make one cubic foot of that object inflammable. It works on such objects as wet wood and leaves, but it also makes sand, stone, bricks, and other nonflammable objects burn as wood would burn. The portion of the object affected by the dust cannot be put out by any nonmagical means. When found, there are 4 + 1d6 pinches.
Alchemical Formula: Earth (any), Fire (any), Transmutation

DUST OF CATASTROPHE

Wondrous item, rare
A creature struck by this dust must make a DC 16 Dexterity saving throw. On a successful save, the target is slowed for one minute. On a failed save, the creature drops anything it is holding and falls prone. For one minute, the target must succeed on a DC 16 Acrobatics check to pick anything up and must succeed on a DC 16 Dexterity saving throw at the end of its turn or drop anything it is holding and fall prone. Each bag of dust is found with 1d10 + 2 pinches.
Alchemical Formula: Earth (any), Agility, Body

DUST OF CLOUD DISPERSAL

Wondrous item, rare
When thrown into any cloud, smoke, dust, or mist, this dust instantly disperses it. This affects clouds caused by spells such as *cloudkill* and *stinking cloud*. The dust leaves the air clean and breathable, though smelling of ozone. Each bag of dust is found with 1d6 pinches.
Alchemical Formula: Air (any), Earth (any), Purity

DUST OF CLOUDS

Wondrous item, rare
When tossed into the air, this dust produces a billowing, swirling, cloud of dust. It fills 16 10-foot cubes. This can be a wall 10 feet wide and 160 feet long, a wall 20 feet wide and 80 feet long, or a 40-foot-by-40-foot cloud. The area within the wall is completely obscured. The dust swirls around for an hour before settling to the ground. When found, there will be between 2 + 1d8 pinches of the dust.
Alchemical Formula: Air (any), Earth (any), Mercury (any), Stealth

DUST OF CONFUSION

Wondrous item, rare
This dust fills a 10-foot cube. A creature that starts its turn within the cube or that enters the cube for the first time on its turn must make a DC 16 Wisdom saving throw. On a failure, the creature is confused, listless, and indecisive. The creature can take no actions, bonus actions, or reactions, and there is a 10% chance that the creature moves in a randomly selected direction. Each bag of dust is found with 1d6 + 4 pinches.
Alchemical Formula: Earth (any) (2 from different sources), Mind

DUST OF CONSUMPTION

Wondrous item, common
This dust makes any organic substance edible. When sprinkled over an organic substance, it breaks it down and allows it to be chewed as if it were tough, tasteless, boiled leather. Substances often have a nasty, bitter taste, but they do provide basic nutrition. Each bag of dust is found with 1d12 + 8 pinches available. One dose is enough to make food for one person for one day.
Alchemical Formula: Earth (any), Plant

DUST OF DECAY

Wondrous item, very rare
This dust causes non-living material to age and decay. When a pinch is applied, it affects up to three cubic feet of material. The non-living material then rapidly ages approximately 300 years. If two pinches are used, objects age up to 1,000 years. Each bag of dust is found with 1d12 + 8 pinches. This dust causes stone to weather, crack, and weaken. In most cases, the dust dissolves wood and other organic materials. Specific effects are left to your adjudication; a safe damage range for a collapsing building is 10d6 bludgeoning damage. A metal container is required to store the dust.
This dust rusts and destroys armor, rope, rations, iron spikes, doors, and other equipment. Note that this dust has no effect on any sort of living organism such as a tree, grass, animals, a human being, or fungi. It causes no damage to undead, but naked vampires are usually not very happy.
Alchemical Formula: Earth (any), Decay (x2 from different sources), Speed

DUST OF DEFORMITY

Wondrous item, rare
When this dust is used, the target becomes hideously deformed, with welts, bruises, warts, horn flesh, twisted cysts, and pores oozing multicolored pus covering their flesh. Their Charisma is reduced to 3.
Those viewing the target must succeed at a DC 18 Wisdom saving throw or be repulsed and unable to bear the appearance of the target.
A *remove curse* or better is required to reverse the effect.
Alchemical Formula: Earth (any), Disease, Transmutation

DUST OF DELIQUESCENCE

Wondrous item, uncommon
This dust, when spread over animal matter that is no longer alive, produces a thick, dark mist for several moments. This mist contains streams and wisps of sparkling silver smoke, and a soft ominous hissing sound can be heard. Several moments later, the dust clears and the material disappears.
This dust has no effect on any living creature and does not affect plant life. It destroys dead bodies, leather armor, and other dead organic matter in one round, leaving no trace. Undead with more than 0 hit points are not affected. Each bag of dust is found with 1d6 + 4 pinches. One pinch is enough to destroy one cubic foot of matter.
Alchemical Formula: Earth (any), Decay

DUST OF DETECT ILLUSION

Wondrous item, common
When sprinkled with this dust, illusionary objects and creatures, optical illusions, figments, glamours, patterns, phantasms, and shadows glow faintly and shimmer as if unreal. After this use, all are immediately detected as such. This allows characters to see an illusionary pit or wall for an illusion, but it does not penetrate the illusion to reveal what is behind it. It negates a creature's displacement ability or reveals a shadow as such, though it does not prevent the shadow (which is partially real) from causing damage.
Alchemical Formula: Earth (any), Sulfur (any)

DUST OF DISPELLING

Wondrous item, rare
This dust breaks all magical effects occurring where the dust is spread. All magical effects are dispelled as if affected by a *dispel magic* cast with successful DC 20 ability check.
It can be dusted over the caster, a magical trap, or over an item. If dusted over an item, it simply suppresses the magic for 10 minutes. Each bag of dust is found with 1d4 + 2 pinches.
Alchemical Formula: Diamond, Azoth (any), Mercury (any), Sulfur (any)

DUST OF DEPRIVATION

Wondrous item, very rare
This dust affects the senses of all living creatures. When used, roll 1d6 on the table below to determine the severity of damage inflicted. Every effect up to the number rolled affects the target. Roll 2d6 to determine the duration of the effect in hours. The dust contains 1d4 + 1 uses for a Medium creature.

TABLE 4–2: AFFECTED SENSES

1d6	Sense	Effect
1	Sight	Vision is blurred. Target has disadvantage on attack rolls and loses any Dexterity bonus to armor class.
2	Taste	Sense of taste is lost
3	Hearing	Target is deafened.
4	Touch	Tactile sense is lost. Target loses 10 feet of movement and cannot take the dash action. Target has disadvantage on saving throws and ability checks that rely on Dexterity and has a 30% chance of dropping anything held any round in which it is used.
5	Smell	Olfactory sense lost.
6	Sixth Sense	No spells, prayers, or spell-like or supernatural powers function.

Alchemical Formula: Earth (any), Mercury (2 from 2 different sources), Body, Mind

DUST OF DISTRACTION

Wondrous item, uncommon
When thrown on the ground, this dust creates the shape of a rat, snake, or fox depending on the bones used. It then lashes out, looking as if it is attacking someone within 15 feet of where the dust was thrown. The dust creation acts for one minute.
However, the shape is just dust and cannot harm anyone. It thrashes and lashes out to draw attention to itself. Weapon and claw attacks pass harmlessly through the dust and do no damage. Creatures can make a DC 14 Intelligence saving throw to recognize the dust as harmless after their first attack.
A creature that attempts a bite attack versus the dust creature automatically hits and must succeed on a DC 16 Constitution saving throw or die at the beginning of its next turn from choking on the dust. *Remove curse* prevents the death. Each bag of dust is found with 1d4 + 2 pinches.
Alchemical Formula: Air (any), Earth (any), Mercury (any)

DUST OF ECHOES

Wondrous item, rare
Those affected by this dust have their sensitivity to sound increased so that even the softest noise sounds like a deafening echo. The target is driven to reduce the amount of noise they make, whispering and moving slowly and quietly. Even hearing sounds at a normal conversational volume is exceedingly painful.
The target has disadvantage on attack rolls and saving throws and advantage on Perception checks that rely on hearing.
This dust is found with 2d4 pinches. The effect lasts 1d6 + 2 x 10 minutes.
Alchemical Formula: Earth (any), Mercury (any), Body, Perception

DUST OF FERTILE GROWTH

Wondrous item, rare
When this dust is spread across any soil in which plants dwell, it has an amazing effect on their growth. It causes one year's worth of growth to occur in one week. This dust has no effect on magical, sentient, or mobile plants. This dust covers up to 1,000 square feet of land.
Alchemical Formula: Earth (any) (x2), Plant, Transmutation

DUST OF FURY

Wondrous item, rare
An intelligent creature actively hostile to the wielder struck by this dust must succeed on a DC 14 Wisdom saving throw or become enraged. An enraged opponent flies into a berserk fury and attacks the nearest creature. An enraged creature has advantage on attacks rolls, and any creature attacking it has advantage on attack rolls. Creatures friendly to the wielder are unaffected. The target may repeat the saving throw at the end of each of its turns, ending the effect on a success. Each bag of dust is found with 1d4 + 2 pinches.
Alchemical Formula: Earth (any), Mercury (any), Emotion

DUST OF THE GRAVE

Wondrous item, uncommon
This dust enhances the connection undead have with the Negative Material Plane. When sprinkled with this dust, undead gain advantage on saving throws to resist the effects of channel divinity. When found, there is usually enough dust to coat 1d12 + 8 Medium undead.
Alchemical Formula: Earth (any), Planar

DUST OF INSTANT ICE

Wondrous item, rare
One dose of this dust freezes up to 1,000 cubic feet of water. Fresh water freezes instantly, but saltwater takes up to 1d4 + 1 rounds to freeze. If there is more than 1,000 cubic feet of water, then the frozen shape does not make a perfect cube, but more of a trapezoidal shape depending on how the dust is dispersed. Creatures made of water are affected by this dust as if under a *slow* spell and take 1d8 cold damage.
Alchemical Formula: Earth (any), Water (any), Cold

DUST OF LIGHTNESS

Wondrous item, uncommon
When this dust is applied to any non-living object, it reduces the weight of the object by half for 12 hours. The dust can be washed or blown off, so care must be taken if transporting objects in a storm. One dose coats one Medium creature or object and 1d8 + 2 doses are found.
Alchemical Formula: Rare Earth, Air (x2), Earth (any)

DUST OF LOOPING

Wondrous item, very rare
This bizarre dust forces the creatures targeted to make a DC 16 Wisdom saving throw. Those that fail their save repeat their previous round. They don't perform the action anew — they repeat the exact same motions and movements. Attacks are dodged trivially; the targets have a −4 penalty to their armor class. Spells are recast, costing the target another spell slot. If no spell slot is available, the creature attempts to cast the spell, but nothing happens. The targets have no control over their actions; they repeat the same actions even if it puts them into mortal danger. A target may repeat the saving throw at the end of each of its turns, ending the effect on a success. When found, this dust has 1d4 uses.
Alchemical Formula: Azoth (any), Earth (any), Mercury (any), Memory

DUST OF MALADWEOMER

Wondrous item, rare
A target coated in this dust must make a save DC 16 Wisdom saving throw. If they fail, it causes all their spells, spell-like abilities, magic items, and magical effects to operate at a minimum effectiveness until the end of their next turn. Spells do minimum damage and have minimum duration. Creatures summoned have minimum hit points and all variable effects are treated as minimum. People affected by magic originating from the target receive advantage on their saving throws. This dust is found with 1d4 + 1 pinches.
Alchemical Formula: Azoth (any), Earth (any), Stasis

DUST OF MIND DULLING

Wondrous item, rare
This dust clouds the mind and makes it difficult for spellcasters to successfully cast spells. Spellcasters (and monsters with spell-like effects) must make a DC 15 Constitution saving throw or find their wits dulled. Spells take longer to cast. A spell that normally takes a bonus action requires an action. A spell that normally requires an action takes one minute. Any longer casting times are increased by a factor of 10. In addition, the target has disadvantage on Concentration checks.
Those affected by the dust are impaired for 1d4 + 1 minutes. This dust is found with 1d8 + 2 pinches.
Alchemical Formula: Earth (any), Mind (x2)

DUST OF NONDETECTION

Wondrous item, rare
Hidden objects or traps sprinkled with this dust are undetectable by magical means of any sort. This does not mean that the item is obscured from view; it simply prevents its detection by magical means. The target cannot be detected or perceived through *clairvoyance*, *telepathy*, *crystal balls*, or any other scrying devices. The target emits no discernible aura, and any predictions of the future neither mention nor account for the target. This dust is permanent until sprinkled with *dust of appearance*, *dispel magic* is cast, or the trap is triggered. This dust can also be sprinkled on a living creature, warding the user against all divination and mental or magical location and or detection for 2d6 hours. This dust can cover one Medium object or creature.
Alchemical Formula: Earth (any), Stealth (x2)

DUST OF PANIC

Wondrous item, uncommon
A creature with Intelligence of 4 or greater struck by this dust must make a DC 16 Wisdom saving throw or drop what it is holding and use its move and a dash action to flee for up to one minute. A fleeing creature may repeat the saving throw at the end of each of its turns, ending the effect on a success. This dust is found with 1d4 + 1 pinches.
Alchemical Formula: Earth (any), Fear

DUST OF PARALYZATION

Wondrous item, uncommon
This terrifying dust paralyzes all who fail a DC 13 Constitution saving throw. Targets may repeat the saving throw at the end of each of its turns, ending the effect on a success. If the target fails this save three times, they are paralyzed for a full hour. This dust is found with 1d6 + 1d8 pinches.
Alchemical Formula: Earth (any), Stasis

DUST OF PLANAR SEVERANCE

Wondrous item, rare
This dust blocks planar connections. It has several effects. Targets can avoid the affects by succeeding at a DC 18 Dexterity saving throw. On a failed save, spellcasters are unable to cast spells or use spell-like effects. Mindless undead have their connections to their home plane severed. They de-animate and drop lifeless to the floor. Planar effects such as *true seeing*, *gate*, *teleport*, *etherealness*, and *blink* are suppressed. An affected creature may attempt a DC 18 Wisdom saving throw at the end of each of its turns, ending the effect on a success. A creature that fails the saving throw each round for a minute has the effect for 24 hours. This dust is found with 1d4 + 1 pinches.
Alchemical Formula: Azoth (any), Earth (any), Planar

DUST OF REDIRECTION

Wondrous item, rare
This powerful dust has an intense effect upon the targets. They must succeed on a DC 18 Wisdom saving throw or be affected. If this save fails, the thing they currently find most important becomes unimportant. If they are fighting, they stop; people eating lose their appetite; whatever task is currently being attempted is ended. The targets remember doing those things, but no longer have any interest in performing or completing the task. Targets may regain interest in the task through normal means after an hour. This dust is found with 1d4 + 1 pinches.
Alchemical Formula: Earth (any), Mercury (any), Sulfur (any), Memory

DUST OF RENDING PROTECTIONS

Wondrous item, rare
When targets are covered by this dust, any magical or supernatural protections and wards are stripped. The target's armor class receives a –2 penalty and any resistances the creature has are removed for an hour. This has no effect on a target's magic resistance or saving throws. It does nothing to remove natural immunities such as a fire elemental's resistance to fire. This dust is found with 1d8 + 2 pinches.
Alchemical Formula: Earth (any), Salt (any), Sulfur (any), Decay

DUST OF REVEALING

Wondrous item, rare
This dust fills an area of about 28,000 cubic feet (28 contiguous 10-foot by 10-foot by 10-foot cubes) or a 10-foot-high, 30-foot-radius circle. The whole dust must be expended for the dust to have an effect. Anything within this area is revealed to be what it truly is. Illusions are made transparent, disguises are revealed, shapeshifters change into their true form, and spells that alter appearance are dispelled. Note that this does not reveal planar creatures, nor creatures out of phase. It just reveals things as they are.
Alchemical Formula: Rare Earth, Earth (any), Fire (any), Perception

DUST OF ROUGHAGE

Wondrous item, rare
A small pinch of this dust added to at least one gallon of water produces an astounding pile of feed. It forms soft, spongy chunks of dry, pasty vegetable matter suitable for feeding 50 Medium creatures for one day. It feeds one-half as many people for every size category increase and feeds twice as many people for each size category decrease: 100 Small creatures or 25 Large ones. The dust is found with 4d4 + 1 pinches available.
In the unfortunate circumstance that a dry pinch is consumed, the imbiber must make a DC 18 Constitution saving throw. On a failure, the creature dies a gruesome death. On a success, the creature is violently ill and permanently loses a point of Constitution.
Alchemical Formula: Earth (any), Mercury (any) (x2), Plant

DUST OF RUST

Wondrous item, very rare
This heinous dust destroys metal. When exposed to the *dust of rust*, nonmagical ferrous metals such as iron and steel disintegrate, rusting apart in one round. Base metals such as nickel, lead, zinc, and copper rust in one round and disintegrate in two rounds. Rare, precious, or alloy metals such as mithril, adamantite, bronze, tin, and aluminum rust and disintegrate in one minute. Certain noble metals such as gold, platinum, and silver are immune to this dust. Magic metal items that are not worn or carried may be ruined, although legendary items or artifacts are not affected. "Magical metal" includes such things as golems, rods, and rings. One preparation covers up to 100 cubic feet or 1,000 square feet of metal.
Alchemical Formula: Earth (any), Salt (any) (x2), Decay

DUST OF SLAYERBANE

Wondrous item, rare
This dust is barely detectable when spread in the air and appears only as a momentary glimmer. Anyone exposed to this dust must make a DC 15 Constitution saving throw or become terribly allergic to the creature whose bones were used in the manufacture of the dust.
As soon as the victim comes within 100 feet of the creature, they experience a violent onset of symptoms. It begins with a sneeze that negates any sort of surprise, and then the eyes water and the nose begins to run. The next round, the victim breaks out in hives that itch painfully.
The reaction is moderately impairing, causing disadvantage on ability checks based on Dexterity or Strength. The victim must succeed at a DC 10 Concentration check to successfully cast a spell. This reaction ends 1d6 rounds after moving more than 100 feet away from the target creature, unless they engaged the creature in combat, in which case blood, sweat, and dander cause the condition to linger until the victim uses an action to clean themselves.
This dust is created from the full skeleton of the creature that the victim(s) are to be made allergic to. Most often, corpses of monsters killed by the monster hunters are used. The reaction is permanent until a *lesser restoration* spell is cast.
Alchemical Formula: Onyx, Earth (any), Body, Disease

DUST OF SLEEP

Wondrous item, uncommon
This powerful dust causes the targets to fall into a comatose slumber. Any creature struck by the dust that fails a DC 14 Constitution saving throw falls into a deep sleep. A sleeping victim can be awakened when a creature uses an action to do so. This dust is found with 2d4 + 2 pinches.
Alchemical Formula: Earth (any), Mercury (any), Stasis

DUST OF SNEEZING

Wondrous item, rare
This dust causes all creatures within its area of effect to make a DC 16 Constitution saving throw or be struck by a sneezing fit. The sneezing fit gives its victims disadvantage on attack rolls, Dexterity-based ability checks, and Constitution saving throws. They can make a saving throw at the end of each round to end the effect. This dust is found with 1d8 + 12 pinches.
Alchemical Formula: Earth (any), Mercury (any), Disease

DUST OF SOLID VAPOR

Wondrous item, rare
This powerful dust has unique properties of stasis and solidification. When tossed into the area of effect of any magical or nonmagical mist or cloud, it begins to harden the vapor into a solid substance. For non-obscuring clouds, this causes the area to become thick and gummy, much like a *web* spell. Those moving through the field each round must make a DC 14 Strength check. Those who fail have their speed reduced by three-quarters while those who succeed have their movement reduced by one-half.
Obscuring clouds become even more dense, hardening into an amber-like substance. Those within the area of effect must make a DC 16 Dexterity saving throw or become trapped in the cloud for the duration. This can be used on a gaseous creature as well.
Those trapped in the solid cloud can still breathe and are simply held in place. The solid nature of the cloud protects them from external attack or damage, but the solid vapor still has all its natural properties. Beings trapped in a solid acid cloud take damage every round they are trapped. This dust has no effect on air or water, only magical and nonmagical mists, clouds, vapors, and other gaseous matter.
This dust lasts for 1d4 + 1 rounds. When found, it has 1d4 + 2 pinches.
Alchemical Formula: Earth (any), Mercury (any), Transmutation

DUST OF THE SPARKLING MIND

Wondrous item, rare
This bag contains white dust that sparkles like thousands of tiny gems. Anyone who uses this dust by snorting it up their nose can communicate telepathically for 1d6 + 4 hours with any other user. The range is 50 feet, and there are 3d4 + 8 uses per bag.
Alchemical Formula: Earth (any), Mercury (any), Telesthenic

DUST OF SPIRIT BINDING

Wondrous item, rare
This dust binds ethereal and noncorporeal undead to the Prime Material Plane. It worsens the armor class of such creatures by five points and solidifies the insubstantial form, causing the creature to take full damage from nonmagical attacks. A downside to this is that it makes attacks from the creatures more physically damaging. Double hit point damage from attacks is dealt, or if no physical attack is given, it gains a claw/claw or slam/slam routine for 1d8/1d8 slashing or bludgeoning damage.
If a body is possessed, this dust paralyzes the body for 3d4 minutes and imprisons the spirit inside the body for the duration. This dust is found with 2d4 + 2 pinches.
Alchemical Formula: Earth (any), Planar, Stasis

DUST OF TOXIN ADHERENCE

Wondrous item, rare
This useful dust is attracted to toxins and poisons as iron is to a magnet. When sprinkled or dusted over a surface, the dust identifies contact and surface poisons, as well as poisons in needles, darts, and injected poisons in traps. This allows certain detection of poison traps and gives advantage on Dexterity checks made to disarm them. Anyone who actually manages to fall prey to the revealed poison, such as an incompetent thief that fails to disarm a trap, receives advantage on their saving throw. This dust can be used to thoroughly test one 10-foot cube for poison, including up to five separate items.
Alchemical Formula: Earth (any) (x2), Toxin

DUST OF TURN RESISTANCE

Wondrous item, rare
When this dust is spread upon undead creatures, energies from the Negative Material Plane are strengthened. All undead affected by this dust receive advantage to their Wisdom saving throws to resist channel divinity effects. If the effect would cause damage, on a failure they take one-half damage and on a success they take none. The dust can cover up to 20 Medium creatures.
Alchemical Formula: Earth (any), Salt (x2), Death

ELIXIRS

Elixirs are usually found in vials with a single, one-ounce dose. Typically, the vials are glass or ceramic, more rarely metal or crystal. Generally, elixir bottles do not have labels, which requires either experimentation or an alchemist to determine the contents. In addition to the standard methods of identification, characters may sample from each container to determine the nature of the liquid inside with a successful DC 15 Intelligence (Arcana) check. Elixirs of the same type, make, and manufacture may be similar in smell, taste, and appearance, but this is no guarantee. In order to encourage experimentation with elixirs, you may have elixirs not subjected to identifying magics be more powerful (maximized effects or duration, etc.) than potions identified using traditional magical or alchemical means. To randomly determine if an elixir is labeled, roll 1d6. On a 1–2, the potion is labeled; on a 3–5, it is not. On a 6, the potion is labeled incorrectly. Roll a second elixir, and that is what is on the label.

Unless otherwise noted in the description of the individual elixirs below, the effects of an elixir last for 1d4 + 4 minutes. In many cases, quaffing a half dose causes the effects to last half as long. It takes an action to open and drink an elixir. The elixir takes effect immediately.

A character can carefully administer an elixir to an unconscious creature as an action by trickling the liquid down the creature's throat.

Alchemists can compound elixirs at low cost, this being their primary advantage over wands and other items. However, this does require time and certain rare materials.

Any two elixirs can be fused into an admixture. This is an extremely difficult process where two magical liquids are combined into one elixir. In order to create a potion admixture, you must succeed at an Intelligence (Alchemist's Supplies) check with a DC equal to 10 plus the DC required to craft the rarer of the two. If successful, you now have a single potion that, when quaffed, provides both effects. On a failure, the potions still combine, but you must roll on the potion miscibility table.

If successful on your Intelligence (Alchemist's Supplies) check, you may choose to roll on the potion miscibility table by choice, adding 5 to your roll. Note that needing to roll this check due to failure does not provide this protection.

ELIXIR OF ABSORPTION

Potion, very rare
After you drink this elixir, you ignore the first 10 points of damage from one particular damage type from each attack until the elixir expires. You may choose or change the damage type as a bonus action. Once you have ignored 220 points of damage or 24 hours after you imbibe the elixir, the effects expire.
Alchemical Formula: Water (any), Body (any) (x2), Protection

ELIXIR OF AGING

Potion, rare
This elixir causes the imbiber to age rapidly. A human subject becomes 2d10 years older. Creatures that drink this elixir with a shorter or longer maximum lifespan than humans age proportionally to their maximum lifespan. The aging can be reversed with *greater restoration* or *wish*.
Alchemical Formula: Water (any), Body (any), Decay

ELIXIR OF ANESTHESIA

Potion, rare
This wonderful elixir has many useful properties. The first and most useful is that it grants a +2 bonus to Constitution checks and Constitution saving throws.
The second effect is that when you imbibe the potion, you gain temporary hit points equal to half your maximum hit points. When the elixir expires, you take damage equal to the number of temporary hit points you lost while the elixir was active.
The third and final effect is that this elixir affects the user by delaying poison. For the duration of the potion, any effect from poison is delayed until the elixir expires, at which point the poison takes effect.
Alchemical Formula: Water (any), Body (any), Healing

ELIXIR OF BALANCE

Potion, uncommon
This elixir grants you superb balance. You gain a +10 bonus to Dexterity (Acrobatics) checks to balance. In addition, if your Dexterity is less than 20, you are considered to have a Dexterity of 20 for Dexterity saving throws.
Alchemical Formula: Water (any), Agility

ELIXIR OF BEAUTY

Potion, uncommon
When this elixir is imbibed, you gain a +10 bonus on all Charisma-based skill checks. If the effects wear off in the presence of someone you manipulated or influenced while under the influence of this draught, then the creature has a hostile reaction and possibly attacks you.
Alchemical Formula: Water (any), Emotion

ELIXIR OF BESTIAL BOON

Potion, rare
When imbibed, this elixir causes you to express your inner animalistic tendencies. Roll on the table below to determine your spiritual animal guide. Your body quickly transforms as you physically express your inner animal nature. This is a visible transformation; you take on the literal forms, colors, and traits of the animal that is your guide. Once a guide is determined, it never changes. Subsequent uses of this elixir always produce the same results. All of the attacks gained are melee attacks and should have their damage adjusted based on your Strength (unless noted otherwise). You are considered proficient in making these attacks.

TABLE 4–3: SPIRITUAL ANIMAL GUIDES

1d6	Animal	Ability and Physical Change
1	Wolf	Add half your level to Wisdom (Survival) checks made to track. You have advantage on Wisdom (Perception) checks that rely on smell. You gain a bite attack that does 1d4 + 1 piercing damage and, on a successful hit, your target must succeed on a Strength saving throw or fall prone. The DC is equal to 10 + your proficiency bonus + your Strength modifier. Your snout elongates, and you grow fur over your body.
2	Cat	Gain two claw attacks that do 1d4 slashing damage each. If both claw attacks hit, add 2d4 slashing damage if not wearing shoes. You may use Dexterity instead of Strength to make these attacks. You have advantage on Dexterity (Stealth) checks. You grow claws and fur, and your pupils become vertical slits.
3	Bear	Gain 2d12 temporary hit points. Gain two claw attacks that do 1d6 slashing damage each. If both claw attacks hit, do an additional 1d6 slashing damage from rending damage. Increase one size category as you grow fur and claws.
4	Hawk	Gain the ability to fly at your normal movement speed. Gain a bite attack that does 1d4 piercing damage. Your arms turn into wings, and feathers grow on your body.
5	Spider	Gain a climb speed of 60 feet. Gain a bite attack that does 1 piercing damage and target must make a Constitution saving throw with a DC equal to 10 plus your proficiency bonus plus your Constitution modifier. On a failed save, the target take 2d6 poison damage and must save again in one minute or fall unconscious. On a successful save, the target takes half the damage and does not have to save again. You grow additional eyes and stiff bristles over your body. Mandibles grow around your mouth.
6	Dragon	Gain a +2 bonus to your Armor Class and a random breath weapon: Roll 1d6; 1–2=fire, 3=acid, 4=lightning, 5=ice, 6=sonic. The breath weapon is a 30-foot cone (fire, ice, sonic) or 60-foot line (acid, lightning). When you use an action to use your breath weapon, each target in the area must make a Dexterity saving throw with a DC of 10 + your proficiency bonus + your Dexterity modifier. On a failed save, the target takes 4d6 of the appropriate damage type while on a success it takes half this amount. The breath weapon has a recharge of 5–6. Your body is covered in scales, and your eyes turn golden.

Alchemical Formula: Water (any), Body, Memory

ELIXIR OF BOUNCING

Potion, uncommon
You gain a spring in your step and can bounce three to 14 feet off the ground on every step. You are resistant to bludgeoning damage from falling, but for every foot you fall, you bounce half that many feet back in the air. Collisions with a ceiling damage you as falling damage. You have advantage on Strength (Athletics) checks made to jump.
Alchemical Formula: Water (any), Body

ELIXIR OF CLARITY

Potion, rare
When this elixir is consumed, a refreshing clarity overcomes you. Your mind becomes clear, dispelling any mind-affecting effects such as *feeblemind* or *confusion*. Your vision also clarifies and grants you *true seeing* for the duration of the elixir.
Alchemical Formula: Water (any), Mind

ELIXIR OF CLOAKING SHADOWS

Potion, uncommon
Once imbibed, this elixir cloaks you in an ever-shifting, roiling web of umbral darkness. Your face, location, and appearance are hidden. The square you are in is considered to be in dim light regardless of the prevailing light level. Darkvision does not pierce this dim light. You can see through these shadows with no drawback. You are partially obscured and have advantage on Dexterity (Stealth) checks made to hide.
Alchemical Formula: Water (any), Stealth

ELIXIR OF CONTROL, ANIMAL

Potion, uncommon
This elixir allows you to empathize with and control the emotions and behavior of one type of beast (cats, dogs, horses, etc.). The number controlled is dependent on the size of the animal. You can control up to 5d4 Tiny animals, 4d4 Small animals, 3d4 Medium animals, 2d4 Large animals, or 1d4 Huge animals. Roll d20 to determine the type of animal that can be controlled by a found potion:

TABLE 4–4: ANIMAL CATEGORY

d20	Type
1–8	Mammal
9–12	Avian
13–16	Reptile/Amphibian/Fish
17–19	Mammal/Avian
20	All

Animals who are well-trained or have good reason to fear or hate you are allowed a DC 16 Wisdom saving throw to avoid the effect. On a failed save, the animal is inclined to view you in a favorable light for the duration of the elixir. Without a way to communicate with the animal, there is no way for the animal to understand your intent. The animal does its best to meet your needs as it understands them. The animal will not harm itself or members of its own kind, though it may threaten them. At the end of the duration of the elixir, the animal is 90% likely to flee in confusion; otherwise, it attacks.
Alchemical Formula: Water (any), Control

ELIXIR OF CONTROL. DRAGON

Potion, very rare
This philter allows you to charm and control a dragon within 60 feet. The dragon receives a DC 18 Wisdom saving throw to avoid the effect. Once under your control, it must willingly follow your commands as if under a *dominate monster* spell for the duration of the elixir, which lasts for 1d4 + 1 hours. After the philter's duration ends, the dragon is 90% likely to be hostile. Roll d20 to determine the type of dragon controlled:

TABLE 4–5: DRAGON TYPE

d20	Color
1–2	White
3–4	Black
5–7	Green
8–9	Blue
10	Red
11–12	Brass
13–14	Copper
15	Bronze
16	Silver
17	Gold
18–19	Evil
20	Good

Alchemical Formula: Water (any), Control, Prowess

ELIXIR OF CONTROL. ELEMENTAL

Potion, very rare
This elixir allows you to influence up to four elementals as if they are under the effect of a *dominate monster* spell. It has a range of 60 feet and allows a saving throw. If you are influencing just one elemental, the saving throw is a DC 20 Wisdom saving throw. If you are influencing more than a single elemental, the DC is 16. If the desired elemental is under the control of another creature, the elemental receives a +2 bonus on its saving throw. Roll d20 to determine the type of elemental controlled:

TABLE 4–6: ELEMENTAL TYPE

d20	Type
1–3	Elemental, Air
4–6	Elemental, Earth
7–9	Elemental, Fire
10–12	Elemental, Water
13	Elemental, Ice
14	Elemental, Lightning
15	Elemental, Magma
16	Elemental, Mud
17–20	All

Alchemical Formula: Azoth (any), Air (any), Earth (any), Fire (any), Water (any), Control

ELIXIR OF CONTROL. GIANT

Potion, very rare
This elixir allows you to charm and control one or two giants. If one is controlled, it must succeed at a DC 18 Wisdom saving throw to avoid the effect. If attempting to control two giants, the DC is 16. While under your control, they do your bidding, treating you as their master in complete obedience. After the control ends, the giant(s) are 90% likely to be hostile. Roll d20 to determine the type of giant controlled:

TABLE 4–7: GIANT TYPE

d20	Type
1–5	Hill
6–9	Stone
10–13	Frost
14–17	Fire
18–19	Cloud
20	Storm

Alchemical Formula: Water (any), Body, Control

ELIXIR OF CONTROL. HUMAN

Potion, very rare
This elixir allows you to control up to eight humans or humanoids that you can see as if they were under the effect of a *dominate person* spell. Each target may attempt a DC 18 Wisdom saving throw to avoid the effect. Roll d20 to determine what kind of humanoids can be controlled:

TABLE 4–8: HUMANOID TYPE

d20	Type
1–2	Dwarves
3–4	Elves/Half-Elves
5–6	Gnomes
7–8	Halflings
9–10	Half-Orcs
11–16	Humans
17–19	Goblinoids
20	Any Humanoid

Alchemical Formula: Onyx, Water (any), Control

ELIXIR OF CONTROL. PLANT

Potion, rare
This elixir allows you to influence the behavior of vegetable lifeforms, including fungi, molds, and monstrous plants such as shambling mounds. You can cause them to remain still or active at your whim, according to their natural limits. Vegetable monsters with an intelligence above 1 are entitled to a DC 16 Wisdom saving throw to avoid the effect. All plants within a 20-foot cube can be controlled for the duration of the elixir. The effect has a range of 180 feet.
Alchemical Formula: Water (any), Control, Plant

ELIXIR OF CONTROL, UNDEAD

Potion, rare

This necromantic elixir acts as a *dominate monster* spell affecting a specific type of undead. You can influence up to the number of creatures shown in the table below. Each target may attempt a DC 18 Wisdom saving throw to resist the effects. Roll d10 to determine the type of undead affected:

TABLE 4–9: UNDEAD TYPE

1d10	Type	Number Controlled
1	Ghast	2
2	Ghost	1
3	Ghoul	4
4	Shadow	8
5	Skeleton	16
6	Specter	4
7	Wight	1
8	Wraith	1
9	Vampire	1
10	Zombie	16

Alchemical Formula: Azoth (any), Salt (any), Water (any), Control

ELIXIR OF CRAWLING

Potion, rare

This elixir grants you the ability to slither like a snake. You can move your full speed even while prone or restrained. You may climb over or up any obstacle that is up to twice your height with no movement penalty. This does not prevent you from walking normally or using your limbs.
Alchemical Formula: Water (any), Agility, Body

ELIXIR OF CURE INSANITY

Potion, uncommon

When this elixir is imbibed, it cures nervous disorders, madness, and other forms of insanity such as mania, depression, schizophrenia, and obsessive-compulsive disorders. Depending on the cause of illness, the cure may be permanent or only last for a few weeks. It does not ward against any future occurrences of insanity.
Alchemical Formula: Mercury (any), Water (any), Mind

ELIXIR OF CURE NERVOUS DISORDERS

Potion, uncommon

When imbibed, this elixir cures common nervous disorders such as generalized anxiety disorder, panic attacks, hysteria, and fear. You are calm and relaxed within one round. You are cured of any fear and receive a +4 bonus on saving throws against fear for the duration of the elixir. The elixir may be habit forming. Depending on the cause of the nervous disorder, the effect may not be permanent.
Alchemical Formula: Mercury (any), Water (any), Stasis

ELIXIR OF DANGER SENSE

Potion, rare

This elixir allows you to detect threats to your life and limb. Any hostile potential or immediate danger within 50 feet is detected. You are alerted by a tingling sensation on the back of your neck or head. The general direction and distance is indicated, as well as a broad type of danger, such as if it is a hazard, trap, or monster. Specifics of what the danger is and exactly where it is located cannot be determined.
Alchemical Formula: Water (any), Perception

ELIXIR OF DEFENSE

Potion, rarity varies

This potion lasts for one minute and provides a bonus to your armor class. The rarity depends on the Armor Class bonus. If found, roll d8 to determine the type of elixir found on the table below. Each additional bonus to the potion requires two more Armor and Protection Essences to craft.

TABLE 4–10: DEFENSE BONUS

1d8	AC Bonus	Rarity
1–4	+1	Common
5–6	+2	Uncommon
7	+3	Rare
8	+4	Very Rare

Alchemical Formula: Water (any), Armor, Protection

ELIXIR OF DEFLATION

Potion, very rare

You change shape when you consume this elixir, becoming thinner until all that remains is a paper-thin, two-dimensional representation. While thin, you may hide or slip through cracks and narrow spaces that have appropriate vertical or horizontal clearance, such as a space under a door.

When quaffed, you must note which direction you are facing. Any target directly to either side of you cannot see you. You have partial concealment from any creature within a 90-degree arc on either side, but not directly to your side. Creatures to your front and back in a 90-degree arc see you normally. You can change your orientation as part of your move or as a reaction.

Your weight (and encumbrance) are reduced to 0 or very nearly such. You gain a glide speed equal to 150% of your walk speed. Glide is like flying, only that you have the option of moving horizontally without losing altitude. You can use your natural ability to jump, of course. This also means that you take no damage when falling any distances, heading to the ground very much like a piece of paper.

There is some risk in using this elixir. The final effect of the elixir is that you take triple damage from any type of attack due to your paper-thin nature. This is treated as a critical multiplier.
Alchemical Formula: Salt (any), Water (any), Body, Planar

ELIXIR OF DEXTERITY

Potion, rare

For the duration of the elixir, you gain a +4 bonus to any Dexterity checks including initiative rolls, Dexterity-based attacks, and saving throws. In addition, if you are hit by a small piece of ammunition such as an arrow or sling bullet and have a free hand, you can use your reaction to roll 1d12 and reduce the damage by that much.
Alchemical Formula: Water (any), Agility

ELIXIR OF DIMINUTION

Potion, uncommon

This magical potion reduces you and all of your gear to a fraction of your normal size. You reduce two size categories. Half of the potion may be consumed to reduce by one size category. This potion lasts between one and two hours (60 minutes + 1d6 x 10 minutes).
Alchemical Formula: Water (any), Body

ELIXIR OF DISPELLING

Potion, very rare

Upon consuming this potion, all magical effects on you are dispelled as if affected by a *dispel magic* cast with a DC 20 spell check. This attempts to break all magical effects, positive and negative. Make a separate check for each effect.
Alchemical Formula: Azoth (any) (x2, each from different sources), Mercury (any), Water (any)

ELIXIR OF DRAGON ATTRACTANT

Potion, legendary
When poured on the ground, this elixir attracts all dragons within one mile. They arrive as if attracted by the sweet scent of food. The elixir wakes dragons from their slumber. All awake dragons arrive within five minutes. Sleeping dragons arrive within 10 minutes. Dragons who wish to resist the odor must succeed at a DC 20 Wisdom saving throw.
If imbibed, you become a delectable, irresistible morsel to dragons for one hour. The radius of attraction increases to two miles. You become the primary target of any dragons that are attracted to the area. To attack another target, the dragon must succeed at a DC 20 Wisdom saving throw.
Alchemical Formula: Diamond, Water (any), Control, Emotion, Mind, Prowess

ELIXIR OF DREAM SPEECH

Potion, uncommon
This strange elixir allows you to ask a question of any being with an Intelligence of at least 4 that is asleep. The sleeping creature hears and begins moving its mouth silently as if in reply. The response appears directly in your mind. You understand the response no matter what language the target speaks. This does not affect dead or undead creatures. The potion lasts for only one minute and allows you to interrogate one target.
Alchemical Formula: Water (any), Dream

ELIXIR OF DREAMS

Potion, uncommon
Taken before bed, this elixir gives you a vivid dream of what you desire most in the world. During this dream, you get some information about the desired item. This may be clues to its location, what guards it, nearby landmarks, etc. Only one thing is revealed per dream. The dream does not fade upon awakening; the dreamer remembers all the details of the dream.
The Game Master determines the nature of the clue. If there is nothing unknown or if the object is magically warded or perhaps does not exist, you suffer a terrible vivid nightmare.
Alchemical Formula: Water (any), Dream, Prophesy

ELIXIR OF ELDRITCH INTENSITY

Potion, very rare
This elixir improves the connection of a spellcaster with the elemental power source of spells. Any spell you cast does maximum damage. In addition, your spell save DC and spell attack modifier increase by +1 for the duration of the potion and you have advantage on Concentration checks to maintain spells. After this elixir expires, there is a 20-minute period during which spellcasting is impossible. There is a small chance that overuse of this elixir can burn out the ability to channel magical energy permanently.
Alchemical Formula: Azoth (any) (x2 from 2 different sources), Water (any), Mind

ELIXIR OF EMOTIONS

Potion, very rare
When this elixir is consumed, you broadcast a strong mental resonance. Each creature you can see with an Intelligence of 4 or greater within a 20-foot radius of you must make a DC 16 Wisdom saving throw. On a failure, you may use an action each round to modify a creature's emotions one step along one of two axes. Each time after the first that you modify the level of emotion of a selected creature, it may repeat the saving throw, ending the effects on a success. Note that each round you may choose which of the affected creatures to affect and along which axis, but all creatures affected in a single round are affected in the same way.
The two axes are described below. Each stage includes the effects of the stages below it.

Fear/Courage: The first stage in the fear direction causes a creature to be frightened. The second causes the creature to run away from you with all possible speed, using their dash action as well as their move. If they remain in your sight and you succeed in pushing them to a third level, the creature becomes incapacitated. A frightened creature can repeat the saving throw if it takes damage. The first stage in the courage direction gives a creature

advantage on saving throws to resist effects that cause fear. The second stage makes a creature reckless; it makes all attacks with advantage and other creatures have advantage to hit it. The third stage puts the creature into a frenzy. A frenzied creature attacks the nearest creature, be it friend or foe, until the frenzy ends.

Hate/Friendship: In the first stage of induced hatred, a creature will not willingly leave a battle that you are part of while you are alive. The second stage of causing a creature to hate you means that it must succeed on a DC 14 Wisdom saving throw in order to attack a creature other than you. A frenzied creature (see above) has advantage on this check. In the third stage, the target is completely focused on you. It may not take opportunity attacks against anybody who is not you and has disadvantage to Perception checks to notice any other creature. The first stage of friendship causes a target to act as if influenced by the spell *charm person*. The second stage means it is susceptible to your instructions as if it were under a *suggestion* spell. The third stage affects the target as if it were under a *dominate person* spell.
Alchemical Formula: Mercury (any) (x2), Water (any), Emotion (x2)

ELIXIR OF FALSE DIVINITY

Potion, uncommon
Your hair sheds golden light in a five-foot glowing ring. The effect lasts for 1d8 + 1 days.
Alchemical Formula: Water (any), Light

ELIXIR OF FORMS

Potion, very rare
You become a being made from a different material for the duration of the elixir. Several different types of elixirs exist, with each providing different effects and requiring different materials. During the duration of this potion, you remain solid, can speak, and your equipment transforms with you. Some examples are provided below:

Fire: You turn into solid flame. Your touch causes 2d6 fire damage and sets anything inflammable aflame. You are immune to nonmagical fire damage and resistant to magical fire damage. You can walk on the surface of lava and magma.
Alchemical Formula: Fire (any) (x3), Water (any), Transmutation

Lightning: You turn into living lightning. You may use an action to cause 2d8 electric damage to any target wearing metal armor within 30 feet. You may move 40 feet as a bonus action. You are immune to lightning damage. If you start your turn in water or enter water on your turn, you take 4d10 necrotic damage.
Alchemical Formula: Fire (any), Water (any), Electricity (x2), Transmutation

Stone: You turn into mobile stone. Your hand-to-hand attacks cause 1d6 bludgeoning damage. If your base damage is already higher, increase the die size by one category. You do not need to breathe for the duration of the potion. You are resistant to bludgeoning, slashing, and piercing damage and immune to poison damage. Your weight triples, giving you advantage on saving throws to avoid being moved.
Alchemical Formula: Earth (any) (x3), Fire (any), Water (any), Transmutation

Undead: Your body becomes undead for the duration of the elixir. You gain darkvision out to 120 feet and are immune to all mind-affecting spells, necrotic damage, disease, exhaustion, paralysis, poison, sleep, and being stunned. You do not need to breathe. However, you are unable to be affected by healing magic during the duration of the elixir.
Alchemical Formula: Azoth (any) (x2), Fire (any), Water (any), Transmutation
Other types of *elixirs of forms* are said to exist. You may discuss with the Game Master what other types might be available.

ELIXIR OF FUR GROWTH

Potion, rare
You grow thick fur over your body that lasts for 9 + 1d4 hours. The fur protects you from cold weather, and you have resistance to cold damage. If you are not wearing armor, your armor class increases by +2.
Alchemical Formula: Water (any), Body, Transmutation

ELIXIR OF GOOD FORTUNE

Potion, very rare
This elixir blesses you with astounding luck. For one minute, every time you roll any dice, you roll twice as many as normal and pick the result you want.
Alchemical Formula: Water (any), Body, Luck

ELIXIR OF GROWTH

Potion, rare
This elixir causes you to increase in size when quaffed. Your garments and other worn and held gear likewise increase in size for the duration of the potion. There are three drafts in the potion. For each one consumed, your size increases one size category. These drafts may be taken separately or together in any quantity.
Alchemical Formula: Water (any), Body, Transmutation

ELIXIR OF HEROIC AID

Potion, rare
This elixir allows you to take heroic action in combat for 1d6 + 2 rounds. For the duration, you receive 5d8 + 10 temporary hit points. You are immune to fear effects and get a +4 bonus to Wisdom saving throws.
Alchemical Formula: Water (any), Mind, Prowess

ELIXIR OF HEROIC FIGHTING

Potion, uncommon
You gain a +2 bonus on attack and damage rolls for one minute. You gain temporary hit points equal to twice your proficiency bonus.
Alchemical Formula: Water (any), Strength

ELIXIR OF HEROIC FIGHTING, SUPER

Potion, very rare
You gain a +3 bonus on attack and damage rolls for one minute. If you bring an opponent to 0 hit points, you may immediately make an additional attack as a bonus action. Opponents have disadvantage on attacks against you. Each round you may choose whether to act on Initiative 20 or on the initiative you rolled. You have advantage on Dexterity (Acrobatics) or Strength (Athletics) checks to escape being grappled or restrained and on Dexterity or Strength saving throws to avoid being grappled or restrained. You gain temporary hit points equal to four times your proficiency bonus.
Alchemical Formula: Water (any), Agility, Body, Prowess, Strength

ELIXIR OF HEROIC LARCENY

Potion, very rare
You gain a +2 bonus on attack and damage rolls for one minute.
This elixir increases your thieving power. You gain a sneak attack that does damage equal to 1d6 times your proficiency bonus. If you already have a sneak attack, its damage increases by this amount. In addition, you may include your proficiency bonus to any Dexterity-based skill check if you are not proficient or double your proficiency bonus if you are. It does not affect your roll if you have expertise.
Alchemical Formula: Water (any), Agility, Body, Prowess, Speed

ELIXIR OF HEROIC SPELLCASTING

Potion, very rare
Any spell slot you expend to cast a spell acts as if it were two levels higher. In addition, your spell save DC and spell attack bonus increase by +2.
Alchemical Formula: Azoth (any), Water (any), Mind, Prowess

ELIXIR OF IMMUNITY, COLD

Potion, rare
You are immune to cold damage and the effects of cold. However, for the duration of the elixir, your skin turns a frosty blue and you are vulnerable to fire damage. This potion lasts for 5d4 rounds.
Alchemical Formula: Fire (any), Water (any), Cold, Protection

ELIXIR OF IMMUNITY, CONTROL

Potion, rare
You are immune to any enchantments, compulsions, or mind-affecting spells. However, for the duration of the potion, your skin turns translucent and you become sluggish. You have a −4 penalty to your armor class as your skin becomes delicate and easy to damage. This potion lasts for 5d4 rounds.
Alchemical Formula: Azoth (any), Water (any), Mind, Protection

ELIXIR OF IMMUNITY, FIRE

Potion, rare
You are immune to fire damage and the effects of fire. However, for the duration of the elixir, your skin turns bright red and you are vulnerable to cold damage. The elixir lasts for 5d4 rounds.
Alchemical Formula: Fire (any) (x2), Water (any), Protection

ELIXIR OF IMMUNITY, METAL

Potion, very rare
This elixir grants you complete immunity to metal. Metal weapons pass harmlessly through your body, and metal armor falls off. You can even walk through pure metal doors and walls. However, for the duration of the potion, your skin turns green and pulpy and you are physically weakened. All damage taken during the duration of this elixir is increased by 2 points per die. This elixir lasts for 5d4 rounds.
Alchemical Formula: Diamond, Earth (any) (x2), Water (any), Body, Protection

ELIXIR OF IMMUNITY, PETRIFICATION

Potion, rare
This elixir grants you complete immunity to petrification from magical effects such as a basilisk's gaze or a gorgon's breath. However, for the duration of the potion, your skin turns metallic and shiny and you become spiritually weakened. You have a −2 penalty to all other saving throws. The potion lasts for 5d4 rounds.
Alchemical Formula: Diamond, Water (any), Body, Protection

ELIXIR OF IMMUNITY, POISON

Potion, rare
You are immune to poison damage and the poisoned condition. However, for the duration of the elixir, your skin turns bright red and you become physically drained. You gain one level of exhaustion. The exhaustion vanishes at the end of the duration. This potion lasts for 5d4 rounds.
Alchemical Formula: Diamond, Water (any), Protection, Toxin

ELIXIR OF INSANITY SHIELD

Potion, rare
This elixir protects your mind from psychic damage and magical and mental attacks by activating a wild insanity on the surface of your brain. You are immune to mind-affecting spells such as *charm person*, *command*, *dominate*, and *phantasmal killer*, etc., and have resistance to psychic damage. When the elixir expires, there is a 1-in-6 chance that you are confused for one minute as the spell.
If you attempt to cast a spell while shielded, you are struck dumb, as if under the effects of a *feeblemind* spell, for one hour.
Alchemical Formula: Water (any), Control, Protection

ELIXIR OF KNITTED BONES

Potion, uncommon
This elixir heals fractures and broken bones. It also heals damage to chitin, teeth, exoskeletons, shells, and bony carapaces. The healing is not instant, but the bones heal correctly. Most fractures heal in a day, but a more serious injury like a broken back could take up to a week to heal.
Alchemical Formula: Water (any), Healing

ELIXIR OF LANGUAGE

Potion, very rare
This elixir, once imbibed, allows you to learn a single language very quickly. You must be exposed to the language for the duration of the elixir. At the end of the duration, you permanently learn the language.
Alchemical Formula: Moonstone, Azoth (any), Fire (any), Water (any), Mind (x2)

ELIXIR OF LIQUIDITY

Potion, rare
When this elixir is consumed, you and all of your equipment splash to the ground as an eight-gallon puddle of liquid. You have a movement speed of 30 feet, and you can traverse small spaces, hide in bodies of water, and travel unnoticed. While in this form, you are resistant to all damage except that you are vulnerable to cold damage.
Alchemical Formula: Water (any), Transmutation

ELIXIR OF LOCATION

Potion, rare
This elixir amplifies your natural sense of direction and allows you to retrace your steps over any distance. This also renders you immune to *maze* spells and other enchantments that attempt to bewilder your sense of direction, but if engaged in this manner, the potion is neutralized. You can also sense true north and depth underground with an accuracy of five feet. The potion lasts for 12 + 1d12 hours.
Alchemical Formula: Water (any), Memory, Mind

ELIXIR OF LOCKPICKING

Potion, rare
When consumed, this elixir greatly increases your mechanical aptitude, granting you preternatural senses and insight. Add 2d10 to any Dexterity check using thieves' tools. If you are not already proficient with thieves' tools, you are considered proficient with them for the duration of the elixir. Note that thieves' tools are still required to pick locks.
Alchemical Formula: Water (any), Agility, Perception

ELIXIR OF LONGEVITY

Potion, very rare
This elixir reduces your age by 1d12 years, restoring youth and vigor. The entire elixir must be consumed to achieve the desired results. It is also useful as a counter to monster-based aging attacks. Each time you drink this elixir after the first, there is a 1% cumulative chance that the effect reverses and all aging removed from previous elixirs is restored over the next 2d4 rounds.
Alchemical Formula: Earth (any), Mercury (any), Water (any), Body, Healing

ELIXIR OF LUCKY FATE

Potion, rare
This elixir makes you especially lucky. Anytime during the next hour, you may choose the result of any one roll that you make, rather than rolling a random result. This effect lasts for one hour or until the luck is used.
Alchemical Formula: Water (any), Luck

ELIXIR OF MAGNETISM

Potion, rare
Once consumed, this elixir causes you to become magnetic. You exude a strong magnetic field out to 30 feet in every direction. Ferrous objects weighing less than 30 pounds are drawn to you. Objects make a ranged weapon attack against you at +6 to hit, doing 1d6 bludgeoning, piercing, or slashing damage as appropriate. You can walk across, hang from, and climb metal surfaces as easily as walking. This elixir lasts for 6d4 rounds.
Alchemical Formula: Earth (any), Water (any), Body, Transmutation

ELIXIR OF MANNERS

Potion, very rare
A totalitarian society developed this powerful elixir to cure inappropriate behavior. After drinking this, you must be polite, respectful, and caring for an entire year. You cannot say negative things or initiate a fight. Unwilling and aware targets that resist may attempt a DC 16 Wisdom saving throw when the potion is administered to resist its effects.
Alchemical Formula: Mercury (any), Water (any), Control, Mind

ELIXIR OF MEMORY

Potion, rare
This elixir allows the alchemist to take a single memory and infuse it into the liquid. They do not lose the memory. When you consume the potion, you gain access to the memory as if it were yours. You know it is someone else's memory, but when recalling the memory, you see yourself in the place of the alchemist.
Alchemical Formula: Water (any), Memory

ELIXIR OF MENTAL COMPOSURE

Potion, uncommon
This elixir allows you to maintain an emotional stability of mind. You are not affected by pain, phobias, or minor distractions. You are immune to effects such as itching, dizziness, and confusion. You receive a +4 bonus to saving throws against mind-affecting spells such as *fear* and *hideous laughter*.
Alchemical Formula: Water (any), Emotion

ELIXIR OF MIND DAMP

Potion, rare
This elixir renders you immune to psychic or magical detection and mental attacks for one week. The includes effects such as *detect thoughts*, *clairvoyance*, *divination*, or *crystal balls*, as well as spells and effects that directly affect your mind such as *confusion* and *feeblemind*. This also prevents you from casting spells for the duration.
Alchemical Formula: Water (any), Mind, Stealth

ELIXIR OF MIRRORED EYES

Potion, rare
This elixir changes your eyes into silver orbs lacking pupils. This does not affect your ability to see. However, light reflects off your eyes, preventing you from being subject to gaze attacks. Targets performing gaze attacks against you have a 20% chance of being affected by their own gaze attack. You also have a disadvantage on Dexterity (Stealth) checks made to hide unless you close your eyes.
Alchemical Formula: Silver, Water (any), Transmutation

ELIXIR OF NATURAL RENEWAL

Potion, very rare
This potion has a duration of one week. During that time, your healing becomes more rapid. For the purposes of healing, treat a short rest as a long rest and a long rest as three long rests. If instead of consuming the potion it is applied to a being that died within the last week, then life is restored. After 24 hours, the risen creature must make a DC 15 Constitution saving throw in order to stay alive. Furthermore, if used as a salve, this potion can be used over the period of two weeks to regenerate a lost member of the body. Any one use precludes the others.
Alchemical Formula: Water (any), Healing, Life

ELIXIR OF NUTRITION

Potion, uncommon
This potion feeds you, protecting you from hunger for one week. This potion also protects against items and effects that cause ravenous hunger, allowing you an additional saving throw versus the effect each time a save is required.
Alchemical Formula: Water (any), Body

ELIXIR OF PERCEPTION

Potion, very rare
This elixir affects you in several ways. It provides a +4 bonus on Dexterity checks to disable traps, a +8 bonus on Wisdom (Perception) checks, you cannot be surprised, and you have an automatic 25% chance to be able to see invisible creatures or illusions that is checked when the illusion or creature is first encountered.
Alchemical Formula: Water (any), Mind, Perception

ELIXIR OF POISON BREATH

Potion, rare
This elixir allows you to spit a terrible poison at a nearby target. Once imbibed, you can hold the poison in your mouth for one minute before it affects you.
As an action, you can spit the venom in a 30-foot line that is five feet wide. Each creature in the line must make a DC 16 Constitution saving throw. On a failed save, the target takes 16 (3d8 + 3) poison damage. A successful save reduces the damage by half. Either way, the target repeats the saving throw at the beginning of its turn on the following two rounds with the same effects each time.
Alchemical Formula: Water (any), Toxin

ELIXIR OF POISON FLESH

Potion, very rare
This powerful elixir turns your flesh to poison. When consumed, you make a DC 14 Constitution saving throw. Failure means you feel ill for the duration of the elixir and gain the poisoned condition.
If you are bitten or attacked and swallowed, the attacker is affected by the poison that flows within your flesh. They must make a DC 10 + one-half your level + your Constitution modifier Constitution saving throw with a DC of 10 + your proficiency modifier + your Constitution modifier against poison. If they fail, they become nauseated for one minute, during which they are unable to attack or cast spells while retching, after which they die. If they succeed at the save, they are nauseated for 1d6 + 1 rounds. A nauseated creature has disadvantage on attack rolls, ability checks, and Constitution saving throws.
Alchemical Formula: Water (any), Body, Toxin

ELIXIR OF POISON TOUCH

Potion, very rare
If mixed with a poison and imbibed, this elixir allows you to poison creatures by touch.
Once the potion and poison are ingested, make a saving throw versus the poison. On a success, you are not affected by the poison at all. On a failure, the poison affects you normally.
In either case, your touch gains the ability to poison targets with the poison you ingested. Anyone touched or struck by your bare hands is dosed with the poison. As part of a move action, you may spread one usage of the poison your skin exudes on a melee weapon.
Alchemical Formula: Water (any), Body, Toxin (2 from different sources)

ELIXIR OF PROTECTION FROM IMMISCIBILITY

Potion, very rare
This elixir protects you from potion immiscibility if those rules are in play. For one minute, you can drink multiple potions without penalty or risk of disaster.
Alchemical Formula: Azoth (any), Water (any), Stasis

ELIXIR OF PROTECTION FROM LYCANTHROPES

Potion, rare
This elixir protects you from the touch of lycanthropes for the duration. Any lycanthrope wishing to attack you with natural attacks (claws, etc.) must succeed at a DC 16 Wisdom saving throw or attack a different creature. Once they save, the lycanthrope can attack freely, but they have disadvantage on these attacks. You are immune to lycanthropy and any saves versus supernatural, spell-like effects, or spells cast by a lycanthrope are made with advantage.
Alchemical Formula: Water (any), Body, Protection

ELIXIR OF PROTECTION FROM MAGIC MISSILE

Potion, uncommon
While this elixir is in effect, you take no damage from *magic missiles*.
Alchemical Formula: Azoth (any), Water (any)

ELIXIR OF PROTECTION FROM MAGIC WEAPONS

Potion, very rare
This elixir protects you from strikes made by magical weapons for the duration. Any attempt to hit you with a magical weapon is made with disadvantage and magic weapons are denied their magical bonuses and effects when rolling to hit and damage.
Alchemical Formula: Diamond, Azoth (any), Mercury (any), Water (any), Body, Protection

ELIXIR OF PROTECTION FROM NOXIOUS GAS

Potion, rare
This potion protects you from noxious and poisonous gases and odors. This also provides protection from strong gaseous attacks. A magical cloud cast at 4th level or lower has no effect on you, and you receive advantage to resist the effects of any such cloud caused by a spell cast at 5th level or higher.
Alchemical Formula: Air (any), Water (any), Protection, Toxin

ELIXIR OF PROTECTION FROM SPIRITS

Potion, rare
This elixir protects you from the touch of spirits for the duration. Any spirit wishing to attack you with natural attacks (touch, etc.) must succeed at a DC 16 Wisdom saving throw. Once they successfully save, the spirits may attack freely, although they have disadvantage on any attacks made against you. You are immune to possession or other mental attacks from spirits and you have advantage on saving throws against any attacks, supernatural abilities, spell-like effects, or spells. Spirits include any incorporeal fey or undead.
Alchemical Formula: Azoth (any), Air (any), Water (any), Protection

ELIXIR OF PROTECTION FROM SPRITES

Potion, very rare
This elixir protects you from sprites and other fey creatures for the duration. You are protected from the touch of fey. Any fey wishing to strike you with natural attacks (claws, etc.) must succeed at a DC 16 Wisdom saving throw. If they make this save, they may attack you freely but have disadvantage on all such attacks. You are immune to fey illusions and glamours (anything that would affect your mind), and a pixie remains visible to you while invisible. Any saving throws made versus a creature of the fey type are made with advantage.
Alchemical Formula: Azoth (any), Air (any), Mercury (any), Water (any), Plant, Protection

ELIXIR OF PROTECTION FROM VAMPIRES

Potion, very rare
This elixir protects you from the touch of vampires for the duration. Any vampire wishing to attack the imbiber with natural attacks (slam, etc.) must succeed at a DC 18 Wisdom saving throw. Once it saves, the vampire may attack you freely but has disadvantage on any such attacks. You are immune to the vampire's energy drain and not susceptible to the vampire's mental influence. You have advantage on saving throws against any attacks, spells, supernatural abilities, or spell-like effects from a vampire.
Alchemical Formula: Azoth (any), Water (any), Protection, Prowess

ELIXIR OF PSYCHIC TRAP

Potion, uncommon
This elixir sets a trap your mind. Any mental contact or mind-affecting spell such as *telepathy* causes 4d8 + 4 psychic damage to the initiator of the contact, attack, or spell and cancels the attack. After the trap is sprung or after 24 hours, whichever comes first, the potion is no longer effective. Note that this only effects spells where you are targeted at the time of casting. Entering a pre-existing spell effect discharges the trap harmlessly and negates the effect.
Alchemical Formula: Water (any), Mind

ELIXIR OF RAINBOW HUES

Potion, uncommon
This thick and syrupy elixir is always found in a metal container. After drinking this elixir, you can turn yourself into any hue or combination of hues desired at will. Any color or combination is possible as long as you can hold the thought in your mind until the color is affected. The coloration is real, not an illusion. One potion contains seven draughts that can be used independently of each other. A draught of the elixir lasts 12 + 1d12 hours.
Alchemical Formula: Water (any), Body, Transmutation

ELIXIR OF RAPID HEALING

Potion, common
While this elixir is active, you regain up to three hit points at the beginning of your turn if you have more than 0 hit points. You do not regrow lost limbs or gain other regenerative powers.
Alchemical Formula: Water (any), Healing

ELIXIR OF RECALL

Potion, uncommon
This elixir provides you with an eidetic memory for 2d6 hours. Everything you see and hear can be recalled with perfect clarity.
Alchemical Formula: Water (any), Mind

ELIXIR OF RECUPERATION

Potion, rare
This elixir completely removes all effects of exhaustion and fatigue, and you are refreshed as if you had completed a long rest except that you do not regain expended spell slots.
Alchemical Formula: Water (any), Body (x2)

ELIXIR OF REFLECTIVE FORM

Potion, uncommon
When consumed, this elixir makes your clothing, skin, and armor highly reflective. This is so distracting that you or anyone standing adjacent to you are granted a +2 bonus to armor class. You are unable to hide or use stealth. You are not affected by this distraction, so you may attack adjacent targets without penalty.
Alchemical Formula: Water (any), Illusion

ELIXIR OF REVENGE

Potion, uncommon
The first time your skin is broken within 24 hours, your blood turns a bright viridian and surges forth in a hemisphere, sizzling like oil in a pan out to a radius of 10 feet. All those within the area must make a DC 18 Dexterity saving throw, taking 5d4 + 5 acid damage on a failure or half as much on a success.
Alchemical Formula: Iron, Water (any), Acid

ELIXIR OF REVIVIFICATION

Potion, very rare
This elixir initially appears as a crystal-clear liquid that has no outstanding qualities. If consumed, it tastes like water. If one drop of a person's blood is added, the liquid turns a brilliant red. Afterward, a creature can use an action to anoint that person's body with the liquid and restore it to life. As long as the body exists and can be found, the elixir restores life to the body. Any permanent damage to the body (lost limbs, etc.) is not healed, but a long-desiccated corpse can be restored to life.
Alchemical Formula: Water (any), Healing, Life (x2)

ELIXIR OF SAFE CONSUMPTION

Potion, uncommon
This elixir renders you immune to all harm and danger from nonmagical food and drink. This protects you from ingested poison and allows you to drink tainted water and eat rotten food or poorly cooked meals without gagging or showing signs of distress.
It does not change the taste of the food.
Alchemical Formula: Water (any), Protection

ELIXIR OF SCENT CONTROL

Potion, rare
This potion allows you to control the aroma your body exudes. You may choose to smell of anything you wish for the duration of the potion, although once you choose the scent, you cannot change it. This potion is fairly cheap to produce, but highly prized by nobility.
Alchemical Formula: Water (any)

ELIXIR OF SCULPTURE

Potion, very rare
This elixir is an alchemical wonder that, when consumed, transforms you
into a living statue made from clay. This is a temporary condition that lasts
only 30 minutes. During this time, anyone may alter or sculpt the living clay
statue, altering its appearance or items.
When the elixir ends, any changes left remain and are permanent. Only
another draught of this elixir or a *wish* spell may alter the results. Note that
you cannot be killed or destroyed while clay and return to some semblance
of life no matter the final outcome or form. If you are smashed down into a
pulp, you still live at least for a short while after changing form. True masters
of sculpture can even alter raw ability and not just appearance.
Alchemical Formula: Earth (any), Mercury (any), Water (any), Body,
Transmutation

ELIXIR OF SHRIEKING

Potion, uncommon
Once consumed, this elixir has two separate effects that may be used. The
effects can be used a total of three times before the duration expires. Using
an effect takes an action.
First, you may shout in a 30-foot cone starting with you. All creatures in
the area must make a DC 16 Constitution saving throw, taking 3d6 thunder
damage and being deafened for one minute on a failure or taking half this
damage and not being deafened on a success.
The other ability is a piercing yell. All creatures within 20 feet of you must
make a DC 16 Wisdom saving throw. On a failed save, targets are stunned
until the start of your next turn.
Alchemical Formula: Mercury (any), Water (any), Transmutation

ELIXIR OF SHRUBBERY

Potion, uncommon
This transformative elixir allows you to change into a green leafy bush as an
action and back at will. The type and shape of bush can vary, from small to
large according to your will. While a shrub, you are resistant to all damage
types except fire and slashing damage. The potion grants this ability for 2d6
+ 2 days.
There is a small side effect. Every time you change into a shrubbery, there is
a 1% chance that you become rooted to the spot, unable to change form until
the elixir expires. Otherwise, you have access to all your senses in plant form
and can move at a speed of 10 feet while polymorphed.
Alchemical Formula: Water (any), Plant

ELIXIR OF SKELETAL VISAGE

Potion, common
Originally designed for medical use, this potion turns your skin, muscles,
organs, and other viscera transparent, leaving only the bones visible. It gives
you the visage of a skeleton. Your skin and flesh remain, turned transparent
by the potion. A particularly astute character may notice that this doesn't
appear to be an actual undead skeleton by noting that the feet do not touch
the floor and through other subtle clues by succeeding at a DC 20 Wisdom
(Perception) check.
If killed while under the effect of this elixir, the effect does not end, but
becomes permanent.
Alchemical Formula: Water (any), Transmutation

ELIXIR OF SKILL

Potion, rare
For the duration of the potion, you are proficient in any one skill or tool of
your choice. If you are already proficient, you have expertise. This works
only for one skill per potion. Each potion lasts for 2d4 + 1 days.
Alchemical Formula: Water (any), Prowess

ELIXIR OF SLEEP

Potion, rare
After drinking this tart, apple-flavored liquid, you sink into a deep, restful
sleep for 2d6 x 10 minutes. You experience the effects of a long rest
combined with a feeling of well-being and peace. This means hit points are
recovered as with a full night of rest and spellcasters can prepare spells.
Unwilling victims are allowed a DC 14 Wisdom saving throw to avoid the
effect. Anyone under the effects of this potion awakens instantly if attacked.
If awakened before the period of rest naturally ends, all benefit is lost.
Alchemical Formula: Water (any), Mind, Stasis

ELIXIR OF SLEEP BREATH

Potion, rare
This allows you to put people to sleep with your breath. For one hour after
consuming the potion, you have the ability to breathe a cloud of sleep gas
that covers a 20-foot square up to 10 feet high up to three separate times.
Each use of the cloud requires an action. As per the spell *sleep*, roll 5d8 to
determine how many hit points of creatures fall asleep.
If the breath is not used at least once before the duration expires, you must
succeed at a DC 16 Constitution saving throw or fall into a deep sleep for
2d6 + 2 hours.
Alchemical Formula: Air (any), Water (any), Stasis

ELIXIR OF SOMATIC REMEDY

Potion, very rare
This elixir renders you immune to slumber. Natural or magical effects
causing sleep fail. This effect lasts for a month. This has no effect on the
body's normal, natural need for sleep.
Alchemical Formula: Azoth (any), Water (any), Mind, Stasis

ELIXIR OF SPINES

Potion, rare
When imbibed, this elixir causes your skin to toughen and turn a dark color
as spikes extend outward from your body in all directions. If you are not
wearing armor, your armor class increases by +1. A creature that hits you
with a melee attack from within five feet must succeed on a DC 16 Dexterity
saving throw or take 2d4 piercing damage from being impaled on spines. At
the start of your turn, any creature that has you grappled or swallowed takes
2d4 + 2 piercing damage. The spikes do not grow if you are wearing heavy
armor, and you cannot don heavy armor while the spikes are present.
Alchemical Formula: Water (any), Body, Transmutation

ELIXIR OF STRENGTH, OGRE

Potion, common
You gain the strength of a mighty ogre. For the duration of the elixir, your
strength is 19 unless it is already higher.
Alchemical Formula: Water (any), Strength

ELIXIR OF SUSPENDED ANIMATION

Potion, very rare
You enter a deep and permanent sleep. It can be broken only by a *wish* or by
the occurrence of a single condition uttered by you just before you imbibe the
elixir. While sleeping, you are in stasis. You do not age, your life functions
cease, and you cannot be harmed.
Alchemical Formula: Diamond, Moonstone, Rare Earth, Azoth (any), Water
(any), Mind, Control, Stasis

ELIXIR OF SWIMMING FISH

Potion, uncommon
This potion grants you a swim speed of 90 feet and a +10 bonus on Strength (Athletics) checks made to swim. It does not provide you with the ability to breathe water.
Alchemical Formula: Water (any), Agility, Strength

ELIXIR OF TACTILE ENHANCEMENT

Potion, uncommon
When this elixir is imbibed, you gain a +10 bonus to Investigation and Perception checks made using your sense of touch. You also take an additional point of damage per die done due to pain.
Alchemical Formula: Water (any), Perception

ELIXIR OF THE ACIDIC PALM

Potion, rare
This elixir causes your hands to secrete a powerful acid. Your barehanded attacks do an additional 1d8 acid damage, and you do 2d8 acid damage to an item you hold. The effect lasts for one minute.
Alchemical Formula: Rare Earth, Water (any), Acid (x2)

ELIXIR OF THE GREEN

Potion, very rare
The bizarre and powerful elixir permanently turns you into a plant-like being that forgoes eating. You acquire your energy from the sun as plants do. After imbibing the potion, you suffer severe convulsions for 1d10 rounds and then fall unconscious for 1d4 days. You must make a DC 5 Constitution saving throw to survive this process. If you fail, you die.
If you survive, your skin becomes a deep, vibrant green and you no longer require food to live. You can process the energy of the sun directly. If denied water, you become dehydrated as normal. If you do not receive at least four hours of sunlight per day, you begin to starve. This transformation is one way, permanent, and breeds true.
Alchemical Formula: Azoth (any), Water (any), Plant, Transmutation

ELIXIR OF THE IRON FIST

Potion, uncommon
This elixir turns your hands and arms into solid iron, and your strength increases to compensate. The iron hands hit as powerful weapons. You gain a magical unarmed melee attack that does 1d10 bludgeoning damage and your Strength increases by 4 to a maximum of 20. You are considered proficient with the attack.
Alchemical Formula: Earth (any), Water (any), Body

ELIXIR OF THE MOLE

Potion, rare
This elixir allows you to dig through earth at your normal movement rate. Your hands and arms change, your skin toughens, and your nails lengthen and become black and gnarled.
You can tunnel through dirt and earth at your normal movement rate or through solid stone at half your movement rate. While traveling underground, it is 80% likely that the tunnel collapses behind you. It is possible for others to travel with you as long as everyone stays within 10 feet of you.
As long as you keep moving, the air stays fresh. If you stop for any reason, the air remains fresh for only one minute. This length of time is halved for every additional person.
The strength, claws, and toughness allow you to make two claw attacks doing 1d4 slashing damage each.
Alchemical Formula: Earth (any), Water (any), Body, Transmutation

ELIXIR OF THE RAINBOW BRIDGE

Potion, rare
Once quaffed, this elixir does nothing unless you concentrate on a bridge. Sometime within the next minute, a temporary bridge forms at a location of your choosing. If you cannot see the location, there is a chance the bridge does not connect well to the location and collapses. See the table below and make an Intelligence check using the DC shown to determine if you are successful in placing the bridge. The bridge must have one support at each end or it dissipates. The bridge can be up to 20 feet wide and up to 200 feet long. The bridge is made of colored force in a rainbow pattern. It lasts for 24 hours unless it is weighted down with more than 50,000 pounds or is subject to *dispel magic*, in which case it dissipates instantly. If you don't create the bridge within 24 hours of drinking the potion, the elixir loses its efficacy.

TABLE 4–11: RAINBOW BRIDGE PLACEMENT DC

Familiarity	DC
Verbal description	25
Visited briefly/seen in dream	20
Technical drawing	15
Visited frequently or spent significant time	10
Have successfully created bridge there before	5

Alchemical Formula: Azoth (any), Water (any), Mind

ELIXIR OF THE REMORHAZ

Potion, rare
Once imbibed, this elixir raises the heat of your skin. A creature that makes a melee attack against you from within five feet takes 2d4 fire damage. You also gain resistance to fire damage.
Alchemical Formula: Fire (any), Water (any), Body, Transmutation

ELIXIR OF THE SCORPION

Potion, rare
Once quaffed, you grow a large scorpion tail from your lower back. This transformation does not occur if you are wearing heavy armor.
The tail has a reach of five feet. It does 1d4 damage and on a successful strike, the target must make a DC 16 Constitution saving throw versus poison. On a failed save, the target takes an amount of damage equal to Xd6, where X is equal to your proficiency modifier. You may attack with the tail as a bonus action using either Strength or Dexterity, and you are considered proficient in the attack.
The tail takes one full round to grow. You may use it at the start of the next turn after you imbibe the elixir.
Alchemical Formula: Water (any), Body, Toxin, Transmutation

ELIXIR OF THE UMBRA

Potion, very rare
This fantastic elixir turns your whole person, including any armor and items, into a shadow. You remain against the wall or floor where the elixir was imbibed until your path is crossed. Once this occurs, you may choose to become the shadow of the person that crossed you. You move with the person and can take no action or move until the elixir expires in 3d8 minutes. Once the elixir ends, you silently appear behind or next to the target you were following.
Alchemical Formula: Water (any), Body, Light, Transmutation

ELIXIR OF TINY FEET

Potion, very rare
This liquid appears to be made of thousands of tiny, tiny feet. Upon imbibing the liquid, you feel nauseous and are poisoned for one minute. At the end of the minute, you vomit up 3d10 diminutive inhuman servants that are about six inches tall. They understand any languages you speak. They follow your commands to the best of their ability for one hour. They have access to simple tools as needed. Each is able to perform the labor of one-half person. They may be commanded to fight, in which case they use the stats of a swarm of insects without a climb speed.
Alchemical Formula: Water (any), Body, Dream

ELIXIR OF TOAD SKIN

Potion, uncommon
This elixir covers you in leaking warts and boils filled with caustic fluid. If you successfully hit a creature with your bare hand, any living target takes an additional 1d4 acid damage and must succeed at a DC 14 Constitution saving throw or become nauseated. A nauseated creature has disadvantage on attack rolls, ability checks, and Constitution saving throws. A nauseated creature may repeat the saving throw at the end of each of its turns, ending the effect on a success.
Alchemical Formula: Water (any), Acid, Body

ELIXIR OF TORPIDITY

Potion, rare
You gain a potent ability to talk others to sleep. The potion has a short duration of 10 minutes, during which time you can speak in sonorous and sobering monotones about any topic at all and cause sleep in listeners. Speaking requires all of your attention, disallowing any other actions, bonus actions, or reactions. All those in earshot must make a Wisdom saving throw to take any action other than listen while you speak. The DC for the save is 20 if they speak the language the imbiber is speaking. If the target understands a language but not the one you are speaking, the DC is 18; if the creature does not understand any language, the DC is 16. A creature that succeeds on the saving throw is immune to the effects of this elixir for the duration. A creature that fails the saving throw must make a DC 16 Wisdom saving throw at the end of each of your subsequent turns. A creature that fails falls asleep for four hours. Anyone attacked while listening or sleeping instantly snaps out of the effect and is immune.
Alchemical Formula: Water (any), Control, Stasis

ELIXIR OF TREASURE FINDING

Potion, rare
This elixir grants you a magical location sense that allows you to locate the nearest mass of treasure within one mile. If you are within one mile of treasure worth at least 100 times your proficiency modifier in value (gp), you can sense the direction of the treasure. Once within 400 feet, you can detect the exact location of the treasure and gain a general sense of how to reach it. Note that this only detects valuable metals such as gold, copper, silver, platinum, gems, and jewelry, not magic items or equipment. Worthless metals and magic items not containing precious metals or gems are ignored. Only lead more than one inch thick or magical wards can block the effect — other intervening material is irrelevant. This potion lasts for 5d4 minutes. When this elixir is combined with any other elixir, it produces a lethal poison.
Alchemical Formula: Gold, Platinum, Water (any), Mind

ELIXIR OF UNDERGROUND AWARENESS

Potion, rare
This elixir grants a +10 bonus on Wisdom (Perception) checks to notice unusual stonework such as traps and hidden doors located in stone walls or floors. You receive a check to notice such features whenever you pass within 10 feet of them, regardless if you are actually looking. You also gain darkvision out to 120 feet, and you can determine slopes and depth underground on a successful DC 15 Wisdom (Perception) check.
Alchemical Formula: Water (any), Perception

ELIXIR OF UNGUIS

Potion, rare
This elixir causes you to grow terrifying and powerful talons in place of your nails. Your fingers lengthen and sharp, hard claws extend from your fingertips. For the duration of the potion, you may use an action to make two claw attacks using either your Strength or Dexterity modifier. You are considered proficient in this attack. On a hit, the claw attack does 1d6 slashing damage. Your Strength increases by 4 to a maximum of 20 for the duration of the potion.
Alchemical Formula: Water (any), Plant, Transmutation

ELIXIR OF VANITY

Potion, uncommon
This elixir enhances one of your physical qualities. This could be perfect skin, a full head of hair, an extra-large nose, or a luxurious beard. You imagine the change when consuming the elixir. The change lasts for 1d4 + 1 weeks.
Alchemical Formula: Water (any), Body

ELIXIR OF VENUS

Potion, very rare
This elixir works much like an *elixir of love*, except it produces undying devotion for the first creature seen after imbibing the elixir. This devotion is complete and stronger than a mere charm spell. It may be resisted with a DC 15 Wisdom saving throw, but if a part of the target is used in the formula, such as a piece of hair or nail clipping, the save is DC 20. A *remove curse* breaks the effect.
The devotion is total as the imbiber now lives life for the purpose of the creature to which he or she is devoted. They are aware of their former lives and state and don't care, thankful that they are now devoted to the person viewed. Individuals who give this elixir to the object of their affection often come to view the final results as a curse.
Alchemical Formula: Water (any), Control, Emotion, Purity

ELIXIR OF VISION OF THE EAGLE

Potion, uncommon
This elixir enhances and improves nonmagical sight. It allows you to see clearly and distinguish objects up to a mile away. You can observe details as if these objects were 10 times closer than they actually are. You can make ranged attacks out to a weapon's maximum range without disadvantage and have advantage on Wisdom (Perception) checks made to see things more than 100 feet away.
Alchemical Formula: Water (any), Perception

ELIXIR OF VITALITY

Potion, very rare
This elixir restores your health and vitality for a week. During this week, you are immune to exhaustion, lack of sleep, starvation, and dehydration. This elixir also protects completely versus poison and disease, and you recover one hit point every four hours.
Alchemical Formula: Sulfur (any), Water (any), Healing, Protection, Stasis

ELIXIR OF YOUTH

Potion, very rare
This potent and scarce elixir reverses aging. Drinking the entire elixir reduces your age by 1d4 + 1 years.
Alchemical Formula: Diamond, Azoth (any), Water (any), Body, Healing, Mind

MISCELLANEOUS ITEMS

Various other wondrous items fall outside the strictures above and have proven themselves useful for alchemy. These are listed below:

ALCHEMICAL JUG

Wondrous item, rare
This alchemical device is extremely useful for the working alchemist. You may use an action to pour out a given quantity of a single liquid. The volume of liquid depends on what liquid is being produced. The jug has the ability to produce only one liquid each day; however, the liquid selected can be poured from the jug up to seven times.

TABLE 4–12: ALCHEMICAL JUG PRODUCTION

Name	Volume
Saltwater	16 gallons
Fresh water	8 gallons
Beer/Ale	4 gallons
Vinegar	2 gallons
Wine	1 gallon
Ammonia	1 quart
Oil	1 pint
Aqua regia	2 gills (8 oz.)
Alcohol	1 gill (4 oz.)
Chlorine	8 drams (1 oz.)
Cyanide	4 drams (1/2 oz.)

Alchemical Formula: not applicable

ALCHEMICAL RETORT

Wondrous item, very rare (requires attunement)
When added to an alchemist's lab, this magical retort cuts the crafting time of any crafted or enchanted alchemical item by one-half. The final calculated time is divided by two, and that is the length of time it takes to craft the item.
Alchemical Formula: not applicable

AUTOMATED ALCHEMIST

Wondrous item, very rare
Three gems are on this vial. The vial produces a magical liquid (potion, philter, or elixir) once per day. The order the three buttons are pushed determines which potion is created. When you use an action to depress the three gems, the vial fills with a potion and deactivates for 24 hours. A potion produced by this item turns into nonmagical water after 24 hours. The potion produced by a given combination is randomly selected, but once a specific combination of gems produces a potion, it always produces that potion. When created, there is no way to control or select which potions the device can create. This vial produces 27 different kinds of magical liquids.
Alchemical Formula: not applicable

BANISHMENT GLOBE

Wondrous item, rare
When this globe is thrown at an extradimensional creature, it banishes them to their home dimension as the wizard spell *banishment* (spell save DC 16).
Alchemical Formula: not applicable

BEAKER OF PLENTIFUL POTIONS

Wondrous item, very rare
This wondrous magical beaker of alchemy creates random potions! Roll 1d4 + 1 random elixirs, potions, or salves. This is how many potions the beaker holds — cursed potions are certainly possible. The potions rolled are layered, in order, within the beaker. Potions are produced with varying frequency. The frequency of potion production is determined by the number of potions within the beaker. Four or five different potions produce two doses of each potion, once per week. Three potions produce three doses of each potion, twice per week. Two potions produce four doses of each potion three times per week.
The doses must be consumed or poured out in order (thus, if *potion of invisibility* and *elixir of fire breath* are rolled, four doses of *invisibility* must be consumed before getting access to *fire breath*). Beakers have a full complement of five potions when created and lose the ability to generate one random potion a month until they are generating only two different potions.
Alchemical Formula: not applicable

BEDROLL OF REST

Wondrous item, uncommon
This alchemically enchanted bedroll provides warm comfort. You are always at a comfortable temperature, never too warm or too cold. It also protects you from insects, rain, snow, and other minor disturbances. You wake alert and refreshed after six hours of rest if you wish, although this does not shorten the rest needed to cast spells. This does not protect against temperatures lower than –40° Fahrenheit or higher than 130° Fahrenheit.
Alchemical Formula: not applicable

BOTTLE OF HECKLING

Wondrous item, rare
This bottle contains a marbled crimson liquid. When uncapped as an action, a chorus of boos, hisses, and insults pours out. A creature other than you that can hear and is within 60 feet must make a DC 16 Wisdom saving throw. Those who fail receive a –2 penalty to attack and damage rolls for six minutes. Each time this item is used, less liquid is contained in the bottle. After three uses, the bottle is empty.
Alchemical Formula: not applicable

BOTTLE OF HOLDING

Wondrous item, uncommon
This useful bottle can hold and organize a vast amount of liquid. It can contain up to 30 units of fluid. A unit is a gallon of normal nonmagical liquid (oil, water, ink) or one dose of a magical or alchemical liquid. The bottle maintains separation between all it contains, and a simple verbal command is required to access the appropriate fluid. As an action, the desired liquid may then be poured out. The bottle always appears empty. If broken, all the contained liquids vanish. The bottle is made of crystal.
Alchemical Formula: not applicable

BOTTLE OF PLEASING ODORS

Wondrous item, uncommon
When uncorked, this bottle produces a pleasing smell and removes offensive smells from up to a 60-foot cube of air.
Alchemical Formula: not applicable

BOTTLE OF PRESERVATION

Wondrous item, uncommon
These bottles appear to be normal and indistinguishable from other bottles. When non-living substances are placed within the bottle, their contents are preserved. Things that are placed within the bottle do not spoil or rot.
Alchemical Formula: not applicable

Wondrous item, legendary
This appears to be a highly burnished bottle. The bottle is corked, and the cork and the bottle are covered with arcane warding runes.
You can open this bottle as an action to attempt to trap extraplanar creatures inside it. Each creature from another plane that is within 30 feet of you at the end of your turn must make a Wisdom saving throw. The saving throw DC depends on the number of extraplanar creatures in the area (see **Table 4–21** below). If the bottle is open at the beginning of your turn, a creature inside make attempt a DC 20 Wisdom saving throw to escape. You may close the bottle as a bonus action.

TABLE 4–13: NUMBER OF CREATURES AFFECTED BY BRAZEN BOTTLE

Number of creatures	DC
1	20
2	18
3+	14

Alchemical Formula: not applicable

BOTTLE. REINFORCED

Wondrous item, rare
This bottle is virtually indestructible. It has AC 30, 50 hit points, and is immune to nonmagical damage.
Alchemical Formula: not applicable

BOX. COOLING

Wondrous item, uncommon
This nondescript steel box can cool a medium-sized room to 50° Fahrenheit. It can also cool any object placed inside to a temperature of –40° Fahrenheit. Cooling takes one minute for every 10° Fahrenheit lowered. This box provides a +1 bonus to Alchemist's Supplies checks if installed in an alchemical lab. The interior temperature is adjustable.
Alchemical Formula: not applicable

BOX. HEATING

Wondrous item, uncommon
This nondescript steel box has the capacity to heat a mid-sized room to 100° Fahrenheit or to heat an object inside the box to a temperature up to 450° Fahrenheit. Heating takes one minute for every 10° Fahrenheit raised. This box provides a +1 bonus to Alchemist's Supplies checks if installed in an alchemical lab. The interior temperature is adjustable.
Alchemical Formula: not applicable

CALTROPS. WALKING

Wondrous item, uncommon
These work exactly like normal caltrops, except every round they move five feet toward the nearest living creature. As soon as they enter an area with a target, that target must save, as must anyone who enters that area this round. They act this way for one minute. After use, they may be collected and reused. They may be used only once per day. The caltrops are not intelligent and do not climb. If they must cross a pit to get to the nearest living creature, they fall in and bunch up at the closest side of the pit.
Alchemical Formula: not applicable

CARAFE OF STEEDS

Wondrous item, rare
This marvelous device contains a violently roiling liquid. When you use an action to pour it on the ground, it produces up to eight mounts. These mounts last for eight hours before they must return to the carafe. These mounts dissipate if they are more than 300 feet from the carafe. The mounts are colorless constructs, not real animals. Roll d20 on the following table to determine the form they take:

TABLE 4–14: CARAFE OF STEEDS RANDOM MOUNT TABLE

Roll	Mount
1–2	Riding Dog
3	Trained Axe Beak
4	Riding Ape
5	Giant Ant
6	Crocodile
7	Pony
8–12	Light Riding Horse
13–14	Heavy Riding Horse
15–16	Warhorse
17	Bear/
18	Rhinoceros Beetle
19	Mammoth
20	Griffon

The creatures are not aggressive and may not be commanded to attack. However, the creatures defend themselves if attacked. The energy in the carafe is unstable, and the type of mount must be checked every time they are poured out. When crafted, there is enough liquid for eight mounts. If a mount dies or gets too distant from the carafe, that liquid is permanently lost, and the number of mounts produced is reduced by one.
Alchemical Formula: not applicable

CASE OF FRESHNESS

Wondrous item, uncommon
This marvelous case is useful in alchemical labs and kitchens. Any herb, plant, fruit, or vegetable stored in this case overnight with one dram of sugar, salt, and 10 carats of pearl is restored to freshness. This reduces an alchemist's monthly upkeep costs by 10%.
Alchemical Formula: not applicable

CAULDRON OF POTIONS

Wondrous item, very rare
This marvelous cauldron produces a single dose of any magical or nonmagical liquid once per day. You use an action to concentrate on the liquid you desire, and the cauldron produces it. There is a 10% that any potion produced is cursed.
There is no way to tell ahead of time if the potion is cursed or not. Not enough of the material or potion is produced to allow an alchemist to learn how to produce a potion from the sample. The potion provided lasts until used or until the cauldron produces another potion.
Alchemical Formula: not applicable

CENSER OF INCENSE OF BURNING

Wondrous item, common
When incense is burnt in this portable censer, add 10 feet to the radius of the incense's effect. In order for this power to function, you must be holding the censer.
Alchemical Formula: not applicable

CLOAK. AEGIS

Wondrous item, very rare (requires attunement)
This rare cloak is designed to protect you while also being a useful weapon. When an attack misses you, you may use your reaction to attempt to entangle the attacker. Make a Dexterity check with the DC equal to the attacker's to-hit roll. If you succeed, the weapon is entangled in the cloak. It may be freed only with a successful DC 21 Strength check or if you choose to release it. While it is entangled, it may not be used to make attacks. If the attack is affixed to the creature that attacked, the creature is grappled.
You may use an action to remove and roll up the cloak, making it into a *+1 club*. In addition, if an attack hits you, you may use your reaction to attempt to parry the attack. Make a Dexterity check with the DC equal to the attacker's to-hit roll. If you succeed, the attack is parried and misses you. If the cloak parries a magical weapon six times, the cloak is destroyed.
Alchemical Formula: not applicable

CLOAK OF EYESTALKS

Wondrous item, very rare (requires attunement)
A series of plates with eyestalks sprout from various places on this cloak. These eyestalks grant you all-around vision. You cannot be flanked or surprised. You receive a –4 penalty to saving throws against any gaze attacks or attacks that cause blindness or otherwise impair eyesight. You receive a +2 bonus to saving throws against attacks that do not affect vision.
Once per minute, you can use an action to draw the cloak around you to activate the second power of the cloak, which is determined randomly from **Table 4–23**. A creature with ongoing effects may repeat the saving throw at the end of each of its turns, ending the effect on a success. A successful DC 18 Dexterity saving throw negates the effects. Note that the effect must be selected randomly.

TABLE 4–15: CLOAK OF EYESTALKS EFFECTS

1d8	Power	Targets
1	*Dominate Monster*	Each creature within 30 feet; DC 18 Wisdom saving throw
2	*Sleep*	Up to 5d8 hit points of creatures within 30 feet, per spell; no saving throw
3	Paralysis	Each creature within 30 feet; DC 18 Wisdom saving throw
4	*Disintegrate*	One randomly chosen creature within 60 feet; DC 18 Dexterity saving throw
5	*Slow*	Each creature within 30 feet; DC 18 Wisdom saving throw
6	*Fear*	Each creature within 30 feet; DC 18 Wisdom saving throw
7	*Inflict Wounds*	Each creature within 30 feet; DC 18 Dexterity saving throw
8	Death Ray	One randomly chosen creature within 60 feet takes 10d10 necrotic damage

Alchemical Formula: not applicable

CLOAK OF LIGHT

Wondrous item, uncommon
This cloak is a dark color on the outside, but the inner lining glows. When you use an action to say the command word, the cloak flares out, shedding light as a torch in a hemisphere. This also makes anyone aiming missile attacks at you from the front receive a –1 penalty to hit until the end of your next turn.
Alchemical Formula: not applicable

CLOAK OF RIGIDITY

Wondrous item, very rare
This cloak hardens when struck by any melee attack, reducing the damage by 2. It also provides total protection from nonmagical missiles. It does this by means of a flexible metal mesh. This negates any opportunity for a saving throw versus lightning damage and causes you to take maximum damage from attacks that do lightning damage if they hit you.
Alchemical Formula: not applicable

CLOAK OF WILDERNESS COMFORT

Wondrous item, rare (requires attunement)
This marvelous cloak has several special features to help people who wander through the wilderness. Three times per day, you can use an action to have it produce enough rations for a single meal. Twice per day, you can use an action to have it produce one gallon of clear, cool water or hot, spiced tea. It protects you from inclement weather and temperatures down to –40° Fahrenheit. At night, it can be used as a one-person tent and bedroll.
Alchemical Formula: not applicable

COPPER FLASK

Wondrous item, common
This flask produces 10 gallons of green-tinged, foul-smelling water once per day. The water is otherwise untainted and safe to drink. When you issue the command as an action, one gallon per round flows out. You may stopper it with a bonus action.
Alchemical Formula: not applicable

CROWN OF AILS

Wondrous item, very rare (requires attunement)
This crown is decorated with nine cabochon gemstones. This crown allows you to touch any nearby creature to discover any ailments that affect it. The crown also has a second and more deadly purpose. You may use an action to remove any of the stones. This infects you with a horrible plague or disease. You will not die of this disease for as long as you possess the gemstone. If the stone is replaced in the crown, you become highly contagious, becoming 75% likely to infect anyone who comes within a 10-foot radius over the next 24 hours. Each gem can be used only once.
Alchemical Formula: not applicable

FABRIC, AIR

Wondrous item, very rare
This fabric weighs nothing. It can be used to construct armor that provides a +2 bonus to armor class. Anybody is considered proficient in armor made from this material. This material is literally without weight. It hangs where it is placed. If wearing a suit of this armor, any damage you receive from falling is reduced by 1 point per die with no minimum.
The cost listed is for one 40-yard bolt of *air fabric*.
Alchemical Formula: Rare Earth, Air (any) (x3), Mercury (any), Transmutation

FABRIC, CHAMELEON

Wondrous item, rare
This fabric blends in with the background. A cloak made out of this material provides a +2 bonus to Dexterity (Stealth) checks. A full suit of clothing (including the cloak) provides a +5 bonus. In either case, creatures have disadvantage on Wisdom (Perception) checks made to see you.
The cost listed is for one 40-yard bolt of *chameleon fabric*.
Alchemical Formula: Rare Earth, Air (any), Mercury (any), Plant, Transmutation

GLOBE, COSMETIC

Wondrous item, uncommon
When you use an action to place this globe in a small bowl of water, the globe quickly dissolves. The water becomes brightly colored. Anyone placing their hands, feet, or face within the bowl is subject to whatever cosmetic procedure they wish (haircut/color, manicure, makeup, exfoliating rub, etc.). Each procedure takes one round, and the water retains its effectiveness for one minute.
Alchemical Formula: not applicable

GLOBE OF OOZES, SLIMES, AND JELLIES

Wondrous item, rare
When you use an action to throw this globe against a hard surface, an ooze, slime, or jelly bursts out, affecting everyone with five feet as if they had suffered an attack from the creature. It then becomes a full-grown, uncontrolled ooze, slime, or jelly of its type. If you fall or are subject to thunder damage while carrying this, make a DC 12 Dexterity saving throw to avoid having the globe shatter on your person. The contents are selected when the globe is crafted, and the globe is destroyed when it is used. The ooze, slime, or jelly can survive indefinitely within the globe.
Alchemical Formula: Azoth (any), Earth (any), Water (any), Body, Transmutation, any 2 essences from the type of ooze to be contained in the globe

GLOBE, WAR SHROUD

Wondrous item, uncommon
When you break this globe, it fills a 40-foot radius with thick, clinging, opaque purple smoke. The area is completely obscured, and even *true seeing* does not pierce the smoke. Anyone in the area when the cloud appears has a five-foot radius of the smoke follow them for the duration and must make a DC 16 Wisdom saving throw. If they fail this save, their movement is halved, they cannot take reactions, and each round they can take an action or a bonus action, but not both. The smoke lasts for one minute.
Alchemical Formula: Air (any), Water (any), Stealth

GLOVES, ENERGY BOLT

Wondrous item, very rare (requires attunement)
While wearing these gloves, you can use an action to fling a bolt of energy at a single target within 60 feet. The target must make a DC 16 Dexterity saving throw, taking 8d6 damage on a failure and half as much on a success. Nothing may be held in either hand; both hands are necessary to fling the bolt. After you use these gloves three times, you cannot use them again until after you complete a long rest.
Each type of bolt requires different materials. Materials and effects are listed below.

TABLE 4–16: ENERGY BOLT GLOVE REQUIREMENTS

Damage Type	Vital Essence	Gemstone
Fire	Fire (any) (x15)	Powdered Ruby
Acid	Acid (x10)	Powdered Turquoise
Ice	Cold (x10)	Powdered Moonstone
Lightning	Electricity (x10)	Powdered Sapphire
Thunder	Pain (x10)	Powdered Agate

Alchemical Formula: Each type of glove requires a gemstone and a vital essence; see Table above.

GOBLET OF PURITY

Wondrous item, rare
This goblet neutralizes any poisons or venoms contained within it. It takes one minute to do this.
Alchemical Formula: not applicable

INK, TOXIC

Wondrous item, very rare
This ink is toxic. Anyone perusing a book for more than one round must make a DC 12 Constitution saving throw in 24 hours or die. For every minute they read the book, the DC increases by 1. The cost produces enough ink to write 20 pages.
Alchemical Formula: Rare Earth, Water (any), Death, Stasis, Toxin

LIQUID IRON

Wondrous item, rare
This small vial contains a flat gray liquid. The liquid can coat up to four Medium objects and bonds with the item completely. This causes the item to be treated as iron for all purposes. A magical item coated in this substance ceases to function. If tossed on a creature, the liquid hardens quickly. The target must make a DC 16 Dexterity saving throw. If it fails, its movement is reduced by half and it receive a –2 penalty on all attack rolls, skill checks, and saving throws. If successful, it receives the –2 circumstance penalty only on attack rolls. The creature can take three minutes to clean off the substance to remove the penalty.
Alchemical Formula: Iron, Rare Earth, Earth (any), Mercury (any), Water (any), Transmutation

LIQUID ROAD

Wondrous item, rare
This small vial contains a gray liquid. You can use an action to create a firm, solid surface in a five-foot square. Each vial contains enough liquid to coat 16 five-foot squares. This is used to create passable surfaces over a swamp, in a pool or river, or even in a magma flow. The surface lasts for one hour.
Alchemical Formula: not applicable

MEDUSA WIG

Wondrous item, rare (requires attunement)
This helm is covered in metal coils that writhe and hiss, each a small replica of a snake. While wearing this item, you can use it make an attack against a creature within five feet. The attack uses your Strength or Dexterity modifier (your choice), and you may add your proficiency modifier. On a hit, the target takes 1d4 piercing damage and is injected with a stored poison. The saving throw against the poison, if any, is 2 higher than normal. If anyone attempts to grapple you while you are wearing this item, you may use your reaction to make an attack with the helm as above.
The wig holds up to 10 doses of poison. Each dose may be from a different poison, but if more than one poison is stored in the helm, then the poison used is determined randomly.
Alchemical Formula: not applicable

MONSTER TEETH

Wondrous item, rare
Alchemists discovered a wondrous ancient secret: The entire record of a being is recorded in its teeth. When you use an action to throw these teeth on the ground, they grow into the creature that they were taken from by the beginning of your next turn. These creatures are under the full command of the alchemist that created them.
The creatures remain in this form for one minute, at the end of which, if they are still alive, they revert to teeth. They can then be collected and reused again after 24 hours pass. Each time they are used, they are created at full health. No other essences can be taken from the creatures used; the bodies must be whole and without major injury (decapitation, etc.) and are destroyed in the process of making the teeth. The alchemist can raise the crafting DC by 5 while making the item to allow the creatures to follow the person who throws the teeth on the ground instead of the alchemist.

Monster teeth are one of the strongest and most iconic items alchemists can create. It ties into them collecting items from monsters in order to concoct their mystic substances, gives the alchemist an interesting and unique ability to use in combat, and creates interesting game choices for the players. *Monster teeth* are an item too important to be overlooked.
Alchemical Formula: Rare Earth, Air (any), Earth (any), Mercury (any), Body, Memory, Transmutation

MORTAR AND PESTLE OF FORCE

Wondrous item, rare
This powerful mortar and pestle allows you to grind the hardest of materials to dust. This decreases the time it takes to craft alchemical items and magic items by 10%.
Alchemical Formula: not applicable

PORTABLE VALISE OF FRUGALITY

Wondrous item, very rare
This marvelous device concentrates the power of consumable alchemical items. For any basic alchemical item such as a potion, dust, powder, or liquid that you have two doses of, you may attempt to produce a third dose of the substance. It requires eight hours and a successful DC 20 Intelligence (Alchemist's Supplies) check. This uses special reagents in order to accomplish this process. There are enough of these reagents to use this device 20 + 5d10 times. A new *valise of frugality* will have 70 uses. For the expenditure of one measure of reagents, this functions as an alchemy lab for 24 hours.
Alchemical Formula: not applicable

ROPE, ENDLESS

Wondrous item, uncommon
This is a small spool of one-quarter-inch silk rope. You can use an action to extend up to 500 feet of rope. To rewind the rope, you use an action to press your hand against the side of the spool and it rewinds at the rate of 100 feet per round. If the rope is cut, it dissipates into smoke. Cutting it does not limit or remove the amount of rope available, however. The spool can always be unwound to a maximum length of 500 feet.
Alchemical Formula: not applicable

ROPE, EXTENSION

Wondrous item, uncommon
When you use an action to issue the command, this 50-foot rope extends 300 feet in length or shortens from 300 feet back to 50 feet. If the shortening command is not given, the extra length rots away after four hours. The rope extends only from one end. The other end is knotted. Untying the knot destroys the rope.
Alchemical Formula: not applicable

ROPE OF IRON

Wondrous item, uncommon
This 100-foot silk rope turns into rigid iron when you use an action to give the command word. If it is broken in either iron or rope form, it becomes a nonmagical silk rope. In iron form, it can be broken with a successful DC 25 Strength check.
Alchemical Formula: not applicable

SHROUD OF SMOKE

Wondrous item, rare (requires attunement)
This cloak appears as a roiling mist or smoke descending from your collar. It has several functions. You can use an action to pull it around you to gain a +2 bonus to Dexterity (Stealth) checks.
You can use an action to utter a command word to cause it to expand and obscure the nearby area as the spell *obscuring mist* three times per day. This cloud lasts for one minute. You can also use it to defend yourself in combat. If you take the dodge action while wearing this cloak, you add a +2 bonus to your Armor Class.
Alchemical Formula: not applicable

SKELETON KEY

Wondrous item, uncommon
When you use this key to attempt a Dexterity check to open a lock, you may add your proficiency bonus and gain an additional +5 bonus to the check. On any roll of a 1, the key breaks.
Alchemical Formula: not applicable

SPHERE, SPLIT-SECOND

Wondrous item, very rare
When you use an action to throw this sphere at a point within 30 feet, each creature within 10 feet of that point must make a DC 16 Constitution saving throw. A creature that fails the saving throw is shunted 1d4 + 1 rounds into the future, when it reappears in the same spot. If the spot is occupied, the creature reappears in the closest unoccupied space.
Alchemical Formula: not applicable

WATERSKIN, ENDLESS

Wondrous item, uncommon
This waterskin holds a half gallon of water. It refills one cup of water per hour until full.
Alchemical Formula: not applicable

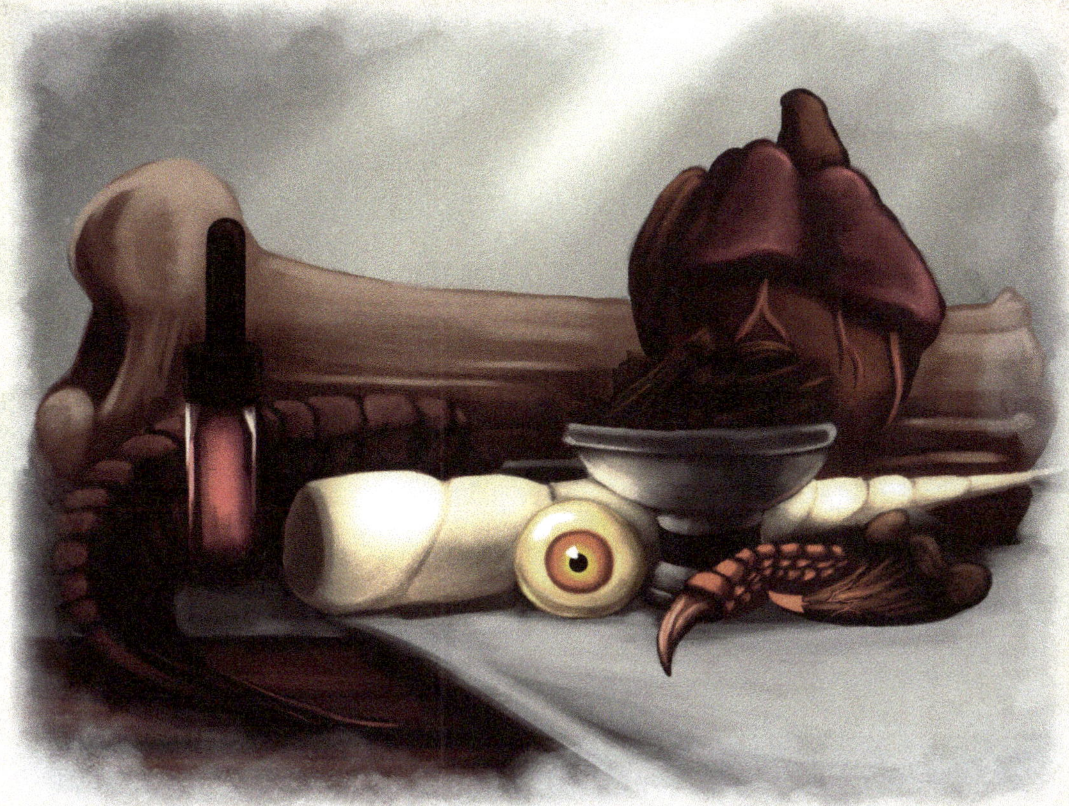

SALVES

Salves are substances that are smeared over a surface for an effect. Within a short period of time, they are absorbed or dry on the item and their effect occurs. They take one action to apply and their effects occur immediately. As with elixirs, salves have a default duration of 4 + 1d4 minutes. If you desire to have a salve's effect end before the duration is expired, most oils are removed easily enough with an appropriate solvent. A mild alcohol wash (i.e., something like wine) works well, as does turpentine. A typical salve container has one usage.

SALVE OF ACCELERATION

Potion, uncommon
This oil grants you increased speed. One application increases your speed by 50%. Moving at this speed is as tiring as moving at the unmodified rate. This oil has a duration of one minute.
Alchemical Formula: Rare Earth, Salt (any), Speed

SALVE OF AGELESSNESS

Potion, very rare
This powerful magic salve is a potent preservative. When applied to the skin of a living being, it halts all decay and aging for the span of one year. The aging process stops and resumes at the end of this period. There are no limits to the length of time this oil can be used, though repeated applications dry and yellow the skin. When crafted, enough is made to cover five Medium creatures. When found, it has 1d4 + 1 doses left.
Alchemical Formula: Azoth (any), Salt (any), Decay, Life

SALVE OF ANIMAL SANCTUARY

Potion, rare
This oil is spread over a Medium or smaller beast with an Intelligence of 3 or less. It creates a magical ward that protects the creature from harm. Anyone wishing to attack the animal must succeed at a DC 16 Wisdom saving throw in order to attack. Melee attacks against the animal are made with disadvantage.
Alchemical Formula: Salt (any), Protection (x2)

SALVE OF ANIMATION

Potion, rare
This strange oil has the wonderful ability to animate objects. One vial animates a single Medium or smaller object that obeys simple commands from its animator.
Once animated, the items are treated as constructs and can complete basic tasks. Stools can walk, suits of armor can pummel and dance, musical instruments can play themselves, but no special forms of movement or other abilities are imbued.
Alchemical Formula: Azoth (any), Mercury (any), Salt (any), Agility, Body

SALVE OF ARCANE SCENT

Potion, very rare
This salve is applied under the nose. It allows a trained caster to smell spells prepared by other casters. It does not detect auras from devices or items. The person sensing the magical energy knows, within a range of 2d4 levels, how many spells or spell-like abilities another caster within 10 feet has prepared or is able to cast. It also allows the caster to determine the schools of various abilities prepared or used. A vial has 6d4 doses and is created with a full 24 doses.
Alchemical Formula: Azoth (any), Mercury (any), Salt (any), Perception

SALVE OF ARMOR

Potion, uncommon
This salve is thin and watery. When applied over a creature's skin, it quickly hardens and acts like armor. The oil lasts for 6 + 2d4 hours. A creature not wearing armor gains a +5 bonus to armor class. There is enough for one Medium or smaller creature.
Alchemical Formula: Mercury (any), Salt (any), Armor

SALVE OF BASIC WEAPON ENHANCEMENT

Potion, rare
This salve grants a temporary magical effect to a weapon. There are a variety of effects that can be applied, and each requires four drams of a different kind of essence. Once applied, this salve lasts for the normal duration unless a character rolls a 1 on an attack. In that case, the salve has been scraped off or ruined somehow and no longer has its effect. Consult the following table for available enhancements.

TABLE 4–17: SALVE OF BASIC WEAPON ENHANCEMENTS

Weapon Quality	Effect	Alchemical Formula
Flaming	+1d6 fire damage	Salt (any), Fire (any) (x4)
Frost	+1d6 cold damage	Salt (any), Cold (x4)
Shock	+1d6 lightning damage	Salt (any), Electricity (x4)
Corrosive	+1d6 acid damage	Salt (any), Acid (x4)
Keen	Increase critical range by one	Salt (any), Purity (x3)

SALVE OF THE BLACK GRAVE

Potion, very rare
This demonic oil burns the very soul out of a body. When sprinkled on a surface in the shape of an X, the next living thing to cross over the X within the next 24 hours must make a DC 20 Constitution saving throw or die. Regardless of the results of the save, the oil works only against the first person walking across the threshold.
The oil is treated as a magical trap and can be located with a DC 20 Wisdom (Perception) check.
Alchemical Formula: Salt (any), Death (x3)

SALVE OF BLASTING

Potion, rare
Any Tiny non-living, inanimate, nonmagical object coated in this oil becomes a bomb that detonates when thrown. Each creature in a 15-foot radius must make a DC 16 Dexterity saving throw. The item is destroyed when it explodes. A creature that fails takes full damage, while a creature that succeeds take half. Damage is as follows:

TABLE 4–18: SALVE OF BLASTING DAMAGE

Material of Object	Damage
Gemstones	6d6 force damage + additional 6 force damage per 1,000 gp value
Glass, ceramic, or bone	2d6 piercing
Metal	6d6 slashing
Soft Materials (cloth, cotton, etc.)	1d4 bludgeoning
Stone	4d6 bludgeoning
Tough Materials (leather, rope, etc.)	1d6 bludgeoning

Alchemical Formula: Earth (any), Fire (any), Salt (any), Transmutation

SALVE OF CAMOUFLAGE

Potion, rare
When this oil is sprinkled over a target, its coloration changes to closely match the environment. This provides a +10 bonus on Dexterity (Stealth) to Hide checks when still, and a +5 bonus when moving. If in combat, this oil provides partial concealment.
Alchemical Formula: Mercury (any), Salt (any), Stealth

SALVE OF CLARITY

Potion, rare
You gain magical insights when this salve is applied to your eyes. You can detect illusions and other magic and know if a creature is an aberration, a celestial, an elemental, a fey, a fiend, or undead. You can also tell if someone is shape-shifted or under the influence of any mind-affecting effect.
Alchemical Formula: Mercury (any), Salt (any), Perception

SALVE OF DISENCHANTMENT

Potion, very rare
This salve removes and suppresses all enchantment and charms on living creatures and objects. Any living creature has all non-permanent enchantments and charms removed. Any object has its magic suppressed for 4 + 1d4 hours. The salve does not detect as magical. Any item that has its magic suppressed does not detect as magical either and generates no aura at all.
Alchemical Formula: Diamond, Azoth (any), Mercury (any), Salt (any), Decay

SALVE OF ELASTICITY

Potion, rare
This powerful salve allows you to shift and shape your body and gear as if it were a singular gelatinous mass. You could flatten a limb or stretch it up to three times its normal length. You could pour your body through a keyhole or slide beneath a door. You may make melee attacks against any targets within 15 feet. You may not extend a limb more than 10 times its natural length.
Alchemical Formula: Mercury (any), Salt (any), Agility, Transmutation

SALVE OF ELEMENTAL INVULNERABILITY

Potion, very rare
This salve provides protection and invulnerability to one type of elemental force. Fire invulnerability protects you from lava flows and forest fires and grants immunity to fire damage. Water protects you from floods, hurricanes, avalanches, and tsunamis and grants the ability to breathe underwater. Earth protects you from mudslides, rockslides, and earthquakes and falling damage. Air protects you from winds, storms, and tornados and grants resistance to force damage. You and the square you are in are completely protected from the elemental effect. Difficult terrain of the appropriate type is ignored; the elements part and do not affect you.
This salve also protects you from elemental attacks of the specific elemental type to which you are invulnerable. Although they are still effective, you gain the resistance to their damage until the salve expires. There is enough in one flask to coat eight Medium creatures or 16 Small creatures. Randomly determine the elemental type that the salve protects against.
Alchemical Formula: Air *or* Fire *or* Earth *or* Water (depending on type, x3 from different essences), Salt (any), Body, Protection

SALVE OF ETERNAL FLAME

Potion, uncommon
A torch soaked in this salve burns for two years. Furthermore, the torch does not emit enough heat to burn or set things aflame. It burns underwater, cannot be blown out, and if snuffed, will relight. Note that the torch does burn down but at a greatly reduced rate.
Alchemical Formula: Fire (any), Salt (any)

SALVE OF ETHEREALNESS

Potion, very rare
This salve seems to absorb light rather than be illuminated by it. Once used, it makes the target ethereal (as the *etherealness* spell). The user can end the effect at any time during the duration and re-enter the Prime Material Plane at will. Each vial contains enough for one Medium creature.
Alchemical Formula: Salt (any), Light, Planar, Stealth

SALVE OF EXPERT WEAPON ENHANCEMENT

Potion, very rare
When applied to a weapon, this salve grants the weapon a temporary magical effect. There are a variety of effects that can be applied, and each requires four drams of a different kind of essence. Once applied, this salve lasts for the normal duration unless a character rolls a one on an attack. In that case, the salve has been scraped off or ruined somehow and no longer has its effect. Consult **Table 4–17** for the available enhancements:

TABLE 4–19: SALVE OF EXPERT WEAPON ENHANCEMENTS

Weapon Quality	Effect	Alchemical Formula
Incendiary	+1d6 fire damage and target catches fire	Salt, Fire (any)(x8)
Freezing	+1d6 cold damage and target's movement is halved and target cannot take reactions until the end of its next turn	Salt (any), Cold (x6)
Electrifying	+1d6 lightning damage and target is stunned until the start of your next turn	Salt (any), Electricity (x6)
Dissolve	+1d6 acid damage and targets armor class is reduced by 1	Salt (any), Acid (x6)
Fast	If you use an action to make an attack with this weapon, you can use a bonus action to make another attack with this weapon	Salt (any), Speed (x6)

SALVE OF FIERY BURNING

Potion, rare
This salve immediately bursts into flame when it comes into contact with air. Each creature within a 10-foot radius must make a DC 16 Dexterity saving throw. A creature that fails takes 5d6 fire damage while a creature that succeeds take half as much damage.
Alchemical Formula: Fire (any) (x4), Salt (any), Body

SALVE OF FORTIFYING

Potion, rare
When applied, this salve hardens the skin of the owner, granting resistance to piercing and slashing damage.
Alchemical Formula: Salt (any), Body, Transmutation

SALVE OF ILLUMINATION

Potion, rare
This salve is usually found inside a dark, opaque, oddly shaped flask. Once opened, the flask turns transparent, and the salve sheds bright light out to 100 feet. The flask counters magical *darkness* and works underwater. The oil can be poured out and used to coat objects, which causes them to glow. The oil lasts for 12 + 2d6 hours.
Alchemical Formula: Fire (any), Salt (any), Light

SALVE OF IMMOBILITY

Potion, rare
This salve has the consistency of thick goop. This goop resists movement, affixing or locking into place whatever non-living, inanimate object to which it is applied. The legs of a stool could be affixed to the floor. Hinges covered in this paste do not swing. This goop affects only the part coated. A door with immobile hinges could be broken through, though the hinges would not swing; they become as solid as a single iron piece. Each flask can coat 25 square feet of material, and the application need not be contiguous. An attempt to force the part to move requires a successful DC 22 Strength check.
Alchemical Formula: Salt (any), Body, Stasis, Strength

SALVE OF IMPACT

Potion, very rare
When applied to a melee or ranged weapon that does bludgeoning damage, this salve gives a +3 bonus to hit and a +6 bonus to damage. The bonus remains with the weapon for 3d4 + 1 rounds. It makes no difference if the item is magical or not.
Each application of oil will treat five pieces of ammunition, two thrown weapons, or one melee weapon. A flask contains 1d4 + 1 applications.
Alchemical Formula: Azoth (any), Rare Earth, Earth (any), Salt (any), Strength

SALVE OF INIQUITY

Potion, rare
This unholy salve does 3d8 necrotic damage to creatures with good alignments on a direct hit. It can also be used to coat a 10-foot square. A good-aligned creature that enters the area for the first time on its turn or starts its turn there takes 2d4 necrotic damage. A good-aligned creature that ends its turn in the area takes 1d4 necrotic damage.
The salve is fairly sweet smelling and appears to be a healing potion. A successful DC 25 Intelligence (Arcana) check or *identify* is required to discover its true properties. If consumed internally, good characters must make a DC 18 Constitution saving throw, taking 6d8 + 6 necrotic damage on a failure or half as much on a success. Creatures with a neutral alignment get an upset stomach, and those with evil alignments treat it as a *potion of greater healing*.
Alchemical Formula: Azoth (any), Salt (any), Death (x3)

SALVE OF INSECTILE BARRIER

Potion, rare
This works as the *salve of protection, insects* but with two crucial changes. The duration is 1d4 + 1 hours and the salve is a powerful insect attractant that calls insects from up to three miles away.
These insects surround and travel with you in a five-foot-diameter sphere. They are harmless to you and disperse at the end of the duration, but a creature that ends its turn within five feet of you takes 2d8 + 2 piercing damage. Any insect control or summoning spells give a Game Master determined bonus to damage for the large number of insects present. Any insects with an Intelligence of 4 or greater receive a DC 16 Wisdom saving throw to resist the attraction.
Alchemical Formula: Salt (any), Emotion, Transmutation

SALVE OF LOOSENING

Potion, very rare
This salve can cover a 10-foot-square area. Webs dissolve and new ones cannot find purchase on any surface coated. Knots are untied; chains, straps, and other restraints fall off. Spells and terrain are unable to entangle or restrain creatures in the area of effect, and doors are unlocked.
Alchemical Formula: Rare Earth, Mercury (any) (x2), Salt (any) Sulfur (any), Body, Transmutation

SALVE OF MAGICAL BACKLASH

Potion, very rare
This salve coats a Medium creature for up to a full month or a Small item for up to a full year. During this time, any attempt to dispel or tamp down the creature's or object's magic is resisted. The spell DC for a successful *dispel magic* against the creature or object increases by +5. An *antimagic field* still prevents the magic from operating outside the creature or object, but does not shut down the magic. A creature benefitting from *water breathing* could still breathe water while within an *antimagic field* and a magical weapon (if coated) would still be magical, but a creature could not cast *magic missile* and the arrow shot from a coated magical bow would not be magical.
Alchemical Formula: Azoth (any) (3 from different sources), Air (any), Fire (any), Mercury (any), Water (any), Salt (any), Sulfur (any), Transmutation

SALVE OF MAKING

Potion, very rare
This salve is a very fluid liquid, approximately three ounces in size. To use it, the bottle is upended and the liquid is dumped out on the ground. The liquid forms the item that the salve contains. The item created is determined by the item destroyed during the salve creation process. The bottle is generally labeled with a picture of the item. Drinking or ingesting the salve has few harmful effects: a bit of indigestion and a few interesting trips to the privy.
Alchemical Formula: Mercury (any), Salt (any), Transmutation

SALVE OF MONSTER REPULSION

Potion, very rare
This salve repels monsters. It can coat up to 5 Medium creatures. Any aberration, giant, monstrosity, ooze, or undead within 80 feet of creatures coated in the salve have a −1 penalty on all attacks, skill checks, and saving throws. Within 40 feet, this penalty doubles to −2. Any creature within 20 feet receives a −3 penalty, and any creature in melee with a coated creature has a −4 penalty on attacks, skill checks, and saving throws.
Alchemical Formula: Mercury (any), Salt (any), Emotion (x4)

SALVE OF PACIFICATION

Potion, uncommon
This salve induces a powerful calm in the user for eight hours. Barbarians and berserkers find themselves unable to enter rage or battle lust in combat. To engage in combat requires a successful DC 16 Wisdom saving throw, although if attacked, the character receives a bonus equal to the damage dealt on this save. Once made, the character may fight for up to one minute at which point the saving throw must be repeated. In addition, stressful situations do not trigger a lycanthropic change in lycanthropes.
Alchemical Formula: Salt (any), Stasis

SALVE OF PILFERING

Potion, uncommon
This salve increases manual dexterity, giving you proficiency with thieves' tools and in Sleight of Hand. If you already have proficiency, you gain expertise.
Alchemical Formula: Salt (any), Agility

SALVE OF POWER

Potion, uncommon
Your Strength increases by +6 for one minute, but afterward you have a level of exhaustion and your Strength reduces by −4 (to a minimum of 1) for two minutes. After the two minutes, your strength returns to normal, but the exhaustion remains.
Alchemical Formula: Salt (any), Strength

SALVE OF PROTECTION, INSECTS

Potion, uncommon
When covered in this salve, no insect or bug, including spiders, scorpions, ants, beetles, centipedes and flies, can touch you. Giant-sized creatures can overcome this effect by succeeding at a DC 16 Wisdom saving throw. If successful, the creature can attack but it has disadvantage on any attacks and you have advantage on saving throws against any effects caused be them. If the Wisdom saving throw fails, the insect is hedged out by the salve and cannot attack. Attacking the insect allows it to automatically succeed at its saving throw.
Alchemical Formula: Salt (any), Emotion

SALVE OF PROTECTION, RUST

Potion, uncommon
This magical salve protects metal from the effects of natural rust and rust monsters, as well as liquids and effects that magically destroy, rust, or degrade metal. Spells that affect the metal without damaging it function normally.
Alchemical Formula: Salt (any), Decay

SALVE OF PROTOPLAST

Potion, very rare
When this salve is sprinkled over a target, the target returns to its natural form. Were-creatures shift into human form, polymorphed or shapechanged creatures return to their natural shape, and beings turned to stone revert to flesh. For the duration of the salve, any natural immunities or resistances (such as a lycanthrope's resistance to non-silvered weapons) are removed. Unwilling targets receive a DC 18 Wisdom saving throw to avoid the effect. The potion contains six doses when created. Using it offensively against a target requires making a successful melee attack against the target.
Alchemical Formula: Azoth (any), Mercury (any), Salt (any), Body, Stasis, Transmutation

SALVE OF REANIMATION

Potion, uncommon
This strange and bizarre salve animates a dead body. However, it does not turn the body into a zombie or create any connection between the original spirit and the body. It simply renders a single corpse ambulatory. The corpse must be dead within the last five days. The corpse continues to rot. It can move at half the movement rate it had while alive, but takes no other action outside of following the person who anointed the corpse with the salve. It cannot be commanded and can take no other actions. It has the same hit point total and armor class it had while alive. This effect does not prevent the target from being raised at a later time. The target is obviously dead, but a well-preserved corpse in a hat and dark glasses can fool a beach house full of people or an assassin.
Alchemical Formula: Salt (any), Body

SALVE OF RESISTANCE, ACID

Potion, uncommon
This salve provides virtual invulnerability to acids. The salve wears off slowly, lasting for a full 24 hours on one Medium creature. It may be used on more creatures or larger creatures with a proportionally shorter duration. The salve absorbs 10d10 + 100 acid damage before becoming useless. This value is divided among the number of targets the salve is used on. Damage is completely absorbed until this limit is reached.
Alchemical Formula: Salt (any), Acid, Protection

SALVE OF RESISTANCE, FIRE

Potion, uncommon
This salve provides virtual invulnerability to fire. The salve wears off slowly, lasting for a full 24 hours on one Medium creature. It may be spread on more creatures or creatures of a larger size to protect them for a proportionally shorter duration.
The salve absorbs 10d10 + 100 fire damage before becoming useless. This value is divided among the number of targets the salve is used on. Damage is completely absorbed until this limit is reached.
This salve may also be constructed in cold and lightning variants by adding Cold or Electricity essence to the formula (the Fire essence must remain in the formula in both cases).
Alchemical Formula: Fire (any), Salt (any), Protection

SALVE OF SCENTLESSNESS

Potion, uncommon
This salve neutralizes all scent. Once applied, you become odorless. This eliminates the ability of monsters and animals to track you or to locate you by smell. A monster that is highly dependent on its sense of smell has disadvantage on attack rolls against you.
Alchemical Formula: Salt (any), Stealth

SALVE OF SCRIBE

Potion, rare
When applied to any surface, this salve renders any text comprehensible as a *comprehend languages* spell, and magic spells are made clear so that spells can be trivially identified. *Glyphs of warding* are revealed, and *illusory scripts* are made clear. One vial covers 200 pages.
Alchemical Formula: Azoth (any), Salt (any), Mind

SALVE OF SCRYING

Potion, very rare
When poured into still, standing water, this salve acts as a *crystal ball*. For the duration of the salve, anyone may use the reflecting surface as a basic *crystal ball*. Some Game Masters may allow additional material components and essences to be used in the crafting of the item to allow the character to simulate a more advanced *crystal ball*. If the water is disturbed, the connection is lost. The water must be calm before trying again.
Alchemical Formula: Azoth (any), Air (any), Salt (any), Sulfur (any), Mind, Perception (x2 from different sources)

SALVE OF SHADOWS

Potion, uncommon
When this salve is used, it coats the user like a shadow, absorbing light. This grants a +10 bonus on Dexterity (Stealth) checks.
Alchemical Formula: Salt (any), Stealth

SALVE OF SHARPNESS

Potion, varies
This salve appears to be the sort that is used to clean and care for weapons. When applied to the blade of any sharp or edged weapon, this salve makes the weapon magical for 3d4 + 1 rounds. The bonus that the weapon depends on its rarity. The materials listed are for creating +1 magical weapons. Multiply these amounts by the bonus to determine the price of more powerful salves. A *salve of sharpness +2* costs 1,500 gp to fabricate and requires twice as many ingredients.
A flask of *salve of sharpness* has 1d4 + 1 applications. The number of applications is determined randomly after successfully creating the salve. Roll d20 on the following table to determine the strength of the oil:

TABLE 4–20: SALVE OF SHARPNESS STRENGTH TABLE

d20	Bonus	Rarity	Cost
1–10	+1	Common	750
11–15	+2	Uncommon	1,500
16–18	+3	Rare	2,250
19	+4	Very Rare	3,000
20	+5	Legendary	3,750

Alchemical Formula: Salt (any), Prowess

SALVE OF STASIS

Potion, rare
There is enough of this salve to coat one Small object. An object coated by this salve is removed from the effects of time and space. It is unaffected by any force or energy short of a *disintegrate* spell. The effect can be dispelled as any magical ward, but the object itself is immune to harm. The coated object exudes a dim rose glow and can be moved, but cannot be touched or manipulated (a chest could not be opened, a potion could not be drunk, a book cannot be read).
The salve does not work on living creatures; however, a living creature in a container would be affected by the temporal stasis.
Alchemical Formula: Azoth (any), Salt (any), Planar, Stasis

SALVE OF STEEL

Potion, very rare
When this salve is used to coat a Medium object, it changes the strength of the object to that of steel. Weight, coloration, texture, and all other properties of the object are unchanged. It is only effective against objects and must set for a minute before it takes effect. It does not affect creatures. There are five doses when crafted, and 1d4 + 1 when found.
Alchemical Formula: Iron, Earth (any), Salt (any), Body, Strength, Transmutation

SALVE OF STONEWALKING

Potion, rare
This thick salve allows items and creatures to pass through stone. An object coated in this salve can be lightly pushed through solid rock as if into pudding. The duration of this salve on objects is permanent and lasts until the salve is washed off. The objects stay where they are placed and may be retrieved by reaching into the stone to retrieve them.
When applied to living creatures, the effect lasts for 3d6 minutes and grants them the ability to swim through solid rock and stone at half their movement speed. This is treated as burrowing, but without disturbing the surrounding materials. The creature's senses are enhanced in no applicable way, so it moves blindly through the rock. If it is within solid rock when the duration expires, the creature must make a DC 22 Constitution saving throw. On a failure, the creature dies and remains in the material, while on a successful save the creature is moved up to 20 feet toward open space and takes 8d6 bludgeoning damage. If 20 feet isn't far enough to move the creature to open space, the creature may repeat the saving throw again with identical results.
Alchemical Formula: Iron, Earth (any), Salt (any), Agility, Body, Planar, Transmutation

SALVE OF THE GREEN

Potion, very rare
This thick green oil allows anyone anointed with it to pass through any vegetation, no matter how dense, at full speed while leaving no trace. It also allows the user to enter any plant and exit from another one time as *transport via plants*.
Alchemical Formula: Earth (any), Salt (any), Planar, Plant

SALVE OF THE MARIONETTE

Potion, rare
When this salve is sprinkled on any Medium or smaller object, it gives you the ability to telekinetically control the object with your hand. You can use your action to control the object, which is treated as an appropriate-sized animated object.
Alchemical Formula: Earth (any), Salt (any), Telesthenic

SALVE OF THE THRESHOLD

Potion, rare
When this oil is carefully applied to a threshold, it damages anyone who attempts to cross. It takes a full minute to apply, and the victims must make a DC 16 Wisdom saving throw when they cross the threshold or enter the square where the salve is applied or take 3d6 damage. When you create the salve, you choose one of the following damage types: acid, cold, fire, or lightning. A creature that passes or fails the saving throw is immune to the damage for 24 hours. The salve retains its potency for one week. It is treated as a magical trap and can be noted with a successful DC 22 Wisdom (Perception) check.
Alchemical Formula: Agate, Rare Earth, Earth, Salt (any), Pain

SALVE OF TIMELESSNESS

Potion, rare
This salve causes material, particularly organic material but also stone and metal, to resist the passage of time. Each object is affected as if the passage of a year were only a period of 24 hours.
There is enough in each flask to coat eight Medium objects or a 20-foot square. Under normal circumstances, this oil never wears off though it can be removed. It is edible and tasteless, allowing the long-term storage of food. It does not affect creatures.
Alchemical Formula: Salt (any), Decay, Stasis

SALVE OF TOTAL COMMAND

Potion, very rare
This salve is thick and gloopy. When smeared across the forehead of a sleeping creature, that creature comes under the control of the person who applied the salve for 24 hours.
The victim has no free will at all and requires commands for all non-automatic tasks. The victim only follows literal direction and is incapable of performing skilled tasks such as spellcasting. Ordering the victim to harm themselves may be done, but this allows the subject to make a DC 16 Wisdom saving throw to break the effect. The victim must be asleep when the salve is applied, otherwise it has no effect.
Alchemical Formula: Salt (any), Control, Mind

SALVE OF TRANSCENDENT FILTH

Potion, very rare
This salve can cover a 10-foot square. The area develops a pile of pure filth. A creature that looks at the area must make a DC 20 Wisdom saving throw. A creature that fails becomes covered in filth and must immediately make a DC 18 Constitution saving throw or become nauseated. A nauseated creature has disadvantage on attack rolls, ability checks, and Constitution saving throws. In addition, the creature has disadvantage on all Charisma skill checks. A creature that succeeds has a –2 penalty on to-hit and damage rolls while able to see the area. The filth decays after one minute.
Alchemical Formula: Salt (any), Body, Decay, Disease, Plant

SALVE OF TRANSPARENCY

Potion, very rare
This salve renders a material transparent like glass. If polished, the substance can be made almost invisible, making it more difficult to find, but the primary purpose of this salve is to turn objects temporarily transparent. The transparency takes one minute to take effect and lasts for the standard duration of the salve. It turns material up to 10 feet thick transparent. The transparency is two-way and does nothing to the structural integrity of the material.
Alchemical Formula: Air (any), Salt (any), Body, Transmutation

SALVE OF TURNING

Potion, uncommon
When this salve is applied to a holy symbol, it increases your ability to channel divine energy. It increases the saving throw DC against your attempts to Channel Divinity by +2.
Alchemical Formula: Salt (any), Purity

SALVE OF WARDING

Potion, rare
This thaumaturgic salve provides protection against all dangers and risks. For 24 hours, any creature that has this paste applied gains a +2 bonus on all saving throws. There is enough salve for one Medium creature.
Alchemical Formula: Salt (any), Body, Protection

SPELL-INFUSED POTIONS

As well as standard potions, a trained alchemist who is also a spellcaster can create a *spell potion*. A spell potion mimics the effects of a spell. Only spells that can be cast on the caster and that have a duration of at least one minute may be made into spell potions. The rarity of the potion (and therefore its cost to create) is based on the level of the spell being mimicked. When you drink the potion, it is as if you had cast the referenced spell upon yourself except that you do not need to concentrate to maintain the effects. You may choose to cast the spell at a higher spell slot if appropriate, increasing the rarity, time, and cost commensurately. Any material components required for the spell are in addition to the base cost to create the potion.

Standard potions follow standard magic item creation rules. Essences can also be used to aid in the crafting of magical items to reduce the crafting cost. The essence, or one of its sub-essences, either must match one of the type descriptors of the item, a spell used in the item, a material component of a spell used in the item, or must be an Azoth essence. Rare Earth and anything that seems thematically appropriate or is described in the text of the item can also be used to reduce crafting costs in this way.

TABLE 4–21: POTION RARITY

Spell Slot Level	Rarity
Cantrip	Common
1st	Common
2nd	Common
3rd	Uncommon
4th	Uncommon
5th	Rare
6th	Rare
7th	Very Rare
8th	Very Rare
9th	Very Rare

CURSED AND FAILED ALCHEMY

Sometimes when crafting items, the process goes awry. Any time a crafting roll for an item fails by 5 or more, there is a chance that the item will be cursed. These are examples of specific cursed alchemical items that can result from the failures. Some may be more likely to stem from attempts to craft certain potions, but this decision is left to the Game Master. In general, these cursed items appear to be a useful potion, although you may decide that an *identify* spell reveals their true spirit.

These items do not have an alchemical formula listed because they can result from mistakes in any number of different attempts that used different formulas. Unless you decide otherwise, these items cannot be deliberately created; they result solely from accidents.

ELIXIR OF AMNESIA

Potion, uncommon
You suffer complete memory loss for 6 + 1d8 hours. You do not forget how to walk, speak, or use any of your other skills, class abilities, or talents, though you may be unaware that you have them. There is a 5% chance that the condition is permanent, requiring a *remove curse* or *limited wish* to restore lost memory.
Alchemical Formula: not applicable

ELIXIR OF BLINDNESS

Potion, rare
You are permanently struck blind upon drinking the elixir.
Alchemical Formula: not applicable

ELIXIR OF BUBBLES

Potion, uncommon
Upon drinking the elixir, a terrible curse befalls you. Each time you open your mouth, a stream of bubbles erupts from your mouth. If you refuse to open you mouths, bubbles stream from your ears and nose.
This effect usually lasts a full eight days, although in rare cases (1% of the time), it is permanent.
Alchemical Formula: not applicable

ELIXIR OF COWARDICE

Potion, rare
This appears to be a *potion of heroism*. Upon imbibing it, you gain disadvantage on all saving throws against fear, and you make all attacks with disadvantage. These effects can be halted with *remove curse*.
Alchemical Formula: not applicable

ELIXIR OF DEAFNESS

Potion, uncommon
You are permanently struck deaf upon drinking the elixir.
Alchemical Formula: not applicable

ELIXIR OF DRUNKENNESS

Potion, uncommon
Upon imbibing the elixir, you are rendered drunk, gaining a –4 penalty on attack rolls and skill checks. In order to cast spells, you must succeed at a DC 10 Concentration check and opponents get a +2 bonus to any saving throws against the effects of your spells.
This effect lasts for six hours, and you have a splitting headache after it wears off. You are unable to take any actions or reactions for three hours.
Alchemical Formula: not applicable

ELIXIR OF GLUTTONY

Potion, rare
Upon drinking the elixir, you are overcome with insatiable hunger and stop whatever you are involved in, including combat, in order to eat. You consume everything you can find for 2 + 1d10 rounds.
Alchemical Formula: not applicable

ELIXIR OF INSOMNIA

Potion, common
A sip of this elixir tastes wonderful and makes you feel fantastic. Once you finish the draught, you feel sharp for a bit. As time wears on, you become more and more weary. When night comes, you are unable to fall asleep or gain the benefits of a long rest. This condition is permanent. Fatigue and eventually exhaustion accumulate. A *remove curse* ends the effect.
Alchemical Formula: not applicable

ELIXIR OF LETHARGY

Potion, uncommon
When you drink this elixir, you take a –2 penalty to your Armor Class, your speed is halved, and you can't use reactions. On your turn, you can take either an action or a bonus action, but not both. These effects last for one minute.
Alchemical Formula: not applicable

ELIXIR OF MADNESS

Potion, very rare
A single sip of this elixir causes you to go insane and act as if affected by the *confusion* spell until a *heal*, *lesser restoration*, or *wish* spell is used to remove the madness. Once a creature is affected, the remaining draught loses all magical properties and becomes a foul liquid.
Alchemical Formula: not applicable

ELIXIR OF PESTILENCE

Potion, very rare
You are cured for 4 points of damage upon drinking the elixir but infected with a debilitating disease. The disease affects you in 1d4 + 1 days. During this time, you are a carrier and infect anyone you come into contact with who fails a DC 12 Constitution saving throw. You then acquire the randomly selected disease. These effects are removed or negated by *lesser restoration*.
Alchemical Formula: not applicable

ELIXIR OF PETRIFICATION

Potion, very rare
A single sip of this elixir turns you to stone. A *greater restoration* spell restores you to mobility and life.
Alchemical Formula: not applicable

ELIXIR OF POX

Potion, legendary
No immediate effect occurs when you imbibe this elixir. One hour after ingestion, however, boils and pus-filled pustules accompanied by a rash cover your body. Your temperature goes up, and you become feverish. Blisters and sores appear where there is friction, and hives cover any remaining skin. This is not a disease but a magical curse. It is not contagious. Every hour after the elixir's consumption, the pox gets worse. For each hour that passes, you must succeed on a DC 12 Constitution saving throw or your Dexterity, Constitution, and Strength drop 1 point. If any of these drop to 0, you die. Each time you succeed on a saving throw, the DC increases by 1. The only cures are a vial of *sweet water* or *dispel magic* followed by *remove curse* followed by *lesser restoration*.
Alchemical Formula: not applicable

ELIXIR OF RAGE

Potion, uncommon
When quaffed, you recover 1d4 + 4 hit points. The next time you are threatened, angered, attacked, stressed, or provoked, you fly into a berserker rage. Each round you must attack the closest creature in sight. Your Strength is increased by 4 during the rage, and the rage lasts for 3d6 + 3 rounds.
Alchemical Formula: not applicable

ELIXIR OF REDUCTION

Potion, uncommon
Your size permanently decreases by one rank. Your gear is not affected. *Remove curse* removes the affliction, and potions and magic items causing growth have a 25% chance of breaking the curse.
Alchemical Formula: not applicable

ELIXIR OF REGRESSION

Potion, very rare
Your body regresses to the physical age of a five-year-old human. Your physical stats are reduced to 25% of their current values, reaching 50% at age 10, and 75% at age 13, and back to their normal values at age 16. You have a –2 penalty to Dexterity until age 14. Your mind is unchanged, and all your equipment is adult-sized. This change is permanent, requiring a *remove curse* within 48 hours or better to cure.
Alchemical Formula: not applicable

ELIXIR OF TRAGIC HEROISM

Potion, rare
Drinking this elixir grants the imbiber the benefits of a *potion of heroism* but also enrages every creatures around you. Any enemy within 100 feet attacks you. Allies who begin their turn within 100 feet of and who do not succeed on a DC 12 Wisdom saving throw become your enemies. An enemy's Strength increases by 4 and it gains a +2 bonus to saving throws for the duration. The effects wear off after one hour or if you drop to 0 hit points.
Alchemical Formula: not applicable

ELIXIR OF VENTRILOQUISM, REVERSAL

Potion, uncommon
After consuming this elixir, a random target within 50 feet of you can make its voice come from your mouth. The random target is instantly made aware of this new ability. This lasts for one minute, during which time you are unable to speak. A creature cannot use your mouth to cast spells.
Alchemical Formula: not applicable

ELIXIR OF VULNERABILITY, FIRE

Potion, uncommon
You become vulnerable to fire damage for one hour.
Alchemical Formula: not applicable

ELIXIR OF WEAKNESS

Potion, rare
Upon drinking this elixir, you are wracked by pain and stunned for one minute. While stunned, your Strength is reduced to a score of 5. These effects last for 4 + 2d10 rounds.
Alchemical Formula: not applicable

ELIXIR OF WORM CALLING

Potion, rare
Upon drinking this potion, you become a target for vermin of all types: crawling insects, rats, bees, hornets, wasps, snakes, worms, and even carrion crawlers, purple worms, and linnorms. Swarms or 1d12 creatures are called every minute for 10 minutes.
Alchemical Formula: not applicable

ELIXIR OF YELLOW MOLD

Potion, legendary
This potion is composed of condensed yellow mold spores extracted into fluid paste. It is a murky yellow in color with milky white clumps. When quaffed, your flesh and organs turn into yellow mold, irrevocably slaying you before your corpse explodes in a 10-foot cloud of spores. Anyone within range must succeed at a DC 16 Constitution saving throw or die.
Some liches use this elixir offensively, turning their regenerating organs and skin into yellow mold.
Alchemical Formula: not applicable

SALVE OF FUMBLING

Potion, rare
The first time you are subjected to a stressful situation (combat, going outside in a major city, going into work, leaving the house), you become clumsy. While clumsy, you must succeed on a DC 10 Dexterity check to hold or pick up an item. If you attempt to move at more than half speed or take an action and move in the same turn, you must succeed at a DC 15 Dexterity (Acrobatics) check or fall prone. This salve wears off in 2d6 days.
Alchemical Formula: not applicable

SALVE OF LIGHTNING

Potion, rare
If you use an action to spread this salve upon a surface, that surface becomes highly charged and attracts lightning bolts for the next 1d4 hours.
If outside, storm clouds gather, heavy rains start, and 1d12 bolts per hour strike at the target. If the target is a creature, it must make a DC 16 Dexterity saving throw for each bolt. A creature that fails the save takes 8d6 lightning damage, while one who succeeds takes half this amount.
A creature that is coated with this salve and moving indoors takes 2d6 lightning damage if it starts its turn or comes within five feet of a piece of metal that has not previously shocked the creature.
Alchemical Formula: not applicable

SALVE OF PHOSPHORESCENCE

Potion, uncommon
When this salve is applied to a living creature, the creature sheds orange-yellow light, making the individual highly visible and shedding dim light out to a radius of five feet. The effect can be removed only by a *remove curse* or similar spell.
Alchemical Formula: not applicable

SALVE OF POISON

Potion, rare
When this salve is applied to a creature's skin, the creature must succeed on a DC 15 Constitution saving throw or take 10d10 poison damage.
Alchemical Formula: not applicable

SALVE OF SCENTS

Potion, common
When applied to the skin, the salve causes a hideous stench for 1d8 hours. The chances for encountering random and wandering monsters are doubled. The stench can be removed with *dispel magic*.
Alchemical Formula: not applicable

SALVE OF SULFUR

Potion, uncommon
When the creature comes under stress or attempts to use the ability the creature believes the salve provides, the salve bursts into flame and causes 3d8 fire damage at the end of each of the creature's turns until a creature uses an action to wash off the salve.
Alchemical Formula: not applicable

CHAPTER FIVE: ALCHEMICAL MAGECRAFT

Some items blend magical crafting and alchemy so closely that they become indistinguishable. These items are a new category of magic item called alchemical magecraft and require proficiency with Alchemist's Supplies and the feat Craft Alchemical Magience (see sidebar). Like other alchemical items, crafting these successfully requires an Intelligence (Alchemist's Supplies) check where the DC is based on the rarity of the item.

The primary types of alchemical magecraft are mineral alchemy, mineral apotheosis, sigils, and talismans. Each of these categories is outlined in this chapter, with individual explanations as to how those items work and who can use them.

<table>
<tr><td>

CRAFT ALCHEMICAL MAGECRAFT FEAT

Prerequisites: Spellcasting and proficiency with Alchemist's Supplies

You have discovered the processes required to blend alchemy and magic seamlessly, granting you the ability to craft alchemical magecraft items.

You can create a variety of alchemical magecraft items. Crafting an alchemical magecraft item takes one day for each 1,000 gp of its crafting cost.

You can also mend a broken alchemical magecraft item if it is one that you could make. Doing so costs half the raw materials and half the time it would take to craft that item.

See magic item creation rules and the specific category of alchemical magecraft item for more information.

</td></tr>
</table>

MATERIAL APOTHEOSIS

Alchemy is not just the creation of items to get you high and melt your opponents' faces. It's the pursuit of purity. The entire endeavor is about taking materials and transforming them into pure substances. And the pursuit of alchemy for some is about reflecting that physical process of material purity into a spiritual one. Material apotheosis is the culmination of that pursuit. Once a material is made so pure that it is no longer the material, but the idea of that material, it can be combined with the soul.

This study is the foundation for all higher levels of alchemy. The materials are removed of all physical and magical properties. The pure platonic ideal that remains takes on a powerful resonance. Some of these substances are used as ingredients in the most powerful alchemical creations. Others can be used to transcend reality. These substances straddle the border of reality, existing with physical mass and subjective philosophical spirituality.

Most appear to be an unreal liquid or solid. Some hum or sing or even pulse, sending off mystical energies. All require special containers as part of the crafting cost — vials made of diamond or woven sacks of translucent ether or other fantastic restraints. These containers cannot be reused. Universal solvents are used in the makeup of these items; see **Chapter Three: Alchemical Items** for more information on crafting universal solvents and their costs and properties.

Even though these are enchanted items, material apotheosis may only be accomplished with alchemy. The crafter must possess the Craft Alchemical magecraft feat, as well as the ability to cast *wish*, and be able to succeed at the Alchemist's Supplies check required to craft a legendary item. Due to the mystical and alchemical processes involved, only one of these may be crafted by any individual alchemist during each lunar cycle.

True metals work on any substance or target, but the spirituality of the alchemist is relevant in the creation and use of elemental transubstantiation. These may be created only by a skilled alchemist and may be used only by the alchemist that created them. This is not magic, but material above divinity. Although our understanding of the basic effects is listed below, the spiritual nature of the creator of the substance must be taken into account, for the effects will be modified by the nature of the alchemist. The nature of these modifications is left up to the whims of the gods (or the imagination of your Game Master). Any individual item may be affected only by one true metal, and any alchemist may consume only one elemental transubstantiation in their lifetime.

TABLE 5–1: MATERIAL APOTHEOSIS

Name	Rarity	Crafting Cost
Apotheosis of Air (Elemental Transubstantiation)	Legendary	101,350 gp
Apotheosis of Earth (Elemental Transubstantiation)	Legendary	101,350 gp
Apotheosis of Fire (Elemental Transubstantiation)	Legendary	101,350 gp
Apotheosis of Gold (True Gold)	Legendary	102,400 gp
Apotheosis of Iron (Elemental Transubstantiation)	Legendary	101,550 gp
Apotheosis of Lead (True Lead)	Legendary	102,150 gp
Apotheosis of Mercury (True Mercury)	Legendary	102,150 gp
Apotheosis of Platinum (True Platinum)	Legendary	121,750 gp
Apotheosis of Silver (True Silver)	Legendary	107,800 gp
Apotheosis of Sulfur (Elemental Transubstantiation)	Legendary	113,800 gp
Apotheosis of Tin (True Tin)	Legendary	103,450 gp
Apotheosis of Water (Elemental Transubstantiation)	Legendary	101,350 gp

APOTHEOSIS OF AIR (ELEMENTAL TRANSUBSTANTIATION)

Wondrous item, legendary

This creates a handful of light crystalline grains that swirl around in different shapes as if blown by the wind. They are multicolored pastels that leave tiny visible burns behind them as they scar the dimensional boundaries with their motion. They require no container, being controlled and contained by your will. If you are killed before the grains are consumed, they fall to the ground as harmless, useless, gray dust.

When they are consumed, you permanently gain a flight speed of 100 feet. You also become immune to falling damage and resistant to all other bludgeoning damage. You gain truesight out to 60 feet.

Alchemical formula: Air (any), Universal Solvent

APOTHEOSIS OF EARTH (ELEMENTAL TRANSUBSTANTIATION)

Wondrous item, legendary

This requires a bowl made from platinum and lead and produces thick, heavy, solid, brown grains that always rest as close to the ground as possible. They exude a scent of rich earth.

Once they are consumed, you gain a +4 bonus to any Strength-based skill checks, saving throws, or attack rolls while standing on or in earth or stone. You can burrow through nonmagical, unworked earth and stone with a speed equal to your base speed. While doing so, you don't disturb the material you move through. You gain tremorsense out to 60 feet.

Alchemical formula: Earth (any), Universal Solvent

APOTHEOSIS OF FIRE (ELEMENTAL TRANSUBSTANTIATION)

Wondrous item, legendary

This creates a one-inch diameter sphere of white flame. It has a luminous aura that radiates out with blues, reds, and greens shot throughout with burning electric lines. It is warm to the touch but not hot.

Once consumed, you become immune to all fire damage and heat effects. You could bathe in magma. You may raise the temperature of your body to catch items on fire. You can do an additional 1d6 + 1 fire damage on any melee attack with a bare hand or a weapon. As a bonus action, you can fling a fire bolt at a target. Make a ranged weapon attack using Dexterity. You are considered proficient in this attack. On a hit, the target takes 1d4 + 1 fire damage. You can also use an action to breathe fire in a 15-foot cone. Each creature in the cone must make a Dexterity saving throw, taking 5d6 fire damage on a failure or half as much on a success. The DC of the saving throw is 10 + your Dexterity modifier + your proficiency modifier. You gain vulnerability to cold damage.

Alchemical formula: Fire (any), Universal Solvent

APOTHEOSIS OF GOLD (TRUE GOLD)

Wondrous item, legendary

This appears as one ounce of a clear liquid with an iridescent blue tinge. Within float countless golden flakes. It radiates a shining golden aura that casts dim light out to 10 feet. When given to any person or used on any corpse, it restores that person to life regardless of the length of time that person has been deceased.

Whether taken by a living or dead person, all wounds heal and all limbs regenerate. If taken or used on a living person, the imbiber is restored to the prime of their lives. Humans return to being 25 years old. A DC 2 Constitution saving throw must be made to survive. The DC increases by +1 per decade for the first century of death, and then by +1 per century after that. If living, the DC increases by +2 for every 10 human-year equivalents you are past your prime.

If this apotheosis is used a second time, the last DC of the Constitution saving throw from the first use of the apotheosis becomes the base DC for the second. For example, a 50-year-old human takes the *apotheosis of gold* and reverts to 25 years of age. This is an age reduction 25 years, so 25 divided by 10 is 2.5, which is rounded down to 2. The DC of the Constitution saving throw increases from 4 to 6. This person succeeds on their DC 6 Constitution check. If they wait until they are again 50 and take the *apotheosis of gold* a second time, then the new starting DC is 6 + 4 or 10. Everyone has to die sometime.

While the resurrection and healing effects can be used on any dead person, the rejuvenation only affects the creator.

Alchemical formula: Gold, Universal Solvent

APOTHEOSIS OF IRON (ELEMENTAL TRANSUBSTANTIATION)

Wondrous item, legendary

This creates one dram of gray, sand-like grains. They are much heavier than they appear and when they shift against each other, they make a sound like grinding stone.

When consumed, you gain a perfect body. Your hit points increase as if you had rolled maximum hit points at each level and your Constitution increases by +6 to a maximum of 24. Your Charisma increases by +2 to a maximum of 24.

You gain control over your body functions, allowing you to speed up your heart rate, control your blood flow, and strengthen and toughen your skin, for example. You gain resistance to slashing and piercing damage. You age at half speed and can go without breathing for up to 10 minutes, requiring one minute to recover.

You can use a bonus action to generate an electrical spark to cause one creature of your choice within five feet to take 1d4 + 1 lightning damage.

Alchemical formula: Iron, Universal Solvent

APOTHEOSIS OF LEAD (TRUE LEAD)

Wondrous item, legendary

You produce one ounce of clear translucent liquid surrounding a smoky gray, spider-web-like cloud that contracts and expands while emitting dim flashes of orchid and alabaster light.

You can mix this substance with paint, mortar, or metal to cover 1,000 square feet. The surface is immune to nonmagical attacks and resistant to all other damage.

Alchemical formula: Lead, Universal Solvent

APOTHEOSIS OF MERCURY (TRUE MERCURY)

Wondrous item, legendary

You produce one dram of fine metallic reddish grains (60 grains). When the grains slide and run across each other, they make soft noises like the ringing of distant brass bells.

Each grain when mixed with molten lead transmutes that lead to purest molten gold. The change is nearly instantaneous. Each grain transmutes approximately 100 pounds of lead.

Alchemical formula: Mercury (any), Universal Solvent

APOTHEOSIS OF PLATINUM (TRUE PLATINUM)

Wondrous item, legendary
You create one ounce of silvery liquid in which swirls a dark vortex that absorbs all light and color. Small particles of colored light appear outside the vial and spiral away into nothingness.
This substance is used to coat one small item. For every application of one ounce, the item gains 5 spell slot levels.
When you are targeted with a spell, you may use your reaction to absorb the spell. If the spell was cast using a spell slot level that is not greater than the number of slots available to store, the spell is absorbed and has no other effect.
You can use an action to discharge one or more spell levels as pure energy at a target you can see within 30 feet. The target takes 1d6 + 1 force for each spell level you release.
You may also use the stored spell levels to cast spells, draining the spell levels from the item.
The item loses one level of spell slot each hour.
An item may be doused in *true platinum* more than once, but each attempt past the first carries a cumulative 15% chance of failure. In the event of failure, the item cannot accept any further doses of *true platinum*.
Alchemical formula: Platinum, Universal Solvent

APOTHEOSIS OF SILVER (TRUE SILVER)

Wondrous item, legendary
You create one ounce of dark silver liquid that appears to contain thousands of insubstantial cubes tumbling throughout the vial.
You can turn this into enough molten metal to make a suit of plate or chain mail armor. The armor made gains a +1 bonus to Armor Class for each quarter ounce added. However, for each dose past the first, there is a cumulative 25% chance of failure. In the event of a failure, no more applications are possible, but the given bonus remains. Because it is applied when molten, the dose must be added in total, and then the failure chance checked.
Alchemical formula: Silver, Universal Solvent

APOTHEOSIS OF SULFUR (ELEMENTAL TRANSUBSTANTIATION)

Wondrous item, legendary
You create a small transparent sphere. Although it is just the size of a pebble, it weighs approximately 25 pounds. A small gold light smolders within the center.
When you consume this sphere, you become immortal. You cease to age and can no longer die. If your body parts are severed or removed, they still continue to live. A heart beats, a head talks, and an arm grasps. The limb reattaches seamlessly if recovered.
It also has the side effect of making your body immune to alteration. New tattoos fade in a week, and haircuts regrow in a few hours.
You no longer age, nor are subject to effects that cause death. You take damage but heal five hit points at the beginning of your turn.
Alchemical formula: Sulfur (any), Universal Solvent

APOTHEOSIS OF TIN (TRUE TIN)

Wondrous item, legendary
You create one ounce of liquid that burns as a gray flame within the bottle. A drop of this substance animates any object less than nine cubic feet upon which it is poured. It imparts no will, ego, or mobility not already possessed by the object. A sword cannot float but could unsheathe itself only to fall on the floor. A stool could walk across the room on its legs. The objects follow your commands as long as they are simple. This animation is permanent. There are 360 drops to an ounce. It is said that this can be useful if one wishes to provide true life to a construct, though one would need the entire ounce to succeed at such a procedure.
Alchemical formula: Tin, Universal Solvent

APOTHEOSIS OF WATER (ELEMENTAL TRANSUBSTANTIATION)

Wondrous item, legendary
You create a dark blue liquid that glows with an eerie green light.
When imbibed, you gain the ability to breathe water and to walk upon any liquid surface (water, clouds). You gain a swim speed double your walking speed and gain immunity to cold damage. As an action, you may breathe a 15-foot cone of freezing wind. Each creature in the area must make a DC 16 Constitution saving throw. On a failure, the creature takes 5d6 cold damage while on a success it takes half this amount. The ground under the cone is covered in ice for 1d4 + 1 rounds. A creature that starts its movement on the ice or enters the ice on its turn must make a DC 15 Acrobatic check or fall prone. A creature that stands up and then begins to move is considered to be starting its movement.
Your health, movement, vision, and mobility are not affected by cold or ice. You gain vulnerability to fire damage.
Alchemical formula: Water (any), Universal Solvent

MINERAL ALCHEMY

Gemstones contain power. Alchemists developed specialized techniques to extract the magical energy inherent in gemstones. Each type of gemstone has certain abilities and powers it and anyone with the Craft Alchemical Magecraft feat may activate. Mineral alchemy is different from other types of item crafting because it requires nothing beyond the material component of the gemstone of an appropriate value to create it. The value of the gem is a representation of its true value, not an indicator of its market value. You must have a gemstone of the appropriate value in order to craft an alchemical mineral; no substitutes are possible. Gem rarity and availability are factors that must be kept in mind when attempting to craft these items.

Once enchanted, gemstones express their inner energies in five different forms: lozenges, which are swallowed; catagemmas, which are applied to the skin; fulminating charges, which are thrown as grenades; flowers, which are possessed and produce a magical scent; and lenses, which are held to the eyes.

A person can use or be under the effect of only a single type of mineral alchemy at a time. An attempt to use or activate more than one type of mineral alchemy causes all active and inactive alchemical gemstones to turn to gray dust due to the conflict of magical resonances.

Lozenges are gemstones and jewels treated to dissolve in liquids and saliva. It takes an action to consume one and the effects begin at the start of the creature's subsequent turn. If not otherwise noted, the duration of a lozenge is one hour. Once used, the gemstone is destroyed.

Catagemma are gemstones or jewels treated so they are absorbed when rubbed against the skin. It takes an action to do so, and the effect begins immediately. If not otherwise noted, catagemma gemstones last for one hour. Once applied and absorbed into the skin, the gem is destroyed

Fulminating charges are gemstones or jewels treated to explode when thrown. They are thrown as a grenade-like weapon. The gem is destroyed once it explodes.

Flowers are gemstones or jewels treated to release a magical odor. Once prepared, these are activated by squeezing them as an action. A flower affects only the creature that initially squeezed it and only if the creature wears or carries it. If not otherwise noted, flowers have a duration of 24 hours.

Lenses are gemstones or jewels treated to be used as a sighting device. They amplify alchemical and arcane energies to allow auras and other normally invisible weaves and patterns to be seen. They are activated by gently squeezing them, similar to flowers. Any creature can look through the lens. If not otherwise noted, the duration of these effects is an hour, which need not be contiguous, being used in one-minute activations. After the gemstone's energy resonance is expended, the gem turns into worthless gray glass.

Name	Rarity	Crafting Cost	Name	Rarity	Crafting Cost
Agate Catagemma of Warding	Uncommon	200 gp	Diamond Fulminating Charge of Blasting	Varies	Varies
Agate Flower of Rapport	Uncommon	20 gp	Diamond Lens of Electricity Control	Rare	2,000 gp
Agate Lozenge of Hydration	Uncommon	20 gp	Diamond Lozenge of Deliquescence	Very Rare	10,000 gp
Alexandrite Flower of Fortune	Uncommon	100 gp	Emerald Lens of Sight	Uncommon	2,000 gp
Amber Catagemma of Sense Restoration	Uncommon	1,000 gp	Emerald Lozenge of Recall	Uncommon	2,000 gp
Amber Fulminating Charge of Lightning	Varies	Varies	Fire Opal Catagemma of Flame	Rare	2,000 gp
Amber Lozenge of Health	Uncommon	200 gp	Fire Opal Fulminating Charge of Flame	Varies	
Amethyst Catagemma of Arcane Shield	Uncommon	200 gp	Garnet Flower of Health	Uncommon	200 gp
Aquamarine Flower of Concord	Rare	1,000 gp	Garnet Lens of Darkvision	Uncommon	200 gp
Aquamarine Lozenge of Wealth	Very Rare	2,000 gp	Hematite Catagemma of Sealing	Uncommon	20 gp
Bloodstone Catagemma of Invisibility	Rare	1,000 gp	Hematite Lozenge of the Warrior	Common	100 gp
Bloodstone Fulminating Charge of Smoke	Uncommon	100 gp	Jacinth Catagemma of the Heart	Varies	Twice gem used
Carnelian Catagemma of Healing	Varies	Varies	Jacinth Flower of Teleportation Stability	Rare	10,000 gp
Carnelian Flower of Courage	Uncommon	200 gp	Jacinth Lens of Spirituality	Rare	2,000 gp
Carnelian Fulminating Charge of Calm	Rare	100 gp	Jacinth Lozenge of Sleep	Very Rare	10,000 gp
Carnelian Lozenge of Poison Neutralization	Uncommon	400 gp	Jade Catagemma of Preservation	Uncommon	200 gp
Chalcedony Flower of Undead Ward	Rare	200 gp	Jade Lozenge of Resuscitation	Very Rare	2,000 gp
Chalcedony Fulminating Charge of Undead Torment	Varies	Varies	Jasper Catagemma of Aegis	Rare	2,000 gp
Chalcedony Lozenge of Strength	Common	100 gp	Jet Lozenge of Death Ward	Uncommon	200 gp
Chrysoberyl Flower of Luck	Uncommon	100 gp	Lapis Lazuli Flower of Morale	Uncommon	100 gp
Chrysoberyl Fulminating Charge of Banishing	Very Rare	1,000 gp	Malachite Lozenge of Feather Fall	Uncommon	100 gp
Chrysoberyl Lozenge of Fate	Uncommon	100 gp	Onyx Fulminating Charge of Chaos	Varies	Varies
Chrysoprase Flower of Nondetection	Uncommon	100 gp	Peridot Flower of Warding	Rare	1,000 gp
Chrysoprase Lozenge of Oratory	Uncommon	100 gp	Peridot Lozenge of Wit	Uncommon	1,000 gp
Coral Catagemma of Warding	Uncommon	1,000 gp	Rock Crystal Flower of Shade	Uncommon	100 gp
Coral Flower of the Mind	Rare	200 gp	Ruby Catagemma of the Burning Touch	Varies	Varies
Coral Lozenge of the Sea	Uncommon	200 gp	Ruby Flower of Warmth	Uncommon	100 gp
Diamond Catagemma of Fate	Very Rare	10,000 gp	Ruby Lozenge of Fire Breath	Varies	Varies
Diamond Flower of Undead Warding	Very Rare	10,000 gp	Sapphire Lozenge of Escape	Rare	10,000 gp
			Violet Garnet of Health	Rare	1,000 gp

AGATE CATAGEMMA OF WARDING

Wondrous item, uncommon
You gain +2 bonus to saving throws versus poison and lightning and the benefits of the spell *protection from evil and good* for one hour.
Alchemical formula: Agate Gemstone (100 gp), Protection

AGATE FLOWER OF RAPPORT

Wondrous item, uncommon
Once activated, this stone releases a pleasant fragrance in a 10-foot radius. You are granted a +4 bonus to Charisma-based skill checks with creatures within the radius. Once someone has spent one minute within this area, you cast *suggestion* on that creature (spell save DC 14). When you do this, the flower loses its powers.
Alchemical formula: Agate Gemstone (10 gp), Emotion

AGATE LOZENGE OF HYDRATION

Wondrous item, uncommon
You are immune to dehydration for 48 hours once the lozenge is dissolved. Also, if exposed to any disease or illness during this time, you receive a +1 bonus on your saving throw to resist the disease.
Alchemical formula: Agate Gemstone (10 gp), Water (any)

ALEXANDRITE FLOWER OF FORTUNE

Wondrous item, uncommon
This scent provides you with good fortune for 24 hours. Once during this period, you may add 1d6 to the result of any die rolled for an attack, skill check, or saving throw after the result is known. When this occurs, the scent is expended and the gem crumbles to dust.
Alchemical formula: Alexandrite Gemstone (50 gp), Luck

AMBER CATAGEMMA OF SENSE RESTORATION

Wondrous item, uncommon
This catagemma restores hearing and sight.
Alchemical formula: Amber Gemstone (500 gp), Healing

AMBER FULMINATING CHARGE OF LIGHTNING

Wondrous item, varies
When you use an action to throw this gem, it explodes in a sphere of electricity. Each creature in the area must make a saving throw or take lightning damage based on **Table 5–2** on a failure or half as much on a success. The crafting cost, radius, saving throw DC, damage, and rarity depend on the value of the gemstone used.

TABLE 5–3: AMBER FULMINATING CHARGE POWER INCREASE

Crafting Cost	Radius	Save DC	Damage	Rarity
200 gp	5 feet	12	1d4 + 1	Common
400 gp	10 feet	14	2d4 + 2	Common
800 gp	15 feet	16	3d4 + 3	Uncommon
1,600 gp	20 feet	17	4d4 + 4	Uncommon
3,200 gp	25 feet	18	5d4 + 5	Rare
6,400 gp	30 feet	19	6d4 + 6	Rare
12,800 gp	50 feet	22	12d4 + 12	Very Rare

Alchemical formula: Amber Gemstone (half the crafting cost), Electricity

AMBER LOZENGE OF HEALTH

Wondrous item, uncommon
You gain a +4 bonus on any saving throws against disease for the next 48 hours.
Alchemical formula: Amber Gemstone (100 gp), Healing

AMETHYST CATAGEMMA OF ARCANE SHIELD

Wondrous item, uncommon
An amethyst combined with some baboon hair and a swallow feather provides protection versus sorcery. This provides a +1 bonus to all saving throws against spells and spell-like effects for the next 24 hours.
Alchemical formula: Amethyst Gemstone (100 gp), Protection

AQUAMARINE FLOWER OF CONCORD

Wondrous item, rare
This fragrance clears your head and improves the attitude of people near you. You receive a +4 bonus to ability checks based on Intelligence and Charisma for 24 hours.
Alchemical formula: Aquamarine (500 gp), Emotion

AQUAMARINE LOZENGE OF WEALTH

Wondrous item, very rare
You gain the ability to detect precious metals for one hour. While you concentrate, you know the distance and direction to the largest concentration of precious metals such as gold, platinum, and silver within one mile.
Alchemical formula: Aquamarine Gemstone (1,000 gp), Perception

BLOODSTONE CATAGEMMA OF INVISIBILITY

Wondrous item, rare
You gain the effects of the spell *greater invisibility* for one minute.
Alchemical formula: Bloodstone (500 gp), Illusion

BLOODSTONE FULMINATING CHARGE OF SMOKE

Wondrous item, uncommon
When this charged gem is dashed on the floor, it produces a 20-radius sphere of thick black smoke. The area is completely obscured. A creature that ends its turn in the area must succeed on a DC 14 Constitution saving throw or be poisoned until the end of its next turn.
Alchemical formula: Bloodstone (50 gp), Toxin

CARNELIAN CATAGEMMA OF HEALING

Wondrous item, uncommon
This catagemma restores lost hit points. The crafting cost, amount of healing, and the rarity depend on the value of the gemstone used in the catagemma.

TABLE 5–4: CARNELIAN CATAGEMMA POWER INCREASE

Crafting cost	Healing value	Rarity
100 gp	1d4 + 1	Common
200 gp	2d4 + 2	Common
400 gp	3d4 + 3	Uncommon
800 gp	4d4 + 4	Uncommon
1,600 gp	5d4 + 5	Rare
3,200 gp	6d4 + 6	Rare
6,400 gp	7d4 + 7	Rare
12,800 gp	8d4 + 8	Rare

Alchemical formula: Carnelian Gemstone (half the crafting cost), Healing

CARNELIAN FLOWER OF COURAGE

Wondrous item, uncommon
You gain a +4 bonus on saving throws against fear and being charmed.
Alchemical formula: Carnelian Gemstone (100 gp), Protection

CARNELIAN FULMINATING CHARGE OF CALM

Wondrous item, rare
This charged gem explodes in a cloud of dust that covers a 15-foot radius. All within this radius have their emotions calmed. It stops rage, fighting, and revelry. Note that although it temporarily makes creatures sedate and non-hostile for one minute, they are not under any compulsion to remain calm and may strike back at those that attack them.
If the targets are under the effect of spells that affect their fighting abilities, such as *bless*, *heroism*, *rage*, or other mind-affecting compulsions, the bonuses from those spells are suppressed for the duration.
Alchemical formula: Carnelian Gemstone (50 gp), Emotion

CARNELIAN LOZENGE OF POISON NEUTRALIZATION

Wondrous item, uncommon
This lozenge neutralizes any poison in your system when it is applied.
Alchemical formula: Carnelian Gemstone (200 gp), Body

CHALCEDONY FLOWER OF UNDEATH WARD

Wondrous item, rare
The scent this gemstone exudes is not detectable by living creatures, but it confuses and confounds those of the living dead that attempt to assault you. Undead creatures have disadvantage on attacks made against you if they are within 10 feet of you. This scent lasts for 24 hours.
Alchemical formula: Chalcedony Gemstone (100 gp), Life

CHALCEDONY FULMINATING CHARGE OF UNDEAD TORMENT

Wondrous item, varies
This charged gem explodes in a circle of radiant light. Each undead creature in the radius must make a Dexterity saving throw. The creature takes radiant damage per **Table 5–4** on a failure, or half as much on a success. The crafting cost, radius, saving throw DC, damage, and rarity depend on the value of the gemstone used.

TABLE 5–5: CHALCEDONY FULMINATING CHARGE POWER INCREASE

Crafting Cost	Radius	Save DC	Damage	Rarity
400 gp	10 feet	10	2d4 + 2	Common
800 gp	15 feet	12	3d4 + 3	Uncommon
1,600 gp	20 feet	14	4d4 + 4	Uncommon
3,200 gp	25 feet	16	5d4 + 5	Rare
6,400 gp	30 feet	18	6d4 + 6	Rare
12,800 gp	50 feet	20	12d4 + 12	Very Rare

Alchemical formula: Chalcedony Gemstone (half the crafting cost), Light

CHALCEDONY LOZENGE OF STRENGTH

Wondrous item, common
This lozenge provides a +2 bonus to Strength-based checks for one hour.
Alchemical formula: Chalcedony Gemstone (50 gp), Strength

CHRYSOBERYL FLOWER OF LUCK

Wondrous item, uncommon
This stone smells mildly of mint. You gain a +1 bonus to saving throws.
Alchemical formula: Chrysoberyl Gemstone (50 gp), Luck

CHRYSOBERYL FULMINATING CHARGE OF BANISHING

Wondrous item, very rare
This powerful charge has two effects. If thrown on the ground, it works as a banishment or exorcism. Extraplanar creatures within a 10-foot radius must succeed on a DC 10 Charisma saving throw or be banished back to their home plane. This DC increases by 1 per 500 gp of the gem's value over the minimum value. A 5,000 gp Chrysoberyl has a DC 20 saving throw.
The gem also has a second use. If a creature attempts to possess your soul while you carry this item, the attacker's soul is instead contained within the gem, trapping them until they find a way free. If the charge is thrown thereafter, the soul is released, and the charge has no other effect.
Alchemical formula: Chrysoberyl Gemstone (500 gp), Azoth (any), Planar

CHRYSOBERYL LOZENGE OF FATE

Wondrous item, uncommon
You gain a +1 bonus to attack and damage rolls for one hour.
Alchemical formula: Chrysoberyl Gemstone (50 gp), Luck

CHRYSOPRASE FLOWER OF NONDETECTION

Wondrous item, uncommon
This powerful scent extends around you and affects the minds of those nearby. Even though their eyes may see you, their minds refuse to notice your presence. You gain a +5 bonus to Dexterity (Stealth) and any checks made to maintain a disguise for 24 hours.
Alchemical formula: Chrysoprase Gemstone (50 gp), Mind

CHRYSOPRASE LOZENGE OF ORATORY

Wondrous item, uncommon
You gain a +5 bonus to any Charisma-based check that relies on your voice for one hour.
Alchemical formula: Chrysoprase Gemstone (50 gp), Emotion

CORAL CATAGEMMA OF WARDING

Wondrous item, uncommon
You gain a +4 bonus on saving throws against charm, enchantment, compulsion, or fear spells or effects for 24 hours.
Alchemical formula: Coral Gemstone (500 gp), Protection

CORAL FLOWER OF THE MIND

Wondrous item, rare
This scent is a marvelous restorative to the mind. You are cured of any magically induced insanity and gain a +2 bonus on saving throws versus mind-affecting spells. You also are resistant to psychic damage.
Alchemical formula: Coral Gemstone (100 gp), Mind

CORAL LOZENGE OF THE SEA

Wondrous item, uncommon
You gain the ability to breathe underwater as the spell *water breathing* for one hour.
Alchemical formula: Coral Gemstone (100 gp), Water (any)

DIAMOND CATAGEMMA OF FATE

Wondrous item, very rare
Your proficiency bonus increases by 1 and you gain a +2 bonus to Strength-based attack rolls and ability checks for the duration. You are resistant to bludgeoning, piercing, and slashing damage. You gain 1d8 + 1 temporary hit points for each 2,000-gp value of the gem, up to a maximum of 5d8 + 5 at a 10,000-gp diamond gemstone. This catagemma lasts for one hour.
Alchemical formula: Diamond Gemstone (5,000 gp), Prowess

DIAMOND FLOWER OF UNDEAD WARDING

Wondrous item, rare
An undead creature must succeed on a DC 14 Wisdom saving throw to approach within 10 feet of you. Once they do, they must succeed at a DC 18 Constitution saving throw to be able to attack you and they have disadvantage on any attacks made against you from within 10 feet. The scent lasts for 24 hours.
Alchemical formula: Diamond Gemstone (5,000 gp), Life

DIAMOND FULMINATING CHARGE OF BLASTING

Wondrous item, rare
This charged gem explodes in a circle of force. Each creature in the radius must make a Strength saving throw. A creature that fails takes force damage per **Table 5–5**, is knocked prone, and is pushed to edge of the radius of the blast. A creature that succeeds takes half as much damage and is not knocked prone or pushed. The crafting cost, radius, saving throw DC, damage, and rarity depend on the value of the gemstone used.

TABLE 5–6: DIAMOND FULMINATING CHARGE POWER INCREASE

Crafting Cost	Radius	Save DC	Damage	Rarity
4,000 gp	10 feet	12	2d10 + 2	Uncommon
8,000 gp	15 feet	14	3d10 + 3	Uncommon
16,000 gp	20 feet	16	4d10 + 4	Rare
32,000 gp	25 feet	18	5d10 + 5	Rare
64,000 gp	30 feet	20	6d10 + 6	Very Rare
128,000 gp	50 feet	24	12d10 + 12	Legendary

Alchemical formula: Diamond Gemstone (half the crafting cost), Prowess

DIAMOND LENS OF ELECTRICITY CONTROL

Wondrous item, rare
You gain control over electrical flows for up to an hour while looking through this gem.
If you create an effect that causes lightning damage, you may cause it to flow in any direction you choose within its range. A lightning bolt you cast may be directed around a circle of targets, for example.
You may use an action to open a gate to the Elemental Plane of Lightning and alter the electric potential between any two targets. Each target must make a DC 16 Dexterity saving throw, taking 4d6 lightning damage on a failure or half as much with a success as electricity arcs between them. While looking through the lens, you have advantage on saving throws against lightning damage and are resistant to lightning damage.
Alchemical formula: Diamond Gemstone (1,000 gp), Electricity, Planar

DIAMOND LOZENGE OF DELIQUESCENCE

Wondrous item, very rare
You may use an action to shift between the Ethereal and Prime Material planes at will. You may spend up to 10 minutes over the course of 24 hours in the Ethereal Plane, returning to the Prime Material Plane if either time limit expires.
Alchemical formula: Diamond Gemstone (5,000 gp), Azoth (any), Planar

EMERALD LENS OF SIGHT

Wondrous item, uncommon
While looking through this lens, you gain a +10 bonus to Wisdom (Perception) checks that rely on sight. The lens is usable for a full hour of use, which does not have to be consecutive. The time is counted in one-minute increments.
Alchemical formula: Emerald Gemstone (1,000 gp), Perception

EMERALD LOZENGE OF RECALL

Wondrous item, uncommon
When this lozenge dissolves, you recover one or more spell slots. The number of spell slot levels is equal to the price of the gem used in preparing the lozenge divided by 1,000. A 4,000-gp emerald allows you to recover four spell slots in any combination of levels. The highest spell slot you can recall using this lozenge is 4th level.
Alchemical formula: Emerald Gemstone (1,000 gp), Memory

FIRE OPAL CATAGEMMA OF FLAME

Wondrous item, rare
You gain invulnerability to nonmagical fire, resistance to magical fire, and advantage on saving throws to avoid fire damage.
Alchemical formula: Fire Opal (1,000 gp), Protection

FIRE OPAL FULMINATING CHARGE OF FLAME

Wondrous item, varies
This charged gem explodes in a circle of fire. Each creature in the radius must make a Dexterity saving throw. A creature that fails takes fire damage per **Table 5–6**. A creature that succeeds takes half as much damage. The crafting cost, radius, saving throw DC, damage, and rarity depend on the value of the gemstone used.

TABLE 5–7: FIRE OPAL FULMINATING CHARGE POWER INCREASE

Crafting Cost	Radius	Save DC	Damage	Rarity
2,000 gp	5 feet	10	1d8 + 2	Common
4,000 gp	10 feet	12	2d8 + 4	Uncommon
8,000 gp	15 feet	14	3d8 + 6	Uncommon
16,000 gp	20 feet	16	4d8 + 8	Rare
32,000 gp	25 feet	18	5d8 + 10	Rare
64,000 gp	30 feet	20	6d8 + 12	Very Rare
128,000 gp	50 feet	24	12d8 + 24	Legendary

Alchemical formula: Fire Opal (half the crafting cost), Fire (any)

GARNET FLOWER OF HEALTH

Wondrous item, uncommon
This scent provides you a +2 bonus to Constitution for 24 hours.
Alchemical formula: Garnet Gemstone (100 gp), Body

GARNET LENS OF DARKVISION

Wondrous item, uncommon
While this lens is applied to your eye, you gain darkvision 120 feet. This lens functions for an hour of use, which does not need to be consecutive. The time is counted in one-minute increments.
Alchemical formula: Garnet Gemstone (100 gp), Perception

HEMATITE CATAGEMMA OF SEALING

Wondrous item, uncommon
Applying this catagemma to your skin protects against bleeding attacks for the next 24 hours. Anytime you are subject to a bleeding effect, the wounds seal quickly and the bleeding stops. In addition, you stabilize whenever you are dying at the start of your turn.
Alchemical formula: Hematite Gemstone (10 gp), Body

HEMATITE LOZENGE OF THE WARRIOR

Wondrous item, common
You gain a +1 bonus to damage rolls for an hour.
Alchemical formula: Hematite (50 gp), Strength

JACINTH CATAGEMMA OF THE HEART

Wondrous item, rare
You gain 10d6 + 10 temporary hit points. The number of hit points depends on the value of the gem used to craft the catagemma. With a base value of 5,000 gp, you gain 10d6 + 10 temporary hit points. For every additional 1,000 gp of value in the gem beyond 5,000 gp, you gain an additional 2d6 + 2 temporary hit points, up to a maximum gem value of 10,000 gp and 20d6 + 20 hit points.
Alchemical formula: Jacinth Gemstone (varies), Body

JACINTH FLOWER OF TELEPORTATION STABILITY

Wondrous item, rare
This flower's scent makes teleportation easier. The next time you cast teleport and do not land on target, add 2d6 + 1 to the roll that determines where you land. Once this is used, the flower turns to dust.
Alchemical formula: Jacinth Gemstone (5,000 gp), Transportation

JACINTH LENS OF SPIRITUALITY

Wondrous item, rare
These lenses fasten to the your eyes and allow you to see into the Astral and Ethereal planes. You also receive a +2 bonus to hit any astral or ethereal creatures. These lenses function for one hour, which does not need to be consecutive. The time is counted in one-minute increments.
Alchemical formula: Jacinth Gemstone (1,000 gp), Perception

JACINTH LOZENGE OF SLEEP

Wondrous item, very rare
You gain three abilities once you take this lozenge.
You can rest for 1d4 + 1 minutes and gain the benefits of a long rest. This includes the ability to prepare and cast a new allotment of spells. You still need to take time to prepare new spells.
You may touch a single living creature with up to eight hit dice and cause it to fall asleep with no saving throw. It sleeps for one minute or until it takes damage or an adjacent creature uses an action to awaken it.
You can breathe out a cloud of *sleepsmoke* filling a 30-foot cone. All creatures subject to sleep in the area must succeed at a DC 18 Constitution saving throw or fall into a restful slumber for up to one minute. A sleeping creature sleeps for one minute or until it takes damage or an adjacent creature uses an action to awaken it.
Once six uses of any combination of the above three abilities are used, the lozenge loses its magical effects.
Alchemical formula: Jacinth Gemstone (5,000 gp), Stasis (x3)

JADE CATAGEMMA OF PRESERVATION

Wondrous item, uncommon
When this catagemma is applied to a living creature, the creature is protected from magical or natural aging for one hour.
Alchemical formula: Jade Gemstone (100 gp), Stasis

JADE LOZENGE OF RESUSCITATION

Wondrous item, very rare
When inserted into the mouth of a creature that has died within the last hour, this pill restores some semblance of life. The creature gains 1 hit point and one level of exhaustion. For the next hour, its movement is limited to five feet, and at the end of any minute that contains strenuous activity, the creature must succeed on a DC 5 Constitution check or die.
Alchemical formula: Jade Gemstone (1,000 gp), Life

JASPER CATAGEMMA OF AEGIS

Wondrous item, rare
When this catagemma is rubbed into your skin, it acts as a shield that absorbs damage. The damage of each attack that hits you is reduced by 5. Once the catagemma absorbs 80 hit points of absorbed damage or after 24 hours pass, it ceases to function.
Alchemical formula: Jasper Gemstone (1,000 gp), Protection

JET LOZENGE OF DEATH WARD

Wondrous item, uncommon
You gain advantage on any death saving throws for the next 24 hours.
Alchemical formula: Jet Gemstone (100 gp), Life

LAPIS LAZULI FLOWER OF MORALE

Wondrous item, uncommon
You experience a temporary increase in your leadership ability. You gain a +1 bonus to any Charisma-based checks, and your allies gain a +1 bonus to saving throws to resist fear.
Alchemical formula: Lapis Lazuli Gemstone (50 gp), Emotion

MALACHITE LOZENGE OF FEATHER FALL

Wondrous item, uncommon
You can use your reaction to fall like a feather. Your rate of descent slows to 60 feet per round. If you land while the lozenge is active, you take no falling damage and can land on your feet. The lozenge lasts for 24 hours, and you can use it as many times as you like within that time period.
Alchemical formula: Malachite Gemstone (50 gp), Flight

ONYX FULMINATING CHARGE OF CHAOS

Wondrous item, varies
This charged gem explodes in a circle of chaotic energy. Each creature in the radius must make a Wisdom saving throw. A creature that fails takes necrotic damage per **Table 5–7** below. A creature that succeeds takes half as much damage. The crafting cost, radius, saving throw DC, damage, and rarity depend on the value of the gemstone used.

TABLE 5–8: ONYX FULMINATING CHARGE POWER INCREASE

Crafting Cost	Radius	Save DC	Damage	Rarity
200 gp	5 feet	10	1d4 + 1	Common
400 gp	10 feet	12	2d4 + 2	Common
800 gp	15 feet	14	3d4 + 3	Uncommon
1,600 gp	20 feet	16	4d4 + 4	Uncommon
3,200 gp	25 feet	18	5d4 + 5	Rare
6,400 gp	30 feet	20	6d4 + 6	Rare
12,800 gp	50 feet	22	12d4 + 12	Very Rare

Alchemical formula: Onyx Gemstone (half the crafting cost), Death

PERIDOT FLOWER OF WARDING

Wondrous item, rare
This scent smells of fragrant oils and petals. You gain a +4 bonus to saving throws against spells and spell-like effects for 24 hours.
Alchemical formula: Peridot Gemstone (500 gp), Protection

PERIDOT LOZENGE OF WIT

Wondrous item, uncommon

This lozenge grants you a razor-sharp tongue that allows you to taunt an opponent. As a bonus action, you can use your voice to enrage an opponent. When you do so, one target that can hear and understand you must succeed on a Wisdom saving throw. The DC is 10 + your Charisma modifier + your proficiency bonus. A target who fails becomes enraged. While enraged, the target must use its action to attack you and cannot take reactions. The effect ends if you fall unconscious or if the creature can no longer hear you. An enraged creature may repeat the saving throw at the end of each of its turns, ending the effect on a success. Each round the creature is enraged, you may continue to use your bonus action to taunt the creature. When you do this, the DC for the target's saving throw increases by +1 to a maximum of 30. Once a creature succeeds on the saving throw or it ceases to be enraged, it is immune to your taunting for 24 hours.

Alchemical formula: Peridot Gemstone (500 gp), Mind

ROCK CRYSTAL FLOWER OF SHADE

Wondrous item, uncommon

This scent cools and refreshes you, maintaining the temperature of 68° Fahrenheit up to an ambient temperature of 160° Fahrenheit. If the temperature rises above 160° Fahrenheit, you feel the temperature rise by 1 degree for each degree it is over 160° Fahrenheit. You are immune to heat stroke and exhaustion and other effects of high temperatures but gain no resistance or immunity to fire damage. Once activated, the effects last for 24 hours.

Alchemical formula: Rock Crystal Gemstone (50 gp), Cold

RUBY CATAGEMMA OF THE BURNING TOUCH

Wondrous item, varies

Your touch leaves searing wounds on opponents. If you succeed on an unarmed strike, the target takes additional fire damage per **Table 5–8**. The crafting cost, damage, and rarity depend on the value of the gemstone used. The catagemma lasts for one hour.

TABLE 5–9: RUBY CATAGEMMA POWER INCREASE

Crafting Cost	Damage	Rarity
4,000 gp	1d6 + 1	Common
4,000 gp	2d6 + 2	Uncommon
8,000 gp	3d6 + 3	Uncommon
16,000 gp	4d6 + 4	Rare
32,000 gp	5d6 + 5	Rare
64,000 gp	6d6 + 6	Very Rare
128,000 gp	12d6 + 12	Legendary

Alchemical formula: Ruby Gemstone (half the crafting cost), Fire (any)

RUBY FLOWER OF WARMTH

Wondrous item, uncommon

This scent warms and comforts you, maintaining a temperature of 68° Fahrenheit down to an ambient temperature of −60° Fahrenheit. If the ambient temperature drops below this, you feel the temperature lower by 1 degree for every degree lower than −60° Fahrenheit. You are immune to frostbite and hypothermia and other low temperature influences such as freezing shock but do not gain resistance or immunity to cold damage.

Alchemical formula: Ruby Gemstone (50 gp), Fire (any)

RUBY LOZENGE OF FIRE BREATH

Wondrous item, varies

You can release a cone of fire as an action. The size of the cone depends on the value of the gem used. Each creature in the area must make a Dexterity saving throw, taking fire damage based on the value of the gem used on a failure or half as much on a success. Your fire breath has a recharge of 5–6, and the lozenge is effective for one hour. See **Table 5–9** below for crafting cost, cone size, fire damage, saving throw, and rarity.

TABLE 5–10: RUBY LOZENGE EFFECTS

Crafting Cost	Size of Cone	Fire Damage	Saving Throw DC	Rarity
2,000 gp	20 feet	1d10 + 1	12	Uncommon
4,000 gp	30 feet	2d10 + 2	14	Rare
6,000 gp	40 feet	3d10 + 3	16	Rare
8,000 gp	50 feet	4d10 + 4	18	Very Rare
10,000 gp	60 feet	5d10 + 5	20	Very Rare

Alchemical formula: Ruby Gemstone (half the crafting cost), Fire (any)

SAPPHIRE LOZENGE OF ESCAPE

Wondrous item, rare

The next time you are grappled, bound, or otherwise physically restrained or subjected to a magical imprisonment effect such as *maze*, *imprisonment*, or *forcecage*, you immediately teleport to a place of your choice that you can see within 400 feet. Once you use the lozenge to teleport, or after one month passes, the lozenge loses its magical nature.

Alchemical formula: Sapphire Gemstone (5,000 gp), Agility

VIOLET GARNET OF HEALTH

Wondrous item, rare

This scent increases your Constitution by +4 and you gain 2d8 + 2 temporary hit points immediately and each time you complete a short rest. It has a duration of 25 hours.

Alchemical formula: Violet Garnet Gemstone (500 gp), Healing

SIGILS

Sigils are magical runes. They are a specialized form of glyph engraved on metal and worn like an amulet. When you use an action to focus on the sigil, you activate its effect. Unless otherwise noted, the effect lasts for one hour. Multiple sigils may be carried and used. Sigils may be activated up to twice daily. Between any two activations of any two sigils, you must not use a sigil for at least six hours. If you attempt a sigil within six hours of having activated a sigil, you fall unconscious and gain a level of exhaustion. Under no circumstances can you activate any number of sigils more than twice a day, even if they are of different types.

Anyone may use a sigil, but the sigil must be made for the use of a specific person. If anyone besides the person the sigil was made for attempts to use the sigil, it has no effect. Anyone with the Craft Alchemical Magecraft feat may also reassign sigils using a process that costs 1,000 gp in raw materials and takes one day. Crafting a sigil also requires the Craft Alchemical Magecraft feat. The crafting cost is given below and the DC for the Alchemist's Supplies check depends on the sigil's rarity.

There are three categories of sigils: silver (uncommon), gold (rare), and platinum (very rare). Examples of several types are given below, although other reasonable sigils can be created. Silver sigils usually contain minor personal effects equivalent to second level spells or less, golden sigils contain more powerful detection and enhancement effects equivalent to 3rd- to 5th-level spells, and platinum sigils contain more damaging and debilitating effects equivalent to 6th- to 8th-level spells in power.

Sigils do *not* directly duplicate spell effects (see potions) but are a type of enchanted rune crafted specifically for a person to achieve a desired end. They are quite popular charms with merchants and nobility who can afford to have them crafted. Certain occupations and jobs also use sigils as tools in order to accomplish dangerous or distasteful jobs.

Note that actual gemstones are required to create these, not carats of gemstone powder.

TABLE 5–11: SIGIL CRAFTING COSTS

Name	Material	Rarity	Crafting Cost
Sigil of Curing	Silver	Uncommon	2,000 gp
Sigil of Dimensional Jaunts	Platinum	Very Rare	18,000 gp
Sigil of Extension	Gold	Rare	6,000 gp
Sigil of Extrasensory Perception	Gold	Rare	6,000 gp
Sigil of Fear	Platinum	Very Rare	18,000 gp
Sigil of Fire Resistance	Silver	Uncommon	2,000 gp
Sigil of Flame	Platinum	Very Rare	18,000 gp
Sigil of Fortitude	Silver	Uncommon	2,000 gp
Sigil of Gusting Winds	Platinum	Very rare	18,000 gp
Sigil of Healing	Silver	Uncommon	2,000 gp
Sigil of Holding	Platinum	Very Rare	18,000 gp
Sigil of Hypnotism	Platinum	Very Rare	18,000 gp
Sigil of Life Detection	Gold	Rare	6,000 gp
Sigil of Light	Gold	Rare	6,000 gp
Sigil of Planar Detection	Silver	Uncommon	2,000 gp
Sigil of Silence	Platinum	Very Rare	18,000 gp
Sigil of Sprightly Stride	Silver	Uncommon	2,000 gp
Sigil of Strength	Silver	Uncommon	2,000 gp
Sigil of Swaddling	Silver	Uncommon	2,000 gp
Sigil of the Sea	Gold	Rare	6,000 gp
Sigil of Tongues	Gold	Rare	6,000 gp

SIGIL OF CURING

Wondrous item, uncommon (requires attunement)
When activated, this sigil begins to cure your diseases. If activated while resting once a day for six days, you are cured of all diseases. While doing this, you automatically succeed on any saving throws against disease. If you engage in activities besides bed rest, it disrupts the healing process. If you are not already cured, you must begin the six-day cycle again.
Alchemical formula: Silver, Water (any), Healing

SIGIL OF DIMENSIONAL JAUNTS

Wondrous item, very rare (requires attunement)
You can use an action to transport yourself to any unoccupied location you can see within 400 feet. Anything held is transported with the user. Once activated, you may make one such jump every minute.
Alchemical formula: Platinum, Air (any), Transportation

SIGIL OF EXTENSION

Wondrous item, rare (requires attunement)
The next spell you cast after activating this charm has its duration increased by 50%.
Alchemical formula: Gold, Azoth (any), Stasis

SIGIL OF EXTRASENSORY PERCEPTION

Wondrous item, rare (requires attunement)
You can detect the thoughts of those within 30 feet and after a period of concentration, sift through them. Each round of concentration produces a more powerful effect. The effects of this sigil last for one minute.

TABLE 5–12: EXTRASENSORY PERCEPTION CONCENTRATION EFFECTS

Round	Effect
1	Detect the presence or absence of thinking creatures.
2	Detect the number and intelligence of each creature.
3	Detect the surface thoughts of a creature in the area. Targets receive a DC 14 Wisdom saving throw to resist if they wish. A failure allows you to try again for the duration. Each time a target succeeds on this saving throw, you take 1d4 psychic damage.
4	Allows you to scan a mind for the answer to a specific question or to get information on a general topic. This can be used only on a target that has had its surface thoughts detected. The target can succeed at a DC 12 Wisdom saving throw to resist. A failure to scan the target's mind allows you to try again for the duration. Every time a target succeeds on this saving throw, you take 2d4 psychic damage.

Alchemical formula: Gold, Azoth (any), Perception

SIGIL OF FEAR

Wondrous item, very rare (requires attunement)
When activated, enemies within 60 feet that can see you must succeed on a DC 20 Wisdom saving throw or become frightened for up to one minute. A frightened creature must move away from you as quickly as possible, using its action to dash. A frightened creature may repeat the saving throw at the end of each of its turns, ending the effect on a success.
Alchemical formula: Platinum, Azoth (any), Fear

SIGIL OF FIRE RESISTANCE

Wondrous item, uncommon (requires attunement)
You are resistant to fire damage and gain a +2 bonus to saving throws made versus fire.
Alchemical formula: Silver, Fire (any), Protection

SIGIL OF FLAME

Wondrous item, very rare (requires attunement)
Once activated, you may use an action to produce a gout of flame. It strikes out in a line five feet wide and 15 feet long. All targets in the area must make a DC 16 Dexterity saving throw, taking 4d6 + 6 fire damage on a failure or half as much on a success. This effect lasts for one minute and allows the user to activate a gout of flame as an action any time during this duration.
Alchemical formula: Platinum, Fire (any), Body, Transmutation

SIGIL OF FORTITUDE

Wondrous item, uncommon (requires attunement)
When activated, this sigil prevents sickness and nausea. For the duration, you are immune to becoming nauseated. If activated while ill, this calms your stomach and nerves, and any penalties from the disease are temporarily eliminated. At the end of the duration, the protection ends. If still under effects that cause those conditions or effects, they return.
Alchemical formula: Silver, Body, Protection

SIGIL OF GUSTING WINDS

Wondrous item, very rare (requires attunement)
When held forth and invoked, a mighty gust of wind originates from the sigil and moves in the direction the sigil is displayed. The 30- to 50-mile per hour winds extinguish small fires and fan larger ones. Small or smaller flying creatures are blown back 1d6 x 10 feet. Medium flying creatures must succeed at a DC 15 Strength check in order to move at half-speed toward the wind. Larger flying creatures are not affected. Vapors and gases are dispersed. Medium and smaller creatures on the ground must make DC 15 Strength (Athletics) checks to move forward at full speed. They may move at half-speed in the area with no penalty. Missile and thrown weapon attacks that pass through the area automatically miss. This effect covers an area up to 20 feet wide and 100 feet long. It lasts for one minute and may be aimed as you desire.
Alchemical formula: Platinum, Air (any), Strength (x3)

SIGIL OF HEALING

Wondrous item, uncommon (requires attunement)
You heal 1d6 + 1 hit points at the beginning of your next turn.
Alchemical formula: Silver, Healing

SIGIL OF HOLDING

Wondrous item, very rare (requires attunement)
Once activated, you can use an action to attempt to paralyze creatures. Each round you may attempt to hold any number of humanoid creatures or up to two non-humanoid creatures that are not constructs or undead. The creatures must be within a 30-foot square centered on a spot within 60 feet of you. Each creature must make a Wisdom saving throw or be paralyzed for one minute. The DC depends on the targets. If attempting to paralyze one or more humanoids, the DC is 18. If attempting to hold one non-humanoid, it is 20, and 16 if attempting to hold two non-humanoids. A creature that is already paralyzed when you target it has its DC increased by +2. A paralyzed creature may repeat the saving throw at the end of each of its turns, ending the effect on a success.
This effect lasts for one minute, and you may target a new group of creatures or the same creatures each round. Targeting a new group frees the old group.
Alchemical formula: Platinum, Stasis (x3)

SIGIL OF HYPNOTISM

Wondrous item, very rare (requires attunement)
When you use an action to hold this sigil aloft, it spins, reflecting interesting pulses of light. All living creatures within 30 feet not allied with you must succeed on a DC 18 Wisdom saving throw or become fascinated. A fascinated creature takes no actions and doesn't move for as long as the sigil is spins. During this time, you may make suggestions to creatures that understand your language. They view that suggestion as reasonable as long as it doesn't result in harming themselves or others they care about. A creature that takes damage is no longer fascinated by your sigil. A creature may use an action to distract a fascinated creature enough to allow it to attempt another saving throw. Creatures that have been fascinated do not recall that it occurred. This sigil spins for up to one minute after it is activated.
Alchemical formula: Platinum, Control, Mind

SIGIL OF LIFE DETECTION

Wondrous item, rare (requires attunement)
You can determine the presence of life in all creatures within your vision. You see connections to the Positive or Negative Material planes. You know how much life a creature has, as well as if it is living, dead, or undead. This vision extends through walls and other obstructions to vision, but is blocked by more than 10 feet of stone, one foot of metal, or a thin sheet of lead. When activated, this ability lasts for one minute.
Alchemical formula: Gold, Life

SIGIL OF LIGHT

Wondrous item, rare (requires attunement)
The sigil sheds bright light in a 60-foot sphere that is visible only to you.
Alchemical formula: Gold, Light

SIGIL OF PLANAR DETECTION

Wondrous item, uncommon (requires attunement)
For the next minute, you know if any creature you can see is an aberration, a
celestial, an elemental, a fey, a fiend, or undead.
Alchemical formula: Silver, Perception

SIGIL OF SILENCE

Wondrous item, very rare (requires attunement)
This sigil silences a single creature of your choice that you can see within
30 feet. When presented to a target, the target must succeed on a DC 10
Charisma saving throw or its lips disappear and appear on the sigil itself for
one minute or until the creature dies. The lips still appear to move, but no
sound comes out, and the target no longer has a mouth. If a target has a bite
attack, breath weapon, or other effect, it no longer functions.
Alchemical formula: Platinum, Body, Transmutation

SIGIL OF SPRIGHTLY STRIDE

Wondrous item, uncommon (requires attunement)
This sigil allows you to be unimpeded by your environment. You treat
difficult terrain as normal terrain and nonmagical plants can't prevent
you from moving or slow you down. You may pass through underbrush,
overgrowth, and briars without leaving a trace. You have advantage on ability
checks made to escape being grappled.
Alchemical formula: Silver, Agility

SIGIL OF STRENGTH

Wondrous item, uncommon (requires attunement)
Your Strength increases by +4 for 1d4 + 4 rounds.
Alchemical formula: Silver, Strength

SIGIL OF SWADDLING

Wondrous item, uncommon (requires attunement)
You gain resistance to bludgeoning damage. You are also kept warm and
protected from nonmagical extremes of cold for the duration. This damage
resistance lasts for one minute but the warmth lasts for a full six hours.
Alchemical formula: Silver, Protection

SIGIL OF THE SEA

Wondrous item, rare (requires attunement)
You can breathe water or other aerated liquids as if they were air. You grow
webbing between your fingers, hair recedes into your body, and your skin
becomes thick and rubbery. You gain a swim speed of 30 feet, as well as
a +10 bonus to Strength (Athletics) checks made to swim. If you are not
wearing armor, your Armor Class increases by +2.
Alchemical formula: Gold, Transmutation

SIGIL OF TONGUES

Wondrous item, rare (requires attunement)
You can read and comprehend any languages, and when you speak to a
creature that understand a language, it can understand what you are saying.
Alchemical formula: Gold, Perception

TALISMANS

Talismans are special items that take pure alchemical gemstones and focus their power. There are only 12 different talismans, one for each type of alchemical gemstone, and each has a different power. In order to create and use talismans, the Craft Alchemical Magecraft feat is required. Though each talisman can be created, only one can be worn at a time and you must attune to it before it functions. The effects are always present while you wear the talisman.

TABLE 5–13: TALISMAN CRAFTING COSTS

Name	Rarity	Crafting Cost
Agate	Rare	20,630 gp
Amethyst	Rare	15,630 gp
Diamond	Rare	9,980 gp
Emerald	Very Rare	13,280 gp
Jade	Rare	20,780 gp
Malachite	Rare	10,780 gp
Moonstone	Rare	20,780 gp
Onyx	Very Rare	12,780 gp
Pearl	Very Rare	20,780 gp
Ruby	Rare	20,780 gp
Sapphire	Very Rare	20,780 gp
Turquoise	Very Rare	45,780 gp

AGATE TALISMAN

Wondrous item, rare (requires attunement by a creature with the Craft Alchemical Magecraft feat)
You gain a +10 bonus to Wisdom (Insight) and Charisma (Deception) checks.
Alchemical formula: Agate, Perception

AMETHYST TALISMAN

Wondrous item, rare (requires attunement by a creature with the Craft Alchemical Magecraft feat)
You gain innate spellcasting using Charisma as your spellcasting modifier. You can cast the following spells without material components:
3/day: *calm emotions, compulsion, enthrall, fear, hideous laughter*
1/week: *antipathy/sympathy*
Alchemical formula: Amethyst, Mind

DIAMOND TALISMAN

Wondrous item, rare (requires attunement by a creature with the Craft Alchemical Magecraft feat)
While wearing this talisman, you can see invisible and ethereal creatures within 60 feet.
Alchemical formula: Diamond, Perception

EMERALD TALISMAN

Wondrous item, very rare (requires attunement by a creature with the Craft Alchemical Magecraft feat)
You have a +2 bonus to Armor Class and all saving throws while wearing this talisman.
Alchemical formula: Emerald, Protection

JADE TALISMAN

Wondrous item, rare (requires attunement by a creature with the Craft Alchemical Magecraft feat)
You may cast *lesser restoration* three times per day without using a spell slot or material components. You have advantage on saving throws versus poison.
Alchemical formula: Jade, Healing

MALACHITE TALISMAN

Wondrous item, rare (requires attunement by a creature with the Craft Alchemical Magecraft feat)
You can breathe underwater while wearing this talisman.
Alchemical formula: Malachite, Transmutation

MOONSTONE TALISMAN

Wondrous item, rare (requires attunement by a creature with the Craft Alchemical Magecraft feat)
You are resistant to cold damage and have a +4 bonus to saving throws against cold and ice and its effects.
Alchemical formula: Moonstone, Cold

ONYX TALISMAN

Wondrous item, very rare (requires attunement by a creature with the Craft Alchemical Magecraft feat)
As an action, you may cast the spell *invisibility* on yourself without using a spell slot or material components.
Alchemical formula: Onyx, Stealth

PEARL TALISMAN

Wondrous item, very rare (requires attunement by a creature with the Craft Alchemical Magecraft feat)
At the beginning of your turn, you heal 1 hit point if you are not at 0 hit points. You can cast *cure wounds* three times per day without using a spell slot or material components.
Alchemical formula: Pearl, Healing

RUBY TALISMAN

Wondrous item, rare (requires attunement by a creature with the Craft Alchemical Magecraft feat)
You are resistant to fire damage and have a +4 bonus to saving throws against fire and its effects.
Alchemical formula: Ruby, Protection

SAPPHIRE TALISMAN

Wondrous item, very rare (requires attunement by a creature with the Craft Alchemical Magecraft feat)
You gain a fly speed of 60 while wearing this talisman.
Alchemical formula: Sapphire, Flight

TURQUOISE TALISMAN

Wondrous item, very rare (requires attunement by a creature with the Craft Alchemical Magecraft feat)
Three times per day, you can move up to 100 feet through wood, plaster, or stone, but not through metal or other harder materials. You leave no trace of your movement through these materials. While within the material, you gain tremorsense 60 feet. You can remain within the material for up to one hour, but after moving 100 feet or spending an hour within the material, you are ejected into the nearest open area. The effects end when you leave the solid surface.
Alchemical formula: Turquoise, Planar

CHAPTER SIX: ALCHEMY IN STRUCTURES

Alchemical mortars are special materials used in the construction of keeps, towers, temples and other permanent stone structures. The walls of ancient buildings were not solid stone or rock. Large 10-foot-thick castle walls often had a mortar-type filler between layers. This material was also packed between the bricks or stone used when constructing the walls. A similar coating was used between outer and inner wooden walls, and indeed is still used today! This binding substance is a mortar, which can be enhanced by alchemical processes.

Each mortar creates about a gallon of small, pebble-sized granules of crystal and stone. These are often multicolored, looking much like small jewels and gems. They are mixed with standard mortars, varnishes, and fillers during construction. Most can be applied to stone and wooden walls.

Batches are crafted in five-pound increments, with each pound covering one 10-foot cube of space. One batch (five pounds) of alchemical mortar will cover a 10-foot-thick wall that is 10 feet high and 50 feet long. Each section of a wall may be treated only by one shroud and one bulwark type. Any other attempts cause the magical energies to conflict and fail. Sections may be treated with multiple ward and stone types. The types are listed after the name. Shrouds and wards affect one side of the wall only, which must be selected permanently upon use.

These alchemical technologies developed in response to magical environments. The desire to create certain areas safe from scrying and teleportation, or to protect a city from flying foes, drove the creation of these items to protect areas. Now, when the characters encounter areas that are warded in certain areas within the game, you can address their existence within the structure of the rules. This also provides options for characters who wish to defend against such techniques being used against them.

These effects are considered magic items for the purposes of *dispel magic*. Each 10-foot cubic section of wall is considered a single item. Suppressing the effect of a mortar does not affect the entire wall, just the section targeted. Because these are alchemical items and have no spell level, the DC for the *dispel magic* check is equal to the crafting DC for the item. Doing enough damage to the wall to destroy it also terminates the effect.

For mortars that have effects that allow for a saving throw, the DC is equal to the spell save DC of the person who prepares the mortar.

Name	Rarity	Purchase Cost	Crafting Cost
Acid Shroud	Rare	Varies	4,000 gp
Arcana Ward	Rare	Varies	5,000 gp
Blade Shroud	Very Rare	Varies	10,000 gp
Clearstone	Uncommon	Varies	4,000 gp
Death Ward	Rare	Varies	1,000 gp
Fire Ward	Rare	Varies	1,000 gp
Fissurestone	Very Rare	Varies	15,000 gp
Flame Shroud	Very Rare	Varies	15,000 gp
Flight Ward	Very Rare	Varies	10,000 gp
Hypnosis Shroud	Rare	Varies	5,000 gp
Ice Shroud	Rare	Varies	5,000 gp
Lightning Shroud	Very Rare	Varies	15,000 gp
Mirror Shroud	Uncommon	Varies	1,000 gp
Mist Shroud	Uncommon	Varies	1,000 gp
Mist Shroud, Acidic	Rare	Varies	10,000 gp
Mist Shroud, Death	Very Rare	Varies	15,000 gp
Mist Shroud, Solid	Rare	Varies	5,000 gp
Mist Shroud, Stinking	Rare	Varies	5,000 gp
Phasing Ward	Very Rare	Varies	5,000 gp
Repairstone	Rare	Varies	5,000 gp
Scrying Ward	Rare	Varies	4,000 gp
Shatter Ward	Uncommon	Varies	1,000 gp
Stalwart Bulwark I	Common	Varies	1,000 gp
Stalwart Bulwark II	Uncommon	Varies	2,000 gp
Stalwart Bulwark III	Rare	Varies	5,000 gp
Stalwart Bulwark IV	Very Rare	Varies	10,000 gp
Stalwart Bulwark V	Legendary	Unavailable	15,000 gp
Swarm Shroud	Rare	Varies	15,000 gp
Teleportation Ward	Rare	Varies	5,000 gp
Terror Shroud	Very rare	Varies	10,000 gp
Time Ward	Uncommon	Varies	1,000 gp
Weather Ward	Uncommon	Varies	1,000 gp
Web Shroud	Uncommon	Varies	2,000 gp
Wind Shroud	Rare	Varies	5,000 gp

ACID SHROUD

Wondrous item (shroud), rare
This mortar causes the wall sections to secrete a powerful acid. A creature that ends its turn in contact with the wall the wall takes 1 acid damage and 1 point at the beginning of its turn for each subsequent turn until it takes an action to cleanse itself. The ongoing damage is cumulative so that a creature that has ended three turns in contact with the wall takes 3 acid damage at the start of its next turn. The acid can be washed off the skin with an alkaline solution such as wine but cannot be removed from the wall.
Objects in contact with the wall take 4d6 acid damage each round of contact. This is enough to dissolve boots, gloves, ladders leaning against the wall, and any other non-living item. Ladders as they dissolve have a cumulative 25% chance per round of sliding down the wall.
This mortar may be applied only to stone walls.
Alchemical formula: Diamond (x10), Turquoise (100), Salt (any)

ARCANA WARD

Wondrous item (ward), rare
This mystical ward protects the wall from magical effects and spells. When the wall is targeted by spells such as *disintegrate*, *stone shape*, or other magical effects, it may make a saving throw using the alchemist's spellcasting bonus against the spell, resisting all effects on a success. This ward may be applied to stone and wood structures.
Alchemical formula: Diamond (x10), Onyx (x100), Earth (any)

BLADE SHROUD

Wondrous item (shroud), very rare
This shroud covers the wall in constantly shifting, razor-sharp piercing stones. A creature or object that starts its turn in contact with the wall or that comes into contact with the wall for the first time on its turn takes 10d6 slashing damage.
This mortar may be applied only to stone walls.
Alchemical formula: Diamond (x10), Ruby (x100), Turquoise (x100), Earth (any)

CLEARSTONE

Wondrous item (stone), uncommon
This stone, when mixed and used to secure a wall, turns the relevant wall sections transparent. This produces a glass-like effect where the contours of the wall are still visible, but it is possible to see through them. This does not affect the composition of the walls; their ability to resist and sustain damage remains the same.
This mortar may be applied to stone and wooden walls.
Alchemical formula: Diamond (x10), Sapphire (x100), Air (any), Earth (any)

DEATH WARD

Wondrous item (ward), rare
This holy ward protects against nefarious hordes of undead. Any undead that approaches within 20 feet or starts its turn within this range takes 1d4 + 1 radiant damage. An undead that touches the wall for the first time on its turn or that starts its turn in contact with the wall takes 3d6 + 3 radiant damage and must succeed at a Wisdom saving throw or gain the frightened condition for one minute.
Alchemical formula: Diamond (x10), Jade (x10), Onyx (x10), Life

FIRE WARD

Wondrous item (ward), rare
This ward protects walls from fire. If the fire comes in contact with the wall, it may make a saving throw using the alchemist's spellcasting bonus against the spell, resisting all effects on a success. In addition, the wall is resistant to fire damage. If using the catching fire rules in **Chapter One: Alchemy Basics**, fires that are used against a wall with this ward diminish on a damage roll of 1, 2, or 3.
This mortar may be applied to wooden and stone walls.
Alchemical formula: Diamond (x10), Onyx (x10), Ruby (x10), Fire (any), Protection

FISSURESTONE

Wondrous item (stone), very rare
This marvelous stone allows you to create portals with your bare hand in the stone. When the mortar is applied, choose a password or one or more items. Anyone who says the password or possesses one of the items may touch the wall as an action and create openings in any section of the wall. These openings can be up to 100 square feet and can travel through the entire length of fissurestone-enhanced walls. This can be used to create portals, footholds, doorways, and passages. If not closed the same way they are opened, these passageways close themselves one minute later. Anyone caught inside is shunted to the nearest open space.
This mortar may be applied to wooden and stone walls.
Alchemical formula: Agate (x100), Diamond (x100), Pearl (x100), Planar, Transportation

FLAME SHROUD

Wondrous item (shroud), very rare
This shroud covers a wall in flames that burn eternally, with no visible fuel source. It is actual fire and produces heat, light, and sets other things aflame. The flame is the color desired by the creator. The wall is immune to any damage from this effect. A creature that ends its turn within five feet of the wall takes 1d4 + 1 fire damage and is at risk for catching fire. A creature or object that ends its turn in contact with the wall takes 2d6 fire damage and catches fire if it is inflammable.
This mortar may be applied only to stone walls.
Alchemical formula: Diamond (x100), Ruby (x100), Fire (any), Pain

FLIGHT WARD

Wondrous item (ward), very rare
This ward protects the interior of a wall from flying opponents. A creature that flies above the wall within 100 feet of it or within 50 feet of the exterior face of the wall is hit with a strong gust of wind. The creature must succeed on an Athletics check or be unable to move toward the interior of the wall. The DC of the check is equal to the spell save DC of the creator of the ward.
This mortar may be applied to wooden and stone walls.
Alchemical formula: Diamond (x100), Sapphire (x100), Air (any), Stasis

HYPNOSIS SHROUD

Wondrous item (shroud), rare
This shroud causes the formation of a fascinating pattern that enraptures anyone who approaches this wall. A creature that ends its turn within 20 feet of the wall must make a Wisdom saving throw. A creature that fails is fascinated for 4d4 rounds. While fascinated, the creature is unable to take actions or reactions. A creature that takes damage may attempt the saving throw again, ending the effects on a success. Once the effects end for a creature, they are immune to them for 24 hours.
Alchemical formula: Diamond (x10), Pearl (x100), Salt (any), Illusion

ICE SHROUD

Wondrous item (shroud), rare
This shroud covers a stone wall with a heavy sheet of ice that never melts. The ice is slick and difficult to climb, adding +10 to the DC of any Athletics checks made to climb the wall. If not wearing appropriate cold-weather gear, a creature that ends its turn within 10 feet of the wall takes 1d4 cold damage.
This mortar may be applied only to stone walls.
Alchemical formula: Diamond (x10), Malachite (x100), Salt (any), Cold

LIGHTNING SHROUD

Wondrous item (shroud), very rare
This shroud coats the wall in arcing electricity. From a distance, the wall seems to sparkle and flash. A creature that starts its turn within 10 feet of the wall or that comes within 10 feet for the first time on its turn must make a Dexterity saving throw, taking 4d8 lightning damage on a failure or half as much on a success. A creature that touches the wall takes 9d8 lightning damage.
If multiple creatures are in a 10-foot square, only one is struck per round. Everyone touching the wall at any time takes the damage.
This shroud may be applied only to stone walls.
Alchemical formula: Diamond (x100), Onyx (x100), Sapphire (x100), Electricity

MIRROR SHROUD

Wondrous item (shroud), uncommon
This shroud causes a defensive wall to become highly reflective. This makes targeting the wall or things behind it more difficult than normal. All ranged attacks made in the direction of the wall have a –2 penalty to hit. Bright lights or other modifiers may cause this penalty to increase. All creatures with gaze attacks must avert their gaze or be subjected to their own reflection.
This mortar may be applied to wood and stone walls.
Alchemical formula: Diamond (x10), Sapphire (10), Salt (any), Illusion

MIST SHROUD

Wondrous item (shroud), uncommon
This shroud covers the wall in mist. This mist obscures the wall and anything within 20 feet. Creatures and objects within this area have partial concealment if five feet from the edge of the cloud or another person, or total concealment if farther away. Variations of the mist shroud exist, but only one may be used on any given wall.
Mist shrouds may be applied to wooden and stone walls.
Alchemical formula: Diamond (x10), Moonstone (x10), Stealth

MIST SHROUD, ACIDIC

Wondrous item (shroud), rare
As per *mist shroud* and a creature that ends its turn within the mist takes 2d4 acid damage.
Alchemical formula: Diamond (x100), Moonstone (x100), Turquoise (x100), Acid, Stealth

MIST SHROUD, DEATH

Wondrous item (shroud), very rare
As per *mist shroud* and a creature that ends its turn in the mist must succeed on a Constitution saving throw or take 5d4 + 5 necrotic damage and become poisoned until one round after leaving the mist.
Alchemical formula: Diamond (x100), Moonstone (x100), Onyx (x100), Stealth, Toxin

MIST SHROUD, SOLID

Wondrous item (shroud), rare
As per *mist shroud* but the mist is very thick. The area is treated as difficult terrain.
Alchemical formula: Diamond (x10), Moonstone (x100), Onyx (x10), Earth (any), Transmutation, Stealth

MIST SHROUD, STINKING

Wondrous item (shroud), rare
As per *mist shroud* and the mist causes all those within to become terribly sick. A creature that ends its turn within the area must make a Constitution saving throw or become nauseated. A nauseated creature has disadvantage on attack rolls, ability checks, and Constitution saving throws.
Alchemical formula: Diamond (x10), Malachite (x10), Moonstone (x100), Disease, Stealth

PHASING WARD

Wondrous item (ward), very rare
This ward protects against planar travelers. This wall is as solid on the Astral, Ethereal, and other planes as it is on the Prime Material Plane. In addition, if the wall is contiguous and encloses an area, the top and bottom are shielded by a dome that is an impenetrable barrier on the Astral and Ethereal planes. This dome is neither visible nor has any presence or effect on the Prime Material Plane, used only to block the passage of planar creatures.
This mortar may be applied to wooden and stone walls.
Alchemical formula: Diamond (x10), Emerald (x10), Jade (x100), Planar, Protection

REPAIRSTONE

Wondrous item (stone), rare
This stone repairs itself as it is damaged. Every time this wall is damaged, if it has any hit points on initiative 20, losing ties, it gains 1 hit point until it is fully healed, when the maximum hit points of the wall increase by 1. The maximum hit points of the wall cannot double more than once per decade. This mortar may be applied to wooden and stone walls.
Alchemical formula: Diamond (x10), Emerald (x100), Turquoise (x10), Healing

SCRYING WARD

Wondrous item (shroud), rare
This ward provides mystical protection from scrying attempts. In order for this to work, all the space to be protected must be enclosed by walls fused with this alchemical mortar. Any open side or passage allows a scrying attempt to succeed. Once the ward is in place, the area is protected from scrying as the spell *nondetection*.
Alchemical formula: Diamond (x10), Onyx (x100), Turquoise (x10), Azoth (any), Protection

SHATTER WARD

Wondrous item (ward), uncommon
This mortar provides protection from blunt strikes. This is particularly effective at resisting battering rams, catapults, and ballistae. This increases the DC to break the wall by +5 and adds 10 hit points per 10-foot cube.
Alchemical formula: Diamond (x10), Onyx (x10), Turquoise (x100), Body, Protection

STALWART BULWARK I

Wondrous item (bulwark), common
This bulwark increases the strength of the wall into which it is mixed. This increases the wall's Armor Class by +1.
This may be applied to wooden and stone walls.
Alchemical formula: Diamond (x10) Turquoise (x10), Strength

STALWART BULWARK II

Wondrous item (bulwark), uncommon
This bulwark increases the strength of the wall into which it is mixed. This increases the wall's Armor Class by +2 and sets the DC to break the wall to 15, if it is not already higher.
This may be applied to wooden and stone walls.
Alchemical formula: Diamond (x10) Turquoise (x25), Strength (x2)

STALWART BULWARK III

Wondrous item (bulwark), rare
This bulwark increases the strength of the wall into which it is mixed. This increases the wall's Armor Class by +3 and sets the DC to break the wall to 20, if it is not already higher.
This may be applied to wooden and stone walls.
Alchemical formula: Diamond (10), Turquoise (x100), Strength (x4)

STALWART BULWARK IV

Wondrous item (bulwark), very rare
This bulwark increases the strength of the wall into which it is mixed. This increases the wall's Armor Class by +4 and sets the DC to break the wall to 25, if it is not already higher.
This may be applied to wooden and stone walls.
Alchemical formula: Diamond (x10) Turquoise (x200), Strength (x8)

STALWART BULWARK V

Wondrous item (bulwark), legendary
This bulwark increases the strength of the wall into which it is mixed. This increases the wall's Armor Class by +10 and sets the DC to break the wall to 30, if it is not already higher.
This may be applied to wooden and stone walls.
Alchemical formula: Diamond (x100) Turquoise (x200), Strength (x8)

SWARM SHROUD

Wondrous item (shroud), rare
This nefarious shroud creates many tiny porous openings in the wall and exudes a strong attractant to various insects. The insects live and breed in the wall. A creature that ends its turn within five feet of the wall takes 1d4 + 1 piercing damage from the biting insects. A creature that actively pesters the insects discovers that each 10-foot cube section of wall has 1d4 + 4 **swarms of insects** within.
This mortar may be applied to stone and wood walls.
Alchemical formula: Amethyst (x100), Diamond (x100), Moonstone (x100), Emotion

TELEPORTATION WARD

Wondrous item (ward), rare
This ward acts as a planar barrier to travelers. Anyone attempting to teleport, phase, or otherwise extra-dimensionally travel across this barrier finds themselves teleported 1d100 miles in a random direction.
Note that this works only if the attempted dimensional travel such as *teleport*, *dimensional door*, or *shadow walk* attempts to cross the wall. If the walls are not completely enclosed, then teleportation is possible.
This mortar may be applied to wooden and stone walls.
Alchemical formula: Diamond (x10), Emerald (x100), Pearl (x10), Planar, Protection

TERROR SHROUD

Wondrous item (shroud), very rare
This shroud causes terrible fear in all who approach. A creature that comes within 20 feet of the wall or who starts its turn within 20 feet of the wall must make a Wisdom saving throw or become frightened for one minute.
A creature frightened of the wall uses its action to dash and moves with all possible speed away from the wall. The creature is heedless of danger and pain as it runs from the wall.
This mortar may be applied to wooden and stone walls.
Alchemical formula: Diamond (x100), Malachite (x100), Moonstone (x100), Fear

TIME WARD

Wondrous item (ward), uncommon
This ward prevents the decay of the wall from age. Wood and stone will not sag, stone will not weather, and the wall is impervious to decay and damage from normal wear, requiring no upkeep. These effects last 500 years unless dispelled or otherwise removed.
This mortar may be applied to wooden and stone walls.
Alchemical formula: Diamond (x10), Emerald (x10), Onyx (x10), Stasis

WEATHER WARD

Wondrous item (ward), uncommon
This ward prevents a wall's surface from sustaining damage from weather. Rain, hail, lightning, and other weather effects cause no damage or wear on this wall.
This mortar may be applied to wooden and stone walls.
Alchemical formula: Diamond (x10), Sapphire (x10), Turquoise (x10), Protection

WEB SHROUD

Wondrous item (shroud), uncommon
This ward covers the surface of the wall with hideous, sticky spider webs. A creature that touches the wall is grappled and restrained (escape DC equal to the spell save DC of the shroud's creator). If the webs are burned off or otherwise removed, they reappear in 10 minutes.
Alchemical formula: Agate (x25), Diamond (x10), Onyx (x25), Stasis, Transmutation

WIND SHROUD

Wondrous item (bulwark), rare
This covers the front of the walls with swirling winds. This protects people standing on the parapets from missile fire, providing partial cover and a +8 bonus to Dexterity saving throws against ranged attacks that travel through the wind. The wall itself gains a +4 bonus to Armor Class against ranged attacks.
Alchemical formula: Diamond (x10), Onyx (x10), Sapphire (x100), Air (any), Strength

CHAPTER SEVEN: SPELLS, SPELLCASTING, AND ALCHEMY

ALCHEMICAL ITEMS AS SPELL COMPONENTS

Arcane formulations concocted in a dark laboratory seething with eldritch power are a staple of fantasy. The following systems allow you to use alchemical items and essences to increase the power of spells. But who wants to stop play to cross reference a spell or item to determine the effect an essence or item has on a magic spell?

No one, that's who.

USING CRAFTED ALCHEMICAL ITEMS TO ENHANCE SPELLS

First, there must be some connection between the item and the spell it is designed to affect. A flask of *alchemist's fire* improves spells that deal with fire and warmth, but is quite useless when used to try to improve a *cone of cold*. Slickshell grenades affect spells that create surfaces; solvents intensify acids. The general rule is that if an alchemical item shares a damage type with a spell's energy type, or they share a common school of magic, then that item can be used to enhance the spell, through the Game Master is the final adjudicator. It's important to remember when doing this that the cost of the component must be burned to enhance the spell, so erring on the side of flexible is encouraged.

Nothing special must be done when preparing your spells for the day. The use of an alchemical item does not add any casting time nor does it prevent the need for the normal material components of the spell. Normally the item is used up, unless enhancing a cantrip (0-level spell). Crafted items, i.e., items not requiring a feat to craft, may affect spells of only levels 1–4.

For every 50 gp or fraction thereof of the retail cost of a crafted item, your Game Master will determine which of the following effects may be added to a spell. Unless noted, each effect may be applied only once:

- You may extend the spell's duration by one round.
- You may increase the effect's radius by five feet.
- You may add 1 point of damage of the energy type of the item to a related spell. Thus, adding a 50-gp alchemical fire to a *burning hands* spell might increase the damage by +1, while adding a 600-gp *alchemist's inferno* would add +12 fire damage.
- A creature that dispels the spell takes 1d6 damage of the energy type of the spell per 10-foot square that gets dispelled. If a 10-foot segment of a *wall of fire* is dispelled, the person dispelling it takes 1d6 fire damage.
- You may apply a related secondary effect of the item to a single target that fails its saving throw versus the spell. For example, you could use an *alchemist's fire* to have a secondary round of burning damage when applied to a *fireball* spell.
- You may reroll one spell attack roll per 50 gp of the cost of the item.
- Increase the spell save DC for the spell by 1 per 100 gp of the cost of the item, to a maximum of 4.
- You may cause a 10-foot square area to gain the quality the item provides. A section of a *grease* or *web* spell could be conjured aflame and burning for the duration of the spell with an *alchemist's fire*.
- You may add +1 to your spell attack, to a maximum of +4.

It is important that a discussion about what items have which effects occur before play. Here are some guidelines for determining how to assign effects.

Each alchemical item has only one of the above effects when paired with a given spell. Only one alchemical modification can be made to each spell. The effects of the items must be similar or related in some way. Opposite effects cause the spell to fizzle: Using a bottle of *alchemist's ice* for a *fireball* will be unimpressive, but using *alchemist's ice* on a *web* spell could add 1 cold damage per round to anyone trapped in the web.

USING CONSUMABLE ENCHANTED ITEMS TO ENHANCE SPELLS

For every 500 gp or fraction thereof of the crafting cost of a consumable enchanted item, such as a potion or scroll, your Game Master will determine which of the following effects may be added to a spell. Unless noted, each effect may be applied only once:

- The duration may be increased as if you used a higher spell slot level.
- The radius of effect may be increased by five feet.
- It may add 1 point of damage per die of the energy type, to a maximum of +5
- You may apply the potion's effect as a secondary effect to targets that fail their saves.
- You may increase the difficulty of a related save by 1, to a maximum of +4

The same guidelines for crafted items apply to consumable enchanted items. Each item has only one effect when paired with a given spell. Only one alchemical modification can be made to each spell. The effects of the items must be similar or related in some way. Opposite effects cause the spell to fizzle.

EMPOWERMENT OF A SPELL USING ESSENCES

Essences themselves can increase the power of spells. Simply using a number of essences related to the effects of the spell causes the following effects. Related essences are associated in some way with the schools of the spell. Necromancy spells could use *wraith dust/death essence*, or *intellect devourer brain/mind essence* could be used to enhance enchantment spells. Certain effects require specific types of essences, while others require essences related to the spell. Instead of the listed effect, you may substitute standardized metamagic effects at your whim.

If this system is too powerful for your campaign, increase the number of essences required or require that they come from a creature with a challenge equal or greater than the spell level it affects. This works best in campaigns where essences are not just freely available for purchase.

Only one set of essences can affect a spell.

TABLE 7–1: ESSENCE EFFECTS ON SPELLS

Effect	Type of Essence	Number of Essences
Admixture	Fire/Acid/Electricity/Cold	2
Amplified	Essence Related to Spell Type	2
Breaching	Prowess	2
Caustic	Acid or Fire	3
Concussive	Pain	5
Discriminatory	Luck	6
Freezing	Cold	6
Glitz	Light	4
Indefatigable	Strength	4
Intensified	Purity	2
Malaise	Toxin	5
Maximum	Prowess	6
Mighty	Prowess	3
Planar	Planar	2
Prolonged	Essence related to Spell Type	2
Quiet	Emotion	2
Reaching	Transportation	5
Reflecting	Illusion	2
Repetitive	Magic	5
Stagnant	Stasis	3
Subdual	Love	1
Thundering	Lightning	3
Tranquil	Stasis	2

Admixture: For any spell that causes elemental damage, using two essences of a different element causes half the damage of the spell to be of the essence type. A *fireball* cast with two acid essences does 3d6 fire damage and 3d6 acid damage.

Amplified: Spells that are cast at range have their range doubled.

Caustic: Spells that cause damage continue to persist and do damage. A creature that fails its saving throw versus this spell takes an additional amount of damage of the type that the spell causes equal to the level of the spell slot used on the round the spell hits and then again on the next round. For example, a *fireball* cast with a 3rd-level slot does 3 additional damage the first round and another 3 damage the next.

Concussive: Any damage-causing spell gains a thunderous burst. This blast causes a creature that fails its save versus the spell to be stunned until the end of the target's next turn.

Discriminatory: This causes spells with area effects to selectively miss targets selected by the caster.

Freezing: This causes spells with cold damage to freeze their opponents, causing their movement to be impeded. This reduces their speed by half, and the target receives a –2 penalty to attacks rolls and Armor Class.

Glitz: Any damage-causing spell gains a brilliant visual effect. A creature dealt damage by the spell that fails its saving throw versus the spell is blinded for a number of rounds equal to the level of the spell slot used. A blinded target may repeat the saving throw at the end of each of its turns, ending the effect on a success.

Indefatigable: Targets have disadvantage on saving throws against the spell.

Intensified: This spell becomes more difficult to resist. The spell save DC increases by +2.

Malaise: This causes any spell that causes damage to sicken the targets. Anyone who fails the saving throw versus this spell becomes ill in addition to the normal save. An ill creature has a –2 penalty on all attack rolls, saving throws, and ability checks for a number of rounds equal to the level of the spell slot used. They may repeat the saving throw at the end of each of their turns, ending the effect on a success.

Maximum: All damage dice are maximized.

Mighty: This increases all the variable numeric effects of the spell by half. This doesn't affect saving throws, nor does it affect spells that lack a random variable.

Planar: This spell affects targets on planes contiguous to the Prime Material Plane. Ethereal and astral creatures are fully affected by the spell.

Prolonged: Spells that have a non-instantaneous duration have their duration doubled.

Quiet: This causes spells to be cast successfully without the verbal component.

Reaching: A touch spell gains a range of 30 feet.

Reflecting: If a reflected spell fails to affect a target in any way, it may instead be directed to affect a nearby target.

Repetitive: This powerful effect causes the spell to repeat itself once cast. The spellcaster unleashes the spell's energy, and the very next round the spell is recast with all the same parameters. New targets are not selected. The spell is cast in exactly the same place the second time. Variable numbers are rerolled. This uses an additional spell slot but does not require an action.

Stagnant: This slows down the effect of an instantaneous spell. It does no additional damage to targets but persists until the start of the spellcaster's next turn. This means it affects anyone who enters the area of effect. If the spell produces a visual effect, it obscures anyone within the area of the spell. It provides concealment to creatures within five feet of the edge or within the cloud adjacent to each other and total concealment beyond that. A *fireball* hangs in the air providing concealment, affecting anyone who enters its area during their turn.

Subdual: This causes any damage-dealing spell to deal nonlethal damage. This effect halves all damage versus dragons.

Thundering: Spells that cause damage deafen opponents. A creature dealt damage by the spell that fails its saving throw versus the spell is deafened for a number of rounds equal to the level of the spell slot used. A deafened target may repeat the saving throw at the end of each of its turns, ending the effect on a success.

Tranquil: This causes spells to be cast successfully without the somatic component.

NEW SPELLS

These spells are available for a spellcaster of the appropriate type who is proficient in Alchemist's Supplies.

TABLE 7–2: WIZARD/SORCERER SPELL LIST

1st level

Spell	Effect
Adhesion	Affix two objects to each other
Buoyancy	Cause objects to float in water
Liquid Sphere	Create a sphere of nonmagical, non-alchemical liquid
Stone Flame	Freeze a small flame

2nd level

Spell	Effect
Acid Cloud	Create an acidic grenade
Acid Mist	Create a caustic cloud of obscuring mist
Acid Scourge	Create an acid whip
Augmented Olfaction	Caster gains scent and increased olfactory ability
Boiling Oil	Pour boiling oil over a target
Corrosive Solvent	Create a powerful acid
Gauntlet	Create a gauntlet of force
Liquid Modulation	Transmutes nonmagical, non-alchemical liquids
Protection from Nonmagical Gas	Protects the caster from smoke

3rd level

Spell	Effect
Acid Bolt	Shoot two bolts of acid doing 6d4 + 6 damage
Burning Blood	Cause a wounded target's blood to burn
Control Fluid	Allows the caster to manipulate and control fluids
Control Vapor	Manipulate gaseous clouds
Disperse Vapor	Cause a gas cloud to dissipate
Hold Vapor	Holds a gaseous cloud or creature in place
Rusting Grasp	Rust ferrous metals with a touch

4th level

Spell	Effect
Acid Storm	Create an increasingly damaging storm of acid
Death Smoke	Create a cloud of blinding, poisonous vapors
Evaporate Fluid	Causes a large amount of water to evaporate instantly
Neutralize Gas	Neutralizes dangerous gases, spores, and attacks
Orb of Containment	Completely contain a small object safely
Preservation of the Flesh	Put some of your life force into a candle
Property Transference	Trade a single trait between any two objects

5th level

Spell	Effect
Abominable Amorphous Amoeba	Loose a horrible creature upon the world
Crystalbrittle	Turn a substance into brittle crystal
Venom Ward	Protect a creature from poisons and toxins

ABOMINABLE AMORPHOUS AMOEBA

5th-level necromancy
Casting Time: 1 action
Range: Touch
Components: V, S, M
Duration: Instantaneous
Target: A prepared glass orb costing 1,000 gp and taking 1d4 weeks to prepare

You prepare a glass orb and fill it with an eldritch alchemical fluid. The crafting cost of the orb is 1,000 gp, and it takes 1d4 weeks to prepare. When you cast the spell, the liquid becomes a terrible living, single-celled creature. You can use an action to throw the orb against an opponent, at which point the sphere shatters and the uncontrolled beast is released. The beast then begins to feed, fueling its awful growth. You are not in control of the creature.

The creature starts with 2d8 hit points and fills one five-foot square. Any creature that starts its turn within five feet of the beast or comes within that distance for the first time on its turn must make a DC 15 Dexterity saving throw. The creature takes 1d8 acid damage on a failure and half as much on a success. A creature brought to 0 hit points by the beast is consumed and dead. A consumed creature cannot be brought back to life. The beast gains hit points equal to the damage taken by its targets. For every 30 hit points the creature has, it covers one additional five-foot square. The creature is an ooze and can share a square with another creature. A creature in the same square as the ooze has disadvantage on its saving throws against the ooze. The ooze has AC 15 and is immune to acid, bludgeoning, piercing, poison, and psychic damage. It is immune to the grappled and prone conditions. It moves at 10 feet toward the closest living creature.

ACID BOLT

3rd-level evocation
Casting Time: 1 action
Range: 120 feet
Components: V, S, M (small arrow dipped into a vial of acid)
Duration: Instantaneous

You create two dart-shaped bolts of flesh-corroding acid. They float near your hand for a moment until rushing forth to strike one or two targets that you can see within range. Each target makes a Dexterity saving throw, taking 6d4 + 6 acid damage on a failure or half as much on a success.

ACID CLOUD

2nd-level conjuration
Casting Time: 1 bonus action
Range: Self
Components: V, S, M (crystal sphere, Rare Earths, 4 drams)
Duration: 3 rounds
Area: 15-foot-radius burst

When this spell is cast, you fill a small crystal sphere with yellow, acidic smoke. As an action, you can throw this at a point within 40 feet. When it strikes a surface, it shatters and fills a 15-foot-radius with yellow acrid fumes. All creatures in the area take 4d4 acid damage. A creature that ends its turn in the cloud takes 1d4 acid damage. The crystal stays filled with the acid fumes for only three rounds. If not used before that time elapses, the fumes become inert and useless. Once thrown, the cloud lasts for one minute unless dissipated.

ACID MIST

2nd-level evocation
Casting Time: 1 action
Range: Self
Components: V, S, M (half an onion)
Duration: 2 rounds
Lightly obscuring smoke pours forth from your hands, filling a 20-foot-radius circle centered on you. At the start of the next round, the smoke turns into translucent acidic green mist and all creatures in the area other than you that breathe must succeed on a Constitution saving throw or take 2d4 acid damage. At the beginning of your next turn, any creatures within the mist must succeed on a Constitution saving throw or take 1d4 acid damage.
This mist is immobile. It can be destroyed with a strong breeze.

ACID SCOURGE

2nd-level evocation
Casting Time: 1 bonus action
Range: Self
Components: V, S, M (7-foot length of string and 3 drops of acid)
Duration: Concentration, up to 1 minute
You create a magical whip made of acid. As an action, you may use it to make an attack using your spell attack bonus. It has a reach of 15-feet and does 4d4 acid damage on a successful hit.

ACID STORM

4th-level evocation
Casting Time: 1 action
Range: 120 feet
Components: V, S, M
Duration: Concentration, up to 1 minute
You create a storm of gelatinous acid rain that covers a 10-foot-radius circle centered on a point within range. All creatures within the area are coated in corrosive acid. The acid can be neutralized by vinegar, wine, or a successful *dispel magic*.
The acid storm becomes more damaging as time goes on. A creature that starts its turn within the area or enters the area for the first time on its turn must make a Constitution saving throw. On the first round, a creature that fails takes 1d4 acid damage, 1d6 acid damage on the second round, and 2d8 acid damage on the third and subsequent rounds. A creature that succeeds on its saving throw takes half this damage. If the target uses an action to cleanse itself of the acid, the progression begins again.

ADHESION

1st-level transmutation
Casting Time: 1 action
Range: Touch
Components: V, S, M (powdered hooves)
Duration: 10 minutes
You choose two solid objects within five feet of you that are not being worn or held that are touching each other. They are affixed to each other for the duration of the spell. The objects can be separated with a Strength check equal to your spell save DC.

AUGMENTED OLFACTION

2nd-level transmutation
Casting Time: 1 action
Components: V, S, M (a piece of dried cabbage and dog dung)
Range: Self
Duration: 10 minutes
Your nose becomes extremely sensitive to odors. You have advantage on Wisdom (Perception) throws that rely on smell. You can locate and identify all liquids and organic materials within 30 feet of you unless they are hermetically sealed.
You gain a −4 penalty to saving throws against being nauseated or scent-based attacks.

BOILING OIL

2nd-level evocation
Casting Time: 1 action
Range: 30 feet
Components: V, S, M (a pinch of sulfur and a few drops of oil)
Duration: Instantaneous
You choose a creature you can see within range and boiling oil pours out on top of the target. The target must make a Dexterity saving throw. On a failure, the target takes 3d8 + 3 fire damage and is blinded. On a success, the target takes half this damage and is not blinded. A blinded creature may repeat the saving throw at the end of each of its turns, ending the effect on a success.

BUOYANCY

1st-level transmutation
Casting Time: 1 action
Range: 60 feet
Components: V, S, M (a small cork and a pinch of bromine salt)
Duration: 10 minutes
Select a number of objects within range that weigh less than 100 pounds total and do not normally float. You cause them to float upon a small layer of bubbles. This allows heavy objects such as gold, lead, stone, or even living creatures to float in water. It can also be used to raise up objects that have sunk.
At higher levels. If you cast this spell using a spell slot higher than first, you increase the total weight of objects you can float by 100 pounds for each level above first.

BURNING BLOOD

3rd-level necromancy
Casting Time: 1 action
Range: 30 feet
Components: V, S, M (a pinch of salt and saltpeter)
Duration: Concentration, up to 1 minute
Choose one living creature you can see within range that has taken unhealed damage from an edged or piercing weapon. The exposed blood of the target turns into burning acid while the spell lasts. At the beginning of each of the creature's turns, the target must make a Constitution saving throw. On a failure, the target takes 2d4 fire damage.

CONTROL FLUID

3rd-level transmutation
Casting Time: 1 action
Components: V, S, M (a small glass tube and a sea sponge)
Range: 30 feet
Duration: 1 hour
You can control the movement of liquids. While this spell lasts, you can use your action to concentrate and the liquid can be moved or turned into any shape.
The liquid can be moved 15 feet per round, floating through the air or running along a surface. You can control only up to a 10-foot cube of liquid.
At higher levels. If you cast this spell using a spell slot higher than third, you can control an additional 10-foot cube of liquid for each level above third.

CONTROL VAPOR

3rd-level transmutation
Casting Time: 1 action
Range: 120 feet
Components: V, S, M (a small glass tube and miniature bellows)
Duration: 10 minutes
This useful spell has two functions. You can control the location, direction of movement, and speed of a body of gaseous vapor or you can create a zone of pure air. You can control or create a 20-foot cube or another shape of the same volume.

For the spell's duration, you can use your action to move any gas or vapor contained within the area of effect up to 30 feet.

Alternatively, you can expel all natural and magical vapor and gas from the area of effect. This allows only the natural background air in — if the air itself is foul, this spell will not produce fresh oxygen. This spell functions against natural mist or gas, spells such as *wall of fog* or *cloudkill*, or even gas breath weapons and creatures in gaseous form! In the event that the gas cloud is a creature, if it is unwilling, it receives a Charisma saving throw versus the effect.

CORROSIVE SOLVENT

2nd-level conjuration
Casting Time: 1 action
Range: 30 feet
Components: V, S, M (include a drop of black pudding, vinegar, and water)
Duration: 3 rounds
You conjure one square foot of strongly corrosive acid on an object or creature you can see within range. If the target is a creature or a worn or held object, the creature can make a Dexterity saving throw to avoid the solvent.

The solvent has the consistency of a slimy paste. If the target is an object, the acid eats through six inches of organic material, four inches of stone, or one inch of metal per round. It can be conjured on the ceiling, but if so, it eats only through the ceiling at half the rate as bits gloop and drip to the floor. If the target is a living creature, it takes 1d4 acid damage per round.

CRYSTALBRITTLE

5th-level transmutation
Casting Time: 1 action
Range: Touch
Components: V, S
Duration: Instantaneous
As an action, you touch a single metal or stone object that is up to two cubic feet and turn it to fragile crystal. This change is permanent.

If the target is a creature or if it is worn or held, make a melee spell attack. If the target is a magical item that is carried or worn, the owner of the item can attempt a Dexterity saving throw to avoid the effect.

DEATH SMOKE

4th-level evocation
Casting Time: 1 action
Range: 120 feet
Components: V, S, M (a crushed spider and a pinch of sand)
Duration: 1 minute
Point your finger at a spot you can see within range and a pellet flies to that spot where it strikes the ground. Thick opaque smoke pours out and covers a 20-foot radius from that center.

The area is heavily obscured. A creature that ends its turn within the cloud must make a Constitution saving throw. A creature that fails takes 5d4 + 5 poison damage and is blinded while a creature that succeeds takes half as much damage and is not blinded. A blinded creature may repeat the saving throw at the end of each of its turns, ending the effect on a success. The cloud always forms on the ground and is 15 feet high.

The material component is a crushed spider and a pinch of sand.

DISPERSE VAPOR

3rd-level abjuration
Casting Time: 1 action
Range: 120 feet
Components: V, S, M (a small cloth fan and a tiny piece of charcoal)
Duration: Instantaneous
When this spell is cast, a 50-foot cube of any gas, vapor, fog, breath weapon, or gaseous creature is dispersed. If the cloud is larger than a 50-foot cube, then an area the size of the area of effect is cleared.

Creatures in gaseous form receive a Constitution saving throw. If they fail this saving throw, they take 6d6 force damage. If they succeed, they take half this damage. In either case they are forced from the area of effect to the nearest open space.

EVAPORATE FLUID

4th-level transmutation
Casting Time: 1 action
Range: 60 feet
Components: V, S, M (a pinch of salt)
Duration: Instantaneous
You vaporize three 10-foot cubes of uncontained liquid within range. The liquid evaporates into the atmosphere, expanding rapidly. This affects water, acid, oil, blood, liquid metals, poisons, potions, and liquid rock — any liquid can be vaporized. When changed out of liquid form, the substance is rendered inert and poses no threat or danger of any kind; toxic and thermal properties are normalized and neutralized. If a portion of a larger body of liquid is vaporized, liquid rushes in to fill the remaining space.

At higher levels. If you cast this spell using a spell slot higher than fourth, you can evaporate an additional 10-foot cube of liquid for each level above fourth.

GAUNTLET

2nd-level evocation
Casting Time: 1 action
Components: V, S, M (a lump of rock crystal)
Range: Self
Duration: 10 minutes
This spell protects your hand. It creates a gauntlet of force that is transparent, silent, resistant, and nonconductive. It is impossible to damage. You can, for example, use the gauntlet to stop a gate or door from closing, removing your hand and leaving the force gauntlet inside. Once your hand is removed, the gauntlet lasts until the duration expires and you may no longer use it.

If you make a melee weapon attack while wearing the gauntlet, the attack is considered magical.

The primary purpose of the gauntlet is to allow the handling of dangerous materials. It protects from extreme heat, acid, boiling liquids, deadly vapors, and more. It is immune to disease, molds, and mummy rot, and nothing adheres to it.

HOLD VAPOR

3rd-level abjuration
Casting Time: 1 action
Range: 100 feet
Components: V, S, M (a small bladder)
Duration: Concentration up to 1 hour
You stop any fog, vapor, gas, or other substance's movement in the air. When this spell is cast, choose a 15-foot-tall, 30-radius centered on a point within range. Any gas, vapor, fog, breath weapon, gaseous creature, natural or magical in nature within the area is held. It does not prevent the movement of creatures in and out of the area of effect.

This works even against magical control and effects such as *gust of wind* that would move the vapor. A gaseous creature that starts its turn in the area or enters the area for the first time on its turn must make a Constitution saving throw. If it fails, it is grappled and restrained until the start of its next turn. While held, creatures able to change or solidify their form are unable to do so.

The material component for this spell is a small bladder.

LIQUID MODULATION

2nd-level transmutation
Casting Time: 1 standard action
Range: Touch
Components: V, S, M (one drop of material to be created)
Duration: Instantaneous
Area: 1 cubic foot of liquid per level
You change 1 cubic foot of one type of liquid into another type of
nonmagical, non-alchemical liquid. Examples of the types of liquids
that can be produced are oil, water, blood, wine, vinegar, and juice.
Creatures are unaffected.
This spell is cast by taking a single drop of the substance to be
produced and putting it on your tongue while touching the liquid to
be transformed. This means there is some danger when creating foul
liquids, poisons, and liquid metals.

LIQUID SPHERE

1st-level conjuration
Casting Time: 1 action
Range: Self
Components: V, S, M (a small clear glass bead)
Duration: Instantaneous
You create a one-gallon sphere of liquid in your hands. The liquid is
at room temperature and cannot be flammable or acidic enough
to cause damage. The sphere rests in your hands, inert. It can be
released or poured into a container. It can be thrown, clumsily, with
a range of 10/20 feet. It does no damage.
This spell often is used to provide the alchemist with fresh water,
ink, dye, juice, cider, soup, and other harmless liquids. Alchemical
liquids may not be created with this spell.
The material component for this spell is a small clear glass bead.
At higher levels. If you cast this spell using a spell slot higher than
1st, the sphere you create can be one gallon larger for each level
above 1st level.

NEUTRALIZE GAS

4th-level abjuration
Casting Time: 1 reaction
Range: 120 feet
Components: V, S, M (a small piece of gauze and some charcoal)
Duration: Instantaneous
You neutralize any harmful gas, cloud, vapor, or fog of any kind in
a 20-foot radius around a point within range. The substance is
rendered totally inert and dissipates within the area of effect.
This spell does not affect creatures.

ORB OF CONTAINMENT

4th-level evocation
Casting Time: 1 action
Range: 30 feet
Components: V, S, M (1,000-gp diamond and a shard of glass)
Duration: 24 hours
When cast, choose a point within range. You create a crystal sphere
up to 12 inches in diameter that surrounds and secures anything
within it. The spell fails if you attempt to secure a portion of a larger
solid object, but can entrap part of a liquid or gas. The sphere is
unbreakable, able to contain any substance no matter how volatile
or inimical to life. Time is suspended within the sphere.
The sphere is immune to all physical attacks, though *dispel magic* can
destroy the orb.
The material components for this spell are a 1,000-gp diamond and a
shard of glass. The diamond shatters when the sphere is created.
You can recast the spell before it ends to renew the sphere using
only a shard of glass.

PROPERTY TRANSFERENCE

4th-level transmutation
Casting Time: 1 action
Range: touch
Components: V, S, M (a small mechanical switch and length of wire)
Duration: Permanent
You touch two nonmagical objects that are each no larger than one
cubic foot. Any single material property can be switched between
the two objects: strength, color, durability, brittleness, melting
points, edibility, weight, etc. Each object retains all other properties.
For example, you could cause a suit of plate armor to become
transparent with a piece of glass. Conversely, a vial could be given
the strength of steel.

PRESERVATION OF THE FLESH

4th-level necromancy
Casting Time: 10 minutes
Range: Touch
Components: V, M (a 1,000-gp candle)
Duration: 24 hours
Before casting the spell, you must create or acquire a candle made
from 1,000 gp worth of rare materials. When you cast this spell, 3d4
hit points flow from you to the candle, and the candle lights. You
cannot transfer more hit points then you currently have; you are
always left with at least one hit point.
The candle burns for the duration of the spell. If extinguished or
destroyed, the spell ends. The lost hit points can be recovered
normally.
If you drop to 0 hit points before the duration expires, you appear to
die. However, when the candle burns down, the borrowed lifeforce
re-enters your body and restores you to life. If you have 0 hit points
and the candle is extinguished before the spell ends, you die.
Some normal wounds are repaired when the lifeforce flows back into
your body, but missing limbs, disease, critical wounds, disintegrated
body parts, limbs trapped in stone, petrification, burn wounds, etc.,
persist. This could mean you immediately perish again. This is also
true if you cannot survive in your new environment. Only one use of
this spell can be in effect.

PROTECTION FROM NONMAGICAL GAS

2nd-level abjuration
Casting Time: 1 action
Range: Self
Components: V, S, M (a silk fan and a 2-inch square of thick gauze)
Duration: 1 hour
A 20-foot-radius sphere centered on you provides total protection
from all nonmagical gases and mists. When they come into contact
with the sphere, they dissipate instantly, leaving nothing but pure
clean air. If air is outside the sphere, the sphere is filled with pure
clean air for the duration of the effect. This spell does not work in a
vacuum or underwater. The spell ends if the sphere comes in contact
with a magical gas.

RUSTING GRASP

3rd-level transmutation
Casting Time: 1 bonus action
Range: Self
Components: V, S, M (a scale or antenna from a rust monster)
Duration: Concentration, up to 1 minute
Your touch corrodes a nonmagical ferrous metal object. If the object
isn't being worn or carried, your touch destroys a one-foot cube
of it. If the object is being worn or carried by a creature, make a
melee spell attack against the creature. If the object touched is
either metal armor or a metal shield being worn or carried, its
takes a permanent and cumulative −1 penalty to the AC it offers.
Armor reduced to an AC of 10 or a shield that drops to a +0 bonus is
destroyed. If the object touched is a held metal weapon, the weapon
takes a permanent and cumulative −1 penalty to damage rolls. If its
penalty drops to −5, the weapon is destroyed.

STONE FLAME

1st-level enchantment
Casting Time: 1 action
Range: Touch
Components: V, S, M (a dram of fine sand mixed with a dram of raw sugar)
Duration: 1 hour
When you cast this spell on a small active flame, the flame freezes into an orange stone while the spell lasts. The stone gives off light as a fire but is cool to the touch. If the stone is broken, the spell ends and the fire is extinguished. If the spell expires, the stone turns back into flame.

VENOM WARD

5th-level necromancy
Casting Time: 1 action
Range: Touch
Components: V, S, M (a few drops of liquid poison and one nail from the corpse of a creature that died from poison)
Duration: 1 hour/level
One creature you touch is immune to the effects of all toxins, venoms, and poisons for the duration of the spell.

VITRIOLIC SPHERE

3rd-level conjuration
Casting Time: 1 action
Range: 30 feet
Components: V, S, M (a drop of stomach acid from a troll)
Duration: Concentration, up to 1 minute
You conjure a bright green sphere full of corrosive acid. Pick a target you can see within range and the sphere flies unerringly toward the target. Upon slamming into the target, the sphere envelops the target in vivid emerald green acid. For the duration of the spell, acid splatters in a 15-foot-diameter sphere centered on the target. A creature that begins its turn in the sphere must make a Dexterity saving throw, taking 3d4 acid damage on a failure or half as much on a success. If the creature targeted by the spell drops to 0 hit points or makes two consecutive successful saving throws, the effect ends.

APPENDIX: MISHAPS

Mixing and creating alchemical items can produce wondrous things. However, a wrong ingredient or a pinch too much of a volatile ingredient can produce a truly horrible event —that might also be spectacularly explosive.

100 ALCHEMICAL MISHAPS

Things may certainly go wrong while you are creating alchemical items. If they do, you may be able to escape the worst by making a saving throw (if allowed). All save DCs are equal to the item crafting difficulties. Roll 1d100 on the appropriate mishap table below to determine what happens, remembering that the event should be the most interesting thing possible. All results are permanent.

TABLE A–1: ALCHEMICAL MISHAP TABLE

1d100	Result
1	Vines entangle you and your entire lab.
2	Noxious fumes cause random vomiting for 1d4 weeks.
3	All metal in the lab takes (1d4 + 1) x 100 acid damage.
4	All magical items are drained of 1d4 charges or suppressed for 24 hours.
5	The item and all materials turn to dust.
6	The item becomes a randomly selected slime.
7	The item becomes a randomly selected ooze.
8	The item becomes a randomly selected fungus.
9	Your hair goes white from fumes. Item is fine.
10	You gain a scent.
11	Explosion! 2d6 force damage.
12	Fire in lab destroys 1d6 x 100 gp worth of equipment.
13	All glass shatters in lab, causing 50d10 gp worth of damage.
14	All leather disintegrates in the lab, causing 10d4 gp worth of damage.
15	Spill! Lab is coated in vermin attractant.
16	Your limbs become invisible.
17	Gravity is permanently doubled in the lab.
18	Item created is a different one of a random type.
19	Disaster causes amnesia.
20	Disaster causes insanity.
21	Lab animates as a Small or Medium construct.
22	Explosion! All flesh in the lab is crystallized.
23	Lab animates as a Large or Huge construct.
24	You change shape.
25	All metal in the lab becomes plated in gold.
26	All metal in the lab quadruples in weight.
27	All creatures in the lab turned to gas.
28	All creatures have the flesh removed from their bodies and become living skeletons.
29	All creatures in the lab age 2d10 years.
30	All magic items are permanently drained of their magic.
31	Creatures in the lab have a random number of their limbs double in length.
32	Lab teleports 10 feet straight up.
33	Explosion! Lab frozen, 6d8 cold damage.
34	Creatures in the lab paralyzed from waist down.
35	All objects and creatures in the lab radiate sunlight.
36	All creatures in the lab are struck blind.
37	Your hands, arms, neck, and torso are indelibly inked.
38	Experiment bubbles over, leaving 20 gray pills that when eaten heal 2d10 damage each.
39	Mishap produces a frozen one-foot cube of human blood.
40	All dead within one mile are raised.
41	Creatures in lab become permanently drunk or high.
42	Disaster produces 1d10 gems worth 100d4 gp each.
43	Creatures within one mile have a chance of gaining the body parts of animals.

44	Explosion! Choking gas; succeed at a DC 18 Constitution saving throw or die.
45	Smoke causes 10d12 gp worth of damage.
46	Creatures within one mile grow mysterious new organs.
47	Creatures within one mile become pregnant regardless of gender.
48	Creatures within one mile grow a second face.
49	Creatures within one mile have their teeth turn into thumbs.
50	Creatures within one mile have a permanently numb extremity.
51	Permanent loss of 1d4 − 1 (minimum 1) hit points.
52	Creatures within one mile gain a permanent scent.
53	Creatures within one mile grow a plant from their body.
54	The lab and everything non-living within it vanishes, then reappears in 1d100 minutes.
55	Explosion! Lab shatters like glass, causing 3d10 slashing damage.
56	One of your extremities doubles in size.
57	Creatures within one mile appear to have skin made from chrome.
58	Laboratory and everything inside it becomes a random solid metal.
59	A dense fog permanently covers the lab, inside and out.
60	The laboratory turns into gingerbread.
61	The laboratory levitates 1d10 feet.
62	The laboratory sinks 2d12 feet into the ground.
63	The laboratory grows bark, repeatedly.
64	The laboratory is packed full of potatoes.
65	The laboratory temperature is raised to 300° Fahrenheit.
66	Explosion! You have a limb or extremity burnt off!
67	An elemental (Small) is summoned.
68	An elemental (Medium) is summoned.
69	An elemental (Large) is summoned.
70	A succubus is summoned.
71	The laboratory and everything inside turns ethereal or astral.
72	The laboratory is coated in contact poison (save or die).
73	The laboratory and everything in it vanishes.
74	The laboratory is transported somewhere interesting.
75	The laboratory is wreathed in darkness.
76	The laboratory collapses.
77	Explosion! Everything in the lab takes 8d10 acid damage.
78	The laboratory travels 5d6 weeks into the future.
79	The laboratory becomes invisible.
80	All trees within one mile animate and become hostile.
81	The laboratory doubles in size.
82	The laboratory becomes transparent.
83	The laboratory turns to sand.
84	Groundwater is rendered toxic in a two-mile radius.
85	The item becomes a nugget of neutronium.
86	The laboratory permanently becomes pleasant smelling.
87	A plague breaks out.
88	Explosion! Sonic blast does 12d12 thunder damage.
89	All food within one mile causes madness.
90	All metal within 500 yards liquefies.
91	Everything within one mile is covered in moss.
92	The laboratory is drained of color.
93	Creatures within one mile are unable to sleep for 2d4 days.
94	The laboratory dissolves into one million insects.
95	The laboratory becomes a gate to another plane.
96	The laboratory is teleported into space.
97	The laboratory is permanently covered in thick webbing.
98	Item created is 10 times more powerful than normal.
99	Explosion! Laboratory disintegrates.
100	Explosion! Everything within a 2,000-foot radius takes 20d8 force damage.

100 RANDOM POTION EFFECTS

Roll on the table below if a random alchemical potion effect is needed. The duration is normally 1d4 + 4 minutes, but the effect can be permanent.

TABLE A–2: POTION MISHAP TABLE

1d100	Result
1	User glows like a torch.
2	User inflates like a balloon for 1d6 rounds.
3	Users skin changes color.
4	User turns to stone.
5	User is enlarged.
6	User is shrunk.
7	User bleeds from eyes for 2d10 + 1 rounds and loses 1 hit point per round.
8	User's gender changes.
9	User is granted a *wish*.
10	User is enraged. Attack nearest target with a +4 bonus to Strength.
11	User's Strength permanently increases by 1d4 points.
12	User is cursed.
13	User ages 1d12 + 24 years.
14	User becomes 1d6 + 1 years younger.
15	User vomits sawdust.
16	User gains resistance to fire damage.
17	User gains vulnerability to fire damage.
18	User gains resistance to acid damage.
19	User gains vulnerability to acid damage.
20	User gains resistance to cold damage.
21	User gains vulnerability to cold damage.
22	User's Dexterity permanently increases by 1d4 points.
23	User can *spider climb* as the spell.
24	User can *comprehend language* as the spell.
25	User can *speak with animals* as the spell.
26	A dragon is summoned that is not under the control of the imbiber.
27	User polymorphs into a dragon.
28	User gains *detect thoughts* as the spell.
29	User is subject to *fear* as the spell.
30	User gains 1,000 XP.
31	User gains double experience points for 24 hours.
32	User gains one pound per round for 1d100 rounds.
33	User's Constitution permanently increases by 1d4 points.
34	User gains one random animal trait.
35	User is *feebleminded* as the spell.
36	User gains luck and gets +4 to all attack rolls and saving throws.
37	User is put to *sleep* as the spell.
38	User can breathe fire as an *elixir of fire breathing*.
39	User can *fly* as the spell.
40	User gains permanent *invisibility* as the spell.
41	User is blinded.
42	User is deafened.
43	User creaks and pops like a squeaky wheel when moving.
44	User's Intelligence permanently increases by 1d4 points.
45	User gains *blur* as the spell.
46	User gains *blink* as the spell.
47	User gains *mirror image* as the spell.
48	User changes race.
49	User is *slowed* as the spell.
50	User is *hasted* as the spell.
51	User gains +4 to Armor Class.
52	User gains a *magic aura* as the spell.
53	User turns into an insect.
54	User is polymorphed into an amphibian.
55	User's Wisdom permanently increases by 1d4 points.
56	User turns into a tree.
57	User turns into a cloud of wasps.
58	User gains the ability to *command* as the spell.
59	User gains *water breathing* as the spell.
60	User is subject to *lesser restoration* as the spell.
61	User is subject to *heal* as the spell.
62	User gains two tentacles.
63	User's hands double in size.
64	User is *silenced* as the spell.
65	User loses all his or her hair.
66	User's Charisma permanently increases by 1d4 points.
67	User's hair turns into precious metals.
68	User becomes gaseous.
69	User is turned into a zombie.

70	User is invisible to non-humans.
71	User gains *water walking* as the spell.
72	User grows a prehensile tail.
73	User grows a tail that grants a bonus action attack that does 1d4 bludgeoning damage.
74	User grows a second face on their body.
75	User gains the ability to *wind walk* as the spell.
76	User's Strength, Dexterity, and Constitution permanently increase by 1d6 + 1 points.
77	User grows a turtle shell.
78	User turns into salt.
79	User is subject to a *stoneskin* spell.
80	User's head grows to double size.
81	User's Strength increases by 1 point
82	User's Dexterity increases by 1 point
83	User can speak only gibberish.
84	User gains infravision.
85	User begins uncontrollably dancing.
86	User attracts vermin.
87	User gains immunity to normal weapons.
88	User's Intelligence, Wisdom, and Charisma permanently increase by 1d6 + 1 points.
89	User can *speak with dead* as the spell.
90	User gains *etherealness* as the spell.
91	User is flatulent.
92	User is subject to *reverse gravity* as the spell.
93	User becomes translucent.
94	User gains *feign death* as the spell.
95	User gains *true seeing* as the spell.
96	User gains one *mirror image* as the spell.
97	All user's ability scores permanently increase by 1d4 + 1 points..
98	User gains *fire shield* as the spell.
99	Roll again; result is permanent.
100	Roll two times. If this result occurs again, user dies.

ALCHEMICAL QUIRKS

There is a 25% chance that any given beneficial item also has a quirk. These quirks last for the duration of the item.

TABLE A–3: ALCHEMICAL QUIRKS

1d100	Result
1	User glows a color.
2	User's skin changes color.
3	User cannot speak due to swollen tongue for 1d4 hours.
4	User receives a +1 bonus on Perception checks.
5	User has tinnitus for the duration of the item or three minutes, whichever is longer.
6	Item works at half power.
7	Item has double duration.
8	User is drunk for 2d12 hours after using item.
9	User loses or gains infravision to 60 feet.
10	This item does not affect humans.
11	This item does not affect demi-humans.
12	User experiences disorientation, imposing a –2 penalty on attack rolls and ability checks.
13	User experiences drowsiness.
14	User glows in the dark.
15	The item is sickening to use. User must succeed on a DC 10 Constitution check to use.
16	User has a random ability lowered by 2.
17	If exposed to air for more than one round, the item evaporates or congeals.
18	The item has an unpredictable effect each time it is used. Roll d10: 1–5, normal effects; 6–8, nothing happens; 9–10, nothing occurs and user is stunned for 1d3 rounds.
19	Explosive! The item has a 75% chance to explode and be ruined.
20	User gets logorrhea.
21	Item is addictive.
22	User's skin acquires a pattern for 24 hours. Roll 1d6: 1–3 is spots; 4–6 is stripes.
23	User is slow and covered in ice.
24	User appears wreathed in phantasmal fire.
25	Hair grows two inches per minute.
26	User's voice sounds robotic, like grinding metal.
27	User's eyes glow.
28	Smoke pours from user's ears and eyes, filling a 10-foot cube each round.
29	All hair falls out (permanently).
30	All water that comes within 10 feet of the user turns to blood.
31	User is confused, as the spell.
32	Item causes 1d4 + 1 rounds of vomiting after use.
33	The item's effect is reversed.
34	User gains a disease.
35	User's hair changes color.
36	User becomes terribly thirsty.
37	User gains a migraine.
38	User's hair turns to snakes.
39	User's hands twist and become useless.
40	User hiccups uncontrollably.
41	User's skin becomes transparent.
42	User levitates one inch off the ground.
43	User's footprints glow.
44	User is covered in scales.
45	User appears to be made of ice.
46	User oozes sweet-smelling oil.
47	An illusionary double of user appears five feet away.
48	User looks like a nearby creature.
49	User begins starving.
50	User becomes dehydrated.
51	User vomits up a random potion at the end of the duration.
52	User experiences a seizure that lasts for 1d3 rounds.
53	User can read the thoughts of any visible creature within 10 feet.
54	User takes a –5 penalty to Intelligence and Wisdom checks.
55	Noise is made when the user moves, such as humming, squeaking, etc.
56	User's skin oozes oil filled with soot.
57	User gains a rash, giving a –1 penalty on attack rolls and ability checks.
58	User loses 2d8 hit points.
59	User has blurry vision for the duration and –1 penalty on attack rolls.
60	User exudes stench that causes creatures within 10 feet that fail a DC 14 Constitution saving throw to have a –2 penalty on attack rolls.
61	User gains tremors that cause –1 penalty on to-hit and damage rolls.
62	User is subject to falls. Succeed at a DC 10 Dexterity (Acrobatics) check when moving or fall prone.
63	Temperature drops 1d4 x 10° Fahrenheit in 30 feet.
64	Temperature rises 1d4 x 10° Fahrenheit in 30 feet.
65	User shrinks proportionately to lost hit points.

66	User is unable to move face while speaking, causing −2 penalty on Charisma-based skill checks.
67	User's eyes turn insectile.
68	Item does not affect men.
69	Item does not affect women.
70	User suffers exhaustion.
71	User is panicked.
72	User is *hasted* as the spell.
73	User's hair turns to wire.
74	User is blinded or deafened for the duration.
75	User develops stutter.
76	User sprouts feathers.
77	User suffers vertigo.
78	Non-humans become invisible to the user.
79	User's fingernails fall out.
80	User's skin acquires a brick texture.
81	User may speak only in tongues.
82	User grows antennae.
83	User's eyes turn black.
84	User grows nonfunctional wings.
85	User stinks of dirty socks.
86	User forgets only his name and his friends.
87	User's AC improves by 2.
88	User hears voices.
89	User sees visions and hallucinations.
90	User becomes covered in runes.
91	User grows a new extremity or limb.
92	User grows mandibles.
93	User's skin oozes honey.
94	User's skin becomes bloodstained.
95	User cannot speak
96	User gains 4d10 pounds.
97	User grows claws, granting two attacks, 1d6 slashing damage each.
98	User can see into the Ethereal Plane.
99	User allergic to item. DC 20 Constitution saving throw or die.
100	Effect of item becomes permanent.

ALCHEMICAL IDEAS

This isn't just a book with lists of treasure. Each item in this book can be used to start a story or add a twist to a story. Below are 100 examples you can expand upon.

TABLE A–4: STORY IDEAS

1d100	Result
1	Local children have been stealing *alchemist's befuddlement* grenades and drinking them to get high. The long-term effects of drinking these grenades are terrible and already one child has died.
2	A nearby ogre kidnapped a group of kobolds and is forcing them to craft *alchemist's fire* to fuel his new war machine.
3	A nearby tribe of wererats has been dumping *alchemist's terror* into the water supply. How will the characters respond to a city of madmen?
4	An alchemist has discovered a way to make *black-light* permanent. She is slowly expanding a permanent globe of darkness from her tower.
5	An angel of retribution has attacked a local church. The priest is being punished for killing good creatures to create *blessed spheres*.
6	People in town are seen with bright stains on their skin. When questioned, they say nothing. They are engaged in a secret underground gaming ring involving *dye bombs* to mark the losers.
7	Firewood in town keeps exploding in searing bursts of flame. A nearby dryad alchemist is seeding trees with *fireburst pellets* to protect her forest.
8	Thieves are using *flash pellets* to stage dramatic robberies. They appear to be immune to the pellets' effects.
9	A popular fashion among youth is using *frost sap* to scar themselves. One youth was seriously injured.
10	A nearby lighthouse suddenly begins shining a dim blue-green light. The town suspects it is haunted, but secretly an alchemist with a vendetta is playing a prank on the lighthouse maintainer by replacing all her oil with *shadow oil*.
11	An earthquake opened a crevice near an important natural resource. The crevice releases a gas that functions as *sleepsmoke*.
12	A new entertainment venue has opened: a skating rink on large blocks of granite covered in *slickshell*. However, the proprietor has been stealing local livestock in order to get enough animal fat to keep his supply current.
13	An alchemist's shop has been closed for weeks and the city wonders why. The god of fungus and slime turned the alchemist into a spellcasting slime in retribution for producing *slime bane*.
14	An alchemist producing *alchemist's kindness* is being harangued by teetotalers. The situation is ready to erupt into violence.
15	Explosions in the cemetery have occurred, leaving shattered remains. A local prankster under the influence of a necromancer has been sneaking into the cemetery and covering bones in *bone bomb* solution. How's he sneaking into the cemetery? He's a vampire.
16	Several adventurers have gone missing. It turns out the *potions of healing* they are buying aren't actually curing anything. They are just extremely alcoholic.
17	A necro-alchemist is coating undead in *death flames*. This scourge must be stopped.
18	The king is dead! But a cloaked figure approaches the party and claims that he has been given *false slumber*. They must rescue him before it is too late.
19	A brave knight disappeared and she is needed for a quest. The knight is a coward who has been using *carnelian flower of courage* to get up the gumption to do quests. Now she's too drunk to do anyone any good.
20	A village seems preternaturally calm in the face of disaster. The mayor is an alchemist and has everyone in the village addicted to a substance of some kind.
21	An alchemical stimulant has been outlawed! Yet citizens are still using it. Who's making it?
22	A wandering alchemist recently sold a number of defective potions in town, and then headed for the hills. Is he a nefarious anarchist working alone, or was this part of a sinister plot?
23	A harmless old lady is selling *black candles* in her candle shop. A curious wizard hires the characters to discover where she is getting her materials to craft such an item.
24	The water in town has suddenly become diseased, and it does not appear to be a normal matter.
25	A thief who uses his ethereal ability to commit crimes hires the party to replace a museum's *phasebound incense* with normal incense.
26	Rats are overrunning the city. That strange smell at night is *stinkstuff incense*. A naga is calling the rats to the city!
27	A merchants' guild is wildly profitable. The characters are hired to find out why. They are using amounts of *buoyancy ointment* to overload their ships.
28	An area has been scoured for a scrying mage causing trouble, and he can't be found. He's using *clarity ointment* to extend the range of his influence.
29	A sorcerer arrived, and the king has taken a liking to her. She's using an ointment of some kind to influence the king. How can she be stopped without drawing the wrath of her new best friend?
30	*Insect repellent* is killing bees, and the beekeeper is hopping mad.
31	The characters are sold fake magic items covered in a paste that creates a false magic aura. Who is at fault? The seller or the merchant he buys from?
32	The characters are approached by some disgruntled townsfolk. A mountebank came into town to sell them *salve of protection, rust*. It worked when he showed it off, but what they bought ruined all the metal they used it on. They want the characters to track down the seller who happens to be a leprechaun.
33	One of the characters' henchmen is using cologne that causes a wild reaction in all those who encounter the party.
34	A thief in plate armor has been committing heists. She's treated the armor with *armor malleability* and *quieting paste* until it's as comfortable as normal clothing. She does it to hide the fact that she's either the queen, a character's mother, or the demure wife of a political figure.
35	Someone used *absorption powder* to turn a moat into paste. The culprit? A traitor who did so for the army that plan to attack in the morning.
36	Healthy people are dying of mysterious heart attacks! No sign of magic is detected. The murderer is injecting a powder into their veins that causes blood clots.
37	Denizens of the forest come to ask the party to track down the alchemist who's seeding their forest with *defoliant powder*. The alchemist is a bitter mountain ogre mage.
38	A well-known public figure begins acting strangely but no enchantment is detected. Who is dosing him with *contrariness powder* and can they be stopped before it becomes permanent?
39	A cult of secrets is dosing its members with *delirium powder*. Several prominent council members joined or are considering joining the cult. Those who are as risk of having their secrets exposed are panicking.
40	An alchemist posts a reward for anyone who can produce a container capable of holding a substance he has invented.
41	A woman asks for help seeking an alchemist who can produce *tincture of wolfsbane*. However, as you travel, you appear to be stalked by a wolf …
42	Who are the characters? Each has an amazing variety of skills, but none of them even knows their own name. They must discover who dosed them with *dust of amnesia* and attempt to restore their memory.
43	An orc force has been making devastating strikes against nearby elven encampments. No one knows how they created stealthy war machines. The tribe's alchemist has learned to produce *dust of blending*.
44	The characters are poisoned with *dust of blighted bones*! They have seven days to track down who killed them.
45	A huge cloud of dust springs up east of town. The party is sent to investigate. An evil wizard and his minions are using *dust of clouds* to cause a distraction to hide the construction of a tower.
46	Farmers and livestock traders are angry because an alchemist producing *dust of consumption* is making them obsolete, feeding the populace with the novel food of flavored rocks.
47	The woods are filled with a mysterious tribe of deformed ogres, and villagers keep disappearing. An alchemist is secretly kidnapping townsfolk and using *dust of deformity* on them.

48 A forest is growing up near town. At first it seems like a boon, but then it begins to encroach upon the road, and traffic dwindles. Will they be able to stop the centaur alchemist using *dust of fertile growth* before the town is overrun?

49 A local tribe of primitives has begun viciously attacking townsfolk. An alchemist has been addicting them to *dust of fury*.

50 A strange hazy chamber is said to drive anyone mad who enters. They just endlessly repeat the same action again and again. It is actually just a large chamber filled with *dust of looping*.

51 The court wizard suddenly becomes weak and ineffective. Can they find the imp dosing her food with *dust of maladweomer*?

52 A high-level party is asked to retrieve an item. Easy right? Except that it's hidden in a chest filled with *dust of nondetection*.

53 A nearby temple is discovered, but everyone who visits leaves in terror. *Dust of panic* coats the floor of the entrance hall.

54 Strange murders are occurring, and the bodies appear to have exploded from within. They are surrounded by a red, pulpy substance. Will the characters discover the noble alchemist who is poisoning his opponents with *dust of roughage*?

55 A gang of mercenary criminals is known for being totally silent while they work. The party is hired to stop them. Can they survive against a group that coordinates their actions using *dust of the sparkling mind*?

56 A village suddenly becomes old overnight. A night hag visited each villager in their dreams and dosed them with an *elixir of aging*.

57 A band of yeti are attacking a southern town. The yeti are actually bandits who quaff *elixirs of fur growth* to hide their identities.

58 A new pugilist is upsetting all the thieves' guild's carefully planned fights. Turns out he had a 2–11 record before this comeback. The party is hired to investigate. Will they discover his use of the *elixir of the iron fist*?

59 A prophecy occurred, and an ancient hero has not awakened from her *elixir of suspended animation*. No one knows what condition was set.

60 Somebody is selling *elixir of super heroic fighting* — cheap! No way they are free of side effects. Not only that, enemies of the characters seem to be snapping them up.

61 The elven archers always win the kingdom's archery competition — but now they have lost to a squad of dwarven archers! They suspect trickery, and their suspicions are correct: the dwarves consumed *elixirs of vision of the eagle*.

62 Animals are setting traps in the forest! A hag alchemist is dosing the woodland creatures with *philters of the awakened mind*.

63 A good dragon is attacking the town! Why? Ask the alchemist in the woods with a *potion of dragon control*.

64 Psionicists are being killed one by one — even powerful ones. The assassin must be using *philter of insanity shield* to protect themselves.

65 An important political figure has fallen in love with an inappropriate person! Can the characters find out who dosed the leader with an *elixir of Venus*?

66 The enemy seems to know every secret plan and all troop locations. Nothing has gone missing. Can the characters find the spy using an *elixir of recall*?

67 The kingdom mandates the use of an elixir on prisoners that causes them to tell the truth when questioned. Protests are occurring. Which side will the characters choose?

68 A rival thieves' guild is using *potions of clairvoyance* and *potions of clairaudience* to outperform the competition. Now they have decided to solve the problem by destroying the alchemist's guild. Can the alchemist's guild be saved?

69 The kingdom's secrets are escaping! At night, a werebat is using an *elixir of dream speech* to spy on the king.

70 A giant is terrorizing a small hamlet, but it turns out that the "giant" is just a gnome suffering from permanent miscibility of an *elixir of growth*.

71 Cheap *potions of invisibility* cause problems on two fronts: a war over a diamond mine and a rash of invisible crimes. Can the characters stop this masterminded plan of a goblin alchemist?

72 An elixir has gone terribly wrong. Spells being cast by the local wizard take physical form and terrorize those nearby.

73 A metal golem is actually an ogre with a permanent *elixir of reflective form*. The confused party may expect a much tougher fight than it is.

74 A cultist gave his minions an *elixir of revenge* for a nasty surprise.

75 A strange shrubbery is seen in several places around town. Will they discover the halfling thief under the influence of an *elixir of shrubbery*.

76 A strange cult is turning people into living skeletons using an *elixir of skeletal visage*.

77 A murderous tiger is attacking a village, but the villagers seem unable to stop it. It has been warded with an *salve of animal sanctuary*.

78 A nearby wererat mage attempted to animate his furniture with *salve of animation* so it would clean itself. But something went horribly wrong and now they won't stop.

79 A mysterious sprite is performing strange curses in the castle. Will the characters discover that she is using a *salve of the green* to enter through the tree in the throne room?

80 The local contest's first prize turned them into a monstrous beast that now terrorizes the area.

81 A vampire used *salve of immobility* to trap the residents of a castle. Can they be saved?

82 A goblin alchemist has received a permanent effect from an *elixir of emotions*, and it has bred true! The resulting scourge of suddenly-powerful goblins must be stopped.

83 A troll alchemist has mastered the formulas for *salve of acid resistance* and *salve of fire resistance*.

84 A shipment of *salve of stonewalking* is en route to those besieging a city. Can the shipment be stopped before it spells doom for those trapped in the city?

85 A statue in the center of town stands up one day and walks out of town. What orders does the construct have?

86 A magma construct being used as a moat has rebelled, and now no one can enter or leave the castle.

87 An alchemist is selling alchemical potions that have a random effect, sepite the fact that they are being prepared properly. What is happening, and why?

88 A noble purchased a *sigil of silence* to use on their spouse, but now finds it is they who cannot speak. Can the characters do anything to help him fix the problem? Do they even care?

89 An alchemist is said to be attempting to create all 13 gem talismans. Since only three can be used at most, what is he planning on doing with them?

90 A fire demon appeared and is causing havoc in a local village. It isn't a demon, but an alchemist who wasn't pure of spirit who attempted to consume an *apotheosis of fire (elemental transubstantiation)*.

91 A character is arrested and dragged before the court. They offer the character freedom if the party can locate the source of the mysterious golden bars devaluing the currency. Can they track down whoever is crafting *apotheosis of mercury*?

92 They characters corner their final opponent. But no matter what they do to kill him, he just laughs and laughs! How can they defeat someone who has consumed a *potheosis of sulfur*?

93 After a mountebank rolled through town, everyone bought new restful mattresses. Only no one is getting any rest at all, and now there is chaos and fighting in the city. Were they tricked or is there something wrong with the *bedrolls of rest*?

94 What's in that *bottle of holding*?

95 In a large city, there's a huge demand for *heating* and *cooling boxes*. However, there are not enough essences to craft as many as people want. Some unscrupulous people are trying to raise hell hounds and yeti — in the same breeding facility!

96 The *cloak of eyestalks* seemed like a great bargain until the stalks seemed to gain minds of their own.

97 All the party's items disappeared in the night and were replaced with potions and elixirs.

98 A series of pools are springing up nearby. What strange subterranean alchemist is causing this?

99 A rash of poisonings has occurred. Can the characters track down the werewolf gnomes producing this new poison?

100 Several politicians are swaying large numbers of people toward violent acts. Can the characters discover the bugbear alchemist vampires behind the act?

NECROMANCER
Games™